LIKE THE
FIRST TIME

LIKE THE
FIRST TIME

Francis Ray

East Baton Rouge Parish Library
Baton Rouge, Louisiana

 St. Martin's Griffin ♏ New York

www.stmartins.com

Library of Congress Cataloging-in-Publication Data

Ray, Francis.
    Like the first time / Francis Ray.—1st U.S. ed.
        p. cm.
    ISBN 0-312-32429-4
    EAN 978-0-312-32429-2
    1. African American women—Fiction. 2. African American businesspeople—Fiction. 3. African American business enterprises—Fiction. 4. Downsizing of organizations—Fiction. 5. Gift basket industry—Fiction. 6. Female friendship—Fiction. I. Title.

PS3568.A9214L55 2004
813'.54—dc22

                                                    2003070879

P1

LIFE TAKES A TURN

Life brings on changes from time to time
Things once before no longer mine.
We often have no choice in what lies ahead
The turns of our lives, we often dread.
Although, life is not promised to you or me
For just this moment God, let it be.
Each day that goes by
Each month I didn't cry.
A year has come and now I see
God allowed The Turning Point *of my life to satisfy me.*
Each day a little longer
Each moment a bit stronger.
Time passes by you see
God allows me, to be set free.
Joy comes within to mend
Faith becomes my true friend.
I will reclaim like before what's mine
It will be better—Like the First Time.

—Valerie Thomas Nesmith
Founder of Read! Write! Celebrate!
In honor of Francis Ray
Poem created: October 28, 2003 & November 1, 2003

LIKE THE
FIRST TIME

CHAPTER ONE

The casualities were running high.

With one eye on the phone on her desk, Claire Bennett sat hunched in her cubicle on the second floor of Middleton Corporation running a diagnostic on the PC she'd just repaired. Helping troubleshoot and repair the thirteen hundred and fifty-two computers at Middleton meant she was always busy, but it also meant she had job security in her hometown of Charleston, South Carolina.

At least it had in the past.

Her fingers stumbled, hitting the wrong key. She clenched her hands in an effort to still the sudden tremor. Surrounding her was an eerie quietness instead of the usual lively debate about the airheads who perpetually screwed up the computers—the otherwise intelligent people who used their CD holders as coasters or spilled soft drinks or coffee onto the keyboards—the muted sounds of no less than three different radio stations, the clatter of computer keys. None of that was happening today. It was as if the entire floor that housed the technical support team of Middleton held its collective breath. Waiting.

Waiting to see who would be next.

Claire's stomach muscles clenched. *Please, not again,* she silently prayed. But she had prayed the last time, to no avail. She put her head down as anguish swept through her. She couldn't lose this job. She couldn't. Not when she was finally seeing her way out of the financial hole she'd dug for herself. But, no matter what, she'd never regret the decisions she'd made to make her parents' life easier. They'd never stopped encouraging her, believing in her, loving her. Helping her older brother, Derek, was another matter entirely.

Just last week Derek had called from Orlando to say he needed a loan to get his car repaired so he could get to work. Even as she wired him the three hundred dollars she could ill afford, she knew she'd never see a penny of it, just as she'd never seen any of the other money she'd "loaned" him over the years. She just hoped and prayed he'd finally grow up and learn to be self-sufficient. Their parents were gone and it was just the two of them. He was her brother and she loved him in spite of his faults.

The shrill ring of the phone startled her, snapping her head up. Her heart thudded. Her mouth dried. She thought of her mother's enormous medical bills that she was still trying to pay off, the gutters that needed replacing on the house, and all the other things she never seemed to have enough money for. She continued to stare at the receiver, debating whether she should pick it up, before realizing it would do little good to ignore the call.

Rubbing her sweaty palm on her khaki slacks, she inched her hand forward. "Tech service, Claire Bennett speaking."

"Claire, please come into my office."

Her breath caught in her throat when she heard her immediate supervisor's tired voice. It remained that way long after the annoying drone in her ear indicated he'd hung up.

For a moment she couldn't move. Then, as if every movement was an effort, she replaced the receiver and stood on legs that refused to stop shaking.

She left her cubicle by rote, her steps slow and deliberate, her gaze fixed on the door at the end of the room as she passed the shell of empty cubicles in her department—the work area of terminated employees who had already fallen to the company's cutback as it tried to save itself from bankruptcy. Desperate to survive, Middleton was cutting its work force by twenty-five percent over the next four months.

She'd worked in this department for two years, had been to co-workers' weddings and baby showers, yet no one spoke as she passed. She could feel their eyes on her and well imagine their thoughts. They felt sorry for her; all were glad it wasn't them. She had been one of the thankful ones yesterday, and thirteen days before. Now, her luck might have run out.

Since Samuel's office was only two doors down, it didn't take long for her to reach her destination. Swallowing the growing knot in her throat, she knocked softly.

"Come in."

The brass knob felt cold against her sweaty palm as she twisted it and entered. Samuel, big, burly and badly in need of a shave and haircut, sat with his arms on his desk. An inch from his clasped hands was a thick white envelope, easily seen since his usually cluttered desk was bare. Lord, how she wished she could turn back the clock so that the hardwood surface would be that way again.

"Cla—" he began.

"I work hard," she blurted, as if that would stall the inevitable. Her hands outstretched, she hurried toward him, determined to make him listen. "Please, Samuel, I need this job."

"Claire—"

"I come in early and take the calls for the weekend no one wants." It didn't matter that she had nothing to do on weekends and no one special in her life. It only mattered that she needed every penny to stay afloat financially. "You know you can depend on me to work any shift. I don't have—"

"Don't you think the others who stood where you're standing have said the same?" he asked her, his usually laughing blue eyes tired. "Don't make this harder on either of us. It's not my call. Your work is exemplary and it says so in here." Picking up the envelope he handed it to her. "Due to realignment your position had been designated as one that is expendable."

"I'll take a cut in salary, a lesser job, anything," she said, her voice frantic.

"They all would." The envelope didn't waver.

Her stomach churning, Claire's fingers closed around the envelope. This couldn't be happening to her. Not again. It wasn't fair. But as she listened to Samuel tell her to clear out her desk by the end of the day, to leave her company-issued cell phone, and continued with the list of items that identified her as an employee of Middleton Corporation, she was forced to admit that she was wrong. It was happening.

There was a roaring in her head. She saw his mouth move, but could no longer distinguish the words. All she could think of was that she stood to lose everything. After two years with Middleton she was once again caught in the downsize crunch that had left her jobless almost three years ago.

For the second time in her life she was being fired.

On the third floor of Middleton Corporation, Brooke Dunlap sat behind her sleek desk of chrome and glass playfully flicking the heart on the eighteen-karat gold bracelet encircling her left wrist. A winsome smile curved her sensual lips and lit her beautiful face as she thought of her future husband, Randolph Peterson III. The list of prospective clients she was scheduled to call that day was the furthest thing from her mind.

Randolph was the man she had been looking for. She'd always said she'd marry a rich man and Randolph was certainly that. Third generation banker, his family was loaded and connected all the way to the governor's mansion in her hometown of Columbia.

Her perfectly French-manicured nail circled the gold heart. The bracelet proved he hadn't forgotten her while on a banking assignment in London for the past five months. She had to admit she had begun to have a few doubts because he hadn't flown home to see her. The arrival of the bracelet by special delivery yesterday quieted any fears she might have had. He cared about her. When they'd talked on the phone last night he'd indicated he would be coming home in a month or so and that he had a surprise for her.

Leaning back in the leather chair that conformed perfectly to her petite body, Brooke extended her slim fingers and imagined a flawless five-karat A-1 diamond on the third finger instead of the peridot birthstone ring her parents had given her on her sixteenth birthday. Randolph's surprise had to be an engagement ring.

Of course, she'd tender her resignation immediately and plan the fabulous society wedding she'd dreamed about since she was seven years old. She wouldn't miss her job or most of the people one iota. There was too much fighting and crap in the corporate world. If she hadn't been so certain she'd find a successful man to marry, she'd have given up and gone back home long ago.

One person in particular she'd be happy to see the last of was her snippy supervisor, Opal Severs. The old biddy was forever on Brooke's case about some nonsense. Then there was all the extra work because of the layoffs. Her parents were concerned about her job, but Brooke had reassured them. She was the manager of her department and brilliant in what she did. No way were the big guys going to fire her.

The phone on her neat desk rang and she picked it up. "Brooke Dunlap."

"Brooke, come into my office immediately."

Brooke's lips thinned with irritation on hearing Opal's crisp voice. Not even eleven o'clock and the old crone was already on her case. "Certainly."

Standing, Brooke picked up her alligator-bound notebook and gold pen. Each time Opal had called Brooke into her office since the layoffs began, the reason had been to assign Brooke more work.

Leaving her office, Brooke smoothed her hand over the side of her rose and navy St. John knit. She could just imagine the jealousy on Opal's austere face when she saw the new couture dress. Opal's problem. Brooke enjoyed having the best her straining credit cards could afford.

Stopping before the door with Opal's name and position engraved on a gold plate at eye level, Brooke toyed with the idea of staying and taking the spiteful woman's job, then just as quickly dismissed it. Being Mrs. Randolph Peterson III was the only position Brooke wanted. She rapped softly on the door.

"Come in."

Brooke blinked. Opal actually sounded happy. She usually wore a perpetually sour expression as if she found no joy in life and wanted everyone around her to feel the same. Opening the door, Brooke was even more surprised to see Opal, legs crossed and arms folded, leaning against the front of her desk instead of sitting behind it in a position of authority, as was her practice. She wore one of the mannish suits she favored, this one a dull gray with a cream-colored blouse that did nothing to complement the older woman's dark complexion or her thin frame.

"Yes?" Brooke inquired.

Her smile widening, Opal reached behind her and picked up a white envelope. "You've been terminated. Effective immediately."

Brooke blinked, too shocked to do anything but stare at her manager.

Opal continued, her voice sickeningly gleeful. "You're to clear out your desk and turn in your cell phone—which I know you're using for personal calls—your laptop that is probably loaded with personal e-mail, your pager, your calling card, and bring all your accounts to me. You have two weeks severance pay and insurance for thirty days. Let's see, there was something else." She tapped the envelope against her narrow chin as if deep in thought. "Oh, yes. The company's credit card."

Terminated. She couldn't be. Not when she had the best sales record in the firm. She'd brought in more new accounts than anyone.

Rage worked its way through the shock and hurt. Somehow Opal was behind this. Only the smug expression on the other woman's face allowed Brooke to keep her anger in check. She wouldn't give her that satisfaction.

Her eyes saying all the things she couldn't, Brooke crossed the room. Opal's triumphant expression turned to weariness. Dispassionately, Brooke watched the other woman gulp. It took every ounce of willpower to gently remove the envelope from Opal's fingers instead of snatching it and cramming it down her scrawny throat.

Going to the door, Brooke opened it, then turned to speak for the first time, "When you dig a ditch for someone, make sure you're not digging one for yourself. Sales will decline and guess whose head will roll next." She had the satisfaction of seeing uneasiness cross Opal's face. "I'll survive and be happy. You'll never do either."

Closing the door, Brooke returned to her office in a daze, the envelope clutched against her chest. Two weeks severance pay wouldn't put a tiny dent in her bills, pay the rent on her condominium, or on her new silver Jag. She spent money as fast as she made it. There was nothing saved. Her checking account was a holding place for her creditor's money.

Brooke shuddered, then sank into her chair. A picture filled her mind. Her, clutching a rusty shopping cart filled with her beloved espresso machine and a pile of her designer clothes, as she begged for change on the streets of Charleston.

There was nothing left to pack.

Claire glanced around her cubicle, as icy fear twisted through her. It was time to leave. She'd already said goodbye to her few friends and turned in everything. She knew she was putting off picking up the box containing her personal belongings as if she expected Samuel to rush back in and say it had all been a mistake. She wasn't being terminated. She had a job. A life.

Fighting tears, fighting misery, she picked up the box, its weight pitifully light. There were only a couple of family pictures, the radio she'd had since college, a black mug with the name of her college in gold letters she'd used to hold odds and ends. Not much to show for two years. For some reason that made her feel even sadder.

She was thirty-nine years old, had worked since she was thirteen, and all she had to show for it were some odds and ends. All her life she'd been taught by her parents that if you worked hard, you could accomplish anything. The American dream wasn't just for the rich or for white people: it was for everyone.

Her parents had been wrong.

Her hands clutched the box closer and she turned to leave. She'd only gone a short distance when her steps faltered and she turned. Every person in the room stood outside their workstation watching her. Tears sparkled in a few of their eyes. They'd been a team, an extended family.

She swallowed repeatedly before she could manage to speak past the lump in her throat. "I'll miss all of you," she finally managed.

A chorus of "good luck" and "take care of yourself" came back to her. Nodding, she continued toward the door, very afraid that luck was something she didn't have.

On the elevator, she punched in three, then avoided the eyes of the two men in business suits. Head still tucked, feeling an odd sense of embarrassment that she hadn't been able to keep her job, she stepped off the elevator as soon as the door slid open, then headed down the brightly lit hallway. She had one more goodbye. Brooke Dunlap.

They'd met six months ago and Claire had immediately liked Brooke. She hadn't treated her as subservient as some in upper level management were prone. Brooke hadn't stopped chatting and joking the entire hour that Claire was there repairing the computer. She was everything Claire wasn't: petite and beautiful, and she could charm anyone, especially men. They'd had lunch at least once a week in the company's cafeteria. Claire always brought her lunch from home; Brooke always purchased hers. Not once had Claire ever seen her check a price of anything.

Shifting the box beneath her left arm, Claire knocked on Brooke's door, then knocked again when there was no answer. She was about to turn away when she heard a barely audible voice tell her to come in. Frowning, because the person hadn't sounded like Brooke, Claire opened the door cautiously. You could almost smell the magnolia; feel her warmth and charm when you heard Brooke's deeply accented Southern voice.

"I'm look—" Claire began but her words stumbled to a halt when she saw Brooke, sitting stiffly in her chair, blinking her eyes. Seeing Claire, the other woman leaned forward, propping her elbows on her desk and let her face fall into her cupped palms.

Claire rushed across the room . . . and saw the letter lying on her desk. "You, too?"

Brooke's head snapped up. Misery and tears swam in her eyes. She slumped back in her chair. "Me, too."

Claire didn't know what to say. She certainly didn't plan to mouth all the things that were said to her, because no matter how skilled, how shining your resume or exemplary your recommendations—it was an employer's market. But Claire had never imagined Brooke would be caught in the crunch. Her sales record was the best in the firm. "I'm sorry."

"I thought you were Opal coming to gloat."

During their weekly lunch date Brooke had told her about her manager's jealousy of her. Claire had been around long enough to warn Brooke against annoying the older woman. But Brooke was young and unfortunately thought the world was reasonably fair. Claire had long since given up the illusion.

"Is there anything I can do?" Claire offered, feeling helpless. She had never been good at comforting people.

Brooke finally lifted her head. Sorrow and pain replaced the perpetual happiness in her dark eyes. "No," she said, her trembling voice barely above a whisper. Then her long lashes swept back down over her eyes.

"Well," Claire began, her hands flexing on the box. Telling Brooke about her own termination suddenly didn't seem like a good idea. "Can I get you a glass of water or something?"

Brooke shook her head, then stood and walked to the window that looked out over downtown Charleston. "I don't know whether to be angry with Opal for being so disgustingly gleeful or the knothead in upper management who let her get away with dismissing me."

"From personal experience I'd say it doesn't make any difference. The results would be the same," Claire offered gently.

Brooke glanced over her shoulder. "Forgive me. I'm thinking about myself when you've gone through the same thing at one time."

Twice, Claire thought, but it went no further. "This . . . it knocks you for a loop."

Brooke nodded, running her hand through her stylishly cut coal black hair. "I guess I better get started." She motioned toward the box in Claire's hand. "Can I borrow that when you're finished?"

Biting her lip, Claire decided to stop hiding the truth. Propping the box against her hip, she lifted the white envelope from inside the box.

Brooke's eyes widened, then she was around the desk, her arms going around Claire. "I'm sorry! Why didn't you say something?" she asked, stepping back to stare up at Claire, who was a couple of inches taller despite Brooke's four-inch heels.

"I didn't want to add to your problems," Claire admitted. "You had enough on your mind."

"All I can say is that Middleton is going to be in trouble without the both of us," Brooke said, trying to smile.

But not as much trouble as *they* would be in, Claire thought, but she left the words unsaid. "You want me to help?" Claire asked, setting down her box. "There's plenty of room in here."

"Thanks." Brooke's hand trembled as she picked up a sterling silver framed picture of her and her parents at her college graduation. "How am I going to tell them?"

"They'll be more concerned about you than anything, from what you've told me about your parents," Claire offered, trying to figure out where to begin packing. Brooke had several family pictures, a collection of crystal paperweights, and an expensive desk set.

"I wish Randolph were here or at the very least that I could reach him." Brooke picked up another picture, this one of her and Randolph wearing formal attire. "With the five hour time difference, he's already left the office. I left a message at his flat."

Claire thought that at least Brooke had a man in her life to call. Claire had no one. Not even a pet. She'd always thought there'd be plenty of time for a family after she climbed the corporate ladder. Her stomach clenched when she compared going home to an empty house with what might have been.

"Why don't you come home with me?" Claire suggested impulsively. "I live in a beachfront cottage on Sullivan's Island. We can keep each other company."

Brooke paused in picking up another framed picture, a frown marring her beautiful face. "Randolph might call."

"I understand," Claire quickly said. Why would Brooke want to spend time with her when she probably had loads of friends? "I'll go find some newspaper to wrap your things."

"I have some," Brooke said, pulling out *The Wall Street Journal* from the chrome wastebasket, then handing a section to Claire. Silently they began clearing the desk. By the time they'd finished they had filled two Saks shopping bags retrieved from Brooke's desk drawer and Brooke was fighting tears again.

"If Opal is behind your termination, then there's nothing that would give her more pleasure than seeing you in tears," Claire told her.

Brooke's head came up. Her eyes narrowed. "She'll wait until hell freezes over." Plopping her Louis Vuitton attaché case on top of the bag closest to her, she gathered the company's laptop, cell phone, calling card, and pager. "I'm going to turn these in to her, then we're leaving. If the invitation still stands, I'd like to take you up on it."

"Why did you change your mind?" Claire asked in surprise.

"I can only hold my anger in so long and then I'm going to explode. I'll have a better chance of not being arrested if I'm on the beach rather than in my condo. Then, too, I'm not ready to hear 'I told you so' from my parents." She sniffed. "They tried to warn me that my job might be in jeopardy, but I didn't want to listen. I thought I was safe."

"No one is safe in corporate anymore." Claire picked up the other bag.

"Claire," Brooke said, her voice frightened, her face pinched, "what are we going to do?"

"Take one day at a time," Claire said, then followed Brooke out of what was once her corner office.

CHAPTER TWO

t didn't take long to reach Brooke's place, an upscale condominium nestled on the banks of the Ashley River with its own marina and river walk. A domed elevator with black grill ironwork dating back to the early nineteenth-century quickly took them to the top and fourth floor. Built on a marshland peninsula, Charleston had very few tall buildings because of zoning laws to preserve the historical beauty of the city. Brooke's place was lavishly furnished with silks and ornate furniture upholstered in the palest earth tone shades.

"Your place is beautiful," Claire said, setting the shopping bag on the sandstone-colored carpet instead of on the hand-painted coffee table topped with a neat stack of fashion magazines and a fresh-cut arrangement of gladiolas in a cylindrical vase near a trio of vanilla candles on a crystal tray. "When I was your age I had a one bedroom with second-hand furniture."

Brooke's eyes misted again. She glanced around the spacious living room. "I may be lucky to have that if I can't find another job."

Once again silence descended between the two women. Claire didn't want to give false hope. It had taken her ten scary months to find another job. "You could do temp work."

"With bonuses and incentives I make way over six figures. Temp work is not going to pay my bills," Brooke said, anger creeping into her voice.

Since Claire understood and remembered her own anger, she didn't take offense. She'd been impossible to live with the first few days after she lost her job. "Be sure and pack a swimsuit in case you want to go swimming."

Brooke started down the hallway, then abruptly turned back. "I'm sorry if I seem to be taking this out on you, and I'm not sure I won't do it again. Do you still want me to go with you?"

Claire nodded. "I know it's not me. I want you to come."

"When did you stop wanting to scream?" Brooke asked, her voice trembling with a mixture of pain, fear, and embarrassment.

Claire had experienced all of them. "Not until I held my Middleton ID badge in my hands."

Brooke's eyes shut, then blinked open. "Ten months. I'll lose everything."

"No, you won't," Claire said, glad this time she could be honest. "Because it won't take you as long." Catching Brooke's arm, she steered her down the hall. "You're bright, energetic, intelligent and somewhere there's a man in personnel who is going to fall all over himself to give you a job."

Brooke immediately perked up. "I've always had a way with men."

Claire smiled at the understatement. "They practically fall at your feet like ripe fruit. The security guard at the entrance to your condo was staring at you so hard after you drove through, he almost closed the gate on me."

"Simpson is a sweetie," Brooke said, entering the last door on the right.

Claire followed. The room was feminine and furnished just as beautifully as the rest of the apartment. Brooke lived well.

As if reading her thoughts Brooke turned to Claire. "I could probably pack the things I own outright in my car. If I don't find a job within a month I'll lose everything."

"Then you'll just have to find one." Taking the bag out of Brooke's hand Claire set it on the floor. "Come on and pack. Then we can both go down to the beach and scream."

C laire pulled into her attached garage and was getting out just as Brooke pulled in beside her. Claire's dusty blue Chevrolet looked more pitiful than ever next to Brooke's gleaming silver Jag. Claire had thought that once she had a handle on the bills she might look into buying a new car. She swallowed the lump in her throat and gathered her things.

"Come on, we can go through the garage."

Closing her door, Brooke picked up her overnight bag. "I didn't know you lived in this exclusive area. I can see just the tip of Sullivan's Island from Randolph's terrace. He has a couple of friends who have homes out this way."

Claire considered that she might not be living here for long, but refused to dwell on it. She'd find another job. She had to.

Unlocking the back door, she moved to one side so Brooke could enter first. "I bought this place for my parents fifteen years ago when the prices weren't so high. You could comfortably fit two of my homes into a single floor of many of the houses on the island. But it was just right for my parents, and they loved the house."

Entering the spotless yellow and white kitchen, Brooke turned to Claire with a smile. "It smells wonderful in here."

"It's the candles," Claire said, closing the door behind them.

"These are beautiful," Brooke remarked, picking up a creamy white candle in a three-inch cylindrical-shaped glass container enclosed in pale netting and tied with a satin ribbon that matched perfectly. A tiny white rosebud peeked from the bow's knot. "Where did you buy these?"

For a moment Claire just stared at the candle Brooke held, then she closed her eyes. "Oh, no."

Immediately, Brooke was by her side, her hand on her arm. "We'll find another job. Don't worry."

Claire's eyes blinked open to see Brooke staring up at her. "It's not that." Setting her things on the counter, she went to the sweetgrass basket filled with carefully wrapped hand-made soaps on the kitchen table. Her hand closed around one of the bars encased in yellow netting with a wire yellow ribbon bow.

"Then what is it?" Brooke came up beside Claire.

"I made these as gifts." Claire never took her eyes from the soap in her hand.

"What!" Brooke's attention snapped back to the basket. She picked up one of the bars. "You're kidding, right?"

Once Claire would have been pleased by the awed appreciation in Brooke's voice, but not as of nine-seventeen that morning. "They were to be gifts to the other members of the book club I belong to. The monthly meeting is scheduled here tomorrow night." Slowly she returned the soap to the basket. "I had planned an elaborate menu of all kinds of seafood to make up for all the times I hadn't been able to have the meeting at my house. I was going to the market early in the morning so everything would be fresh." Her eyes shut briefly. "Now I can't."

"How much do you think it would cost?" Brooke asked slowly. "Maybe together we co—"

"No, but thank you. You need all your money." Claire swallowed. "So do I. It wouldn't make sense for me to spend money when I don't know how long it will take before I find another job."

"This is just so unfair!" Brooke said, anger creeping back into her voice.

"You won't get an argument from me. Come on I'll show you to your room."

Leaving the bright yellow kitchen, the women passed through the large family room, which continued the color scheme. The sofa and overstuffed chair were upholstered in neutral khaki and taupe, while the accent pillows and table skirt of the pedestal end table were done in a bold tropical fabric with a yellow background. The three French doors were topped with cornice boards in the same bold fabric. Through the glass, the peaceful blue Atlantic was endless beyond the glistening sand dunes.

"The sandy beach stretches for three miles along the Atlantic side of the island. We'll go out later if you'd like," Claire said. "My parents loved the island and the ocean. Evening was their favorite time here."

"This place is fabulous," Brooke commented, stopping to stare at the vastness of the ocean. "Property values here must be through the roof."

"They are." Claire continued to the first door down the short hallway.

"There are only about two thousand homes here. They're all on at least a half-acre lot. I understand houses sell very quickly. I was lucky. If it hadn't been for Gray, the mortgage company wouldn't have loaned me the money and the sale might have fallen through."

Brooke stopped and stared. "Gray? You aren't talking about Gray Livingston, are you?"

Twin furrows marched across Claire's forehead. "You know Gray?"

"Girl! Every single woman between the age of eighteen and sixty in Charleston knows *of* Gray." Sighing, she entered the sunny bedroom. "That is one fine man. I'll tell you a little secret. If you promise not to tell anyone."

Claire had no idea why her body tensed. "All right."

Brooke sat on the white iron daybed that had once belonged to Claire and pulled Claire down beside her. "Well, you know my theory that you can fall in love with a rich man as easily as you can a poor man."

"Yes," Claire said, her hands clenched in her lap.

"I thought about Gray Livingston being that man." Brooke confided. "I did my research on him. I knew all about the Livingston mail-order catalogue business that his grandfather started, that Gray has been the CEO for the past year since his grandfather's death, and I know about Gray's very public and messy divorce after three short months, two years ago. Then I met him and changed my mind."

"Why?" Claire asked, unaware of the challenge in her voice. Gray was six-foot-three and heart-stopping handsome with piercing black eyes. His slender nose flared slightly over a mobile mouth that easily curved into a smile. His chin was determined. In her opinion, he was much better looking than Randolph and had a self-assurance about himself that put you at ease instead of making you feel as if you weren't worthy to be in his presence, the way Randolph had made her feel the one time she'd met him.

"He has the looks, the money, the prestige." Brooke ticked off the items on her fingers. "Lord knows his body is to die for and he has all the qualifications on my short list, but when he looked at me there was nothing there. No spark. Nothing. He probably forgot about me as soon as he turned away."

Claire stared at Brooke in disbelief. "Men fall all over themselves for you all the time."

"He didn't." Brooke wrinkled her nose. "It might have hurt my feelings if his reaction to the other women in the room wasn't the same. Of course behind his back they were whispering about his ex-wife, Jana. According to the juicy gossip she pops back in town every now and then from wherever the current jet-setter hot spot is to warn other women off. Seems she was here a few weeks ago. Talk is she wants him back." Brooke leaned closer to Claire. "Is it true that when he found her and her lover in their bed he tossed both of them out of the house naked?"

"I don't know." Claire glanced away. Conversation about Gray and his ex-wife always made her unbearably sad. She'd seen pictures of his beautiful ex-wife, but had never met her and hoped she never would. The last time she'd seen Gray was at her mother's funeral. "The Gray I knew was caring and fun-loving. It must have hurt him terribly to be betrayed by his bride. Gray is very loyal and, although you might not expect it, sensitive."

"A cheating bride would certainly dent a man's ego and his pride. The couple of times I've seen him, he's always been with a different woman. Guess his ex's plan is working," Brooke confided. "It's going to take a special woman to get him to the altar again."

"Perhaps." Standing, Claire walked to the closet and took out three padded hangers. "The dresser drawers are empty. The connecting bathroom is through there."

Opening her overnight bag, Brooke took out two sundresses and reached for the hangers. "So how do you know Gray?"

Obviously Brooke wasn't going to let the subject drop. In any case, Claire reasoned, it was better than thinking about not having a job and all the bills she needed to pay. "My parents worked for his grandparents from the time I was eight until they retired about five years ago. I was always there after school, but especially during the summer. Each summer from the time he was ten Gray would come down from Atlanta where he lived with his parents and sister for at least a month to learn the business."

"Talk about missed opportunity," Brooke said, hanging up the dresses.

Claire blushed. "Gray never thought of me that way."

Brooke picked up her French lingerie, frothy bits of nothing that cost dearly. "Well, you certainly must have made some kind of impression if he helped you get this place for your parents."

"He did it for them. They thought very highly of each other." Becoming uncomfortable with the conversation, Claire went to the door. "If you don't need anything I want to make a couple of calls."

"I'm fine." Brooke opened the drawer and sniffed appreciatively. "But before I leave Sunday I want to know how you keep the scent in the room. My expensive candles certainly haven't done it."

"Sachets beneath the pillows, back of each dresser drawer, and on top of the armoire," Claire explained.

"I suppose you made them, too," Brooked said, a teasing smile on her face as she walked back to her case.

"As a matter of fact, I did," Claire told her and this time she let herself feel proud. "My mother was allergic to a lot of different additives in soaps and scents, and since she loved her 'smell goods,' as she called them, she started experimenting with making her own. She taught me. She always said a house and a woman should smell and look beautiful."

"Sounds like my kind of woman." Brooke hefted her bulging bags of cosmetics.

Claire had to smile. "Daddy always used to complain that my mother was going to put him in the poor house with all the different fragrances and oils she used to buy, because she always believed in buying the best. But I can't count the high number of times I saw them walk hand-in-hand on the beach. They were devoted to each other."

"My parents are the same way." Brooke placed her cosmetic bag on the counter in the bath and came back out. "That's the kind of marriage I want, and I plan to have it with Randolph."

Claire wished there was someone to share her trials and triumphs with. A twinge of envy coursed through Claire and she quickly pushed it away. "You're going to call him again?"

Brooke glanced at her slim diamond watch. "I think I'll wait. It was probably best that I didn't reach him. Randolph doesn't like emotional women."

A frown worked its way across Claire's brow. "But surely he'd understand in this case?"

"I think he would, but I'm too close to jeopardize things." Brooke picked up her empty case. "After we're married, if I have a problem I'll cry all over his Italian suit, but not now."

"Whatever you think best," Claire said, but she recalled the times her father had comforted her mother when she'd been upset about something or another. From talking with her mother, she knew he had been the same caring way before they were married. "I'll go make that call. When you're finished you can come into the kitchen."

"See you in a bit." Brooke started to the closet with her empty case.

Claire went to the kitchen, glanced at the basket of gift items, and felt her eyes fill with tears. She had to call Lorraine. Besides being the president of the book club, she was also Claire's mentor and friend. How was she going to tell a woman she respected and admired that life had slapped her down again. That this time she wasn't sure if she could get back up.

orraine Averhart was restless.

She picked up a fashion magazine only to toss the issue down before she opened it. Fridays were always her day to regroup, to reenergize. For the past year she'd purposefully planned her schedule that way. After rushing to meeting after meeting, both church and civic, on the other six days, she needed some quiet down time. Usually she found something to occupy her mind, some task she hadn't completed, but not today.

Arms across her waist, she gazed out the terrace door of the great room. A limestone walk led the way to the rectangular swimming pool fifty feet away. The life-sized Grecian statue at the far end signaled the beginning of the three informal gardens filled with roses, ferns and wildflowers and four murmuring fountains. Usually she enjoyed the way the dew settled on the roses, the shifting shapes as the sunlight probed its way though the giant oaks, but not today. She was unaware of the sigh that drifted across her lips.

Her French Renaissance dream home was the height of luxury and comfort. Even her mother, after all the years of having nothing but bad things to say about her marriage, finally admitted Lorraine's home was a showcase. She hadn't set out to impress her mother; her goal had been to have a home her children, and husband Hamilton, could relax in and enjoy.

Lorraine shifted from one low-heeled sandal to the other and sighed again. Hamilton was out of town on business more than he was home these days. Their two oldest children were grown and gone. Their youngest, Stacy, might as well have been. A sophomore journalism major at Howard, Stacy had settled in nicely to being away from home and was enjoying living on her own. Justin and Melissa, the two oldest, had jobs in financing in New York and Baltimore, respectively, which kept them away. She missed her children and understood they were forming their own lives apart from their parents. She understood that and was proud of them.

She just wished she could see where her life was going.

Empty nest syndrome, Hamilton had said. But it was more than that. The feeling had been nagging at her for months. It had burst into her consciousness four months ago after Margaret, her oldest and dearest friend, died, and it refused to leave.

Lorraine blinked away the tears. Margaret wouldn't have wanted that. Even as cancer ravaged her body, she'd refused to let it destroy her spirit. She had been so full of happiness and laughter. She'd always had time for everyone, but never took time out for herself. And when she did, it was too late. The saddest part of saying goodbye to Margaret was in knowing she'd died without fulfilling her dream.

The dream they'd shared.

After years of talking about opening a floral gift shop they'd finally decided to stop letting family, friends and all of their other obligations stand in their way. They both loved flowers, but Margaret's family owned a wholesale florist in Akron. She knew the business backwards and forwards. Lorraine's business experience was nowhere as in-depth, but she'd worked in a gift shop in high school and college and loved it.

Lorraine would never forget the excitement in Margaret's voice the afternoon she called to say she'd found the perfect location. She'd pick up

Lorraine the next day and take her to see for herself. They'd never gone. After their conversation Margaret and her husband had gone by her doctor's office for her biopsy results.

Lorraine's eyes darkened with pain. Margaret had fought so hard. When it became apparent that she would never get well, she made Lorraine promise not to let their dream die. But Lorraine didn't know where to begin. The two years of art she'd taken in college before she'd dropped out to marry Hamilton certainly wouldn't help. Margaret had the business expertise and the contacts. Without her, the shop would remain a dream forever. But giving up Margaret and their dream was hard.

Turning away, Lorraine stared at the room behind her. The French Country décor was picture perfect. The glow of the pale golden walls and warm sable floors pulled the Louis XVI furniture together in soft coherence. She'd carefully chosen each piece. A full-time maid that Hamilton insisted on ensured that their home would remain immaculate. They had come a long way from the tiny walk-up apartment they'd lived in while Hamilton worked on his M.B.A. at Columbia in New York.

They'd been as poor as the proverbial church mouse, and had almost starved, as her affluent parents had predicted. That was thirty-eight years ago, and now Hamilton was president of his own company, Corporate Revitalization. He was brilliant at turning around companies on the verge of bankruptcy. In the unsettled economy, his services were in high demand. He'd been in Memphis for the past week, guiding another firm from the brink of disaster.

And that left her in this big empty house by herself.

On the oval table across the room the phone rang. Unfolding her arms, Lorraine walked over to pick up the receiver. Absently she fingered the velvet-soft petals of the orange and ivory roses in the floral arrangement in a Baccarat crystal vase. "Hello."

"Hi, Lorraine. It's me, Claire."

Immediately Lorraine straightened. The happiness that had been in Claire's voice when they'd spoken last was gone and in its place was an unmistakable sadness. "Claire, is something wrong?"

After a brief pause, Claire softly admitted, "I got caught in downsizing again."

"Oh, Claire, I'm so sorry." Lorraine took a seat on the creamy white silk sofa, the hem of her brightly colored sundress fluttered, then settled around her ankles.

"For some reason, I knew I would be asked to go," Claire told her. "I just felt it once we started hearing that the company had hired a revitalization expert to come in."

Lorraine's eyes shut briefly. She distinctly remembered Middleton as one of the companies Hamilton had been a consultant to a few months ago. In that capacity, he would have made suggestions to revitalize the company, and that often meant a reduction in the work force. Of all the people to lose their jobs, Claire was probably the worst.

"But I'll find another job. I have to." There were equal amounts of determination and desperation in her voice.

"You'll make it, Claire." Lorraine fervently hoped she was right. "You aren't the kind of woman to give up."

"I used to think so, but now . . ." Claire's voice trailed off.

Lorraine ached for Claire and felt somehow responsible. "The last three years have been rough with you losing your father, then your job and shortly thereafter your mother being diagnosed with Alzheimer's. If you weren't at your part-time job, you were with your mother." Lorraine folded one arm across her waist and leaned back against the sofa. "You made her last days more comfortable by keeping her at home. I admire you for that."

"No matter what, I'll never regret doing for them," Claire said, her voice tired. "I have to keep the house. They both cherished and loved this place so much. There are so many good memories here."

"You will," Lorraine said. For some odd reason, she again thought of Margaret, who had always done for someone else, then died before she could achieve her own dream. Lorraine shook the thought away. "I insist on having the book club meeting here tomorrow evening. I'll call all the members and tell them of the change."

"I knew you'd say that," Claire said, sounding relieved. "You're such a good friend. I don't know what I would have done after Mama died if not for you and the book club."

Lorraine thought of Hamilton, with Middleton's accounts spread over his desk, and shook her head. "I feel the same way about you. That's why I wouldn't take no for an answer."

"You were pretty persistent," Claire said, a small smile in her voice.

"There was something about you that drew me to you. Still is." From their first meeting at church a little over three years ago, Lorraine had immediately liked the shy, sensitive Claire and purposefully sought her friendship. "Please come to the meeting."

"Thank you, but I don't think I'd feel up to it, but if you'll be home tomorrow I'd like to drop off the little gifts I made for you and the members."

"You probably don't feel like getting out," Lorraine said with understanding. "Why don't I come by this afternoon and pick them up and save you a trip into town?"

"You sure it wouldn't be too much trouble?" Claire sounded relieved.

"Not at all. I'd love to see you and visit for a while." Lorraine glanced around the empty room again.

A weary sigh drifted through the phone. "I may not be very good company."

"All the more reason for me to come," Lorraine said. There was certainly nothing to keep her home. "I can pick up dinner if you'd like."

"No, I'll cook," Claire told her. "A friend from work is here for the weekend. She lost her job today, too."

Worse and Worse. Neither one of them would want her there if they knew Lorraine's husband was probably the cause of them losing their jobs. "Is six all right?"

"It's fine. You know the address." Claire gave her directions after crossing Ben Sawyer Bridge. "It's easy to find."

"I'll find it, don't worry. Should I bring anything?" Lorraine offered.

"No, thank you. I have it covered."

"See you at six." Lorraine hung up the phone. *Hamilton, I love you, but your job stinks,* she thought with a sigh.

CHAPTER THREE

Claire left Brooke setting the table when the doorbell rang. "Must be Lorraine. I'll get it." Claire left the kitchen and went to the front door. She tried to smile when she saw her friend. "Hi, Lorraine."

"Hello, Claire." Lorraine greeted her. She was a tall, striking woman. In her late fifties, she had a smattering of gray in her layered auburn hair. She wore a big white shirt with screen-print roses and red capri pants. Like Brooke, Lorraine had an innate sense of style and, despite her wealth, she was unpretentious and friendly.

"Glad you made it all right." Claire stepped back.

"You gave excellent directions." Seconds after Lorraine stepped over the threshold, she lifted her face and inhaled deeply. "Whatever that scent is, I love it."

"Pear vanilla," Claire informed her, and closed the door.

Lorraine glanced at the living room and dining room flanking the entrance foyer that led to the family room in the back of the house. "Claire, your home is lovely. So warm and vibrant."

Claire flushed with pleasure. "Thank you. Yellow was my mother's favorite color. Now it's mine."

"It's so peaceful and natural." Lorraine cast appreciative glances as she followed Claire through the great room.

"Mother believed less was better and kept the space open with scatter rugs on the hardwood flooring throughout the house. We all liked walking on the beach and the neutral furniture can take it and no one had to worry about tracking in sand," Claire said as she entered the kitchen to see that Brooke had finished setting the table.

Introductions were quickly made and in a matter of minutes the women were sitting down to a dinner of spicy spaghetti with thin slices of link sausage and homemade spaghetti sauce. Claire was thankful she'd already made the pound cake for the meeting. She topped it with ice cream and plump strawberries. At least she could offer her two friends a decent meal. Finished, they cleaned up the kitchen, put away the food together, then sat around the small table sipping coffee and talking.

"I hope the book club members like the little gifts." Picking up a medium-sized red gift bag, Claire handed it to Lorraine. "These are for you."

"Claire, thank you." Smiling, Lorraine pulled out a bar of rose-shaped soap, a jar candle, and potpourri. "They smell wonderful." She touched a manicured nail to the satin ribbon on the potpourri. "And look too beautiful to use. This is too much."

Claire was already shaking her head as Lorraine tried to give the items back. "You encouraged me to join the book club, had meetings in your home when it was my turn because you knew I couldn't afford to feed them, and helped me after Mama died. I wish it was more."

"You certainly know my weakness." Lorraine sniffed the scented soap and candle. "Smells like a mixture of peach blossoms and vanilla. I love candles, and bath and body products."

"Me, too." Brooke sat across from them at the small table. "I can't believe Claire made them."

Lorraine's attention snapped to Claire. "You *made* these?"

Claire folded her hands in her lap and repeated what she'd told Brooke, then finished by saying, "This is the first time since Mama died that I felt like making them." A bit embarrassed by the way Lorraine was staring at her, she shifted in her seat. "I just wanted to give the women something special for letting me be a part of the book club."

"She made them all perfumed soap." Getting up from the chair, Brooke returned with the sweetgrass basket and set it on the table. "If it wouldn't be rude, I'd accidentally misplace one in my bag."

"I made some extra if you want one," Claire said.

"I'll take one." Brooke quickly accepted with a smile. "Since I'm not in the book club, I'd like to pay you."

"Mama would be ashamed of me if I charged my friends. I'm just glad you like them." Claire glanced from Brooke to Lorraine, still finding it difficult to believe that two such sophisticated women, who were used to the best, liked her products.

Lorraine picked up a bar of soap in the nylon bag and brought it to her nose, then inhaled and closed her eyes for a moment. "Hmm. The women are going to go crazy over the soaps. You're sure you won't come?" She turned to Brooke. "You're welcome as well."

Both women quickly declined. "Please explain and tell them that I'll try to make it next month," Claire said.

"No trying. I'm letting you miss this time, but next month I want you there." Lorraine smiled across the table at Brooke. "There's always room for one more."

Brooke shook her head and picked up her glass of sweetened iced tea. "Thank you, but I think I'll pass."

"If you change your mind about tomorrow night, or joining, please feel free to contact me. Claire knows the phone number." Lorraine stood. "Do you want me to take the soap in the basket and return it?"

The coiled basket had been made by her great-great-grandmother. It was one of the few things that had passed from one generation to the next. "I'll pick it up."

"You'll do no such thing," Lorraine said firmly. "I'll bring it by one day next week."

"Thank you." Claire walked her friend to the door, fervently hoping by then she'd have a job.

What am I going to do?

Claire had pondered the question all night, and as she watched the sun slowly rise, turning the Atlantic into a sparkling blue jewel, she still had no answer. Her severance pay was for only two weeks, and her unemployment check wouldn't come even close to paying the mortgage payment. She couldn't lose the house. She'd promised her parents. They were proud that they owned land that served as an entry point for their ancestors. The house would be the beginning of a legacy that would be handed down through her to her children and her children's children.

At least that was her parents' hope. But there were no children, and it didn't appear as if there would be any.

There was no man in her life, and never had been. She'd always been shy and a loner. One of the reasons she had chosen to major in Computer Science was that she dealt with machines better than with people. She had viewed working overtime and on holidays as a way of reaching her goal of being financially independent by the time she was fifty. Marriage and family would come, but she was too busy trying to rise in her profession to date. Now, at thirty-nine, she had done neither.

Getting up from the bed to go into the kitchen, Claire caught a glimpse of her reflection in the mirror over the dresser in her bedroom. Everything about her was ordinary: her face, her eyes, her mouth, and her nose. She'd never stop traffic the way Brooke did and she certainly didn't have the air of confidence or poise that Lorraine possessed. She didn't have that sparkle, that zip.

For some odd reason, she thought of Brooke's comment about her missed opportunity with Gray. It would be laughable if it weren't so implausible. By the time he turned thirteen and was almost six feet tall, girls were after him. He could have had his pick. The daughter of the cook and the chauffeur wasn't even in the running . . . not that she wanted to be.

Annoyed with herself for letting her mind wander to something so totally off base, she left her bedroom and headed for the beach. Perhaps a walk would clear her head.

---

er hand clenching the cell phone, Brooke paced the floor and waited for Randolph to pick up. It was barely ten minutes after four on Saturday morning. This was her third time trying to reach him since she'd set her alarm clock for four AM. Last night she kept getting his machine. Every time she'd think he might be out with another woman, she'd glance at her gold bracelet on her wrist. He must have been too tired to check his messages last night and simply forgotten this morning.

Randolph cared about her. He'd told her numerous times. Once she talked to him everything would be all right. Perhaps he'd even ask her to marry him now and she wouldn't have to worry about finding a new job at all. She'd be too busy planning her wedding.

"Peterson."

Hearing Randolph's voice, Brooke felt tears sting her eyes. She blinked them away. Randolph didn't like emotional women. "Randolph, thank goodness. I've been trying to reach you since yesterday."

"I had a lot of work to do and I had the machine on. I was trying to finish this morning, but the phone kept disturbing me," he grumbled.

Brooke tried to remember how Randolph hated being interrupted. "I'm sorry, but something terrible has happened."

"You're dumping me?"

Brooke blinked. "No, honey, you know I love you . . . it's something else. Yesterday I was laid off."

"What! What did you do?"

She was almost as shocked by his second question as she was by his first. "I didn't do anything! It was my supervisor, Opal Severs; she's always had it in for me. Because Middleton is going through restructuring, she probably put my name at the top of the list to go. The hag."

"Restructuring doesn't work that way, Brooke. Upper management has some say-so in the leveling process, but consultants usually have the final say on the positions that are expendable."

Her hand tunneled though her hair in rising irritation. Randolph could be so . . . so analytical and logical at times. "Randolph, we're talking about my job. They only gave me two weeks' severance pay."

"You'll find another position. You're smart, savvy, and gorgeous. I can think of several companies that would snap you up."

She perked up. "Which ones? Can you call them?"

"You don't need me to do that, dear. One of the reasons I'm so crazy about you is your resourcefulness. You'll find another job and be back in management before I get home. Now, I have to run. These reports are due Monday morning and I want to make sure they're on time and correct. The bank president and the board will be there. I need to make a good impression."

"But Randolph—"

"You'll do fine. I really must get back to those reports. I'll call later. Bye."

"But . . ." Brooke's voice trailed off as she realized he'd hung up on her. How could he have done that to her? Cell phone in her hand, her mind reeled with confusion. She'd thought he'd be sympathetic, offer encouragement. He'd done none of those things. She tried to hang on to his promise that he'd call later. Laying down on the bed, she snapped out the light, put her arm over her eyes and wished she could call her mother.

Randolph hung up the phone and turned. She was still there. He went from semi-aroused to full arousal in the next breath. She wasn't as beautiful as Brooke, but she was more exotic, more alluring in an openly sexual way. She'd proven it last night. There wasn't any sex act she wasn't willing to do.

He didn't feel the least bit ashamed that he was being unfaithful to Brooke. He might care for her, but he wanted a wife who was on an upward career path. Having a beautiful, intelligent woman as his wife would be a great business asset. But in the meantime, there was no reason to deprive himself of sexual pleasures.

A real man couldn't be expected to remain celibate the way a woman did. His father certainly had his little affairs. Women on the side were almost an honored Southern tradition. And this one he'd picked up at a party at the American Embassy last night was stunning. A jet-setter, she was in between husbands and beds. Randolph couldn't believe his luck.

A half smile on her mouth, she walked over to him. Red nails trailed along his chest, down his stomach, over his groin. The contact was just short of pain. Air hissed through his teeth, then he forgot all about the pain as she dropped to her knees and expertly took him into her mouth.

"J-Jan-aa," he moaned raggedly, forgetting everything but the woman in front of him. He'd heard she could sap a man's soul. He was more than willing to let her try.

Claire fixed a breakfast she didn't want, because she had a guest. However, seeing Brooke's unhappy face Saturday morning around ten, Claire wasn't sure the younger woman was hungry either. "You still can't reach Randolph?"

Brooke's lower lip trembled, then she pulled out a wrought-iron chair and sat down at the table. "We spoke briefly. He was working on a report. He's going to call later."

Claire wasn't sure how to respond. Wouldn't a man in love with a woman want to comfort her at a time like this and put her first? "Did you give him this number?"

Brooke, who had been looking down at her hands in her lap, lifted her head. Misery swam in her teary eyes. "He has my cell."

"Of course." Claire hated that Brooke, who always was so lively and self-assured, was so unhappy. "Have you spoken with your parents yet?"

Brooke swallowed. "I think I'll wait."

A change in subject was definitely in order. "The biscuits are homemade and so are the peach preserves. I'll be offended if you don't eat. Afterwards we can take a walk along the beach and I can show you around Sullivan's Island."

Brooke picked up a biscuit and put it on her plate, but she made no attempt to eat. "I think I'll stay in my room and wait on the call from Randolph."

"He can reach you just as well while you're out," Claire said, opening the preserves and putting a heaping tablespoon on Brooke's plate. "I feel a scream coming on and I might need a reference in case they try to arrest me."

Finally, Brooke looked at Claire. "What if I'm screaming just as loud as you?"

"We'll be in the cell together until Lorraine springs us," she said, happy at least that she could find a smile and that she had a loyal friend like Lorraine.

Brooke picked up her fork and cut into her ham. "Works for me."

I t was close to five that afternoon when Claire pulled back into her garage. They'd been gone longer than she had intended, but as the day had worn on and Randolph hadn't called, Claire had been determined to take Brooke's mind off him. Claire reasoned that other men might be able to accomplish that goal. She certainly didn't have any experience getting men's attention, but thankfully Brooke had achieved that on her own.

Every place they went, Fort Moultrie, the lighthouse, the beach, men noticed Brooke. She resembled Halle Berry and had the same flawless caramel skin and flirtatious smile. The sadness Brooke couldn't hide gave her a certain vulnerability that had men gravitating to her like metal shavings to a magnet. The straight white strapless sundress with high-heeled sandals probably helped. Claire would have broken her neck in heels half that height.

A couple of them even tried to talk to Claire, but since she had never received that kind of attention before, she was sure the reason was because they were trying to get next to Brooke. Claire hadn't minded. By the time they were on their way home, Brooke's smile was back and she had five phone numbers in her little Fendi bag.

"What are you going to do with those numbers?" Claire asked as they entered the house through the garage.

"What I always do." Brooke took them out of her purse and threw them in the trash beneath the sink. "I used to try and say no thank you, but found it was simpler to just take the number and discard them later."

Shaking her head, Claire washed her hands in the sink and pulled two glasses from the white glass-front cabinet. She'd definitely never had that problem. "Does that happen when you're out on a date with Randolph?" Claire could have kicked herself when she saw the shadow return to Brooke's eyes.

"Yes, but Randolph is the only man I want," Brooke said firmly. "We love each other."

Claire wondered if Brooke was trying to convince herself when the phone rang. Brooke, who was closest to the extension on the end of the yellow tiled counter, reached for the phone, then abruptly stopped. Claire knew she had remembered that Randolph didn't have Claire's home phone number.

"I think I'll go lay down for awhile."

Watching her friend leave, her head bowed, her shoulders slumped, Claire felt a distinct dislike for the absent Randolph. She picked up the phone. "Hello."

"You're a hit."

Claire frowned on hearing the excitement in Lorraine's voice. "A hit?"

Laughter flowed through the line. "Your bath products. The ladies went nuts over the soaps." She laughed again. "I think a few of them were a bit jealous when they saw the candle and potpourri you had created for me."

"I'm glad they liked them." Claire's mind wandered to Brooke.

"Like is too mild a word. We agreed, hands down, that yours were the nicest mementos of any book club meeting." Lorraine's voice became subdued. "They felt guilty in accepting the gifts when I told them your situation."

"I didn't want their pity or for them to feel sorry for me," Claire said, a bit defensively.

"I know. I was shameless I'm afraid, and told them if they couldn't accept your gracious gift I'd be happy to donate it in their name to the women's shelter Monday when I go to volunteer." Amusement returned to her voice. "There were no takers. They were still talking and sniffing when they left fifteen minutes ago. I've been trying to call you ever since."

"Brooke and I went out for a while."

"Well, I won't keep you. I just wanted you to know you're definitely a hit and your talents are appreciated."

Just not in the right way. Claire shook off the thought. There would be no self-pity. "Thanks. Is Hamilton home?"

"He called this morning. He'll be home tomorrow." Excitement rang in Lorraine's voice. "Hopefully he'll be home for a while this time."

Claire knew Lorraine's husband was a certified turnaround expert. It suddenly hit Claire that he might have had something to do with Middleton. Even if he hadn't worked on Middleton, there were others just like her that he had caused to lose their jobs. They were names, not people with hopes and dreams, to him.

"Claire, is everything all right?" Lorraine asked as the silence lengthened.

"I was just remembering what Hamilton did for a living."

A sharp intake of breath came clearly through the phone.

"But I remembered something else that's even more important. You and your friendship. I'm glad we're friends and nothing will ever happen to change that."

"Thank you. That means a lot." Thankfully she heard the relief in Lorraine's voice.

"Let's stop before we get soppy. Thanks for the call. I'm going to run out and get an early Sunday paper to check the want ads." She wasn't giving up. Monday morning she planned to be ready to hit the ground running.

"Good luck."

There were those two words again. "Thanks." Claire hung up and added. "I'll need it."

CHAPTER FOUR

Brooke's Jaguar wouldn't start Sunday morning.

Helpless, Claire watched as Brooke finally gave up and stopped flicking the key. The engine had initially tried to turn over, then there'd been only silence. That had been two minutes ago. It seemed longer. Brooke had cursed, pleaded and kept trying, as if her will alone would make the engine spark to life and stay that way. Muttering something Claire couldn't understand, Brooke dropped her head onto her hands, clenched around the steering wheel. Defeat radiated from her.

Claire bit her lower lip. She didn't know if Brooke had talked to Randolph and the conversation hadn't gone any better than yesterday's, or if he hadn't called at all. After seeing the miserable expression on Brooke's face when she came into the kitchen this morning, Claire hadn't had the heart to ask. Now her prized car was giving her grief.

"Maybe it's the battery," Claire offered. "Once mine did the same thing and John had to put a new battery in it."

Brooke slowly turned her face toward Claire. "Who's John?"

"My mechanic." Claire made a face. "He's kept my car running these past nine years, when I thought the best I could do was shoot it and put us both out of our misery."

Brooke didn't smile as Claire had hoped, but she did lift her head. "No one is touching my car but a certified Jaguar mechanic."

"Service departments are closed on Sundays. Even if one were open, it would be very expensive to have your car towed back to Charleston," Claire pointed out.

"Not for me," Brooke said, lifting her head a fraction further. "I never pay full price for anything when a man's involved. I got this car at the dealer's price. He showed me the papers."

Considering what had happened with men yesterday, Claire felt Brooke was probably telling the truth. "You're welcome to spend the night and call them in the morning."

Brooke was already shaking her head. "I better get home." She opened the glove compartment and pulled out her Operator's Manual and began flipping through it. "I have Roadside Service." Finding the number, she called, then tapped her fingernails on the steering wheel as she listened to the recorded message. After a minute or so she hung up. "They're backlogged. May take three to four hours to get someone over here."

She tossed the cell phone back into her purse. "I guess you can call your mechanic, but he'd better know what he's doing or he's not touching my car."

"He does," Claire assured her. "I'll just go inside and call him. It's not nine so he might not have left for church yet." She stopped at the door. "I'll ask John to bring a battery just in case."

"It had better be a certified battery," Brooke called out.

Claire went inside the house without answering. Brooke probably wouldn't know a certified battery from any other, just like Claire didn't. John would. He was the best in the business.

John Randle was heading out the door with his two children for Sunday school when his cell phone rang. Pulling it from his belt loop he checked the number. "Wait a minute, kids. I need to see what Claire wants."

"Maybe she wants me to come over so she can bake me some more cookies," Amy offered hopefully, her sweet face wreathed in a wide grin which showed her missing two front teeth.

Mark rolled his eyes. "Like she's gonna want to bake you cookies after you wasted your milk all over the floor the last time she baby-sat us."

"It was an accident," Amy said, sticking out her lower lip.

"That's enough, you two. It's Sunday." John gently separated his children. Amy might be four and Mark eight, but she held her own and wasn't above driving home her point with a right cross. She had spunk just like her mother. Linda had been gone almost five years and he still missed her smile.

"Hello, Claire, what's up?"

"Good morning, John. My friend spent the night and now her new Jaguar won't start. She really needs to get back to Charleston. Her car service can't come for at least three hours," she quickly explained. "Can you please come over and take a look at it?"

He glanced down at his children in their Sunday best ready for Sunday school. He was getting pretty good at plaiting Amy's thick black hair that reached past her shoulders. His mother had pressed out her dress so there were no wrinkles this time. Mark looked like a little gentleman in his dark pants and white shirt and tie. Amy's wouldn't stay that way, but their leather shoes were polished to a high shine. He tried to take care of his kids, but occasionally life got in the way.

It wouldn't be the first time he'd had to leave them. They'd grown up in the church. Both sets of grandparents would be there, and Pastor Collins and his wife were Mark's godparents. But it still bothered John when he was called away on business even though that same business made sure his children were well taken care of. Being a single parent wasn't easy.

"Just a minute." He held the phone to his chest. "Claire has a friend who needs my help to get her car started. Will you two be all right and behave if I drop you off at Sunday school?"

"I'm always good, Daddy," Amy said, staring up at him with those big brown innocent eyes that reminded him so much of her mother.

"Yeah, when you're asleep," Mark cracked. His sister's penchant for trouble was well known. "I'll watch her, Dad. You know my class is next door."

"Thanks, son." John briefly squeezed Mark's shoulder, and again marveled how tall he'd gotten in the past year. John lifted the phone back to his ear. "I'll go by the garage and pick up the wrecker in case I have to put it on the flatbed."

"It might be the battery," Claire said. Her voice sounded odd.

John's mouth twitched. People always thought of the battery when a car wouldn't start. But since Claire was more astute than most people and had the same problem once, he'd listen. "I'll bring one."

"Ah, John do you have a certified Jaguar battery? Brooke is kind of . . . well, particular about her car."

Since John had clients who felt the same way about certified parts for their cars, he wasn't surprised. "I do, just for cases like this. The battery is bigger for a Jaguar, so I always keep one in stock."

"Wonderful. I'll tell her so she won't worry."

"Be there in about thirty. Bye."

John deactivated the phone. "I need to change into my work clothes. Mark, read to Amy while I'm gone."

"Why can't I read to him?" Amy wanted to know.

"Because you don't know some of the words in the lesson?" was Mark's comeback.

"I do so know them!" Amy said, belligerently.

Quick as a wink Mark opened his Sunday school book and pointed. "What's that word?"

John paused and watched as Amy's brow furrowed in concentration. "P–a–t–i–e–n–c–e. Pa . . . pa," she started trying to sound the word out, then she looked up at her brother with a smug grin on her angelic face. "It's the word that comes after me," she said triumphantly.

His lips twitching, John continued to his bedroom without waiting for Mark's reply. *Thank you, Linda,* he thought, taking off the jacket to his suit. *We have two wonderful kids. I just wish you were here with me to see them.*

Brooke was pacing in front of the garage when she spotted the shiny black wrecker with a flat bed rumble down the two-lane road. *He better know what he's doing.* She'd called roadside service again to make sure the wait hadn't changed. It hadn't. This time she'd been hoping to have a man in customer service answer. Men usually fell all over themselves to help her.

Then why hadn't Randolph called back?

He's busy, Brooke almost shouted aloud. Or perhaps he'd forgotten her cell number. She'd switched services a couple of weeks ago and had a new number. Of course, she'd told him and written the number in the letters she'd sent him. He'd probably misplaced the number. Of course he had. Randolph loved her.

The lumbering vehicle pulled to a stop just as Claire came out the back door in the garage. Brooke had gone in once for a glass of juice while she waited and seen her going through the want ads.

"John made good time," Claire said, heading for the truck.

Brooke grunted. Thirty minutes was far less than the time the auto club had said, but she had always been the impatient type. She just hoped he had worked on a foreign car before.

His steel-toed brogans were topped by long, well-muscled jean-clad legs topped by an impressive chest in a pristine white tee shirt. He was built, and ruggedly handsome. Brooke could imagine him on a hopped-up motorcycle with black leather pants, leather vest, and a bad attitude. Some women would probably find him attractive, but he was too rustic, too blue collar for her.

She glanced at Claire to see if they might be an item and saw the same warm smile Claire had for every man she met. A woman as pretty as Claire deserved a good man to love her. When this mess with their jobs was settled, Brooke was going to help Claire jump-start her love life.

"Hi, Claire. Miss." Stopping in front of Claire, the man tipped his baseball cap to both of them.

"Hi, John. Thanks for coming." Claire turned to Brooke. "Brooke Dunlap. John Randle."

"Ms. Dunlap," he said, his voice smooth and mellow. He extended his large hand.

"Mr. Randle," Brooke said, taking her cue from him as she found her hand briefly encompassed in his wide, calloused one.

"If you'll give me your key, I'll check your car."

Brooke pulled the keys from the pocket of her flared sundress and dropped them into his hand. She noted his nails were trimmed, and clean. "Thank you. I appreciate you coming. I'm not sure what I would have done," she practically crooned.

Out of the corner of her eye, Brooke saw Claire blink, but Brooke kept her expression vulnerable and helpless. Although it galled her to do so, she decided she had to go into her "poor little me, I need a big strong man" act. With four uncles and a doting father, she'd discovered at an early age that men responded well to weak women.

John slid his long, muscular body behind the wheel of the Jag and attempted to start the car. Nothing. Getting out, he lifted the hood and began checking underneath. When his head popped around the hood he had a half-smile on his face. "You may be right, Claire, about the battery. Everything else looks all right. I'll see if a booster will get it going."

"Claire said you would know what to do," Brooke gushed, touching his arm lightly as he passed. The muscles beneath were warm and solid. For a crazy moment she wanted to let her hand linger.

John's eyes widened at the contact and it was all Brooke could do to withdraw her hand and act casual. She hadn't expected the jolt or the sudden coldness in his black eyes that made her want to slink away.

"When I give you the signal, try to start it," he told her. Was it her imagination or had some of the warmth left his voice?

Brooke's smile was strained as she said, "Of course."

"What are you doing? I thought you didn't trust him with your car." Claire whispered as John continued to his wrecker.

"Ensuring that I get a discount," Brooke said, absently rubbing her tingling hand on her thigh as she went to sit in the car.

John connected the cable to the car and after a few seconds gave her the signal. Nothing happened. Waving at her to stop, he got out and came back to her. "The battery isn't taking a charge. It will have to be replaced."

Although Brooke had expected as much, it was still a shock to hear. "The car is less than six months old."

"The dealership will probably reimburse you. I'll give you a receipt and store the battery in your trunk so they can see it was needed," John said.

"Thank you," she said. "I hope this won't cost too much."

"Three-fifty should cover it."

Brooke's eyes bugged. She was actually at a loss for words. But not for long. "That's ridiculous."

"Double service charge for Sunday plus the cost of the battery. Foreign car parts aren't cheap," he said calmly.

"You're supposed to be Claire's friend."

"I am, but I have a family to think about."

"Well, I pity them," she snapped.

His eyes narrowed. "Ms. Dunlap, do you want me to put the battery in or not?"

"Put the damn thing in," she said tightly.

He didn't budge. "Will that be cash, check or credit card?"

Brooke had never wanted to inflict bodily harm on someone more. Not even her old boss had gotten to her this badly. "Credit card."

Claire's worried gaze went from Brooke's angry face to John's unhurried steps taking him to the side of the wrecker. She was caught between two warring people who were friends of hers. Feeling responsible, she went to try and correct the problem.

"John, I didn't know about the double time. I'll pay it."

He stopped with the battery in his hands. "With a car like that she can afford it even if she doesn't get reimbursed."

"That's just it; she can't," Claire said. "She was laid off Friday."

He stared down at Claire a long time, then asked, "What about you?"

Claire glanced away. "The same."

Setting the battery down, he pulled off one glove and placed his hand on her arm. "I'm sorry, Claire. If there's anything I can do, just name it."

She looked back at him. "Give Brooke a break."

He pulled his glove back on. "I might consider it if she hadn't tried to pull that little helpless act of hers instead of being honest. She might be beautiful, but she needs to learn that all men aren't going to salivate over her because she smiles at them."

"Desperation made her act that way. I've worked with her for several months and I've never seen that side of her," Claire said. "Please."

"I'll think about it."

Claire sighed. There was nothing more she could do.

As if she knew what she was looking at, Brooke watched John's every movement as he installed the battery. Finished, he reached inside the car and turned the key. The engine purred to life. After putting the old battery in her trunk, he went to the wrecker and came back with a clipboard.

Brooke had the credit card ready. He took it, copied the information and handed her the bill to sign. She practically snatched both from his hand and quickly signed her name.

He took his time tearing off her receipt. "Thank you."

She jerked the carbon copy out of his hand and stuffed it into her pocket without looking at it. "I'm having the dealership's service department check my old battery first thing tomorrow morning."

Undisturbed, he turned to Claire and said, "Call if you need me for anything."

"Goodbye, John, and thanks."

"Anytime," he said and went to his wrecker.

Infuriated, Brooke watched John pull off. "How can you call that rude money-grabbing man your friend?"

"Because he's kept my car running and charges me a fraction of what another mechanic would charge," Claire told her.

"He makes up for it by overcharging the rest of us," Brooke said. Then, as if realizing what she had implied, her eyes widened. "Please forgive that crack. He just made me so angry."

"I'll pay for the double time."

"You'll do no such thing. Either the dealership or my salesman is going to eat this." Getting in her car, Brooke slammed the door.

"Please drive carefully."

"Don't worry. I want the satisfaction of getting in John's face and telling him he was wrong about my car. He won't ignore me then." She backed out, then sped down the road.

Claire watched Brooke speed away, wondering if John ignoring Brook had added to her irritation with him. Letting down the garage door, she went inside to continue looking through the want ads.

E verything was ready.

Lorraine checked her makeup in the mirror, then glanced around the bedroom to see the ecru duvet turned down, the flickering flame of the candle Claire had given her on the nightstand. The soft scent of peach-vanilla filled the room. She'd lit it for the book club meeting, but had liked the way the fragrance had scented the room so well she'd brought it to the bedroom.

She might be fifty-eight and Hamilton fifty-nine, but thank goodness they still enjoyed a healthy sex life. Or perhaps the desire was still there because they saw each other so infrequently these days. In the last month he'd been home exactly seventeen days.

The doorbell rang, breaking into her thoughts. *Hamilton.* She whirled to rush out of the room and race down the wide hall. Years ago, when the children were growing up, with their hectic schedules, they'd established the routine of him taking a taxi to and from the airport. The children might be gone, but she still had a full calendar.

Halfway down the spiral oak staircase, the front door opened. Joy splintered through her. "Hamilton!" She ran the rest of the way.

Hamilton glanced up, happiness replacing the weariness in his face. As always, he was conservatively dressed in a tailored navy pinstriped suit with a silk tie and white shirt. He never appeared in public without a suit or a sports jacket. His briefcase and luggage fell from his hands and he opened his arms.

Laughing, she went into his arms as she always had, with love and complete devotion. Their lips clung, their bodies welcomed each other.

"I missed you," he said.

"Not as much as I missed you." It was a ritual they had always gone through when he returned after a business trip. She was thankful that it was still true after years of marriage. Some of her friends and associates weren't as fortunate.

Her hand resting on his strong jaw, she smiled at the man she had defied her family to marry. "Did everything go all right?"

"Great, but it took longer than I expected. I think I could sleep for two days."

"Let's eat first," she said. Curving her hand around his waist, she headed for the kitchen. She'd already set the table and put the serving dishes out as well. "You never eat right while you're working." And she always waited to eat with him.

"There are some things I miss more than food," he said, nibbling on her ear.

She laughed and leaned in closer. "You won't get an argument from me, but first you eat."

"You smell wonderful. New perfume?"

One of the things she'd always liked about Hamilton was that he noticed things about her. "Soap. Claire gave it—" She stopped abruptly and bit her lower lip.

Frowning, he lifted her chin with his thumb and forefinger. "What is it?"

"She worked for Middleton. She and her friend were laid off Friday."

He touched her arm gently. "Lorraine, I'm sorry it happened to your friend, but I look at expenditures and ways of making the company more efficient. The bottom line is saving the company and that often means cutting jobs."

"I know." Lorraine swept her hair back behind her ear. "We've gone through this before, but it still bothers me. Especially when it hits this close."

Concern entered Hamilton's eyes. "She doesn't blame you, does she?"

Lorraine shook her dark head of hair. "No, she's too good and too practical for that."

He looked at her closely. "But you blame me?"

She saw the glimmer of hurt in his eyes and instantly sought to soothe. "I love you," she said and hugged him. "But I'd be a liar if I denied that sometimes I wish you had chosen a different profession."

"But it's given us a good living. The kids were able to go to the best schools. You've all had the best of everything. Just like I promised you when you married a dirt poor kid from a town in Texas no one had ever heard of."

After all these years Hamilton's background still bothered him. It was the one area in their marriage that they had not been able to overcome or openly discuss. "Things never mattered. You did."

His arm around her waist, he started for the kitchen again. "Your parents didn't think so. They didn't want their baby, their only daughter, not having the lifestyle she had always been accustomed to."

"They're very proud of you."

"Because I've proven to them I could give you even more than they had," he said, taking a seat as Lorraine put the tossed green salad on the table and served the lemon herb chicken with rice. "We both know their opinion of me is tied to my financial success."

Since he was right, there was no sense denying it. She took her seat. "Mine and the children's aren't."

He reached for her hand and grasped it. "You're the best part of me. I couldn't do it without you behind me. There's a certain comfort in knowing you're always here that helps me get through the day. You make this house a home worth coming back to."

Hamilton had grown up with parents who had died the summer he graduated from high school. Home was important to him. She understood that, but this was the first time hearing him say it almost made her feel trapped.

"Eat. So you can get back to nibbling," she teased, trying to shake off the return of the depressed mood that her life was missing something, a mood that had plagued her since Margaret's death.

Grinning, Hamilton picked up his salad fork.

B rooke did something she never had done in all of her twenty-five years. She sat by the phone and waited for a man to call. She'd never had to. Men had always catered to her. First it had been her father, and his four brothers. It had probably helped that her father was the oldest and the first to get married and have a daughter. There was always a pair of arms to hold her, to give her what she wanted. They couldn't give her what she wanted now.

Arms wrapped around her body, Brooke stood and looked out her window to the marina. Usually she enjoyed looking at the boats and all the activity, but not today. Why didn't he call?

She'd been home for more than four hours and she'd yet to hear from Randolph. He had to know she was upset about losing her job. He should want to comfort her. She'd always known he wasn't as demonstrative as the men in her family, that he tended to be more rigid in his thinking, but she had accepted it as the way he had been brought up. She'd met his parents once. They had been polite, but cold. They didn't even appear to like each other.

Glancing over her shoulder at the silent phone she decided she couldn't take this waiting another second. Just as her hand reached for the phone it rang. She snatched it from the cradle.

"Randolph."

"Hello, Brooke."

He sounded as he always did: cool, calm and in total control.

"I've been waiting for your call."

"Sorry, something came up," he said carelessly.

She couldn't believe her ears. "And it was more important than what I'm going through?"

"There's nothing I could have done to change your situation," he replied, a bit of annoyance creeping into his voice.

"I needed you." She wrapped her arm around her waist. "Is that all you can say?"

"What do you expect from me, Brooke? I'm thousands of miles away in another country. You'll just have to handle it yourself."

"When two people care for each other, I thought they handled things together."

"Don't get accusatory and take that tone with me," he said. "It's not my fault you lost your job."

She gasped, hurt and growing angrier by the second. "Why don't you just come out and tell me that since I lost my job you've lost interest. I'm no longer an asset."

"There's no need to become snide. We're both intelligent people, we both know the score. We were drawn to each other because of our upwardly mobile positions."

"And now that's changed." Her eyes clamped tightly shut. He was being as callous as she had been in searching for a man with money in the bank instead of one with love in his heart. She'd erroneously thought she'd found both. "I thought you loved me."

"I do care. Things are just hectic here at the moment. We'll see how things are when I come home," he placated. "I wouldn't have sent you the bracelet if I didn't care."

He cared, not loved. He always managed to wiggle out of saying the words. She fumbled to unclasp the bracelet from her wrist. "I'll mail the bracelet back to you tomorrow."

"Please, Brooke, don't be hasty. You'll find another position and we'll laugh about this one day."

"I doubt that."

"You're just down at the moment because of what happened. You'll bounce back."

"And then things will be back to the way they were?"

"Exactly."

Her sarcasm had gone right over his head or perhaps he just thought she was that needy. "Goodbye, Randolph."

"Bye, Brooke. Keep your chin up."

Hanging up the phone, she hefted the bracelet in her hand. Perhaps she wouldn't send it back after all. After wasting seven months of her time she deserved something, if no more than a reminder of how she'd been dumped by a callous man. For the first and last time.

Her mind went to John. Another man who thought to use her. She wasn't about to let him get away with charging her such an exorbitant price. First thing Monday morning she was going into the dealership.

No man was ever taking advantage of her again.

CHAPTER FIVE

Claire tried to remain optimistic Monday morning as she started out with a list of prospective jobs. She filled out applications, waited up to an hour to be seen by Human Resources personnel. In between interviews she called to check on Brooke and found out little more than she'd taken her car in and learned the battery had been the problem. She hadn't sounded too happy. Claire had hung up without asking about Randolph and headed for the next business on her list.

By Thursday, Claire was beginning to feel her job search was hopeless. More and more companies were laying off people in her field and employers could take their time and pick from a long list of applicants.

Sifting through the mail she'd picked up from the mailbox in front of the house, she came through the back door to the garage. Seeing the electric bill, her shoulders slumped even further. The next letter was from the home care nursing facility that had provided care for her mother when Claire was at work. She didn't have to open the envelope to know the balance remained over five thousand dollars.

It might have been cheaper to put her mother in a nursing home, but the thought had never entered Claire's mind. Although it broke her heart for her mother to look at her and not know her, she seemed to take pleasure being near the water, walking on the beach. Claire didn't regret her decision, although at the moment she had the urge to go into her room, get into bed and pull the sheet over her head.

Tossing the bills into the basket on the kitchen counter, she shut her eyes. How was she going to survive? She'd been desperate enough to call her brother last night and ask him to repay her.

"You wouldn't have to ask if I could," Derek said. "It makes me feel less of a man to ask, but you know how things are. The white man is still trying to keep a brother down."

It was an excuse he'd used since high school when their parents had asked why he couldn't find a job.

"You don't have to pay me back all of the money at once. If you could send two-hundred dollars now and, when you get paid, another hundred, it would help."

"You know I would, Baby Sis, if I could," he said. "With the economy being so bad, car sales are down. I'm barely making ends meet."

"I really need the money, Derek. Please." She'd been desperate enough to beg.

"You'd have it if I had it," he said, then his tone almost became defensive. "You sound like you don't believe me."

"I just need the money."

"I ain't got it, I told you. You're the one with the college education. You're the one Mama and Daddy always bragged on."

The taunt hurt. Everyone had expected her to succeed and she was floundering. "I better go, Derek. Goodbye."

She'd hung up and gone through the want ads again. She had to find a job that would pay her enough to keep afloat.

Now, she wasn't so sure that would happen. She glanced around the kitchen. Thankfully, she'd already paid the house note for the month, but what about next month?

She had to face reality and the very real possibility that she might have to sell the house. It hurt her every time she thought of doing so. Her parents had been so proud of her, so sure she would be the first one in their family to make something of herself, the first one to leave her mark.

They had been so wrong.

The doorbell rang, and Claire pushed away from the cabinet. Opening the front door, she was surprised to see Lorraine grinning from ear to ear. It almost didn't seem fair when her life was going down the tube. "Hello, Lorraine, come on in."

"I have some great news," Lorraine said, coming inside and following Claire into the great room and taking a seat. She placed the sweetgrass basket on the table in front of them. "Last night it was my turn to have the women over for bridge and I put the bar of soap you gave me and the candle in the guest bath. The women went just as crazy as the book club members."

"That's nice," Claire said absently, her mind on paying bills.

"Nice? It's fantastic," Lorraine said, her enthusiasm growing. "Your soap smells fabulous, lathers like a dream and, best of all, it doesn't dry out the skin." Lorraine held out her hand as if to demonstrate her statement.

Claire glanced at Lorraine's hands because she was wiggling her fingers in front of her face. At any other time she'd be happy for Lorraine's visit, but not now. "Thanks for returning the basket. Did you want another bar of soap?"

"In a manner of speaking." Lorraine placed her purse beside her on the couch. "The women were clamoring to know where I had bought the soap. I told them I wasn't ready to divulge my source at the moment, but I'd let them know something soon."

Claire tried to remember how many bars of soap she had left. She'd given Brooke two bars and a scented candle. "You know you can have what's left to give them. I'm sorry, but I don't have time to make any more."

"Who said anything about giving them away? I want to sell them."

Claire blinked. "What?"

Lorraine laughed. "Sorry. I'm just so excited that it's difficult for me to make sense. I've thought about opening a specialty shop since I was in college, and after using your products, I've decided that you and your products would make a great addition to the store." She paused and drew a breath. "After the women left last night the idea came to me. I could hardly sleep I was so excited. I would have been here earlier but I had a meeting I couldn't get out of."

"You want me to make products for you?" Claire asked, still trying to understand what Lorraine wanted from her.

"For us," Lorraine clarified. "I want us to be partners."

"Me?"

"You," Lorraine said. "You can make your wonderful soaps, candles, and potpourri. The moment customers walk in and smell how heavenly the store is, they'll want to buy your candles. We'll have crystal, brass and porcelain gift items to complement them. Can you make anything else?"

"Yes, moisturizing cream, lotion and bath gel, but—"

"Perfect," Lorraine said, cutting Claire off.

Claire stared at her friend. She'd always considered Lorraine level-headed. "You can't be serious."

"I most definitely am." Lorraine pointed to the potpourri on the table, the unlit candle in the center. "Women and men want their homes to smell good and they're willing to pay top dollar."

Claire stood. "Thank you, but no. I'm not wasting a penny of my money on anything so reckless. A few women might like the things I made, but that doesn't mean there would be enough customers willing to buy the products."

Lorraine came to her feet as well. "I disagree. There's already a demand for your products. All we have to do is tap into it."

"Making large amounts costs money." Claire folded her arms around her waist.

"I'll stake you. You can pay me back when the profits start rolling in."

In Claire's mind that suggestion made the possibility even less appealing. "I'm not gambling with your money. I appreciate all you've done for me, but the answer is no."

"Claire, please sit down. I want to tell you something."

Reluctantly Claire took her seat. She needed to look for a job, but Lorraine was too good a friend not to listen to her.

Lorraine sat beside her. "My dearest friend, Margaret Holmes, died four month ago with cancer. She was a wonderful energetic woman who was always ready to help someone. She'd always wanted a flower shop. I wanted a gift shop. We decided to combine the two. Margaret put off opening the shop to help her oldest daughter plan her wedding. After that she took on the chairmanship of a charity ball and, after that, her sister wanted her to help decorate her new home." Lorraine's eyes misted. "I was just as busy with my family and other obligations.

"There was always a reason for us to put our dream on hold. We always thought there would be time. Then Margaret went for her checkup and her pap came back class four." Lorraine swallowed the sob in her throat. "She was gone in less than six weeks. I don't want to die without living my dream."

Claire tensed with fear. "Are you sick?"

"No. I'm sorry if I upset you, but I feel as if I'm putting my husband, the church, my social obligations, everything ahead of what I want . . . to open a gift shop. I thought with Margaret's death my chance had ended. Now I know that's not true." Lorraine stared at Claire. "Working together, you and I could make that happen. Your products would make the shop unique. This is my second chance, maybe my last chance to live my dream."

Claire saw the longing in Lorraine's face, and vividly recalled how it had felt to have your dream snatched away. "Lorraine, you know I'd do anything for you, but I just can't do this. I can't go chasing possibilities."

"This will work, Claire. I feel it," Lorraine insisted, her voice vibrant. "Just go with me to visit a few of the specialty shops in the area and in Charleston and compare your products to theirs. Please. Just for a couple of hours."

Claire had planned to go through the want ads again, but she couldn't forget how Lorraine had befriended her and helped her. "I'll go, but I'm not promising anything."

A wide grin on her face, Lorraine came to her feet. "Fair enough. Let's go."

Claire wandered in a daze through the cosmetic department of a specialty store near the historic district. She couldn't believe a candle in a plain glass jar cost $45.

"Well?" Lorraine asked, standing beside her. "What do you think about bath and beauty products now?"

"I haven't been shopping for anything but the basic necessities in over three years, but if I wasn't looking at the prices I wouldn't believe it," Claire replied.

Lorraine pointed to the cylindrical candle in Claire's hand. It was enclosed in a gold organza bag with matching satin ribbon. "Tell me the difference between that and yours."

"Packaging and price," was Claire's prompt response.

Lorraine nodded. "Exactly."

"From the first my mother always bought the best natural and essential oils she could afford." Claire put the candle on a glass hexagon display shelf and picked up one in a silver tin and turned it over to look at the bottom. "I'm familiar with the ingredients listed. It may sound complicated, but it's not."

"Mrs. Averhart, do you and your friend need any help?" asked a young saleslady in a short black miniskirt and black knit top.

"No, thanks, Karen. We're still looking."

The ebony-skinned saleslady smiled. "Call if you need me," she said, then walked away.

Taking Claire's arm, Lorraine pulled her to an area with a soap display on a round two-tier shelf. She picked up a package of three bars of guest soap and turned the box over. "Thirty-two dollars. I've purchased this brand before. It doesn't lather or moisturize my skin any better than yours."

Claire picked up a fat squat jar that looked like it contained creamed honey. "Body wash. One of the key ingredients in this is honey, which contains amino acids and vitamins A and C. It protects and moisturizes the skin. You can buy the base for the bath gel unscented and colorless from a number of manufacturers and add your own fragrances, essential or natural oils, or make your own from scratch." She glanced around the open, lighted area with lots of glass shelving and exotic flower arrangements. "This place is making a killing."

"Hi, Lorraine," greeted a fashionably dressed woman in her late fifties. "I see you like Aswan Bath Gel, too."

"Hello, Holly. Holly Hunter meet Claire Bennett, a friend of mine." Lorraine introduced, then continued. "I do, but I've discovered another product that makes my skin feel softer and doesn't dry it out. The women in my book and bridge clubs were ecstatic after using it."

"Really? What's the name?" the woman asked, her eyes glittering with greed. "Do they sell it here?"

Lorraine glanced around as if to ensure that she would not be overheard, then leaned closer. "No, and I'm not at liberty to say at the moment where it's sold, but rest assured when the announcement is ready to be made public you'll be among the first to know."

"Oh, please. You have my number."

"I certainly do. Goodbye, Holly," Lorraine said, leading Claire out the double glass doors of the store and onto busy King Street. A horse-drawn carriage ambled by.

"I haven't said I'd do it yet," Claire felt compelled to point out as they started down the most famous street for shoppers in Charleston. In the three-storied buildings dating back to the nineteenth century, the storefront windows displayed everything from pawned goods to rare antiques.

Lorraine looped her arm through Claire's. "I'm afraid I can't help but feel optimistic. I was a bit hesitant when Margaret suggested we go into business together. She showed me that the discriminating buyer would appreciate the high quality and uniqueness of our shop. I wanted to show you that there are women eagerly waiting for the next product that is going to pamper their skin, especially those of us over fifty."

"Mama always said a woman shouldn't wait to take care of her skin," Claire said.

"She was right. But unfortunately most women think their skin will miraculously remain unlined and smooth without any protection or care." Lorraine dropped her arm and reached into her bag to pull her car keys from her purse. They'd been lucky enough to snag a rare parking spot near the store. "Next stop is a beauty boutique on the other side of town. I want you to be thoroughly convinced this is going to work."

"There's some place else I'd rather visit."

Lorraine activated the lock on her Mercedes. "Where?"

"A person who takes excellent care of her skin and buys the best of everything Brooke."

B rooke was happy to get a call from Claire and Lorraine asking if they could come over. She'd done nothing but mope around the house since Sunday. She'd called her parents soon after getting off the phone with Randolph and told them about losing her job and Randolph.

"We'll be there in an hour," her father said. "Your uncles, those who can make it, will want to come, too."

She'd started crying. She couldn't help but think that that was the kind of unconditional support she had expected from Randolph. It had been difficult, but she had told them not to come. She appreciated the offer, but she was twenty-five. She'd get another job.

The next day she'd received a FedEx letter with checks totaling over two thousand dollars from her parents and uncles. It had simply read, "We love you and if you need more, you only have to ask."

There had been more tears and a greater determination to find a job. Instead of looking at the sales in the newspaper, she'd pulled out the employment section. Unfortunately, Claire had been right about it being an employer's market. She hadn't received one call from the twenty resumes she'd faxed or e-mailed.

The doorbell rang and she hurried to answer it. Lorraine and Claire took a seat in the hand-tied ten-thousand-dollar Italian leather sofa she'd just had to have. She sat in the matching chair. "Were you out doing book club business?"

"*Our* business hopefully," Lorraine replied.

Claire scooted to the edge of the buttery-soft ivory cushion. "You know the products I made. Lorraine seems to think we might be able to make money selling them. We just left an upscale store after checking out their merchandise and prices."

"Sounds reasonable. Beauty products are a multi-billion-dollar industry," Brooke said. "Women's magazines are full of ads with products for women that will make them feel and look sexier, prettier, and healthier."

"But we don't have money for that type of advertisement," Claire said, the seed of hope that had sprouted dying.

"You don't have to," Brooke said, uncurling her bare foot from underneath her. "Marketing has changed dramatically in the last ten years with infomercials, the home shopping network, the web, and all the other ways to sell. Let me show you." Picking up the TV control she turned on the forty-two-inch TV she kept in a beautiful cherry armoire.

Claire leaned forward, switching her attention from the spokeswoman for the herbal fragrance bath set of five products, to the counter on the bottom left-hand side which showed the number of units being sold. "The number is changing by the second. I can't believe it. My mother and I have never bought anything in our lives that we couldn't see or touch. Even with the products, she was able to get samples first. When she worked for Livingston, the other household staff used to tease her about not helping them all keep their jobs by buying from the Livingston catalogue."

"Many women are too busy these days to shop in stores, or for one reason or another they can't get into the store," Lorraine pointed out. "Most large specialty stores, like Saks, have personal shoppers for just that reason. There may not be a Neiman's or a Bergdorf here, but many women order from their catalogues or online."

Claire turned to her. "Then to reach those customers we'd need a similar established outlet they already trust."

"You just said we couldn't do TV or magazines," Lorraine reminded her.

"I was talking about the Livingston Catalogue," Claire said.

Lorraine's eyes gleamed with excitement. "Then you're in."

Claire glanced back at the counter. "I'm in."

With a squeal of joy, Lorraine hugged Claire. "I knew it! I just knew it."

"Congratulations. This calls for a drink." Brooke stood and went to the bar. At least somebody's life was on the right track.

Lorraine was bubbling over with happiness. She couldn't wait to tell Hamilton when he arrived home from work that night. She'd prepared a special dinner of grilled salmon and had a bottle of his favorite wine. Hearing the key in the door, she went to open it. "Hi."

He smiled into her face and kissed her on the mouth. "Hi, yourself. What's got you so happy?"

"I'm going into business with Claire," she blurted.

The smile on Hamilton's face slid away. "You're doing what?"

Uneasiness coursed though Lorraine. "Claire and I are going to open a gift shop."

He walked past her and placed his attaché on top of the slate gray marble on the kitchen island. "This is rather sudden, isn't it?"

"In a way, yes. But I've always wanted a gift shop since I worked in one in high school and college. Margaret and I had the idea to open a floral gift shop . . . then she became ill," she explained. "She made me promise not to let our dream die."

"Margaret is gone and you know nothing of what it takes to run a business," he pointed out.

"I can learn," she told him.

He didn't appear convinced. "You've never mentioned this before."

"You were so busy with the Anderson account that I decided to wait. Then Margaret became ill and I forgot about it." She reached toward him. "Now I have another chance."

He folded his arms instead of taking the hand she offered. "Businesses go bankrupt every day, Lorraine, with people running them with far more experience than you or Claire have."

Hurt splintered through her. She let her hand drop to her side. "I realize that, but I believe this can work. Claire's products are wonderful. We went to Saks and several other upscale shops today and did some comparative pricing," she told him. "I really want to try."

Arms still crossed, Hamilton leaned back against the island. "At least Margaret had some retail business experience in management. You and Claire have none. Besides, you can't possibly think you can compete against Saks' buying power or their clout in advertising."

"We don't plan to. We'll specialize in what we do, and do it well," she said, not understanding why he was being so stubborn.

"What about your social obligations, this house, me?"

Suddenly she smiled and went to him. So that was the problem. "You'll always come first. I just want you to support me the way I've always supported you."

His mouth firmed. "I was making a better life for all of us. You don't need to work. Isn't it enough that I need you to be here for me?"

"This isn't about my feelings for you or the life we have; it's about fulfilling a dream of mine."

If anything his expression became sterner. "Are you saying I haven't made you happy? You aren't satisfied being my wife?"

Lorraine felt the conversation slipping from her control. "No, not at all. You have your work. I want mine."

"I see." He turned and picked up his attaché case. "I think I'll go shower before dinner."

"Hamilton," Lorraine called and he glanced back over his shoulder. "I love you. Please, I don't want to fight."

He quickly came back and took her in his arms. "I just don't want to think that what we have isn't enough for you."

"Ham—"

"No. I have to leave in the morning and I don't want us to be at odds over this." He kissed her softly on the lips. "Let's talk about it when I get back."

"All right, Hamilton," she agreed, but she wasn't giving up on the dream she and Margaret had begun. She loved him, but this was something she had to do for herself.

CHAPTER SIX

Claire had a plan. It just wasn't working.

After four days of trying to contact Gray at his office in Charleston he still hadn't accepted any of her calls. It looked as if getting an appointment with the CEO of Livingston Catalogue was next to impossible. Fifteen years ago, when she needed the clout of his name to help convince the bankers to give her a loan, she'd simply gone by his grandparents' home where he lived. He had been much more accessible then.

Looking at the stack of bills in the basket in the kitchen, she decided to try the same method. She had no idea if he still lived there or not, but it beat sitting around doing nothing. Grabbing the gift basket of products, she went to her car.

It didn't take her long to arrive at the Livingston home in the cobblestone streets of the Battery. Tall and imposing, the house was an impossibly beautiful, three-story mansion, all the more so because an African American family had lived in the historic neighborhood for forty years. Many of the homes, preserved since the antebellum era, were built by African craftsmen, bond and free. Gray's grandfather had started the catalogue business by sending products from Korea, while he was stationed there in the Army, for his wife to sell. Once home he'd kept his contacts and expanded. Now Gray ran Livingston Catalogue.

Her heart thumping in her chest, Claire opened the black wrought-iron gate and walked up the stone walkway to the door. Neatly trimmed hedges hugged the house. Monkey grass ringed colorful borders of begonias and caladiums. She moistened her lips. She had no idea if Gray was home or if she'd even get past the front door. She just knew she had to try. She rapped the brass lion's head with a sweaty hand.

The heavily carved, recessed door opened almost immediately. Her hand clenched around the basket handle.

The woman who answered the door wore a gray uniform with a white apron. "Yes."

Claire recognized the round friendly face at once. "Good evening, Mrs. Martin."

The elderly woman peered at her a long time, then a slow smile washed across her lined face. "Claire?"

"Yes, ma'am," Claire said, relieved to see that the woman who had worked during her mother's tenure was still the housekeeper. "It's Henry and Nancy's daughter."

Sadness entered the woman's eyes. "It still grieves me when I think of them being gone. We were talking just the other day about them and how fine they were. Always proud of you and what you did for them."

"Thank you. I tried."

"You're a whole sight better than most children these days. Including mine, which I haven't heard from in weeks." She squinted up through her thick bifocals. "What you doing here?"

Claire's mind veered back from Mrs. Martin's daughter, Prudence, who, like Derek, hadn't been able to wait to leave Charleston. "I need to see Gray . . . Mr. Livingston. Is he here by any chance?"

"Sure is. He's working in that study as usual." Mrs. Martin stepped back onto the terrazzo floor of the spacious foyer. "Come on in. It's muggy out there today. Can I get you something to drink? I remember you liked strawberry lemonade."

Claire was touched she remembered. Everyone had always watched out for her. "No, thank you. It's good to see you, Mrs. Martin. Is the rest of the old staff still here?"

The robust woman grinned, showed a gap-toothed smile. "Just like that bunny on television; we just keep going and going. Added some help, but the rest of us old timers are still here. Although I sometimes wish I could rest these old bones like your parents did, but what would I do all day? But 'least I got a job to be thankful for."

"I'm glad." The Livingstons were kind, down-to-earth people who had always treated their employees with respect. She tried to remember that as she glanced down the hallway.

"You go on, baby, and when you finish talking with Gray, you come on back to the kitchen and say hello to the others," Mrs. Martin said. "They'll be as glad to see you as I am."

"I will," Claire replied. *If Gray doesn't throw me out first.*

Gray was racing against a deadline. But what else was new? He divided his time between his grandparents' home and his new place in Columbia. The move had been necessary when he'd opened a second warehouse six months before. Livingston was growing and he planned to keep up with demand.

He never paused when he heard the soft knock on the door. He assumed it was one of the servants. His grandmother never knocked. "Come in."

He didn't look up from going through the quarterly reports, expecting whoever had come in to say what they wanted. When they didn't, he lifted his head and saw a pretty woman with cinnamon-hued skin and a death grip on a basket. Her straight black hair was pulled away from her face that was free of makeup. Her unpainted lips were sweetly curved. His dark eyes narrowed as his gaze ran over her slim, shapely figure. There was something vaguely familiar about her, but none of the women he knew dressed in simple cotton shirtwaist dresses or wore low-heeled flats.

"Yes?" He pulled his reading glasses from his face.

Moistening her lips, she took another step closer. "Hello, Gray."

The voice, the shy innocent voice, made the face click into place. Gray smiled and leaned back in his chair. "Hello, Claire."

"Mrs. Martin let me in. I know you're busy, but I just have to talk with you. It's important."

He motioned for her to have a seat. The last time she had come to him had been for her parents. They were gone now. "What can I do for you?"

Instead of taking a seat, she set the overflowing basket on his desk. "I made these. I want to talk to you about putting my bath and beauty products in your catalogue."

Gray felt instant disappointment. He wouldn't have expected Claire to be the kind of person who would attempt to use him for her own benefit. Old friend of the family or not, he didn't want to be used by anyone again. "I don't handle product placement in the catalogue." He picked up his glasses and returned to the report. "You know the way out."

"Please, Gray. Tell me what I have to do to have them in your catalogue," Claire said, her voice trembling.

Gray glanced up, remembering the shy young girl who used to stare at him with huge worshipful chocolate brown eyes. If he spoke to her, she'd drop her head and chew on her lower lip. He'd always liked her because she appeared so open and honest. Now, she was just another woman wanting him to do something for her.

"Please. Tell me," she pleaded.

"All right." At least that would get her to leave. Closing the folder, he clasped his hands on top. "Can you deliver five thousand products to my warehouse within the next ten weeks before the final catalogue is printed? Can you sell the products to me at a sixty to seventy percent discount?"

"No, I . . . I can't." Stunned, Claire sank into a leather burgundy side chair in front of his desk. "What am I going to do?"

"Keep your day job," he advised briskly, picking up the file again.

Claire blinked, then swallowed. "I wish I could have. I was laid off ten days ago."

Gray tried to feel nothing, but couldn't quite manage it. Seeing her blink, he absently set the folder aside. He didn't deal well with tears. Well, that wasn't true. Jana had pleaded and cried and he had felt nothing but disgust. He'd heard she was in London. He didn't care where she was as long as she stayed away from him.

Not wanting to remember how big a fool he had been with his ex-wife, Gray reached into the basket Claire had set on his desk and picked up the first thing he touched—creamy rose-shaped soap enclosed in netting with a rosette bow. A light fragrance drifted out to him. "How much do you plan to sell this for?"

The blinking stopped. She chewed on her lip, then dropped her head. "I have no idea."

"Well, you better get one." Gray tossed the soap back into the basket. Claire's head came up. "How?"

Now he was the one blinking. Her directness caught him off guard. He remembered himself sitting in that same chair as his grandfather drilled the catalogue business into his head. He'd been scared, but determined to learn and to make his grandfather proud of him. "Don't do another thing until you come up with a business plan. That means everything from production time and cost to your core audience."

Claire dug inside her worn, black imitation leather purse for a pen and paper. "What else?"

If she didn't look so eager and earnest, he might have told her to get a business manual, but he found himself ticking off advice about everything from inventory to budget to a marketing plan.

Gray finished thirty minutes later. "Find your strength and know your weaknesses, and above all remember customer service is key."

Claire put her pen and paper away, then stood. "Thank you, Gray. You've been very helpful."

Standing, he picked up the basket. "Don't forget this."

Smiling, Claire shook her head. "It's my gift to you for being so nice. You've given me a lot to think about. Goodbye and thanks again."

The door closed softly behind her and Gray was left wondering if she'd make it. He found himself hoping she would. At least she was willing to put forth the effort, unlike a lot of people he'd met.

Gray was barely settled in his chair when the door opened again. Corrine Livingston breezed into the room, looking as lovely as usual in a raw silk natural-colored suit, her gray hair perfectly coiffured, her back straight despite her seventy-eight years. His grandmother was a five-feet-three-inch dynamo. Fiercely loyal, she didn't suffer fools. She kept the whole family on their toes.

"Hi, Grandmother. I thought you were out shopping."

"I just returned. Helen says you've been in here all afternoon. I came to remind you that we're having guests for dinner and not to be late."

Gray wrinkled his mouth. He wasn't looking forward to an evening with the Franklins even if he was president of the bank they did business with. "Is Sherry coming with her parents?"

His grandmother shot him a look. "You don't think she'd miss an opportunity to try and interest you, do you?"

Gray grunted.

"Oh, how lovely." Bending, she started going through the assortment in the baskets. "Don't tell me women have started sending you gifts."

"It was a gift, but not in that way. It's from Claire Bennett." He proceeded to tell her about Claire's visit.

"I always liked the family, with the exception of the son. Always had an excuse ready for not working."

His grandmother hesitated, something unusual for her. "You haven't received any more packages from her, have you?"

Gray's mouth tightened. There was no need to explain who she referred to.

"No."

She nodded. "That woman has some serious issues."

An understatement if ever there was one, Gray thought. He'd been completely snowed by Jana's vulnerable act partly because it was obvious that her father could barely stand to be in the same room with her. He didn't learn why until it was too late.

Gray had thought he was saving her when he married her, that his love would heal her. Instead she'd nearly destroyed him. He'd never give any woman that much power over him again.

"Enough unpleasantries." His grandmother picked up a candle in a clear container and turned it over in her hand. "Are you going to help, Claire?"

He picked back up his folder. "With the new warehouse opening in Columbia, I'm busier than ever."

"That's not what I asked you."

Sighing, Gray glanced up at his grandmother. She was patiently waiting for her question to be answered. "She doesn't know the first thing about running a business."

"Then she came to the right place." Corrine picked up the basket. "Don't forget, dinner at six."

Gray rocked back in his chair. He might not be able to get out of dinner, but Claire was on her own.

Claire was excited.

She couldn't wait to get home and invite Lorraine and Brooke over the next morning. As soon as she served them coffee, she told them of her visit with Gray. "I met Gray yesterday afternoon and although he's not going to put my products in his catalogue, I can see why. We need to develop a business plan."

"That's exactly what Hamilton said," Lorraine told them. "We put discussing the business on hold until he returns from a business trip next week." She sighed. "Margaret had all the business knowledge."

"We have Gray," Claire said. "If we all work together we can develop a business plan."

"Whoa." Brooke held up her hands. "Claire, forgive me, but I don't see why you called me. I have nothing to do with this."

Claire shoved her coffee aside and braced her arms on the table. "One of the key elements Gray mentioned was a good marketing plan. You're the best when it comes to marketing. I didn't have time to discuss it with Lorraine, but I'd like you to come on as a consultant or partner."

"I think it's an excellent idea," Lorraine said.

Brooke was momentarily speechless. "You really want me to be a part of your business?"

"Yes," Claire said, her gaze intent. "We can be our own bosses and we won't have to worry about being laid off again."

Brooke didn't have to think long. "Partner, and I'm in."

Claire stuck out her hand. The three women clasped hands warmly.

"Now," Claire said, handing each a spiral notebook. "If there are no objections I will be the production manager and design the Web site, Lorraine will be the financial manager, and work with Brooke on marketing and public relations. We can all work on the package design and logo. Can you meet here tomorrow afternoon at three? I'll fix dinner."

Lorraine looked up from writing. "You didn't waste any time."

"I've wasted enough time."

The next evening the women sat around the kitchen table after dinner with products in the middle as they tried to come up with a name and a logo. They'd already worked out a business plan for Lorraine to be the principal investor with the majority of the profits returning to her to repay the loan.

"Then it's agreed that we have a limited number of products in each of the four lines," Claire said. "Triple-milled, perfumed bath soaps; creamy body moisturizers; luxurious hand lotions; foaming bath gels; skin-conditioning shea butter and aromatic candles. How about fragrances?"

Brooke pushed two bars of soap with her pen. "One fragrance for each line of products. That way the wearer has an overall layer of fragrance."

"I've seen brands with one fragrance and different scents of lotions, soaps and body creams," Lorraine told them. "But I think they were more fruity smells."

"You're probably right. Three of our product lines will be a mingling of floral scents like gardenia and honeysuckle, and the fourth a mixture of pear and orange, but what I had in mind is to make each fragrance distinct." Claire leaned over on the table and picked up the open jars of naturally scented shea butter and body cream. "The shea butter is a great moisturizer, but it can be a little greasy. A black woman might want to put it on her elbows and knees to deal with dryness in those areas—"

"You mean ash?" Brooke cut in and the women laughed.

"Ash, then, but not all over her body. Would she want to have two competing scents?" Claire asked.

"No," Lorraine said. "They should come in a complete set with their own fragrance, as you suggested."

"I've been thinking about the names of the products as well as the business," Brooke said, leaning back in her chair. "We want something that when women hear the name they think of luxury, pampering and that special man."

"Every woman doesn't need a man," Claire said quickly, unsure of why Brooke's comment had struck a nerve.

"She may not need one, but most women want one," Lorraine said quietly.

"Exactly! And although I've sworn off men at the moment, there are a lot of women out there who are still looking for Mr. Right and finding Mr. Wrong." Brooke made a face.

"But we don't want to forget that there are also a lot of women out there, who for one reason or another aren't looking for a man and are content with their lives," Claire said, trying to be analytical. "Just look at the three of us and how different our views are on men. Lorraine, do you take care of your skin and wear fragrances for yourself or Hamilton?"

"Both."

Claire turned to Brooke.

"For myself and to entice," Brooke admitted. "We don't have to ask you why or for whom."

"I did it for myself, but I always thought I'd find a man one day, get married and have a family." Claire sighed. "I may have waited too late."

"No, you haven't," Brooke and Lorraine protested at the same time.

Lorraine continued. "One of my friends just had a healthy baby at forty-two. They're coming out with more and more studies of women having healthy babies later in life."

"Who knows?" Brooke said with a mischievous wink. "You might meet Mr. Right when he comes in the shop to buy a gift for his sister or his mother."

"Maybe," Claire replied, but she wasn't convinced. She had waited too long. "My mother's maiden name was Bliss. I'd like to submit it for the name of the store since she sort of got us started and brought us together."

"Bliss. For you . . . for him . . . for always." Brooke mused.

The three women shared a grin. "Ladies, we have a name and a slogan," Lorraine said. "Tomorrow I'm going to start looking for a place."

"I didn't think Hamilton was coming home until tomorrow night?" Claire asked.

"He isn't."

"Don't you want to wait and discuss it with him?" Claire bit her lower lip.

"Opening a floral gift shop was my and Margaret's dream. Opening Bliss is mine," Lorraine said quietly. "For the first time in my marriage I'm going to do something completely selfish and think of what I want."

"Well, go on with your bad self," Brooke said with a laugh.

Claire said nothing. Independence was one thing. Creating a problem in your marriage was quite another.

thought we were going to discuss this before you made a decision. Have you gone crazy?"

Hamilton's response wasn't the one Lorraine had been hoping for when she told him about her new business venture. The scrumptious meal she had prepared to smooth the way hadn't helped.

Aware that she had a death grip on her dessert fork, she placed it beside the key lime pie she no longer wanted. "Hamilton, please try to understand. This is something I've always wanted. I understand your hesitancy, but Claire is consulting with Gray Livingston."

"Consulting doesn't mean he'll be there on a day-by-day basis when problems are sure to rise. Now is not the time for the inexperienced to go into business," he told her evenly. "I consult and deal every day with multi-million-dollar companies that are in financial trouble and they have an executive who has a lot more business sense than you and knows how to run a company."

His remark hurt, more so because he had no confidence in her. "Then you can help us make the right decisions," Lorraine countered. "I'm sure Claire and Brooke would welcome any suggestions you have."

"My suggestion is to give up this idiotic idea." He tossed his napkin on the table, his favorite dish of veal forgotten. "If you're becoming bored with the house perhaps you should take up a hobby."

Lorraine's eyes narrowed. "Just because I want to go into business for myself doesn't mean I'm bored. I didn't call you bored when you wanted to go into business for yourself."

"That's different and you know it," Hamilton riled. "A man is supposed to take care of his family, and that's just what I've done." He paused and leaned in closer. "Is this some kind of hormone thing?"

Lorraine closed her eyes, counted to ten, then counted to ten again. When she opened her eyes Hamilton was watching her as if she were a ticking time bomb. "It's not a hormonal imbalance. I am not bored with this house or my life. I simply think my life can be better and I plan to see that it is."

"I forbid it, and I don't want to talk about it anymore." Hamilton picked up his napkin and went back to his food.

Lorraine felt anger, but most of all she felt shut out, as if what she wanted didn't matter. They'd had arguments before. What couple married as long as they had been didn't? But Hamilton had always been reasonable. Until now. Why couldn't he at least try to see her side of it? Whatever the reason, it was obvious he wasn't going to give in.

"I don't need your permission, you know," she told him.

Hamilton's head jerked up. He stared across the table at her.

She hadn't wanted it to come to this. "I'd like your support, but I plan to do this with or without it."

"I refuse to let you take the money out of our account," he told her, his voice rising.

Lorraine's hands began to tremble and she clasped them to steady them. "Very well. I'll use the money from the trust fund my grandmother left."

Stricken, he stood. "Then there's no more to say."

She watched him walk away, and clamped her teeth together to keep from calling him back. Hamilton had always been sensitive that she'd come from an upper-middle class family while his family had been poor. Consequently, she'd left the money for the past twenty years in a mutual fund. She'd never wanted her husband to feel he couldn't take care of his family financially.

Now, she had anyway.

Lorraine cleaned up the kitchen, then slowly climbed the stairs to their bedroom. Hamilton wasn't there. This time the turned down bed seemed to mock her. Feeling miserable, she prepared for bed, then turned off the overhead light and crawled between the scented sheets, leaving only the lamp on Hamilton's side of the bed burning. This was not how she'd wanted the night to end.

The bedroom door opened. She raised up in bed to see Hamilton going to the bathroom. He never paused or looked in her direction. Moments later she heard the shower. After a nerve-wracking ten minutes, he came out in his silk pajamas. When they were first married he'd worn only thread-bare cotton bottoms. On the first night back from his out of town trips, neither of them bothered with sleepwear.

Slipping between the covers, he turned and looked at her a long time. "You won't change your mind?"

"I can't," she whispered.

Something flickered in his eyes, then it was gone. "Then I guess there's nothing else to say." He turned away from her and snapped off the bedside light, throwing the room into darkness. "Good night."

"Good night," she whispered, her throat stinging with unshed tears. She'd hoped he'd understand, but regardless, she wasn't willing to give up her dream or her promise to Margaret.

Lorraine wasn't sure why she found herself at the cemetery the next morning battling tears and despair. Her lower lip tucked between her teeth, she walked over the freshly mowed grass toward Margaret's grave. A tear rolled down her cheek. She dashed it away. Tears, she realized, that were for both of them. But if there was one friend who would understand what she was going through, it was dependable, always-to-be-counted-on Margaret.

Lorraine was almost up the slight incline before she caught a movement out of the corner of her eye. Head down, hands in the pockets of his dress slacks, Thomas Holmes, Margaret's husband of thirty-five years, was making his way to Margaret's grave site on a little hill. A fresh batch of tears streamed down Lorraine's cheeks. She felt so bad for him and so utterly helpless. Margaret had filled all of their lives with her warmth and love. Lorraine missed her, but how much more did Thomas miss the woman who had been devoted to him?

Not wanting to intrude, she stopped and waited for him to continue on, thinking she could go back to her car and wait. He'd come from another direction. He'd never know she was there.

When he was almost at the stone monument of an angel with arms and wings outstretched, he stopped. His hands came out of his pockets to swipe across his face, again and again.

Lorraine felt her own tears. Not stopping to think that he might not want anyone to see him crying, she rushed to him, her arms open to give what little comfort she could. "Thomas."

He looked around wildly. He blinked as if to clear his vision.

Lorraine hugged him to her as best she could. Thomas was six-feet-three of brawny muscles from playing football back in his college days. He had gone on to play professionally and marry his high school sweetheart, Margaret. Both had come from affluent families in Ohio. After his football career was cut short by a knee injury, they'd relocated to Charleston. She'd heard Thomas say more than once that it had been the best thing that could have happened to him because he was able to get in on the ground floor of the real estate boom in the low country and he and his family had met so many wonderful people who accepted them despite their being Yankees.

"I miss her, too," Lorraine said, then eased back to look into his red-rimmed eyes. "I'm sorry. I'll come back later."

"No." He caught her hand, swallowed. "Each day I think it will get easier, but it never does."

"You loved her and she loved you," Lorraine said.

He briefly squeezed her hand. "She loved you, too. I'm glad she was loved."

"Come on. Let's go sit." Silently they continued to the curved stone bench beside the grave. Margaret's name was engraved in the white marble at the base of the angel. Fresh flowers were beneath. "Lilies were her favorites."

He nodded, seeming to have forgotten that her hand was still in his. "I came up the other day. Every year in May I'd take her to see the thousands of spider lilies that bloomed in the Catawba River."

"How are the children?" Lorraine asked. They had two married daughters. One lived in San Francisco, the other in Seattle.

"Good. I promised I'd visit soon." He started to swipe his face again, then blinked as he realized he held her hand. He looked at their clasped hands, then at her for a long time. "Sorry."

For some odd reason Lorraine felt almost embarrassed. She freed her hand. "Don't be."

"How's Hamilton and the children?" he asked.

"Fine." Lorraine thought of the strained breakfast with Hamilton that morning and felt like crying again.

"Then why do you look so lost?" he asked, staring down at her.

Surprise widened her eyes. No one, at least no man, had ever been able to read her like Hamilton. It was rather frightening that one could.

"I didn't mean to pry," Thomas quickly said, his hand going to her shoulder to comfort her the same way she had him.

It was that undemanding touch that pulled the story from her. "I've decided to go on with the gift shop as I promised Margaret. Instead of flowers we'll have bath and body products made by a friend and one of the three partners. Hamilton is adamantly against opening Bliss." By the time she finished, she was drying her eyes with Thomas's handkerchief. "I thought he'd understand."

"Lorraine, I can't tell you what Hamilton's reasons are, but I do know a lot of men feel as if women shouldn't work. It's almost a status symbol. My mother and Margaret's certainly didn't," he said.

"Mine didn't either, but Margaret had planned on working in our shop." Lorraine dried the last of her tears. "You were supportive of her and had helped her find a location."

"It was impossible not to catch her excitement. She almost drove me crazy looking for the right spot. I own several properties, but none of them were right until she walked into one of my lease properties on East Bay Street." His lips curved at the memory, then his shoulders slumped. "Then we went to the doctor's office."

Each sought the other's hand at the same time. "That's why I can't let

Hamilton stand in my way." She shook her head to keep the tears at bay. "The hardest part of saying goodbye to Margaret was in knowing she didn't get a chance to live her dream. I'm doing this for the both of us."

"She'd like that," Thomas said quietly. "And I'm going to help you."

She turned to him, a bit astounded. "What? How?"

"I take it you haven't found a location yet?"

She shook her head. "No."

"The place is still available. I didn't have the heart to put it back on the market, and now I know why. Margaret's dream will live on in some way when you open your shop," he said. "East Bay Street has almost as much draw as King Street, but, to me, it's more quaint without all the hustle and it's in the French Quarter. There, shoppers can leisurely browse and buy. Being near Waterfront Park and Charlston Harbor will ensure a lot of foot traffic."

She couldn't believe it. It would be a perfect location. That was prime real estate and very much sought after. "Thomas, I can't . . . I don't know what to say."

He stood, then reached for her arm. "I'll walk you to your car, then I'll come around and you can follow me to see the place. If you like it, it's yours."

"I'm sure I'll like it. Thank you, Thomas. Thank you so much."

His smile was sad, but it was there. "Thank you for being a friend to both of us."

Together they went back down the hill, both of their hearts just a little bit lighter.

Less than thirty minutes later, Lorraine stepped inside the property and felt excitement sweep through her. No wonder Margaret had loved it on sight. The front of the store was bright and already had glass cases in which to display their products. The floor was hardwood. Foot-wide shelving three feet high ran along each side of the door and would be perfect for displays. A dusty twenty-light glass chandelier hung from the ceiling. It would glitter like a jewel when cleaned.

"In the back, there's a sink and storage area." Thomas gestured with his hand. "Go on and take a look."

She didn't need any further urging. In the back room, she could already imagine shelving to hold their merchandise. A small refrigerator, microwave, and coffee pot for those occasions when, she was positive, they'd be too busy to go out for lunch.

Almost giddy with excitement, she rushed back out. "We'll take it."

His forced smile was heartbreaking.

Lorraine instantly felt remorse that she was so happy when . . . "On second thought maybe I should look at other properties—"

"Please." In two long-legged strides he was in front of her. "I want you here. I need to move on and this would help. We can go by the office and sign the lease."

Signing a lease was an irrevocable step.

"You want to talk to Hamilton about it first?" he asked, as if sensing her unease.

Lorraine glanced around the shop, loving it more with each passing second. The likelihood of them finding another location in such a high-traffic and desirable location was slim to none. "How much?"

"Fifteen hundred dollars a month," he said, then continued when her eyes widened at the low cost. "To go to two thousand dollars after the first year, then increase by five hundred dollars the next with increments built in."

"You could easily get five times that amount," Lorraine said.

"But I wouldn't have the satisfaction of seeing the same delight and happiness in their eyes that I saw in yours and Margaret's." He held out his hand. "Deal?"

"Deal." There was no turning back.

CHAPTER SEVEN

What was he doing here?

Gray had asked himself that question several times since he'd parked his sports car in front of Claire's house. If Claire needed money all she had to do was sell the place. The beachfront cottage was a prime piece of real estate, but he suspected its value was in what it represented to Claire as an achievement rather than what it would bring if she sold it. Her parents hadn't been shy about telling him how proud of their daughter they were. She'd started a home place, something her father had wanted to do, but never had the financial means. Claire's parents' home on Sullivan Island had probably meant that much more because of the location. The island had been a major port of entry for African slaves. A few years ago a six-foot historical market was placed near Fort Moultrie to honor those who had arrived in bondage. With Claire's strong sense of family, she's do everything possible to honor her parents' wish.

Gray sighed and stuffed his hands into the front pockets of the slacks of his tailored suit. He was well acquainted with being relegated to carry on the family traditions. Neither his father nor his two sisters wanted to run Livingston Catalogue, nor had his cousins. He'd never understood their reluctance and gladly accepted that he was the chosen one. He understood Claire's determination to keep her parents' home, but it would take more than that to succeed in the rough economic climate.

Indecision was not a trait Gray was familiar with. He had an analytical mind that cut through the crap to find what was essential and necessary to get the task done. He hesitated this time because he didn't want to see the light go out of Claire's eyes again and to know he was the cause. Yet, he also vividly recalled her face shining with hope when she left his study. He just hoped that during the past week reality hadn't kicked her in the teeth.

Enough stalling. He jabbed the doorbell.

The door opened. A mixture of pleasant scents he couldn't define welcomed him. Staring up at him was a petite, beautiful woman in a white shorts set. "Hello. Is Claire in?"

The woman tilted her dark head to one side and sighed. "I'm definitely losing my touch."

"I beg your pardon?"

Shaking her head, she waved his words aside. "Never mind. Inside joke. Claire is in the kitchen doing her thing."

A bit puzzled about the woman's reaction and what Claire's "thing" was, Gray followed her a bit cautiously, then came to an abrupt halt just inside the family room. Claire was pouring a creamy white substance from a quart measuring cup into rose shaped molds on a folding table, while another woman was placing clear glass containers on another table. It looked like an assembly line. A third table was laden with soaps, candles and a shrink-wrap machine.

"Who is it?" Claire asked, absently moving to another mold.

"Our business advisor," replied the woman who had answered the door.

Claire jerked around, sending a stream of thick, creamy liquid across the table. "Oh!"

Gray quickly crossed the room and reached for the container. "Sorry."

"Stay back," Claire advised, lifting one hand to punctuate her statement. "I can clean up the floor and the table a lot better than I can you." Setting the measuring container down, she reached for the nearby roll of paper towels.

"Point taken." He stayed where he was.

Claire kept throwing glances at Gray as she cleaned up the spill. Sticking his hands in his pockets again, he debated his visit. He had no idea why he always made her jittery.

"Brooke Dunlap and Lorraine Averhart, my business partners. Ladies, Gray Livingston."

He shook the women's hands, then nodded toward the tables. "Does all this mean you have a business plan?"

"It does." Claire offered him a small, shy smile and pointed to a black folder with red lettering on the occasional table in the living room. "Bliss."

"Your mother's maiden name. She'd like that," he said.

Surprise and delight widened her dark brown eyes. "How did you know?"

For a moment he simply stared. He'd never noticed that her eyes were so deep, nor the color so soothing. "I guess I remember your father saying once it was her maiden name and that's what she was. Bliss. I'd forgotten it until now." Probably because he'd thought he had that in his marriage and had been proven so very, very wrong.

Sadness touched her face. "They loved each other very much."

"And you," Gray said.

Claire felt herself being pulled in by the sound of Gray's voice and had to mentally shake herself to break free. She made a production of disposing of the paper towels in the trash can. Once the wax dried she'd clean up the rest. Gray always had the power to shake her. "Would you like to see what we've done?"

"Very much," he answered easily. "Grandmother used the products you left and said they're among the best she's had."

"Told you," Lorraine said with an emphatic shake of her head. "Women will be clamoring for Bliss."

"We already have a location on East Bay Street with reasonable rent, thanks to a contact of Lorraine's. It's old and quaint and beautiful," Claire told him. "We plan to fill it with products that will pamper a woman's body from head to toe."

"And make a man's hands itch to get them on her?" Brooke said with a saucy laugh.

Claire blushed, but managed not to duck her head. "Brooke is the director of marketing and is looking for the Man of Bliss to put on the Web site I'm designing."

Gray's dark eyebrow lifted. "Why not a woman?"

Claire's unpainted lips twitched. "Same question I asked."

"Because although a lot of women are going to be buying the products for themselves, many of them will have a man in mind," Brooke explained. "I want to find a man with the kind of raw sensuality that makes a woman want to buy the products in hopes of finding her own Man of Bliss."

"He's got to be spectacular," Lorraine said, her gaze going to Gray.

"Look dynamite in a tailored suit or jeans," Brooke said, studying Gray as well.

"The kind of man that makes a woman look twice, maybe a third time," Claire added thoughtfully, sizing Gray up as well.

Gray folded his arms and shook his head. "Not in this or any other lifetime."

The women laughed. "Come on, I'll show you what we plan to do," Claire began, just as the doorbell rang.

"I'll get it," Brooke said. "Maybe it's the FedEx guy and we can talk him into posing for the Web site," she tossed over her shoulder.

She was still smiling when she answered the door. On seeing the man standing there it instantly disappeared. "Yes?" she asked crisply.

"Is Claire in?" John asked.

Brooke was considering saying no when a little girl with sparkling black eyes stepped in front of John and sent Brooke a gap-toothed smile. There was a dark smudge on her amber-hued face, her white canvas tennis shoes had seen the worst of a mud pile, and she'd lost one barrette from her thick black shoulder-length plaits. "Hi, I'm Amy and I'm four. Claire is going to baby-sit me and Mark while Daddy goes to work."

Brooke wondered how such a sweet child could have a grouch for a father.

John's large hand lifted to rest gently on the little girl's shoulder. "Hold on, honey, we don't know if Claire's in or if she can baby-sit."

"Dad, I told you I can handle it if you're going to be gone just for a couple of hours," Mark said, his hand on the strap of his backpack.

Brooke switched her attention to the little boy, a three-foot-high version of his father, but without the disapproval Brooke always saw on his face. Mark was as neat as the little girl was ruffled. His white shirt was tucked neatly into his pressed jeans, his tennis shoes snow white.

John's other hand came to rest on his son's shoulder. "I appreciate it, Mark, but it may be longer. I won't worry if I know you and Amy are with Claire." He looked at Brooke. "Is she home?"

With three pairs of eyes looking at her Brooke couldn't have lied to save her life. "Yes, please come in." She retraced her steps back to the living area. "Claire, you have three visitors."

"Oh, my," Amy said and started toward the table.

"No, you don't," John said with a laugh, scooping up his daughter.

"Hi, John," Claire said, coming forward and making the introductions.

With Amy still in his arms, John glanced around the room. "I wanted to see if you could keep the kids for a couple of hours. They've already had their supper, but I see you're busy."

"Never too busy for a friend," Claire said.

"Just what is it you're doing here?" John asked, looking around in confusion.

Claire's eyes sparkled with excitement. "Making bath and body products," she replied. "We're going into business."

"Wow. That's big news," John told her with a wide grin on his handsome face. "You'll be great."

"That's what we're counting on," Claire said, smiling at her partners.

"I'll keep my fingers crossed. About this baby-sitting thing, are you sure you can do it with all you have going on?"

"I'm sure," Claire replied.

Obviously still troubled, John rubbed the back of his neck. "You know how inquisitive Amy is. I don't want her to mess up things."

"I'll be good, Daddy," Amy said, both hands on her father's cheeks.

Brooke found herself saying, "Inquisitiveness is a trait that should be nurtured, not stifled."

John turned, and if looks could kill, she'd be knocking on the Pearly Gates.

"She'll be fine," Claire said into the thick silence. "She can help. So can Mark."

Brooke refused to look away from John. The arrogant jerk. His wife was probably away from home on purpose.

Finally John turned to Claire. "I'd appreciate it. Mom and Dad are at church. I should be gone two hours tops."

"Go. I have your cell number." Taking Amy from him, Claire put the little girl on the floor. "They'll be fine and you know I love having them."

John hunkered down in front of Amy and took her hands in his. "Be Daddy's big girl and mind Claire. Don't touch anything except food and water."

She giggled. "What if I have to go to the potty?"

John's lips twitched. "Smarty." Giving her a one arm hug he pulled Mark to him with the other. "Take care of each other." Pushing to his feet, he started for the door.

Brooke watched him leave, her gaze unerringly going to his butt. Tight. In those jeans he was sin walking. Her face heated along with other unmentionable parts of her body. Her dislike of John increased tenfold, but she didn't look away until the door closed and she noticed Claire watching her. Brooke flushed with embarrassment. What was she thinking with the man's children there? Besides, she'd sworn off men.

"I was just checking to see if he might be a Bliss candidate." The lie made her feel worse.

"You think?" Claire asked, then said to Mark, "Please take Amy to the kitchen and you both can have a cookie and milk."

"I'll pour," Mark said, and caught his sister's hand and went toward the kitchen.

"I definitely think he has possibilities," Lorraine said, emptying out the last oblong-shaped soap from its mold.

Gray chuckled. "Poor man. But, for what it's worth, you ladies seem to have a solid plan and are on the right path to succeed."

The women beamed at him.

"Coming from you that means a great deal. Without your help this wouldn't have happened," Claire said, continuing to smile brightly.

Gray shook his head. "It was you, Lorraine and Brooke who did the work. You didn't sit around whining. You rolled up your sleeves and simply did. That takes guts."

"Thank you. I hope you can come to our opening," Claire said, her voice and eyes full of hope.

"If at all possible I'll be there," he assured. "I guess I better let you ladies get back to work. I'll see myself out."

Claire watched him every step of the way. The door closed. Air fluttered between her lips on a sigh.

"I think he kind of likes you," Brooke whispered to Claire.

Claire's heart leaped. "Of–Of course he likes me. I told you what he did for my parents."

Brooke rolled her eyes and looked at Lorraine. "With any other woman I'd think she was being coy, but Claire's too honest."

"I think it's sweet," Lorraine said, coming around the table.

Claire frowned at the both of them. "What are you two talking about?"

"Amy didn't waste any milk and I put the glasses in the sink, Claire," Mark said, coming back into the room with Amy.

Claire faced the children. Amy had a new smear—chocolate—on her cheek. "I see you found the cookies all right."

Amy pouted. "Mark only let me have one."

"Too many sweets can rot those beautiful teeth that are going to come in during the next months," Brooke said, squatting down in front of the little girl. "I'm Brooke. How about we go get you cleaned up and then you can help me?"

Amy's eyes widened. "Really?"

"Really." She came to her feet, then glanced back at the quiet boy. Something about him tugged at her heart. "Would you like to help, too?"

"Yes, ma'am."

She held out her other hand. The little boy quickly came to put his hand in hers.

An hour later they had finished wrapping the soap taken from the molds, left the freshly poured ones to set, and made plans to start on candles in the morning. They'd do one to two products a day for each of the bath and body sets.

"I think we can call it a night," Claire said, stretching her arms over her head. "Mark, get out your homework. Amy, why don't you draw a picture for your daddy."

Amy raced for the backpack she'd left in the kitchen. Mark followed at a more sedate pace.

Brooke's gaze followed the children. "Amy has got to take after her mother. Poor woman, whoever she is."

"Their mother died when Amy was less than four months old," Claire said quietly.

"What?" Brooke jerked her head around. Her eyes briefly closed. "Oh, Lord. I'm so sorry."

Claire placed her hand on her shoulder. "You couldn't have known. John works hard to be both parents and give them a good home. He's a wonderful father."

Lorraine joined them, shoving the strap of her purse over her shoulder. "Goodnight, partners. I'll be back in the morning."

"Good. After we pour the candles, we can go to the shop and meet with the contractor about the shelves," Claire said. "I hope Hamilton doesn't mind you spending so much time here."

Lorraine's smile wavered, then firmed. "Hamilton is a wonderful husband."

Frowning, Claire walked Lorraine to the door. "Lorraine, is everything all right?"

"Of course. I'll see you tomorrow."

Claire watched until Lorraine pulled off, then closed the door and went to the kitchen. She was more than a bit surprised to see Amy in Brooke's lap giggling. The rapt adoration on Mark's young face was totally expected. He was a male.

Brooke glanced up. "I've got the kids. You can work on the Web site."

"You're sure?"

"Positive."

"I'll be in my bedroom if you need anything."

Claire went to her desk and had just clicked on the computer when the phone rang. "Hello?"

"Hello."

Gray. Her heart actually fluttered.

"I hope I'm not disturbing you."

"No," she quickly answered. "Brooke is watching the children while I work on the Web site."

"Does John know he's a Bliss candidate?"

She smiled into the phone. "Not yet."

"You're probably aware of this already, but try to make the site as user-friendly and inviting as possible."

"It doesn't hurt hearing it again. Thanks."

"Well . . . ?" He paused as if he wanted to say something else. "Good night, Claire."

"Good night, Gray," she said and hung up with a big smile on her face.

D addy!" Amy launched herself out of her chair as soon as she heard the doorbell. Brooke caught her around the waist as she dashed by.

"Whoa." Amy had enough energy for six people. "Let's make sure it's your daddy before we open the door." Taking the little girl's hand, Brooke went to the front door and opened it.

"Daddy!" Amy squealed and threw herself at him.

John plucked her up into his arms. "You behave?"

She giggled. "Didn't you tell me to?"

He had a smile on his face when he turned, but it slid away when he saw Brooke. "Hi, Mark," he said to his son in an effort to ease the awkwardness.

"Hi, Dad," Mark said. "She really was good this time. Brooke let us help with the products they're making, then told us stories while Claire worked on the Web site."

"You finish your homework?"

Mark's head went down. "Almost."

John's laser gaze sliced through Brooke. "Don't worry, son. We'll finish it at home."

Brooke immediately felt guilty. "It's my fault," Brooke tried to explain. "I guess time got away from me."

He set Amy on her feet. "Go get your things while I find Claire and thank her."

"Here I am," Claire said, coming into the foyer. "You're right on time. Did things go all right?"

"Fine." He reached for Amy's backpack. "Thanks again, Claire. Good night."

"Good night," the children called back as their father hurried them to his truck.

"Good night." Claire was still frowning as she closed the front door. "You two still having problems?"

"He thinks I'm an irresponsible dimwit and he's right," Brooke said with a disgusted sigh as she followed Claire back into the family room.

Frowning, Claire paused. "What happened?"

Brooke was almost afraid to confess her blunder. Claire would undoubtedly think the same thing. "I never got around to helping Mark finish his homework." Brooke shoved a hand through her short hair. "The time got away from me. I tried to explain, but John just stared a hole in me. Surely the teacher won't mind one night," she said, but it came out more as if she were seeking reassurance than a statement.

It wasn't to be. "Mark is in accelerated classes. He's always been at the top of his class since he was in kindergarten. He's an exemplary student and child."

Brooke groaned. She'd already figured out he was smart. She'd only had to tell him once how to pack the baskets and products. He could put the labels on as well as she could. "I messed up."

"Don't be too hard on yourself," Claire told her gently.

Brooke thought of Mark dropping his head when his father had mentioned the homework. He hadn't looked at her or blamed her. He was a good kid. "I better get out of your hair. I'll see you in the morning." Grabbing her oversized bag, she headed for the door.

"I'll see you in the morning. Sleep well."

"Night," Brooke called as she went to her car, her thoughts troubled. She'd let Mark down. Superimposed over the image of Mark was his father's tightly controlled anger, his disgust. No one had ever looked at her that way. His son might have forgiven her, but he never would.

CHAPTER EIGHT

When you mess up, you really mess up.

Brooke stared at her credit card bill and felt her muscles tense. Not because of the amount she owed, although it was considerable, it was the charge from Randle Garage that held her attention. No wonder her salesperson at the Jaguar dealership had said he'd be happy to send her a check to cover the charges.

"Ninety-seven dollars."

A brief call to her salesperson had confirmed her suspicion. John had only charged her the wholesale price of the battery. She felt lower than a snake's belly after the way she'd acted toward him. Not helping Mark with his homework only compounded the feeling.

Grabbing her purse, she was out the door. She had a stop to make before she went to Claire's.

Twenty-two minutes later Brooke pulled up in front of John's garage, which was located off the access road near a strip shopping center. There were eight bays in the prefabricated structure, with an attached office to the left. Despite it being a little after nine, the bays were all full and several cars were parked in an adjacent parking area, waiting, she supposed, for their turn.

Brooke parked beside a Lexus and went inside the office. Several people were sitting around the waiting area, watching the TV mounted on the wall or flipping through magazines. She went straight to the waist-high counter. The three men in blue overalls behind it greeted her almost simultaneously, grinning for all they were worth and all asking if they could help.

Brooke's natural smile widened. Seems she hadn't lost her touch after all. "Thank you, gentlemen," she said. "Is John in?"

All three looked taken aback. One with the name of Greg stitched on the pocket of his blue overalls spoke first. "You a relative or something?"

There was no mistaking the hope in his voice. She definitely hadn't lost her touch. "No relations. No interest."

His smile widened. "I'll show you."

"I can show her," the one with the name Fred said.

"Both of you have tune-ups to do, so I'll show her."

That brought a heated debate about who would take her until a frigid voice brought the argument to an abrupt halt. "Enough."

Brooke and the three men jumped in response. She didn't even try her smile out on John. He was immune.

His mouth in its usual disapproving line, he stared coldly at her. "Come with me." Without waiting for a response, he spun on his heels and started for an open office door behind the counter.

No "please," just an order. She thought of putting her hands on her hips and giving him a piece of her mind, then remembered the credit card bill. Sighing, she followed him through a door into an office area that was as neat as the rest of his business. On the wall behind him were family pictures and framed artwork by Mark and Amy. Mark's pencil drawing of a house was neatly drawn, whereas Amy's was just lines, but both were in a place of honor.

"What is it you want?"

She hadn't expected it to be easy. "I came to apologize." She pulled the credit card bill from her pocket. "I didn't know until I got home last night and opened my mail. Thank you."

He had almost hoped she had come to chew him out about how rude he'd been last night. He didn't want anything to soften his opinion of what a spoiled brat she was. "You're welcome." He sat in his chair and pulled a folder toward him.

He heard her sigh and glanced up. The same unwanted feelings punched him in the gut. She was beautiful. The little cropped top showing off her smooth stomach made his hands itch.

"I wanted—" She paused as a brief knock sounded on the door.

"Come in," John said, irritated because it meant she would have to be in his office longer than he wanted. He didn't want her there, not with her sexy body and her expensive perfume trying to twist his insides.

Greg, one of his mechanics, stuck his head in the door. Behind him John could see Fred and Kent trying to look in as well. He didn't need two guesses to figure out why. "You need something?"

Greg came in, grinning like fool and throwing glances at Brooke. "Excuse me, miss."

"No problem," she said brightly.

"What is it, Greg?"

"Ah, just wanted to know if you wanted to send for takeout at Marty's for lunch."

John glanced at the clock on the wall in front of him. They never decided on lunch this early. "Fine."

Greg was barely out the door before there was another knock. John gritted his teeth.

Fred popped in, once again nodding to Brooke. "The parts came in for the 'Benz. Thought you'd want to know."

He did, but it could have waited. "Thank you."

"Miss," Fred said with another nod.

"Fred," she replied.

Fred's eyes lit up.

"Goodbye, Fred, and tell the others I don't want to see another person unless the building is on fire."

The grin faded. "Yes, boss."

With her sultry looks, she was the cause of the men coming into his office. She couldn't be more than five foot, two inches, which was worse because it made a man feel protective toward her. Being built on the lush side made her lethal.

"You have a friendly group of men."

"They're acting like idiots," John spat out. The way she was dressed, the way she looked at them that encouraged their behavior. Linda would have never acted that way. As soon as the thought materialized, John cursed himself for comparing his wife to a shallow person like Brooke.

"If that's all, I'm kind of busy."

"I really am sorry about Mark's homework. Claire told me what an exemplary student he is. I hope I didn't mess up his record or anything."

Since there was obvious concern in her voice, John let himself bend enough to say, "We finished it after we got home."

"He wasn't sleepy this morning, was he? I wouldn't want him getting in trouble because of me."

His son wouldn't be the first male nor the last to get in trouble over Brooke, John imagined. He certainly didn't plan to join the list. "We weren't that much over his bedtime."

Brooke smiled at him and John felt the kick he'd experienced the first time she'd smiled at him. "If that's all . . ." He let his voice trail off.

She sighed, causing her lush breasts to rise over the neckline of her square top. John barely kept from crumbling the folder in his hands. "There was one other thing. Claire and Lorraine think it's a good idea and it would really help the business."

He racked his brain, but couldn't think of anything he could do to help their business. "What is it?"

She took another of those breaths and bit her lower lip. "We want you to be the Man of Bliss."

"What?"

"I know it's asking a lot, but we need a man to exemplify all the attributes of what women look for in a man, to go on our Web site," she explained, bracing both hands on his desk and leaning toward him. "You'd really be helping us out if you'd do it. The pictures could be taken on the beach."

"No. I don't have time for such foolishness."

"Foolishness." Brooke jerked upright. Her black eyes flashed. Her small-fisted hands braced themselves on her hips. "Foolishness because we want to make a success of our lives? Foolishness because we don't want to be caught in a job crunch again? Foolishness because we believe in each other? If anybody knows what it is to open their own business, you should. Thanks for nothing."

She hadn't gone two steps before shame hit him. "Wait," he called when she was almost at the door. She didn't stop. John was forced to round the desk and grab her arm. An electric spark shot up his arm. He jerked his hand free. Her eyes rounded. Her mouth opened in a sound-less gasp.

Hell. That's all he needed. To be attracted to a selfish flirt like Brooke.

Folding her arms beneath her breasts she glared up at him. John didn't know if she was punishing him or not. He just tried to keep his gaze from dropping below her neckline. "I do know what it is to start out on your own. I might not have had the courage if it hadn't been for Linda. She believed in me."

Her hands dropped to her sides. "Your wife?" Brooke asked gently.

John nodded, not knowing if he'd mentioned Linda to remind himself or to try to explain. "Mark was eighteen months old at the time and we had one bay. She brought him to work with her and made it seem easy. She never stopped believing in me."

"She sounds like she was a wonderful woman," Brooke said softly. "Claire told me about her. Do Mark or Amy take after their mother?"

A grin came to his face. "Both. Amy has her tenacity and love of life. Mark has her brains and sweet disposition."

"Thank goodness," Brooke said, then her eyes widened as she realized what she'd implied. "I didn't mean—"

"Yes, you did," John said cutting her off.

She grinned up at him.

He found himself grinning back at her. His smile died as he continued to stare down at her. He didn't want to be attracted to her. Turning, he strode back behind his desk as if that would protect him.

"Please reconsider," Brooke asked. "We're scheduled to sign the lease today and afterward we're going over to meet the contractor. Having the Man of Bliss would be one less problem."

"Dressed like that?" he blurted before he could stop himself. He could have gladly bitten off his tongue.

Brooke glanced down at herself, then back at him. "What's wrong with what I have on?"

In that micro-ribbed white tank top and hip-hugging black cropped pants with strappy low-heeled sandals, she'd have the poor man eating out of her hand. The thought occurred to him that she might have had the same idea when she came to see him.

"I asked you a question."

"Sorry, you're a grown woman, not a four-year-old who attracts dirt like a magnet."

Her posture relaxed. "Amy is so sweet. You should have seen her helping us."

His children hadn't been able to stop talking about Brooke. He came to a quick decision. "The children and I try to spend time together every Saturday morning. How about if I come over around nine and we can take the pictures on the beach behind Claire's house?"

Brooke flashed him another heart-stopping smile. "It's a date. Bye and thanks again. Really. You won't be sorry." Opening the door she was gone.

John sank down in his chair, hoping she was right that in trying to prove himself immune to Brooke and help Claire, he hadn't made a big mistake.

She had to keep trying.

"Everything is going well," Lorraine told Hamilton as they sat at the breakfast table in the bay window nook of the kitchen. "We've made a lot of progress in stockpiling supplies. You should see what we've done."

"I'm rather busy at the moment." Hamilton sipped his coffee with one hand and made a notation with the other on his PalmPilot.

Desolation swept over her. From the earliest days of their marriage they had decided that the breakfast table would be a time for them to discuss matters as a family. Even when he was his most rushed, Hamilton had never broken that rule until now.

"Hamilton, please."

His hand paused briefly with the pointer. "I'm taking a flight out tomorrow to Washington for the Isaac account. I hope you didn't forget to get my suits from the cleaners."

She had forgotten his suits. "I thought things were going well."

"Just some minor complications I have to clear up." Setting the cup in the saucer, he picked up the PalmPilot and stood. "I may be late, but I'm sure you have other plans."

He left before she had a chance to say anything more. She let her head fall forward into her palm. He just didn't, or wouldn't, understand.

When he came back through on his way to the garage, she lifted her head. "Why are you punishing me?"

"I have no idea what you're talking about."

"Don't lie," she said, coming to her feet. "At least be man enough to admit what you're doing."

Irritation crossed his face. "What do you want from me?"

"To be happy that I'm doing something that I enjoy. I'm busy doing something I love, not having an affair."

Eyes hard, Hamilton stepped closer. Lorraine didn't step back. He had always been possessive and jealous, but he would hurt himself before he'd harm her or the kids.

"Is that what this is all about?" she asked. "You're afraid that there's some other man out there?"

"Of course not," he said as if the thought wouldn't cross his mind in a million years.

Lorraine couldn't decide if he was telling the truth or not. Acting on instinct, she went to him and despite the stiffness of his body, the coldness in his face, she slid her arms around his waist and held on. "I love you. Have always loved you. This has nothing to do with the way I feel about you. It has to do with my trying to find my own way."

"I thought you had already found it with me," he said tightly.

"Hamilton, don't."

"I'll be late."

Closing her eyes, she slowly released her hold on him and straightened. He turned away as soon as he was free.

"Hamilton," she whispered to the closed door. "Why won't you try and understand?"

Turning away, she fought the tears threatening to spill from her eyes. She was not going to cry. Why couldn't Hamilton be as understanding as Thomas? She never thought she'd compare her husband to another man, but it was becoming increasingly difficult not to do so. Thomas couldn't seem to do enough for them. He'd had the utilities turned on almost immediately, found a cleaning service, and even located a contractor to paint and build lighted recess shelving.

The phone rang and she picked it up. "Hello."

"Good morning, Lorraine."

Her face brightened instantly. "Good morning, Thomas."

"Sorry to be calling so early, but I may have found a couple more glass cases for you at a reasonable price. Would you like to go look at them?"

She reached in the drawer beneath the countertop for a pen and paper. "Just tell me where."

"I'm still at home and can pick you up in about five minutes."

"I'll be ready." She always dressed and put on makeup when she got up, a Southern tradition in her home.

"Great. I'll see you in a bit."

Lorraine hung up the phone and went in search of her purse, wondering, not for the first time, why couldn't Hamilton be more like Thomas.

Claire woke up with a smile on her face. She felt more refreshed than she had in months. Getting out of bed to shower and dress, she kept telling herself it was because the plans for Bliss were going so well. While that was true, a small part of her admitted it was because of Gray. Sitting at the breakfast table sipping her coffee, she could admit that she had had a crush on him since she was thirteen.

Before then he had just been the Livingston's grandson who came every summer to learn the business. But between one summer and the next he'd changed. His body had developed muscles, his voice deepened, and he'd grown four inches taller. She hadn't been the only one to notice. There always seemed to be girls about the house. Although they'd used the excuse of visiting with his female cousins who were often there, it had been plain they came to see Gray.

However, she was not about to delude herself into believing that Gray was being anything more than nice. She'd never had time for many friendships. It was interesting that the loss of her job caused her friendships to deepen with Brooke and Lorraine, while also renewing her acquaintance with Gray. Proof that you never knew where a blessing would come from.

The doorbell interrupted her thoughts. A bemused smile on her face, Claire went to answer.

"John agreed to be the Man of Bliss," Brooke told her as soon as Claire opened the door.

The women squealed and only pulled apart when Lorraine drove up. They both ran to the car to tell her the great news.

"Isn't that wonderful?" Brooke said.

"Yes," Lorraine said, her eyes overly bright. "I've been with Thomas, and I just purchased two more cases for Bliss."

"We're on a roll!" Brooke declared. "Things couldn't be better."

Claire grinned.

Lorraine promptly burst into tears.

CHAPTER NINE

never imagined it would come to this."

Claire and Brooke exchanged helpless looks as Lorraine sat between them on the sofa. After her outburst she'd told them everything. "If you want to drop out or cut back on your time we'd understand," Claire offered, putting a comforting hand on her friend's shoulder.

"Sure," Brooke chimed in. "You could be a silent partner."

Tears rolled down Lorraine's cheeks. "I don't want to be a silent partner. This was my idea."

"Then tell Hamilton to get a grip and run your life the way you want," Brooke said, obviously still irritated at men in general.

"If only he could be as understanding as Thomas." Lorraine cried harder.

Claire shot an annoyed look at Brooke. "Lorraine, you're in an unenviable situation. As difficult as it is, you have to decide what you want the most . . . to make Hamilton happy or stay with Bliss. We can't tell you what to do."

Brooke opened her mouth, but closed it when Claire shook her head. "Whatever decision you make, we're behind you."

"You'd still be a part of Bliss," Brooke assured, following Claire's lead. "Like Claire said, we're behind you."

"I've always put Hamilton and the children first. He's never had to doubt my love or faith in him." Lorraine straightened. "Perhaps he needs a little reminder. Let's see how he likes it when I'm not there for him to pick up his clothes from the cleaners, pack his suitcase or prepare his favorite meals."

"I like it already." Brooke grinned.

Claire's expression brightened. "I recall Mama going on strike when Daddy was popping off about how he could take care of himself. In less than a week he was singing her praises and helping around the house."

Lorraine dried her tears. "Hamilton won't capitulate so easily. But I'm not giving in either." She came to her feet. "We better get going or we'll be late for the appointment to sign the lease and then meet the contractor."

An hour later they signed the lease on the property. Thomas gave them the key and a bottle of chilled vintage champagne.

"Let me be the first to congratulate you." He shook hands with Claire and Brooke, and hugged Lorraine.

"Thank you again, Thomas," Lorraine said, slowly straightening. "Your support means so very much."

"I want to see you happy, Lorraine."

"She will be," Brooke said, casually drawing Lorraine away from Thomas and heading to the door with the bottle of champagne. "See you later."

The three women left Thomas's office, then drove in their separate cars to Bliss to meet the contractor. Brooke popped the trunk of her car and removed a wicker basket.

"What's that for?" Claire asked as they started down the street toward the shop.

Brooke smiled. "You'll see."

Standing in front of the glass-front store Lorraine removed the key from her purse, then looked at the other women. "I think we should do this together." Claire's hand and Brooke's hand settled on Lorraine's as she turned the key and opened the door. They walked in together.

"We did it," Claire said, turning around in a circle. "We did it!"

"We certainly did, and I think this calls for a celebration." Setting the picnic hamper on the counter, Brooke removed a bottle of Cristal and three glasses. "Randolph's favorite, but it's good stuff. We'll save Thomas's for the opening night."

Claire took her glass. "What do we drink to?"

"Success, what else?" Brooke said, filling their glasses.

Lorraine lifted her glass. "To the success of Bliss."

Repeating the toast, the women clinked glasses and drank.

Claire took another sip of the golden liquid, decided it wasn't half bad and finished it off. "I could get used to this."

Brooke recorked the bottle. "Randolph might have been a rat, but he knew how to live. I miss that."

"Not for long," Claire said. "Bliss is going to be the place for the discriminating buyer for bath and body products for herself and her home. The Web site is almost finished. I'll upload the pictures of John as soon as you take them and have them developed."

"Me?" Brooke's eyes widened in alarm.

"You're the PR person, you know what will entice a woman." Claire wrinkled her nose. "Besides, we can't afford to pay a professional photographer. You can use my thirty-five-millimeter."

"I have a digital," Lorraine piped up. "It was a Christmas present from Hamilton. He'll help, whether he wants to or not."

The door opened and a slender man dressed in a chambray shirt and jeans entered. "Hello, ladies, I'm Ralph Hendrix, the painter."

The young man's gaze briefly touched Lorraine and Claire before it settled on Brooke and stayed. Smiling she walked toward him, her hand out, her smile dazzling.

Lorraine and Claire hung back and watched Brooke do her thing.

The table wasn't set.

Hamilton frowned, then anger began to build. He had known this would happen. With a quick twist of his wrist he checked the time. Seven-fifteen. He turned and saw the note propped against the coffee machine.

Snatching it up he read it once, then twice, not believing what he was seeing.

Since you didn't know what time you were coming home and you're leaving in the morning I decided to spend the night at Claire's. Your suit is in your closet. You'll have to pack yourself. I'm sure you won't mind. Love, Lorraine. P.S. Have a safe trip.

Tossing the note aside, he flipped through the phone book, then dialed. He paced as the phone rang for a fourth, then a fifth time.

"Hello," answered a voice filled with laughter.

"May I speak with Lorraine?"

"Who is calling please?"

"Her husband," he snapped, his hand clenching on the cordless phone. There was a brief silence then Lorraine picked up.

"Hamilton, is everything all right?"

How could it be when she wasn't home? "I want you to come home."

"Are you ill?" she asked, her voice sounding strange.

He hadn't meant to frighten her, but panic had seized him as soon as he read her note. "You should be at home."

"Hamilton, I never complained once when you had to work late or go out of town on business. You, of all people, should understand what it takes to get a business running."

"You're my wife." She was his life.

"I'm also a person who wants to achieve something on her own," she said quietly. "Besides, I thought you wouldn't mind my not being there."

"That's idiotic. Come home this instant."

"I'm afraid I can't do that."

"Why?" he demanded.

"Because we're celebrating the signing of the lease with a bottle of Cristal."

"You've been drinking?" he gasped. Lorraine never had more than a glass of wine.

She giggled. "We all have."

"I knew this was a mistake. I'm coming to get you and bring you home."

"No."

He was heading for the garage when that single word stopped him in his tracks. "What did you say?"

"No. Hamilton, you had your chance. Now it's my turn. I never dragged you home from a business meeting."

"That's not a business meeting."

"It's a celebration, and I know you've had plenty of them when you've closed a big deal," she told him, her voice becoming less mellow and more sharp with each sentence. "If you don't want to give me the same support I gave you, then that's your decision. I love you, but I'm not coming home. Have a good trip, and don't forget to take your sinus medication."

The line went dead and Hamilton stared at the phone. She'd hung up on him. His dependable, steady-as-a-rock and unflappable wife of thirty-eight years had hung up on him.

What was he going to do?

Y̶ou want me to call a cab?" Claire asked, seeing the misery on her friend's face. Perhaps the price for Lorraine's independence was a bit high.

"No," she said, leaning her head back on the sofa. "I won't heel because Hamilton thinks I should. I was there for him. He has to learn to be there for me."

Claire came to her feet. She hurt for her friend and had no idea how to help except to be there for her. Her experience with men was too limited to attempt to give advice. "Brooke, put the Cristal away and let's all go for a walk on the beach to clear our head. Then we can get back to work."

"I think I liked you better before you became a general," Brooke said, but she unfolded her legs from beneath her on the other end of the sofa, then pulled Lorraine up beside her. "Come on, Lorraine, and I know the perfect spot to scream out your frustration and anger and no one will think about calling the cops."

Looping arms, the women left through the French doors and walked down to the beach.

T̶wo hours later Lorraine was as miserable as ever.

The women were sitting around a card table labeling soap. The trash can by Lorraine had a growing number of discarded tissues inside. Just then Lorraine plucked another one, and tried to stem the moisture from her eyes.

Claire had said she wasn't going to give advice. At the time she had meant it, but the more she saw of Lorraine's misery and remembered the wonderful marriage she had, the more she wondered if Lorraine's decision had been the best one. She stayed out of people's business because she didn't want to be involved. She'd always been shy and unsure of herself. Losing herself with an inanimate computer had been the best choice for her.

But with the birth of Bliss that would no longer be possible. She'd have to learn to reach out and help people. She might not know much about relationships, but she knew not talking wasn't going to solve anything.

"Lorraine, I'd give anything to have what you have with Hamilton."

Lorraine looked up at her and tears spilled unheeded down her cheeks.

Going to the bedroom, Claire returned with her purse and car keys. She pulled Lorraine to her feet. "You and Hamilton can be at odds when he's in town, but not when he's about to go out of town on a trip tomorrow."

"I don't want him to think he's won."

"Do you want to live with the possibility that something could happen to either of you and your last conversation was in anger?" Claire asked quietly.

Lorraine flinched and tucked her head. "No."

"Where're you two going?" Brooke asked, coming from the kitchen with a glass of Evian.

"Lorraine is going home. I'm driving her car," Claire answered. "You're up to following me in your car and bringing me back."

"Takes more than a couple of glasses of Cristal to do me in." Brooke set the glass on a coaster and grabbed her own purse.

Claire wished the same could be said of Lorraine. Claire had a feeling that she'd drank more because of the problems with her husband. "Lorraine, I've admired you from the first time I saw you. Surely you can think of another way of showing Hamilton your independence without making yourself miserable, and possibly driving a wedge between you two. You love him."

Lorraine sniffed. "But does he love me enough to accept the new direction my life has taken?"

Closing the front door, Claire took Lorraine to her car and put her in the passenger seat. "You'll never know hiding at my house. If I've learned anything it's that hiding from life is a mistake."

Hamilton didn't know what to say.

"Good evening, Hamilton," Claire said. "We finished earlier than we anticipated."

Hamilton stared at Lorraine, her face set, standing between Claire and another woman he didn't know. He stepped back from the doorway. "Come in."

"I don't believe you've met Brooke Dunlap, former marketing manager for Middleton," Claire said, finally releasing Lorraine's arm.

The third partner. Beautiful, but he didn't like the way she was dressed with her midriff showing. Perhaps she was the bad influence on Lorraine. Claire had always impressed him as quiet and a homebody. "Ms. Dunlap."

"Mr. Averhart," Brooke said, studying him just as closely as he was studying her.

"Good night, Lorraine. We'll see you in the morning," Claire said, then to him, "Have a good trip, Hamilton."

"Thank you. Goodnight."

Wordlessly, Lorraine started up the stairs. She knew it drove him crazy when she gave him the silent treatment.

"Haven't you anything to say?"

"I'm home. Doesn't that say enough?"

It said something, but he wasn't sure what. He followed her into their bedroom and saw the mess he'd made of packing his clothes. Lorraine had always packed for him. He fully expected her to stop and straighten it out, but she walked past without glancing at the suitcase on the bench at the foot of the bed.

Feeling as if his life was spiraling out of control, Hamilton sat on the edge of the bed and stared at the closed bathroom door. His forte was bringing sanity to chaos, but for the life of him he couldn't think of what to do or say to make his marriage the way it was before Lorraine got the ludicrous notion to go into business for herself.

He ran his hand distractedly over his head. It certainly wasn't the money. Her parents might have judged a person by the number of zeroes or the lack thereof, in a person's checking account, but Lorraine had never done so. She'd been happy eating the cheap, greasy hamburgers he could barely afford while they were students at Baylor University in Waco. Later when they'd married, there had been a lot of spaghetti, beans, and macaroni. She'd laughed once and commented that she ought to write a cookbook for young couples on a budget.

Money wasn't the reason, but what was? The only answer that kept coming back to him was that she was growing tired of him. Their life was no longer enough to keep her happy. Just the idea made his world tilt.

The door opened and she came out wearing a long V-neck silk nightgown that clung to her firm breasts before slanting over her flat stomach, then molded over her rounded hips. His body hardened. He'd wanted her the moment he'd first seen her. Didn't she realize how much he loved and needed her?

Passing within arm's length of him, her perfume reached out and punched him in the gut. Climbing into bed, she pulled the covers up over her bare shoulder. "Good night, Hamilton."

He wanted to go to her—pull her into his arms, kiss her, love her—but he wasn't sure of her reaction. He'd fully expected her to give up her plan to open a shop once she saw that it was putting a strain on their marriage.

She was home, but that was all that could be said.

"Hamilton, could you cut off the overhead light, please?" she asked.

He was across the room in no time and flicked off the switch. "You feel all right?"

"I've been better."

He didn't think, he just went to her. Lorraine was never sick. He rested his hand on her forehead. "Should I get you something?"

She turned over on her back and stared up at him. "Yes. You."

"Lorraine." Her name tumbled from his lips as he pulled her to him, his mouth finding hers. There was a faint taste of the wine she'd drank, but there was also the much sweeter taste of Lorraine.

His hand swept up the curve of her waist to her breast. His hand closed gently over the soft mound. They moaned together. He moved over her and found her wet and hot. There was a sweet desperation in their lovemaking this time . . . as if both were aware of the trouble in their marriage and afraid.

Afterwards, he pulled her close and listened to the reassuring sounds of her breathing as she slept. His arms tightened possessively.

He still had time to get her to change her mind and come home. He just had to be smarter.

Nothing was taking his wife away from him.

CHAPTER TEN

nviting a man to lunch shouldn't be so difficult.

Her hands bracketing the telephone on the kitchen counter, Claire stared at it as if she'd never seen one before. In the past half hour since she'd come up with the idea of asking Gray to lunch Saturday, she'd been staring at the phone a lot. She might be relatively decisive in trying to tell Lorraine what to do, but not when it came to her own life.

A little lunch to thank him for all he'd done for Bliss was all she had in mind. The idea seemed a good one earlier; now it had her worried. Gray was used to the best money could buy. Perhaps a simple lunch at her house tomorrow wouldn't appeal to him. Perhaps he already had plans.

Claire closed her eyes and leaned her head against the glass-front cabinet. She was doing it again. Running from life. Opening her eyes, she picked up the phone and dialed before she had a chance to let doubts stop her again. She'd memorized the number from all the times she'd tried to call him.

"Gray Livingston's office. May I help you?"

Claire's hand clamped and unclamped on the receiver. She'd forgotten one important fact. She'd never gotten past his secretary in the past. "I, er . . ."

"Yes?" the smooth voice coaxed.

"This is Claire Bennett. May I leave a message for Gray? Mr. Livingston," she hastily added.

Warmth resurfaced in the woman's voice. "Good morning, Ms. Bennett. Would you like for me to see if he's available?"

Claire blinked. "Yes, please, thank you," she quickly said. She was still trying to figure out how she had gotten through so quickly when Gray came on the line.

"Hi, Claire. How is Charleston's newest entrepreneur doing this morning?" There was warmth and laughter in his deep voice that went through her like a sunshine.

"Fine, and how are you doing?"

"Can't complain, but it's early yet," he answered.

She smiled as she knew he'd intended her to. "I won't keep you. I wanted you to know that the lease went through. The contractor is scheduled to start painting and putting up the shelves today and by next week we should be able to start moving products in."

"This calls for a celebration. How about I take you to dinner tomorrow night?"

"Dinner?"

He laughed. "Dinner, or supper as Granddaddy refers to it."

"Actually, that's why I called. I wanted to invite you to lunch here tomorrow if you're available."

"I'm available. What time?"

She tried to slow her heartbeat. "Around twelve. We should be finished with the photo shoot around then."

"Photo shoot?"

"John consented to be the Man of Bliss. Brooke is going to take the pictures on the beach."

A chuckle came through the line. "So Brooke talked him into it."

Claire's brow arched in surprise. "Yes, but how did you know?"

"Instinct. There's the other line. See you tomorrow. Bye."

"Bye," Claire said, hanging up the phone and puzzled over Gray's comment. Then the answer came to her. Brooke had a way with men. For the tiniest of seconds Claire wished she had some of Brooke's allure and self-assurance.

———

H ave a safe, successful trip," Lorraine said, removing her keys from her purse.

Hamilton looked around from straightening his silk tie. "Where're you going so early in the morning?"

"To Claire's." She expected the closed expression on his face, but was still disappointed to see it. Last night they had made love, held each other while they fell asleep, but this morning they were at odds again.

"I see." He went to his suitcase. "Thanks for repacking for me."

She sighed. "You're welcome." It was on the tip of her tongue to tell him that he was going to have to do things like packing for himself from then on. Instead she walked over to him and went into his arms. "I'll miss you."

"I'll miss you more."

They fell so easily into the pattern when there were no harsh words between them. "Go kick butt at Isaac."

"Yes, ma'am. I should be gone four or five days. When I get back, we'll talk."

It didn't take a mind reader to know what they would talk about. "We'll talk."

His arms still around her he asked, "You think you could stay until the taxi comes?"

"You aren't due to leave for another hour."

His hands went to the top button on her blouse. "I know the perfect way to pass time."

"Hamilton, intimacy won't solve anything."

He pressed against her, letting her feel his arousal. "I think you're wrong about that."

Then he proceeded to show her.

J ohn had made a mistake.

He tried to keep from staring at Brooke when she opened the door to Claire's house, but it was extremely difficult. She was the most exquisitely beautiful woman he had ever seen. She had on a floral bikini top and some kind of flimsy wrap over the high-cut bottoms. She twisted his insides and made his body and hands yearn to touch, to taste her. "Morning," he managed to mumble.

The smile on her face wavered, then blossomed again. "No. I'm not going to let you spoil this perfectly glorious day."

"Sorry," he managed. "Guess I'm having second thoughts about this."

"It will be fun," she assured as she stepped back.

John entered, but remained silent

"Morning, John," Claire said, coming out of the kitchen. "I thought you were going to bring Amy and Mark with you."

"I got to thinking about us being busy with the pictures and thought it wouldn't be a good idea to let Amy have free run of the beach without me watching her." He stuck his hands in the pockets of his jeans. "Is this all right? You didn't say what to wear."

Brooke's gaze tracked slowly over his body. By the time she finished he was glad he hadn't tucked his plaid cotton shirt into his jeans.

"Fine," she finally said.

"John, would you like some coffee or juice before we get started? I have a coffee cake," Claire offered.

"No." He hunched his shoulders. "I'd kind of like to get this over with."

"Sure," Brooke said with brisk efficiency. "We'll go down on the beach and get started. Claire, you and Lorraine come down later."

This was getting worse and worse. Three women watching him make a fool of himself, and one of them he had the hots for.

"You two go on," Claire said. "Afterwards we'll have lunch. Just so you won't think you'll be outnumbered, I invited Gray."

John didn't have to look at his watch to know it was a little after nine. "It's going to take that long?"

Brooke heard the panic in his voice and automatically reached out to soothe him. The muscled warmth and the little jolt that traveled up her fingertips had her hastily withdrawing her hand. "It won't be that bad."

"Easy for you to say since you won't be in front of the camera," he groused.

"That's not exactly true." Claire folded her hands in front of her and moistened her lips. "I know you're the marketing guru, Brooke, but I've been thinking and it seems to me that a man on the Web site would draw the women, but a man touching a woman would really sell the products."

"What!" Brooke shouted.

The half-smile on John's face died a swift death.

"Not that way," Claire quickly said, her face suffused with hot color. "Perhaps a hand on a shoulder, an ankle, to show how touchable and irresistible a woman's skin is after she's used the products. Then we'd have one with Brooke by herself with this blissful look on her face held up to the sun, a half smile on her lips. The afterglow effects of the products. I—" Claire snapped her mouth shut. Brooke and John were looking at her as if she'd sprouted two heads and wings. "It was only an idea."

John refused to look at Brooke. He tried to shove his hands deeper into his pockets, and hunched his shoulders to give some relief to his tight jeans. He'd always suspected Claire was an innocent.

The doorbell sounded. Claire looked relieved. "That must be Lorraine." She beat a hasty retreat to the front door and opened it. "Gray."

"I know I'm early, but I couldn't resist seeing the photo shoot."

Her shoulders slumped. "There may not be one."

Coming inside Gray closed the door. "Why?"

Claire cast a swift glance to where Brooke and John stood. Brooke was fidgeting with the camera Lorraine had left the night before. John was staring out toward the ocean. "I–I think I may have embarrassed them by what I said."

Gray smiled easily. "I doubt that."

"Everything was going so well." Claire chewed on her lower lip.

Without thinking Gray placed both hands on her shoulders and turned her toward him. "Stop shredding your lip."

Her eyes widened, but she did as he requested.

"Good. Now tell me exactly what you said."

She thought about tucking her head, but squared her shoulders instead. No more hiding. Her gaze locked on Gray's left ear, she repeated exactly what she'd said. The slight tightening of his hands on her shoulder inexplicably made her want to lean closer even though he was displeased with her.

"Claire."

His voice sounded deeper somehow. Once again she had the urge to lean. "Yes?"

"You didn't embarrass them."

She finally met his eyes. "I didn't?"

"No."

Taking her by the arm he went to join Brooke and John. "Morning, Brooke. John."

"Good morning," they greeted, but they both appeared distracted. John kept hunching his shoulders and Brooke seemed to find something immensely interesting about Lorraine's camera.

"It was just a suggestion," Claire said again.

"I think it was an excellent one," Gray said.

"It has merit," Brooke admitted reluctantly, lifting her head. "But I think we should use another female model."

"I don't," John stated flatly.

Brooke speared John with a look that would have made a lesser man slink away. He appeared unfazed. "You're the one who was talking about all the fun it was going to be, how you couldn't afford to hire a model. Was it just talk?"

"I'm not prepared to do a photo shoot."

"You were born prepared," he said, his gaze running appreciatively over her body. "You're flawless."

Brooke inhaled sharply.

Claire stood frozen, eyes and mouth wide open with surprise. Gray just grinned.

"Let's go. I have things to do," John snapped.

Opening the sliding door, he started toward the beach. *Why the hell had he said that to Brooke?*

"Ready, Brooke?" Claire asked when the other woman simply stared after John.

"You're going to owe me for this." Handing over the camera, she started after John.

"This should be interesting," Gray said as he ushered Claire after them.

Why couldn't he be flabby, with calluses on his feet and a receding hairline? But if he had been, she wouldn't be in this predicament. She couldn't even blame Claire. It wasn't her fault that for some ungodly reason John ignited a spark of interest in her. He wasn't her type, but that didn't seem to matter to her body.

"What do you want me to do next?" he asked.

Put your shirt back on, Brooke thought. "Go for a swim."

He didn't even glance behind him at the rushing water. "If I do, you're coming in with me."

She stared at him. He stared right back. He wasn't backing down, and she'd already learned he didn't push worth a damn. She took a deep steadying breath. "Unsnap the top button of your jeans."

"Oh, my!"

She ignored Claire's outburst behind her. She folded her arms across her chest as John simply stared at her. "Open them just a bit, like you're pulling them off or putting them back on."

John's dark eyes narrowed and Brooke felt her nipples tighten. *Damn.* It got worse when he slowly did as she asked, never taking his eyes off her. "You see a woman on the beach you want. You take what you want. You can feel the warmth of her skin, the resiliency of her flesh, you can taste her lips."

Something hot flashed in John's eyes causing Brooke to swallow. There was a promise there, quickly banked. He didn't want the attraction any more than she did. *Good.*

"Now move like you're on the prowl." She directed him through several more poses that caused her to mouth to dry and her body to heat. The scoundrel!

"I think that's enough of me." John put his hands on his lean hips. "Why don't we get you in these shots so we can finish this up?"

Brooke swallowed. She didn't want him touching her. Just watching him was difficult enough. "This is raw silk."

"I'm sure you have lots more."

The words were almost sneering, as if she was a spoiled brat. Her chin angled. "All right, big boy, you asked for it." With no more warning than that she ran full tilt toward him. He caught her as she jumped. Her arms locked around his neck, her legs around his narrow waist.

"Gymnastics for seven years," she said, her smile smug. She stared down into his eyes and knew she'd miscalculated again. She began to shiver.

"Celibate for eight months," he said through gritted teeth.

Her jaw dropped.

"Don't play unless you're going to put out the fire."

Blushing—and she never blushed—Brooke tried to scramble out of his arms. John's arms tightened, holding her effortlessly.

"What's the matter, found someone you can't tease and charm?"

She stopped immediately. "If you want a fight, you've come to the right place." She spoke over her shoulder. "Claire, put in a new card, make sure it's on auto focus, then shoot at will." She curled her body tighter around John's. "Let's see who hollers uncle first."

She was all over him, her hands, her body, her lips. He wasn't shy about where he put his hands, his body, his lips either. They went from him holding her to them being on the sand, water washing over them, her body arched, their lips inches apart. She was on top in one shot, the position reversed in the next.

Claire took shots with John's hand on Brooke's ankle, splayed against her bare abdomen, her thigh.

"I'm out of cards," Claire said, her hands shaking as much as her legs. She'd never seen anything as erotic as Brooke and John. It was a wonder the water lapping against them as they lay entwined in each other's arms wasn't steaming.

Applause sounded. Claire looked around to notice for the first time that the shoot had attracted a crowd. Brooke, lying on top of John, her legs sandwiched between his, jerked her head up. She rolled to her feet, her smile shaky.

"Thank you," she said with remarkable calm as John slowly came upright behind her. Her gaze flickered to him as he walked past her to pluck his shirt from the sand and give it a brisk shake. "You've just seen the photo shoot for Bliss, the newest name in women's bath and body products. My partner will give you the Web site address. Goodbye."

Brooke started toward Claire's house to more applause. As she passed John, he draped his shirt around her shoulders. "I think it's a draw."

"You would." She continued toward the house, planning to stay as far away from John Randle as possible.

CHAPTER ELEVEN

ooks like it's just the two of us for lunch," Claire said.

Brooke and John had already left when they arrived back to the house. On the answering machine was a message from Lorraine saying she had to attend a called meeting of the Women's Club.

"Do you need any help in the kitchen?"

Claire had to smile despite the nervousness that had steadily increased on learning they would be alone. "I don't imagine you've had very much practice in the kitchen."

Folding his arms, Gray leaned against the counter. "You'd be surprised."

She looked at him again in his wheat-colored tailored sports jacket and tobacco brown slacks. As always he remained impeccably groomed from head to toe. "Plates are in the first cabinet. Flatware is in the drawer beneath."

Pushing away from the counter, he began setting the table. They worked easily together. In minutes they were seated, the food blessed, and she was heaping shrimp salad on their plates. "Please help yourself. I thought there'd be more of us."

"I'm glad there isn't."

Her fork wobbled.

Gray seemed not to notice. "I enjoy down time. I'm around people all day long. Going from meeting to meeting, inspecting the warehouse, talking to employees. It's nice to relax."

"But I don't think you'd give it up."

"Bite your tongue," he said with a chuckle as she picked up a slice of French bread. "I never wanted to do anything but run the business. It fascinated me, from the acquisition of merchandise to telemarketing."

"It must be nice doing what you enjoy and are good at," Claire said, unaware of the wistfulness in her voice. Gray wasn't.

"I've been blessed to discover what I wanted to do at an early age. For some, it just takes a little longer."

Claire tilted her head. "You wouldn't be trying to cheer me up, would you?"

Gray leaned closer. "You can point a person in the right direction, but they have to take the first step themselves, then the next, to achieve their own success. I'd say you're on your way." He smiled. "Those photos should certainly heat up your Web site."

Heat spread across Claire's face. "It didn't come out as I envisioned."

Gray's mouth lifted in an amused grin. "I think that's an understatement. Brooke and John were just as surprised."

"What do you mean?"

He leaned back in his chair. "They're attracted to each other and fighting it tooth and nail."

Claire's mouth gaped. "Brooke and John? I thought they were just caught up in the moment."

"That they were. They probably came near to melting your camera lens."

Heat climbed up her neck again. She bit her lip.

"You always did that whenever I spoke to you when I visited my grandparents during the summers."

She tucked her head.

"That, too."

"I—" Her voice trailed off. She didn't know what she'd planned to say. He placed his hand briefly on hers. "Forget it, and forgive my bad manners." He picked up his fork. "If you need any help uploading the photos I'd be happy to help."

"Thank you, but I can manage." The idea of Gray sitting with her as she went through those sensual photos made her twist uneasily in her seat. "I want Lorraine and Brooke to see them first."

"What about John? Did you get a release from him?"

She paused. "No, I didn't think of it."

"I don't know him. He doesn't appear to be the type to cause trouble, but it's best to try and circumvent problems. You can download the pictures to him so he can view them at his leisure and fax a release at the same time."

"But there isn't any need for a release. John's a friend."

"Money changes people." His eyes went cold. "It's best to protect yourself going in."

Claire wondered if he was thinking of his ex-wife. The newspapers had reported that she hadn't signed a pre-nup, but because of the adultery that she hadn't been able to deny, and the short length of the marriage, she'd gotten very little. "All right."

Gray's lips pursed in exasperation. "People will use you, Claire, if you aren't careful. Believe me, I know."

Her heart went out to him. What must it be like to always be on guard? Just as she had, people probably looked at the wealth and position Gray had, but not at the heavy responsibility he carried. "I'm sorry."

He looked at her sharply. "For what?"

"For being one more person who thought of using you to help themselves."

His hand closed over hers again. He felt the leap in her pulse and refused to believe it was anything except nerves. "You quickly proved me wrong. You want to work for what you want, not have it handed to you." Casually, but reluctantly, he released her and went back to his meal. "Bliss will be good for you."

Gathering her scattered thoughts, Claire said, "I think it will be successful."

He looked her in the eyes. "That's not what I meant." He went on at her puzzled look. "You've always been shy. I remember asking you to join us for a swim or to go to the beach, but you always refused."

"I wanted to," she blurted, then gasped at her revealing blunder.

"Why didn't you?"

Because my brother said all you wanted to do was get in my panties, she thought, staring at her salad. She'd been shocked and so pleased by the invitation. She couldn't wait to tell Derek. He'd quickly set her straight. There was only one reason why the grandson of a millionaire would want to date the daughter of the hired help.

"Claire?" Gray said gently.

She looked up at him. There had always been something compelling and comforting about Gray. It was the intense way he looked at you. "I didn't have a swimsuit."

"Do you have one now?" he asked softly without missing a beat.

She had to swallow before she could say, "Yes."

"Good. When would you like to go swimming?"

She was tempted, but there was no way she was going to let Gray see her in a swimsuit after seeing how gorgeous Brooke had been in hers. "Thank you, but I'm pretty busy at the moment."

His dark eyes narrowed for a split second, as if he didn't believe her. "You're going to give me a complex if you keep turning me down."

Claire tried to decipher whether he was still being the friendly mentor or something different, and decided to take it as the former. "I'm just trying to ensure that your faith in me and Bliss is justified."

Gray sat back, his face closed. "I've taken enough of your time. Thanks for a wonderful lunch." He rose to his feet.

Claire slowly followed, feeling as if she had just shut the door on something wonderful. "You haven't had dessert yet. It's pecan pie with vanilla ice cream. Your favorite."

"Perhaps some other time." Gray stuck out his hand. "Goodbye."

Claire's throat clogged. She extended her hand. His closed warmly over hers. "Goodbye."

Releasing her hand he left the dining room and headed for the front door. She watched him with an uneasy feeling that he wasn't coming back. Somehow the luncheon had gone terribly wrong.

He opened the door and stepped out into the hot sun and went down the walk toward his black Porsche.

"Gray, wait!"

Shoving his hands into his pockets, he turned. "Yes?"

Claire could read nothing in his enigmatic gaze. She caught herself chewing on her lip, then stopped. She'd always been quiet, but she had a feeling this time if she stayed quiet she'd lose something precious. "The painters should be finished by Tuesday. I'd like to show you the shop."

"Thank you, but my schedule is rather busy."

Formal, polite enough to cut and leave you bleeding, he turned and started toward his car again.

"I look terrible in a swimsuit."

Claire had clamped her eyes shut the moment she'd blurted the heart-wrenching words. She prepared herself for his callous laughter, the sound of his car starting, but nothing prepared her for the gentle touch of his hand on her chin. Just two fingers that stroked, then lifted.

Her eyes slowly opened. He was so close. His gaze riveting. "I'd ask you to let me be the judge of that if I thought you'd change your mind, so how about I meet you around eleven Tuesday at Bliss, then we can have lunch. I'll clear my schedule."

"I'd like that."

"Until then." He turned and went to his car. Claire's hand touched her chin as he drove away. *Careful, Claire*, she warned herself. Gray was just being nice. Just because he hadn't liked being rejected didn't mean he felt anything special for her. She just had to keep remembering that.

They were worse than she had imagined.

"Wish I had been here yesterday," Lorraine said, regret in her voice.

"I wish I hadn't been," Brooke groaned. Seeing the pictures again was worse than last night when Claire had e-mailed them to her.

Lorraine's gaze remained glued to the computer screen. "I'll never forgive Bessie Hendrix for calling an unnecessary meeting to discuss a menu change for the annual banquet."

"I sent John a download and faxed a release form yesterday," Claire told them. "I have yet to hear from him, but I checked and he has read the e-mail."

Brooke's flesh heated at the thought of him seeing the pictures, reliving as she had relived last night, their bodies molded to each other. She'd forgotten their bet five seconds after John buried his face in the crook of her neck. The sneaky bastard.

"If he returns the release, the hard part will be deciding which to use," Claire said thoughtfully. "Of course I still need to get a photo of Brooke by herself."

"How about this one?" Lorraine pointed on the screen. "Maybe we could crop John."

Brooke felt a spiral of heat shoot through her. Her head was thrown back, her knees bent with John between them, his hands on her thigh.

"I think this one should go on the site as is." Claire turned to Brooke. "What do you think?"

"I think I was crazy to do the photo shoot." She straightened. "I need a glass of water."

The women looked at each other, smiled and nodded. That photo was definitely going on the site.

Brooke decided on raspberry lemonade instead of water. Eyes closed, she rolled the glass loaded with ice across her forehead. She'd pulled some crazy stunts in her life, but none had backfired on her so badly. Who would have ever thought she'd be attracted to the silent, arrogant type? Or that he'd have hands that sent shivers through her body and make her crave more?

Her eyes opened and she gulped her drink. No man had ever gotten the best of her. She'd always been able to hold the edge. Even with Randolph. She had cared for him, but she was honest enough to admit he'd hurt her pride more than her heart when he dumped her. And what did that say about her?

And she knew how little John thought of her.

"You don't know me," she said aloud, then groaned. Now he had her talking to herself. The man was a menace. Thank goodness they didn't have to do any more photos. And if she had her way the ones Lorraine and Claire were so pleased with would never go up on Bliss's Web site.

She brightened. Claire was a pushover at times. All Brooke had to say was that she felt uncomfortable . . . which was the truth . . . with them being on the site and Claire would let her redo them. With another man, of course. Delighted with her plan, Brooke rinsed the glass and put it in the sink. Hurrying back to the family room where Claire had moved the computer, she accidentally brushed against a basket on the counter, sending it and its contents spilling to the floor.

"Shoot!"

Bending, she began picking the letters up. Her eyes caught the return addresses. She realized what the letters were. Bills. It didn't take much to see that Claire was behind on paying them. Claire had never said a word. She just worked hard to get the Bliss products out, to help Brooke and Lorraine realize their dreams.

Claire clearly hadn't had an easy time of it, but she was still resilient enough to fight and not be bitter. Bliss was their way out. Was she that insecure, to let a man intimidate her and spoil all of their chance for success? Pushing to her feet, Brooke replaced the bills and the basket and went to the den.

"I had a great idea." She gestured toward the picture that was still up on the screen and was gratified when her body only shivered. "Let's turn the photo around and focus back on the woman, as Claire suggested earlier. What if the woman is not responding to the man's touch so much as to the products he's smoothing on her body? It's the products that put that look on her face. The man is immaterial. We'll call that line BTS."

"BTS?" Claire repeated, a frown working its way across her brow.

"Better Than Sex," Brooke explained. Claire's mouth hung open. Lorraine smiled and nodded.

"With African American and Puerto Rican blood, my father and his brothers are about as macho as they come. My single uncles love women and if one told them that she had a product that made her feel better than sex, they'd stand on their heads to prove her wrong."

"So the woman in a relationship would get the benefit of her man's added attention, and the one not in a relationship would benefit from the products themselves," Lorraine mused aloud.

"Exactly," Brooke said, getting into her plan. It would also send a message to John that he wasn't *all that.* "We've already used the essential oils in the products and affixed the ingredients labels. We'll give them lush, exotic names like meringue-whipped body cream or soufflé moisturizing bath and shower gel."

"They sound like food. The women won't know whether to eat them or apply them," Claire said, a frown darting across her brow.

Brooke's grin was pure sin. "Yeah. If they have a man in their life, he can do both."

"Oh, my," Claire said, but she was grinning.

John scrubbed his shaky hand over his face as he sat in front of the computer screen Sunday night.

After a full day with the children and church, he'd finally had a chance to download the photos Claire had sent. But as the first photo materialized, he admitted he had purposely waited to view them. He'd had a feeling they would go straight to his gut. He'd been right.

Brooke had been all over him like a heat rash. He wished she was all over him right now. He'd wanted to rattle her and had ended up being the one rattled. Her body might seem fragile, but she was resilient and supple, her skin as soft as velvet. He'd dared to taste and had felt the punch all the way to his toes.

The lady took no prisoners.

He looked at the picture of both of them on their knees, his arms wrapped around her, her head on his shoulder. Lust hit him hard. He couldn't look at them without remembering that he wanted her until he ached. A part of his mind had kept it together for the simple reason he'd enjoyed touching her, feeling her response to him which she'd been unable to control. He wondered what it would take to push her beyond that control?

"Daddy."

John shot up from his chair, almost tipping it over in his haste to stand. "Amy, what's the matter? I put you to bed an hour ago."

"I'm thirsty," she said, rubbing her eyes. Amy hated going to bed.

John scooped her up in his arms, careful to block the computer screen behind him in his corner office in the den. He'd set it up there so he could keep an eye on the children while they did homework or read. He wasn't much on television.

"Let's get you some water, then you're back to bed."

"Whatcha doing?"

Innocence and love stared up at him from Amy's big brown eyes which reminded him so much of her mother. He wasn't getting tangled with a woman who was only out for her own good. The children were already fascinated with Brooke and had asked about her as soon as he'd picked them up yesterday. Thankfully he'd had a cold shower by then and no longer felt like knocking his head against the wall. He'd been able to answer in a reasonable tone. He'd told them she was busy with the business and he'd take them to the shop when it opened.

When Brooke wasn't there, he silently added. Brooke was definitely off limits.

"Nothing important. Nothing at all," he finally answered. There was no way he was going to let whatever it was he was feeling for Brooke go any further. "Let's get that water and get you back into bed."

CHAPTER TWELVE

Hamilton had a lot of time to think while he was gone.

Although he saw travel as a necessary part of his business, he didn't enjoy being away from his family and seldom left his hotel if it wasn't business related. He much preferred to stay in his room, order room service and work on his current project. In his years as owner of Corporate Revitalization LLC, based in Charleston, he hadn't always been able to solve all his clients' problems, but that was to be expected. However, the number was low enough that he remained one of the top turnaround experts in the country.

So why couldn't he turn his own marriage back around?

Hamilton glanced out the window as the cab wound its way through his affluent, tree-studded neighborhood. Every two- or three-story house was immaculate with sweeping flowerbeds and lush St. Augustine grass. There were no junk cars rusting at the curb, no patches of dirt dotting sun-baked grass in the front yard, no faded, dingy curtains on dirty windows or pieces of mismatched furniture inside that no one else wanted. He'd worked hard to leave that life behind and take care of his family the way his parents never had.

Hamilton's hand flexed on the knee of his charcoal Valentino trousers. Neither of his parents had had time for him. He was someone to cook the meals or a way to get government assistance, but never someone to love. He'd sworn that his children would never have to be ashamed of him or wear hand-me-down clothes or go to bed cold or hungry. He'd succeeded with the one woman who always had faith in him, the one woman he loved desperately. But now he wasn't enough.

"Here you are."

Hamilton glanced up and saw that the cab had come to a stop in the circular driveway in front of the house. He'd bought the spectacular two-story mansion with its gracefully arched windows and four fireplaces as a twentieth wedding anniversary gift. Lorraine had loved the house on sight, but had said it was too expensive. He'd put a contract on the house that very day and redoubled his efforts to grow his business. His family would not have to do without.

"Sir, this is the address you wanted, isn't it?" the cabbie asked, his arm on the back of the front seat as he turned to look at Hamilton.

"Yes." Hamilton got out of the cab and pulled his wallet from the inside pocket of his double-breasted suit. He handed the driver the fare and a generous tip. Picking up his suitcase, he went up the three flagstone steps. Unzipping the side pocket of his smaller carry-on, he took out the house key on a gold chain with a picture of Lorraine and their children grinning at him. It had been a present when he went into business for himself and began traveling so much. They'd said they always wanted him to remember them waiting at home for him.

His hands closed over the picture. That had changed. The children were gone and if he wasn't careful Lorraine would be also. He stuck his key into the lock and opened the double door. Usually Lorraine would be there, but now he wasn't sure what to expect. He'd called her as usual, but both had been careful to skirt around the issue of her shop. In the past, they'd always talked over their problems, but he wasn't sure about this time. Lorraine was displaying that stubborn side of her personality that he had forgotten. The same one that had allowed her to defy her parents to marry him. He just hoped and prayed she wasn't beginning to regret that decision.

He stepped into the wide, white marble-tiled foyer, unaware that he was holding his breath. He paused, listening. She wasn't there. The loss hit him hard. Head bowed, he slowly started toward the stairs.

"Hamilton."

He whirled and saw her. His heart thudded with sheer joy. She was rushing toward him, her face radiant and happy. It wasn't too late. She came into his arms just as she always had. His arms tightened as they always had.

He came to a quick decision. He'd bide his time and let her see for herself how foolhardy her venture was. He'd hate for her to fail, but she'd get over it. However, he didn't think he would get over losing her.

"I missed you."

"Not as much as I missed you."

Tucking her arm through his, she started toward the kitchen. "I was in the garden cutting flowers for the table." Picking up the basket overflowing with vibrant pink, yellow and white blossoms she'd left on the sofa table, she tried not to show her nervousness. She and Hamilton had to talk. "Have a seat. After I put the flowers in a vase, we can eat."

"Let me wash up and I'll help."

She watched Hamilton loosen his tie, remove his suit coat, then wash his hands over the kitchen sink all the while trying to gauge his mood. Perhaps she should wait until after dinner to tell him about the store's progress. Taking a diamond-cut crystal vase from the cabinet, she began arranging the roses, zinnias and cornflowers. "How did it go?"

"Well, I think." Opening the oven, Hamilton took out the standing rib roast and placed it on the waiting rack on the countertop. "They finally believed me when I said now isn't the time for expansion, not with the tight economy. There'll be some layoffs and they'll have to tighten their belt, but they should be able to stay afloat and after the next six months begin to see a small profit."

Lorraine placed the bouquet on the table with hands she had to force to remain steady. "But aren't some companies expanding and doing well?"

Hamilton wasn't fooled. He paused in slicing the roast. "There will always be certain businesses that will flourish, but they're in the minority. You've seen and heard about the biggest companies in the world going under because they tried to expand too quickly."

She picked up the serving dishes and filled them with new potatoes and fresh snapped green beans. "Wasn't that also due to greed, book-keeping problems, and poor management?"

"In part, but the problems started when some very business-savvy men made the wrong decision and refused to admit their mistake and get out. Instead, they stayed until it all crumbled." He set the white porcelain din-nerware on the table. "It takes just as strong a person to concede when they realize it's the only way."

He was talking about her. "It also takes a strong person to stick to their convictions," Lorraine countered.

"But they have to count the risk." Turning away from her he placed the flatware beside the plates, pleased with the weight and the polished sheen of the Waterford stainless. The table was perfect and a far cry from the chipped plates and jelly jar glasses he'd grown up using. "This looks good. You always make coming home such a pleasure." Leaning over he kissed her on the cheek, then pulled out her chair.

"Thank you," Lorraine said and took her seat.

Hamilton took his seat, said grace, then placed his crisp linen napkin in his lap. "Your skin felt a little warm. You're all right?"

"Yes, why?" She served him the potatoes, then the fresh snap beans.

"Just wondering. One of the executives mentioned that his wife was having a difficult time going through menopause and she's about your age."

Lorraine stared at him in disbelief then seriously thought of dumping the dish over Hamilton's head. The only thing that saved him was that she'd have to clean up the mess. "Why do you insist that I'm going through menopause?"

"I only asked because I'm concerned. I didn't mean to make you angry," he quickly said.

Her mouth tightened. "So, in between discussing the company, you discuss your wives."

Apparently her sweet tone didn't fool Hamilton. The wary look in his eyes remained. "You may not like what the facts and figures are telling you, but you can decipher them," Hamilton told her cautiously. "Women are different. Loving them is not always enough to understand them."

The anger that had been building died in Lorraine. Hamilton had no idea she'd harbored the idea of having her own shop for so many years.

She'd just have to give him time to get used to the idea. "And what did you say to the executive?"

"That if he loved his wife as much as I loved mine, he'd do whatever it took to keep her happy."

Lorraine studied Hamilton. Maybe he was trying. "Right answer." She casually picked up her wine glass. "I was thinking about asking your help in testing a new concept we've come up with."

"I don't know anything about bath and body products."

"But you do know about pleasing a woman," she said and watched Hamilton's head snap up. "We're going to have a limited supply of products we're going to market as making a woman feel BTS after applying them."

He fell hook, line and sinker. "BTS?"

"Better Than Sex," she practically purred, then set a jar of Jasmine Crème Brûlée moisturizing cream in front of her. "Since I'd hate for us to be sued, I thought I should test the products out."

Hamilton put his knife and fork down, came around the table and picked up the jar. "Why don't we go find out?"

"Don't you want to finish your dinner?"

He pulled her to her feet. "Later."

Smiling, she let Hamilton take her upstairs.

John couldn't believe it. But the sudden cessation of noise, the hard thump in his heart and the uncomfortable fitness of his jeans said otherwise.

"Hello, John. Hope I'm not disturbing you."

John slowly straightened from under the hood of the Mustang he was giving a tune-up and watched Brooke saunter toward him in what looked like giraffe-print mules trimmed with the exact rose color of the Chanel bag hooked over her shoulder. The short black jacket and hip-hugging pants she wore today covered her body, but only fueled his imagination because he knew the lush curves and silken skin underneath and how good she felt when he touched her. "This is a restricted area."

"This won't take long." She pulled out a folded sheet of paper from the calf leather bag shaped like a bowling bag. "We need your signature before we can put the pictures up on the site."

"You've seen them?" he asked before he could stop himself.

Her answering laugh stroked his body in ways he didn't want to think about. "Of course. I *am* head of the marketing for Bliss."

John studied her face, trying to read if she was as affected by the almost erotic photos as he had been. When she appeared unfazed, he could have shaken her. He'd felt her, tasted her, he knew when a woman was aroused, and she certainly had been. "Which ones do you plan to use?"

"The ones that epitomize that, with Bliss, a woman doesn't need a man."

His head snapped back. "I beg your pardon?"

She sighed as if he were a dingbat and reached inside the bag again for a pen. "Bliss products make a woman feel pampered. After seeing the photos I decided on the perfect way to use them. We're marketing a special line called BTS. Better Than Sex."

His mouth dropped open. He couldn't help it. Around him he heard the shocked and outraged comments and affronts from the other men in the garage who had halted work the instant Brooke had walked into the work area. The unnatural quietness was what had caused him to look up in the first place, to see what had caused the oddity.

She would make him look like an ass. He could go off on her for her affront on his manhood or he could be just as blasé as she was. Or he could be as smart as his parents always thought he was. "Maybe you should do a line of BTS products for men and use the same photos?"

Her beautiful black eyes flashed. Dead hit. The men hooted.

"That's an idea." She glanced around the shop. "Would any of you like to consider doing a photo shoot with me in a bikini to prove that point?"

Tools clattered on the concrete floor as the men rushed toward them. Smiling she reached into her purse again and took out a pad. "It's a bit hot in here. Could you please hold my jacket while I write down the information I'll need?" Without waiting for an answer, she pulled it off and handed it to him.

There was a great intake of breath as the men saw the sheer blouse over the white, low-cut lace bra. John felt lightheaded.

"If you could please give me your name and contact information for—"

"Enough! Get back to work."

Shoving her black jacket back at her in hopes she'd put it on, John grabbed the release, scrawled his name on the bottom and handed it back to her. "You got what you came for."

Taking her time, she replaced the release, the pad and pen back in her purse. "I always do for as long as I want it."

She walked off, and John knew she knew that there wasn't a man watching her who wouldn't give his soul to be walking off with her. Including him.

B rooke was fuming. Not even the frigid blast from her air conditioner vents could cool her down.

Arrogant, egotistical ass. And those were his good points. She whipped around another car with steely precision and nerve. Her father and four uncles had taught her how to drive and how to play hardball. John would think twice before he messed with her again.

She shot through a tiny opening between two cars and took the road to Sullivan's Island. Claire needed the release to finish designing the Web site. Brooke had volunteered to get John's signature because she had wanted to be the one to tell him he wasn't *"all that."* She pulled up next to a motorcycle cop at a stoplight and had the nerve to smile at him.

Another thing the Dunlap men had taught her: never flinch. The policeman smiled back and pulled off ahead of her. Since Brooke had learned on her own when not to push her luck, she eased off the brake and gently pressed the gas pedal. While rushing to a sale at Saks was perfectly justifiable, letting her irritation at John rule her actions and getting a ticket was not.

Use the pictures for Bliss products for men—her Aunt Fanny. As if to say she had no sex appeal. She'd shown him, and afterwards left him staring after her, wanting something he couldn't have. She'd practically felt the heat pouring off him.

The only thing she hadn't quite been able to do was remain unaffected. She twisted in the seat as her body remembered and wanted. "Damn your hide, John Randle. I'm going to get the best of you yet."

H e usually gave very little thought to women.

Gray leaned back in his chair in his office on the fourth floor of the Livingston Catalogue Company and knew that had been his philosophy before his marriage. It had changed when he met Jana Carpenter, a vivacious, beautiful, well-educated and accomplished woman who spent a great deal of time working with various charities in Virginia. Her wealthy father owned several thoroughbreds and she was an exceptional equestrian. He hadn't learned until three months after their marriage that she'd used her exceptional riding skill with a few of his business associates. Gray had come home unexpectedly and caught her and one of the men in bed.

Throwing both out of the house hadn't released his anger, nor had tossing the bedding. By the time Gray had tossed the mattress out the balcony window onto the front lawn, she and her lover were gone. Naked, the man certainly hadn't had his key on him so Gray reasoned he must have had a spare hidden under the fender of his Corvette.

An observant policeman had stopped them a few miles away when he noticed the woman with a sheet draped around her. Gray couldn't believe she had actually called from the police station for him to come get her and bring her some clothes or the lie that Allen had forced her.

Not in the position he'd caught them.

After the phone call he'd gone to her closets and gathered up an armload of clothes and hadn't stopped until her closet and lingerie drawers were bare. The lawn under the balcony had been littered with clothes. Since her adultery had barred any claim for alimony, and Gray had owned the house before they were married, she had no claim to community property.

Filled with rage when it became clear to her and her greedy lawyer that she wasn't going to get anything remotely close to the millions she'd expected, she'd sued him over the loss of her designer clothes. His lawyer had argued, and the judge agreed, that as a young husband Gray had been too emotionally upset to deal with the situation and simply tried to provide Jana with a way to clothe herself. How was he to know that in an affluent neighborhood such as his that people would come onto his property and help themselves?

Outside the courtroom she'd gleefully told him every sickening detail about the affair. "That wasn't the first time Allen and I had had sex. And he wasn't the first. I've slept with more men than I can count, before and after our marriage, and in every imaginable position. There's nothing I won't do to a man to get him hard. It doesn't matter who they are as long as they can pleasure me." She had laughed nastily. "The night of our engagement party an old boyfriend was waiting for me at my apartment. We were at it all night. Every time you flew back here while we were dating then engaged I had a man waiting. The pool boy on our honeymoon I did for kicks just to see if I could. He was better in bed than you could ever be."

He'd wanted to choke her. Instead he had walked away without looking back.

He'd been such a guileless fool, but he had learned his lesson about women. They were for casual flirtations, nothing more. So then, why was he gradually becoming involved with Claire?

Getting up from his desk and his daily mountain of paperwork, Gray stared out the window. From this vantage point he could see the warehouse and loading docks. He and his grandfather before him had chosen this office location on purpose. Neither wanted to forget what Livingston meant to them, to forget that with the wealth came the responsibility of maintaining the high standards of the products they offered and taking care of the backbone of Livingston, their employees.

So why was he thinking about Claire instead of the reports due out by the end of the day? The women he usually dated were beautiful, sophisticated, and well connected. Claire was pretty, painfully shy, and teetering on the brink of financial disaster.

But she wasn't giving up or looking for some man to bail her out. She was doing that herself, fighting to get her life together with guts and determination. He had to admire her even if he didn't understand why her refusal to go swimming with him had hurt him.

Just as he didn't understand why her quiet admission that she didn't look good in a swimsuit should make him want to hug her. He knew she'd made the admission because she'd sensed him pulling back. He also realized how much it must have cost her to expose herself that way.

She wanted them to be friends. He felt in his gut that she hadn't had many in her life.

But what did he want from her? She couldn't hide any better now than she had as a teenager her shy worship of him. He had no illusions that many women were after him because he was wealthy and successful. He dated them for the same reason. He was as shallow as they were, but he was becoming increasingly tired of the pretense.

Maybe he needed a friend as well.

CHAPTER THIRTEEN

Claire had nothing to wear.

No matter how much she shoved the clothes around in her closet she couldn't find anything but the simple, casual, and inexpensive clothes she'd always worn. There was nothing new or exciting she'd bought on impulse, but never had an occasion to wear. Probably because she didn't do impulse.

She'd always been the practical, logical one. Derek was the one who leaped without looking, never calculating the risk to himself or anyone else. Not practical Claire. She'd thought being that way would save her from all the financial problems and erratic job history of her older brother. It hadn't. A college degree hadn't kept her from being laid off twice.

She closed her closet door. She hadn't purchased anything but the basic necessities for the past three years. Any extra money had gone to her mother's medical care, then to maintaining the car and house. She glanced around her bedroom with its pale yellow walls and white trim, the gauzy white curtains at the French doors. Luckily she'd furnished the house when she had been pulling down six figures at her first job, but even then her mother had insisted on buying well-made pieces on sale and doing the draperies and pillows herself.

Claire sighed. She had nothing to wear that hadn't been worn several times, and none of it light and bright. Call her crazy, but she wanted to look nice and not have Gray ashamed of her when they went out to lunch. She knew Gray well enough to know he wouldn't think less of her, but she'd be miserable the entire time.

How was she going to face Gray tomorrow? He never looked less than perfect. Calling and canceling was out, especially after what happened the other day after she'd refused his offer to go swimming. What was she going to do?

The ringing of the doorbell pulled Claire from her unhappy thoughts, and she went to answer the door. Wouldn't it be nice, she thought, if it was her fairy godmother who would change her out-of-style drab clothes into the latest chic fashions? Her shoulders slumped lower. If she'd ever had a fairy godmother, she'd long since deserted her.

Opening the door she saw Brooke. Her spirits plummeted even lower. The younger woman wore a beautiful white sheer blouse. She would never have to worry about finding something to wear. "Hello, Brooke."

She stalked past Claire, pulling a sheet of folded paper from her bag. "Got it and your tab is mounting. He's such an ass."

Claire eyed the beautiful blouse again. She'd never worn anything like it, hadn't really thought about it until Gray. "Brooke, where did you buy that blouse?"

"Saks. But I set him straight," she said, continuing into the family room to toss her purse on the sofa.

Claire grimaced. "Do you think they might be having a sale?"

"Probably." Brooke folded her arms. "He can be so insulting. Thinks he's God's gift to women."

"Do you think we could go and find out?"

"I guess. . . ." Brooke slowly unfolded her arms and stared at Claire. "You want to go shopping?"

"Gray is taking me to lunch tomorrow after I show him around Bliss."

Brooke screamed, then grabbed Claire, and jumped up and down. "Mama always said, still waters run deep."

Claire flushed and barely kept from tucking her head. "We're just friends."

"Yeah, right." Brook grinned devilishly. "I can't begin to tell you how many times I used that line with my mother and she never bought it either."

"It's the truth," Claire said, defending herself. "I just want to have a nice dress."

Brooke's expression became serious. "You may find something since they're already bringing in the fall merchandise. I went by the other day just to torture myself."

"How much do you think I'll need?"

"You can probably get a nice sheath for around one-fifty."

Claire's eyes bugged. "One-hundred-and-fifty dollars!" She closed her eyes and shook her head. "I can't afford that."

"We can always use my plastic."

Claire opened her eyes. "Thank you, but I'm not charging anything. I'll just have to cancel."

"Are you crazy?" Brooke yelled, snapping Claire's head around. "Gray is one of *the* most eligible bachelors in the state, not to mention he's rich, handsome, and has a great bod."

"That's not why I'm having lunch with him."

"I know that and Gray is smart enough to know that as well." Brooke caught Claire's hand and dragged her toward her bedroom. "Enough talk. Let's look in your closet."

"I already looked," Claire said as they entered her bedroom.

Brooke dropped Claire's hand and began going through Claire's meager selection of clothes. Less than a minute later she turned with a look of stunned amazement on her face.

"I've never gone out much so there's never been a need to buy clothes except for work. Mama was sick the last months of her life and when I wasn't working I was home," Claire said, feeling the uncomfortable need to defend her pitiful wardrobe.

"You don't buy clothes because you *need* them," Brooke told her. She kneeled to inspect the six neatly stacked boxes of shoes on the floor. Finished, she pushed to her feet. "We're going to the store and getting you a dress and a pair of high-heeled sandals if I have to knock you over the head to do it."

Brooke was so serious and outraged on Claire's behalf she couldn't be offended. "You're a good friend, but I'm not taking your money. Maybe there's another way." She picked up the phone on the nightstand. "Can you please give me a minute to make a phone call?"

"I'll file the release and work on the product labels," Brooke said, and left.

Saying a quick prayer, Claire took a deep breath and dialed her brother's work number. The receptionist at the used car dealership where he worked connected her immediately.

"Derek Bennett. If you want a car you've called the right man."

"Hello, Derek."

There was a slight pause. "Hi, Claire. I thought you were a potential customer."

Hearing the disappointment in his voice, her hand flexed on the phone. "Sorry." She took another breath to steady her jumpy nerves. Maybe this time it would be different. "I . . . I . . . was wondering if you could wire me a hundred dollars of the money you owe me."

"Damn, Claire. I already told you I don't have it. Don't you think if I had the money you wouldn't have to ask? I hate borrowing money from you."

Claire's hand gripped the phone cord, but she refused to back down. "I really need it, Derek. You promised you'd repay me this time. Remember?"

"So I'm a little late," he said, his irritation obvious. "Not everyone can be perfect, you know. You were Mama and Daddy's favorite. You're the one that went to college."

You didn't want to go to college. They had to beg you to finish high school. "I don't want to argue."

"Who's arguing? I just get tired of people always coming down on me cause I'm going through some bad times. If I had it, I'd send it to you. You know that."

She wished she could say she did, but since she wasn't absolutely sure, she didn't say anything.

"You believe me, don't you?" Derek asked.

"Yes." She didn't want to get into a disagreement over it. "Thanks anyway."

"No problem. Once you open that shop you told me about, you should be raking in the dough. I told the guys here that my little sister was opening her own business. I'm proud of you. Gotta run. Bye."

"Bye," Claire murmured, but Derek had already hung up the phone. What was she going to do?

Brooke took one look at Claire's face when she entered the room, and immediately stopped affixing labels on the three wick candles and stood. "Come on, we'll just go check out a couple of shops. I'd call Lorraine, but she said Hamilton was coming home and she was going to spend the day with him."

"I can't afford much."

"It doesn't cost anything to look."

Claire soon discovered that while it didn't cost to look, she couldn't afford the clothes. There had been several dresses that she would love to have had, but they were way out of her price range. Those in her price range, she didn't want.

As they left the fourth boutique in Towne Centre, she decided that she'd had enough. "Thanks, Brooke, but I don't want to visit another store. We've wasted enough time. We have inventory to complete, labels to print and affix."

"What about the dress for your date with Gray?"

"Getting ready to open Bliss on time is more important." Leaving the shopping center, Claire headed for Brooke's car. Opening the door to the Jag, Claire sank heavily into the passenger seat.

"Claire—"

"Please, Brooke, can we just drop it?" Swallowing the lump in her throat, Claire was thankful when Brooke started the car without another word.

This could blow up in her face, but she was doing it anyway.

Brooke walked into Gray's office and hoped she hadn't read him wrong the couple of times she'd seen him. He had the kind of presence women and men noticed and reportedly the kind of intelligence that had taken Livingston to even greater profits since he was CEO. "Thank you for seeing me."

He came around the beautiful oak desk with the easy grace of a man sure of himself and one used to wielding authority. "You said this concerned Claire?"

Brooke relaxed a little bit more. She hadn't read him wrong. There was genuine concern in his deep voice and on his handsome face. "She doesn't know I'm here and she wouldn't be pleased if she found out."

His piercing black eyes went glacial. "I have no intention of lying to Claire."

His temper made her feel even easier. So whatever was going on between them wasn't one-sided. It would be fun to see which one stopped fighting it first. "Neither do I. I admire Claire and consider her my friend. She has a sense of honor and fair play that you don't find in many people these days."

Hitching up his tailored slacks, Gray perched on the corner of his antique desk. "Go on."

"I don't suppose you'd give me your word that what is said between us goes no further than this room." The arch of his brow was Brooke's answer. She sighed. "Thought so, but I can't let her be hurt."

Gray came to his feet. Brooke leaned back in her chair, the image of an avenging angel coming to mind. His five-thousand-dollar tailor-made Brioni suit didn't do anything to make him look less lethal. "Is Claire in trouble?"

"No, no. It's nothing like that." She shoved her hand through her hair, then decided to go for it. "Suppose a certain woman had a date with a sophisticated man-about-town, but say this certain young woman's closet is as bare as Mother Hubbard's cupboard? This certain young woman is too stubborn and too independent to let her friends play fairy godmother, but this certain young woman really wants to go out with the sophisticated man. The friend of this certain young woman is afraid she'll cancel the date."

Gray studied her, then said, "That would be a tragedy. I can assure you I'll do everything possible to prevent it from happening." He held out his hand to her.

Taking it, Brooke rose. "She's very proud and a good friend. I haven't had many female friends."

"You picked a good one."

"I think so, too."

He nodded. "I'll take care of it from here. And as you wanted, our conversation will not leave this room."

She smiled up at him. "I knew I wasn't wrong about you."

Claire was standing in her closet when the phone rang. She'd carried in a box of soap and hadn't been able to resist going through her clothes again. Perhaps she and Brooke had overlooked something. The phone rang a fourth, then a fifth time.

"You want me to get that?" Brooke yelled from the other room.

Claire jumped guiltily. Brooke had returned a short while ago after running an errand. She was working while Claire loafed. "No, I'll get it," she called, then crossed to the phone on the bedside table. "Hello?"

"Hi, Claire, it's Gray. You sound off. Is everything all right?"

"Fine." She tried to infuse some enthusiasm into her voice. "I was just thinking about tomorrow."

"What a coincidence. That's the reason for my call."

Claire perched on the edge of the bed. He was going to cancel. "Yes?"

"Something has come up at the plant in Columbia and we may have to change plans for tomorrow."

She hoped her disappointment didn't come through in her voice. "I understand. You're a busy man and have a company to run. You can drop by some other time."

"I told you you're going to give me a complex," he said, then continued, "I still want to see the shop and have lunch, but I have to leave directly afterwards to inspect the plant. Would you mind if we eat someplace my jeans won't look out of place?"

A relieved grin spread across Claire's face. "That's fine. There's a nice little seafood place nearby."

"Great. See you tomorrow at eleven."

Smiling, Claire hung up the phone. Casual she could handle. Then another thought struck. She hurried out of the room and didn't stop until she found Brooke.

"That was Gray on the phone and we're doing casual for lunch, which

I can handle, but I think I want to wear a little makeup and do something with my hair. Can you help?"

"Can a duck quack?" Brooke asked and both women burst into peals of laughter.

CHAPTER FOURTEEN

They'd forbidden her to set foot in Bliss before ten-forty-five.

Parking her car, Claire got out and started toward the store. She couldn't help the furtive looks she kept throwing at the storefront windows to catch a glimpse of the new her. She still couldn't believe the woman looking back at her was her. Brooke hadn't been bragging. She'd expertly used her bulging bag of cosmetics to make Claire's eyes appear deeper, a bit of rouge to emphasize her high cheekbones—courtesy of her great-grandmother who was Cherokee, then cut and styled her thick hair—courtesy of her African ancestors—into a wedge cut. The change had been dramatic.

But best of all Brooke hadn't said one word about all of Claire's talk about Gray just being a friend. Neither had Lorraine when she arrived this morning. She had just set about helping with her transformation. They didn't want Claire working in the shop and mussing her hair or ruining her makeup.

They told her she was not uncrating boxes of products and getting the shop ready before her date with Gray, and that was an order. Claire smiled. After all these years of being alone, it was nice to have two wonderful friends.

Still smiling, Claire turned the street corner and came to an abrupt halt. A group of women were standing in front of Bliss, pointing and laughing at something in the window. The first thing that went through her mind was that they were laughing at the products. Dread coursed through her as she hurried up the sidewalk to peer over their shoulders.

In the display window was a twenty-four-by-eighteen-inch picture of Brooke by herself with her head thrown back, looking sensual, with a caption underneath that said, "Pamper yourself with Bliss." On the other side of the door was another promo piece for the new line of bath and body products and a photo of Brooke and John together with the words "Is it the man or the Bliss? You'll never tell."

Claire gasped.

"Same thing I thought when I saw it," the woman in front of Claire said with a wide grin. "I'll certainly be back for the grand opening."

Claire turned to go inside the shop, then stopped. "Please do," she said and extended her hand to the woman who had spoken. "I'm Claire Bennett, one of the owners of Bliss. We'll have samples of the products available at the grand opening."

"Can we sample him, too, and see for ourselves?" one of the women asked.

Claire laughed before she could stop herself. "You'll have to ask him."

She was still smiling when she unlocked the front door and entered the shop. Brooke and Lorraine hadn't wasted their time. Beside the window display, they had already put out one complete line of products.

"The window display is a hit," she said as Brooke and Lorraine came out of the back through the swinging white louvered doors.

Brooke grinned. "People have been stopping by all morning."

"It's just what we needed to get a buzz going." Lorraine's eyes sparkled. "I can certainly attest to Brooke's marketing savvy about men."

Claire's eyes widened at the implication. She couldn't keep the blush from spreading from her neck upward.

Brooke wrinkled her nose, viciously tore open another box and began pulling out bath and shower gel in cylindrical plastic bottles. "She's been grinning and bragging like that ever since we arrived and put up the pictures. If I had known that, I might have waited."

"I thought you'd be happy I'd test-marketed your theory. Hamilton certainly was."

Brooke plopped a bottle on the glass shelf none too gently. "Not when *I* can't test-market it."

"I think I'll take the Peach Meringue body cream home tonight," Lorraine said, placing a jar of the product on a shelf.

Brooke shot to her feet. "Claire, don't you think it's in very poor taste for Lorraine to rub it in when we can't do our own test-marketing?"

Claire opened her mouth, closed it, then tucked her head. "I . . . I . . . er . . . don't think there's a possibility for comparison in my case."

There was dead silence for five full seconds. "You couldn't be!" Brooke rounded the counter. "Tell me you aren't," she asked in disbelief.

Claire wanted to slink away. There should have been at least one man she'd met in her thirty-nine years who she'd cared about enough to be intimate with.

"There's nothing wrong with waiting, Claire," Lorraine said from directly beside her. "Is there, Brooke?"

Claire lifted her head to see the astonished look on Brooke's face before it cleared. "No. No, of course not."

"I didn't have many dates in high school because I wanted to get an academic scholarship so I could go to college. Then in college I needed the grades to maintain the scholarship and to get the best possible job afterwards." She shrugged and placed her purse on the countertop beside a grouping of Honeysuckle Passion candles. "I always thought there'd be time for marriage and children."

"There is and I don't want to hear you say otherwise," Lorraine told her firmly.

"Then, Claire, you *can* do your test-marketing," Brooke said wink.

"What's this about Claire doing test-marketing?" a deep voice from behind them asked.

The women spun around to see Gray. Claire swallowed hard. Not so much from embarrassment, although she was. She'd never seen him in faded jeans that looked as if they'd been poured on and a white Polo shirt that stretched across his wide chest. Thoughts of test-marketing popped into her mind.

A smile lifted the corners of Gray's sensual mouth. "Ladies, I've been around enough women in my family to know that look."

Brooke managed to speak first. "We were just startled, that's all."

"Because you were caught talking about men," he correctly guessed.

The women's jaws dropped.

Gray laughed and as always Claire was fascinated by the way it softened his face. It made her want to curl up in his lap and sigh. Closing the door, he started toward her, the laughter still lurking in his eyes when they suddenly narrowed. Claire tensed in spite of herself.

"You look beautiful."

She stared wordlessly at him as pleasure spread through her, but she'd be darned if she choked on the first compliment she'd ever received from a man. "Thank you."

He glanced around the shop. "Looks good. The window display should bring customers in by the droves."

"They've been stopping all morning," Lorraine said.

"Brooke's idea," Claire added, feeling more at ease. "I think the women want to meet the man almost as much as they want to sample the product."

A snort came from Brooke's direction. Spinning on her heel, she went back to shelving products. "Once he opens his arrogant, egotistical mouth they'll be running for the hills."

Gray's eyebrow lifted. "I thought you and John got along very well."

Brooke's gaze clashed with Gray's. "Even you can make a mistake."

"I stand corrected," Gray said, then turned to Claire. "How about the tour and we can go to lunch before the place gets too crowded?"

She showed him around the shop, then they were ready to leave. "Would you ladies like to join us?" Gray asked.

"No, thank you," Brooke and Lorraine said in unison.

Gray opened the door with one hand and placed the other one on the curve of Claire's small waist. "We'll be going then. By the way, Brooke, if you hadn't thought to do so, I'd trademark the captions beneath the photos and any other ideas regarding 'test-marketing.'"

Claire tensed. "Just how long were you standing there?"

"Not nearly long enough."

Trying to decipher what he meant, Claire let Gray usher her out the door and down the street.

The restaurant was once a barbershop and still had the original pounded tin ceiling and hardwood floors. It also had some of the best fried cheese grits, she-crab soup, and pan-fried catfish sandwiches in the city. Claire and Gray just managed to beat the rush and snag a table on the patio surrounded by lush greenery and colorful flowers.

"I'd forgotten about this place until you mentioned it," Gray said, digging into his shrimp sautéed with scallions and mushrooms with gusto. "Good choice."

"Glad you approve," Claire said as she dined on pasta salad with grilled vegetables. "Thanks for the tip about the copyright."

"No problem. Comes with being in the business." He tore off a chunk of French bread. "The three of you complement each other very well. It's not easy forming a working relationship."

Claire sipped her raspberry iced tea. "I wish I could do more besides just making the products."

"Don't sell yourself short," Gray told her. "Without the products there'd be no Bliss. And don't forget you came up with the first marketing idea."

Down went Claire's head. He wished again that he'd caught the women's conversation earlier. Like he'd said, he surmised they were talking about men. What he didn't say was that it was probably about men *and* sex. Somehow he didn't think Claire had very much experience with either.

"What are you going to test-market?"

She choked on her tea that she'd picked up again. The tall glass hit the wooden table with a plop. She blinked those big beautiful brown eyes of hers at him, then bit on her lower lip. He had the strangest urge to bite it for her.

"Test-market?" Her voice sounded strained.

"Is there anything I can do to help?"

Her eyes went wide again and he knew without a doubt he'd been right. Brooke didn't appear the shy type and Lorraine was too sophisticated. Claire, on the other hand, had probably led a very sheltered life.

"Ah, no."

For some reason he didn't want to let it go. "Why don't you tell me about it?"

She opened another package of crackers. Her salad was almost gone and she still had two crackers left on her plate. "It–it's kind of complicated."

"Claire," Gray said, putting his hands on her to stop the nervous motion and giving into the need to touch her. Her skin was smooth and soft. Her hand jerked, then stilled. "Men are going to come into the shop to buy gifts for the women in their lives. You'll have to talk to them."

She twisted in her chair and slowly withdrew her hand. "You probably think I'm terribly naïve."

"I think you have a whole world out there waiting for you and it's going to be interesting to see you discover it." He picked up his fork and was glad to see her do the same. He didn't speak again until she'd finished her meal. "When is the grand opening?"

She placed her napkin on the table and settled back. "We're aiming for mid-September."

"From what I saw today, you'll be ready." He shoved his empty plate aside. "Would you like dessert or coffee?"

She shook her head. "No. The food was delicious. Thank you."

"My pleasure. I enjoyed being with you," he told her, then placed a bill on the table.

She flushed as warmth radiated through her. She'd never met a man as complimentary or as caring as Gray.

He stood. "Shall we go?"

Claire reached for her purse, but couldn't make herself pick it up. Gray had more confidence in her than she had in herself. She had to stop running from life. She was a grown woman. Talking about sex shouldn't embarrass her. She stared up at Gray. "Before we go I'd like to tell you about the marketing plan we were discussing."

"All right." He sat back down.

"We propose that using certain Bliss products on a woman's skin is BTS. Better Than Sex. For many women this will be a moot point as they lead very satisfying lives without men, but for others it presents an intriguing possibility and a challenge to the men in their lives. We believe that these men might take exception to our claim and try to prove it false."

Gray didn't appear shocked. What he looked like was interested. Claire's body heated.

"Is that what the test-marketing talk was about?"

She refused to look away. "Yes."

"Interesting concept. I hope you know I'm available to help in any way I can."

Claire didn't know if he meant what he said as a come-on or if he was just being concerned. "Thank you." She stood and picked up her purse.

"Excuse me."

Turning, she saw three women sitting at a table behind theirs. "Yes?"

"We overheard what you just said and wanted the address of the store and the name of the product," one of the women said.

Claire took a business card from her purse. "It will have the trademark BTS."

The woman laughed. "My husband will have a fit."

"And you'll both reap the benefits," Gray commented with a smile.

The women whooped, then the one who had spoken looked at Gray and said, "Looks like you'll be reaping your own benefits."

Claire didn't blush, just walked out of the restaurant with Gray, hoping the woman's prediction might come true.

John, it's your mother on the phone."

John straightened from beneath the hood of the car to see the receptionist standing in the doorway connecting the garage and the waiting room. Concern knitted his brow. His mother didn't call during the day unless it was important. "Tell her I'll be there as soon as I wash up."

With a wave, Samantha disappeared back inside the office. Quickly washing his hands, John followed and indicated to the receptionist that he'd take the call in his office. "Hi, Mama. Everything ok?"

"Well, baby, that's what I called to ask you."

Since his mother only called him "baby" when only she and his father were around and when she was in a good mood, the tension trying to knot his shoulders disappeared. "Mama, I have no idea what you're talking about."

"You should have told me and your daddy," she chided gently. "Seems everybody knew but us. I wouldn't have believed it if I hadn't seen it for myself. Of course it kind of shocked me for a minute."

Frowning, John took a seat behind his desk. "Told you what?"

"Your picture with that woman for Bliss."

He came to his feet. "You *saw* that picture?"

"Me and a lot of members at the church," she told him. "Sister Brown's daughter, Mary, works down the street from the store and was passing on her way to work this morning and saw you. That girl's the worst gossip. She probably spent the next hour calling everybody she could think of."

John closed his eyes and thought of his hands around Brooke's beautiful little neck. She'd scammed him.

"You know Mary likes you. She was probably jealous it wasn't her even as she told everybody who'd listen that the pictures were shameless."

Maybe he'd hang Brooke up by her toes first.

"Well, after Sister Hopkins called and said what Mary said, I got my hat and had your daddy take me down there myself. I had to drag the old rascal away from the picture of that woman of yours over to the other side to look at your picture."

He almost got hung up on "that woman of yours" before he realized he had a more critical matter—that of his sixty-five-year-old conservative father seeing Brooke in one of those provocative poses. So many conflicting emotions ran through John's mind he couldn't sort them all.

"I have to tell you, I just about hung my head."

John's own head fell. His parents had always been so proud of him. "Mama—"

"Then I heard what a woman beside me said and I have to tell you I had to hold tight to my religion."

"Mama—"

"That woman said you were probably gay and the whole thing was faked."

"What!"

"You better believe I set her straight. I told her you were my son, you were not gay and even if you were, it was none of her business. I told her you were a widower and had two beautiful children and owned your own business. Your daddy added that he was your father and proud of it."

Worse and worse. His parents had to defend him.

"You'll never imagine what happened then."

He was afraid to ask, but didn't have to.

"Women started giving me their phone number for you to call them," his mother said cheerfully. "You know I loved Linda, but we both know as sweet and loving as she was she wouldn't want you and the children to be alone. After women start seeing that picture you'll have more women than you can shake a stick at. Hold on, baby, your daddy wants to say something."

"Mama—"

"Hello, son. I know you're grown, but if I were you, I'd stick with your first choice."

"My first choice?"

"The woman in the picture."

Brooke's life was definitely in imminent danger.

CHAPTER FIFTEEN

By the time John rapped hard on Bliss's door he was angrier than he had ever been in his life.

The pictures of him and Brooke prominently displayed in the window, the stares and whispers of the women standing around him, didn't help. Seeing Brooke behind the counter, cool and calmly sipping bottled water, laughing with Lorraine while she had single-handedly screwed up his life sent him over the edge.

A red haze filled his vision. The glass rattled under his knuckles.

Brooke glanced up. The frown beginning to form on her beautiful face was replaced by shock. She slowly lowered the bottle of Evian from her red lips.

That's right, sweetheart. Time to pay.

Lorraine followed the direction of Brooke's gaze, said something to her he couldn't understand, then started for the door. Brooke's hand on Lorraine's arm stopped her and she came around the counter instead.

If he hadn't been so angry he might have given her points for facing him. At the moment all he wanted to do was get his hands on her neck.

"Hi, John. Come to congratulate us on the success of our marketing campaign?" she said sweetly as she opened the door.

"You—"

Ignoring him, she spoke to the women gathered outside the door, "Ladies, as you've probably already guessed, this is the man in the picture." She gave him a thorough once over and John clenched his teeth tighter. "What do you think? Was it the Bliss products or him that put that smile on my face?"

Amid the laughter and suggestive comments that made the tips of his ears burn, John took Brooke's arm and pulled her inside. "You—"

"We still have an audience," she said through clenched teeth, her smile never wavering. "We can talk in the back."

John slanted a look at the women with their noses practically pressed against the glass, and at Lorraine who was warily watching him, and he started toward the back of the store.

"Brooke—"

"Don't worry, Lorraine, I have a black belt in karate," she said when she passed as she allowed John to pull her along.

The swinging door closed behind them. John glanced down at her, felt the softness of her skin and scoffed at the idea. Brooke barely came to the middle of his chest. "You have a lot of explaining to do. You told me the photo was going on a Web site."

"If you think I'm going to discuss anything with you while you're manhandling me, you're mistaken."

John released her arm. He'd forgotten he held it. "Talk."

Brooke straightened the turned-up collar of her yellow sleeveless blouse while John tried to refrain from shaking her. "The contract you signed gave Bliss use of the photos in any way we saw fit to promote the products. It was in the contract."

"You know darn well I didn't read it," he shot back.

Her eyebrow lifted regally. "As a businessman, you know better than to sign anything you haven't read first."

"You conned me." The fact that she was right only added fuel to his anger. "People at my church are talking about that picture. My parents have even been down here."

Uncertainty flashed in Brooks eyes. "They have a concern about the pictures?"

"Wouldn't your parents?"

She glanced away before he could read any emotion in her face. He was about to press another point when he heard a sound that was suspiciously like stifled laughter. He couldn't believe it. "You think this is funny?"

She stopped laughing, but her mouth twitched. "My father and uncles would probably take you out on my uncle's fishing boat and use you for bait, but I'll explain that it's just business. I'll be happy to talk to your parents and tell them the same."

"I don't want you anywhere near my parents or my children."

Brooke took an abrupt step back from him, the hurt in her face unmistakable.

Impulsively John reached out for her to apologize and seconds later found himself flat on his back. When the stars cleared he saw her standing over him, her hands braced on her hips. "You're the nastiest man I've ever met and I feel sorry for your parents, and for Mark and Amy that they have to put up with anyone like you." She stuck her nose in the air. "No man puts his hands on me unless I want them there. Remember that."

She whirled to leave and he came off the floor in one controlled rush. She might know karate, but he'd been wrestling since he was Mark's age and he hadn't always fought fair. An instant after he grabbed Brooke around the waist, the pointed heel of her sandal speared the top of his foot.

She didn't fight fair either.

It took all of his strength to control her without injuring her or letting her injure him. He finally managed to pin her to the wall with her arms over her head. After she tried to make a eunuch out of him, he stepped between her legs to protect himself. It was the wrong move to make.

He knew it.

From her sudden intake of breath, she knew it.

He stared down at her. Her warm breath fluttered across his mouth with each breath, and each time her lush breasts stroked his chest. There was nothing he could do to prevent his arousal or her from feeling it. He might have been able to extricate himself if her gaze hadn't gone to his mouth. He lost it.

His mouth crashed over hers. She met him with the same fierce desire. She was fire and passion in his arms, burning him up and he was gladly consumed. His tongue mated with hers in the boldly erotic way he wanted his body to mate with hers. He greedily searched her mouth's sweetness as his hands boldly roamed over the soft curves of her body.

He'd die if he didn't touch her skin. His hand slipped under her blouse. He moaned when his hand closed over her lush breast. It lovingly filled his hand and emptied his mind. He had to taste. His head bent.

"Brooke?"

Claire's hesitant voice was like a bucket of cold water. Still, it took long seconds for him to control the wild hunger racing through him. He stared down at Brooke. Her eyes were closed and he didn't know if it was from embarrassment or if she was still fighting the need clawing through her.

"She'll be out in a minute."

"John, I—"

"Please. Claire."

He heard the louvered door swing shut, then took a deep, shuddering breath and straightened. He groaned on seeing Brooke's blouse hitched up over her tempting breast in a flimsy piece of cloth imitating a bra. Swallowing, he reached out and slowly covered up the temptation with hands that refused to stop trembling.

Why should they? She had almost blown the top of his head off. If he ever got inside her . . . He stepped back from the lure of her body.

John knew he should just leave, but somehow he couldn't. She looked vulnerable with her eyes closed, her hands clenched at her sides. He didn't manhandle women.

"I'm sorry. I didn't mean for this to happen." He rubbed his hand over his head. "I'm not sure how it happened."

Slowly her eyes opened. Passion still shimmered in their depths. "I think it best if we don't see each other again."

She had drawn first blood again.

"Fine by me."

Picking up his baseball cap from the floor, John plopped it on his head and strode out. Claire and Lorraine stood just outside the door. He didn't know quite how to excuse his bad behavior. "I didn't mean for that to happen. I'm sorry." He left, knowing he was going to be a lot sorrier if he ever saw Brooke again.

She was nothing like the women he was used to, and he had never wanted any of them the way he wanted her.

Bad. Very bad.

The moment John left, Claire and Lorraine hurried into the back. Brooke was on the floor, her arms wrapped around her updrawn knees. The two women knelt in front of her.

"Are you all right?" Lorraine asked gently.

"I wouldn't have come in, but Lorraine said he was angry and we heard the noise," Claire said. "I didn't mean to embarrass you."

Brooke finally lifted her head and leaned it against the wall. "I'm a disgrace to the partnership."

"Nonsense," Lorraine said. "You're two attractive, single people."

"All you did was kiss him," Claire soothed.

"And proved without a shadow of doubt that our products might be good, but they can't make my body burn the way John just did. And I could just kill him for that."

The Livingston distribution plant in Columbia was a little over an hour and a half drive from Charleston. Gray had planned the inspection for next week, but Claire had changed his mind. His fingers tapped on the steering wheel as the Porsche ate up the road.

Claire had changed his mind about a lot of things. Her innocence, her vulnerability, her sense of fair play drew him to her. He enjoyed being with her. Seeing her made him forget to be cautious. He liked seeing those tell-tale blushes on her beautiful face.

She was beautiful, not pretty as he'd always thought. That beauty came from within as much as it did without. And he'd bet his portfolio that she had never been intimate with a man.

So where did that leave them? He could control his zipper, but he had healthy desires.

Flicking on the turn signal he pulled onto Gordon Livingston Drive, named after his grandfather. Buying up the ten-acre tract for the second distribution center and making sure he had room for expansion allowed him certain privileges.

His grandfather had blustered about the name, but Gray had seen the shine of tears in his eyes. On the other hand, his grandmother had wanted to know why her street, Corrine Boulevard, was in the back since she was the one who actually sold the products when he'd been stationed in Korea. Gray had explained to her that her street would wind through the entire complex and link everything one day, just as she was the link that held the family together. She'd asked for his handkerchief to blot her own teary eyes.

The guard on duty stepped out of the white gatehouse even before Gray rolled to a stop in front of the double white steel bars. No one was going to crash through his gate.

"Good evening, Mr. Livingston. Good to see you again."

"Good evening, Cecil." Accepting the clipboard, he signed himself in. He never made exception for himself or his family. He handed the clipboard back. "Everything all right with security?"

"Yes, sir, and the loads are moving in and out on schedule. No vandalism."

"Good. Please call ahead and have Peters meet me at the loading dock. Tell him to be prepared for a full inspection."

"Yes, sir."

The gates swung open and he cruised through. For the time being, he'd have to put thoughts of Claire on hold. All fifteen of the loading dock spaces had an eighteen-wheeler parked in front. He bounded up the steel steps leading inside the first of two warehouses.

"Thinking about getting on the road again, Gray?"

"Hello, Carl," he said as the brawny figure of his old friend approached. Carl Sanders was six feet of solid muscles and had hands the size of dinner plates.

"I'm leaving in thirty, heading down to Jacksonville. Remember those good times we had?"

"Good and wild," Gray said with a wry twist of his mouth. Carl could outdrink, outcurse, and outfight any man who had the misfortune to cross him. "I thought grandmother was going to have granddad fire you and scrub my mouth when I came back from that trip to Texas, chewing tobacco, when I was sixteen."

"Made a man out of you." Carl moved a wad of tobacco from one cheek to the other.

Gray stuck out his hand to greet the best driver Livingston employed. His safety and delivery record attested to that. Gray, Sanders's wife and his adult children had long since given up trying to get him to kick the chewing habit. His comeback was that he had to die of something. "Good to see you."

Carl nodded toward Gray's knit shirt, softly washed jeans and loafers. "Gotta say you look better out of those fancy suits you've been wearing since they made a big shot out of you."

Gray slid four fingers into the front pocket of the jeans he'd had to scrounge in his closet to find. "I plan to do a full inspection of the plant."

Carl eyed his boss. "You could walk though a pile of manure and come out squeaky clean and smelling like a rose, just like your grandmother. Pull the other leg."

"I do believe you're insinuating your boss is not telling the truth."

Carl shook his dark head and smiled. "You don't have to lie. You're good enough at twisting the truth and leaving out to make lying unnecessary and not as much fun."

Gray folded his arms across his broad chest. "I think you've just insulted me."

"And I think you were hiding something, and I want to know what her name is?"

Gray's expression didn't change. Out of the corner of his eye Gray saw the plant supervisor hurrying toward them. "You better hide yourself. Peters is bearing down on us and if I'm not mistaken, no type of tobacco is to be consumed on the premises. I signed the memo myself."

"Damn. Later."

"Later," Gray said with a smile. What good were rules if you couldn't bend them once in a while for a friend? he thought as he greeted the plant supervisor. The thing that bothered him was, how had Carl known there was a woman involved?

Hamilton had known this would happen.

"Hamilton, sweetheart, I won't be home until around ten tonight. I can't wait to tell you how fabulously the day went."

His finger jabbed the delete button on the answering machine. Lorraine knew how he hated coming home to an empty house. Before she had the crazy idea of opening a shop, she had kept those times to a minimum. Now, that had changed.

He glanced at his diamond encrusted Rolex. Six-thirteen. Setting his attaché case on the granite counter he went in search of the food Lorraine always left on those rare occasions she would be gone when he arrived. The refrigerator was well stocked, but there was nothing with a note attached with heating instructions. Closing the door, he stalked to the phone and jabbed in her cell number.

"Hello, Hamilton. Can you hold on a minute?"

She'd sounded breathless. Why was she breathless? His hand gripped the phone tighter. Lorraine was too honest to even think about having an affair. But he'd also thought she was thoroughly happy and satisfied in their marriage.

"Sorry, it's been hectic here."

"Where are you? Why aren't you home?"

"I'm at the store," she told him. "We decided to put the Web site address in the window since there's been so much attention for the window display. We're already getting hits. Claire is setting up a chat for Friday night to discuss the products. Isn't this wonderful?"

"I want you to come home immediately." There was a long silence. "Lorraine, did you hear me?"

"Hamilton, the other night . . . I thought you understood."

"It's you who doesn't understand," he told her, refusing to be swayed by the memory of her beneath him, loving him so sweetly, so completely. "Your place is here at home with me."

"The products—"

"I do not want to hear about some idiotic marketing plan that claims to be better than sex or some soap that lathers better than the rest. All I want to know is when you're coming home."

There was an unnerving moment of silence, then, "With that attitude I may not come home at all."

A frisson of fear raced through him. He forced himself to relax. "Lorraine, don't be silly. Just come home."

"To think I was considering bringing home Peach Meringue tonight."

He thought he heard her voice hitch, but couldn't be sure. At least she hadn't forgotten about his dinner. "Thanks for thinking of bringing home dessert, but there's nothing else. Stop somewhere for takeout."

"Hamilton."

He was sure she was going to ask for forgiveness. Lorraine had always been sensible, if a bit stubborn. He was prepared to be magnanimous in his victory. "Yes?"

"Don't hold your breath." The phone disconnected.

Hamilton leaned heavily against the cabinet, the receiver still in his hand. As soon as the bookstore opened tomorrow he was going to pick up a couple of books on menopause. He wife was definitely going through a change.

guess I won't need this after all." Lorraine removed the jar of Peach Meringue whipped body cream from her oversized bag and placed it back on the shelf.

"Is there anything we can do?" Claire asked, turning from the computer screen in the back room.

"You name it and it's done," Brooke said, concerned as well.

Lorraine shook her head. "I feel so stupid after all the talking I did today. Our night meant nothing to him."

"It's a sad fact, but men think with their gonads and women with their hearts," Brooke said philosophically. She glanced at Claire. "Perhaps you should have canceled your date with Gray. You're already worried that he didn't ask you out again."

"I think I'd rather live life than be afraid of it," Claire told her. "If he doesn't ask, I'm considering asking him."

Brooke bumped her shoulder against Claire's. "Lorraine, I think we've created a monster."

"I agree with Claire. Hamilton may be acting like a total ass, but I love him and refuse to regret that love although I'm very angry with him at the moment." Lorraine folded her arms. "When I mentioned the Peach Meringue he thought I was talking about dessert and asked me to bring takeout."

"Typical," Brooke made a face.

"What are you going to do?" Claire asked.

Lorraine unfolded her arms. "Teach Hamilton a lesson. I won't be treated like an imbecile, and he can't run my life." She picked up the jar she had just placed on the shelf. "I'm taking the Peach Meringue home after all and I plan to rub it all over my body in full view of my husband, then go to sleep. Alone."

Brooke nodded with approval. "Dirty, but effective."

"You're sure you want to do that?" Claire asked, a thoughtful expression on her face.

"Yes, and I'm not going to let you talk me out of it."

Claire leaned back in her chair. "On the contrary, I was going to suggest you take the bath and body gel and the soap as well. When Hamilton goes in the bathroom in the morning faint traces of the fragrance will linger through the night. He'll remember and regret."

Brooke whooped. "You might be a later bloomer, but you learn fast."

Claire smiled. "I'm trying."

CHAPTER SIXTEEN

Bliss was taking shape.

Claire, Lorraine and Brooke had put in twelve-hour days to ensure they met the opening date. After the excitement of the first day they decided to keep the interest in the products high by intensifying the displays.

On Wednesday, Brooke had been able to "borrow" a claw-foot tub from an antique dealer a couple of doors down to place beneath her photo. They'd filled the tub with packing peanuts to resemble soap foam. On a tray across the tub was an assortment of bath and beauty products. Nearby, one of Brooke's peach-colored negligees was draped over an antique vanity chair from Lorraine's bedroom. In front of the tub was the caption, "Step into Bliss."

The next day, beneath the picture of Brooke and John, the scene was seductive instead of relaxing. A faux fireplace was constructed out of material purchased at a home improvement store and placed against the structural wall so it wouldn't impede the view into the shop. On top of the mantel were two crystal candlesticks and a crystal frame with a small picture of Brooke and John. Directly in front were a crystal decanter and two wine glasses on a sterling silver tray. The caption read, "A Blissful Night Ahead."

Beneath all the crystal and the tray was a discreet price tag. They wanted the customer to be able to create her own blissful area at home using products and merchandise from Bliss.

By Friday, they were nervous and excited about the chat that night. By tacit agreement, they didn't discuss the men in their lives as they worked to get everything ready. Lorraine was the only one who could actually claim a man and she was being cordial, tempting Hamilton every chance she got, and leaving him to his own devices in taking care of himself.

A growl sounded over the soft sounds of the jazz playing on the radio. Claire smiled and rubbed her stomach. "Sorry."

Lorraine stretched her arms over her head. "Don't be. I'm hungry, too."

"I refuse to eat another sandwich." Brooke leaned against the shelf she was filling. "I say we treat ourselves to a nice lunch where we can sit without our elbows and knees knocking against each other."

"The card table isn't so bad," Lorraine said, then wrinkled her nose at the look of disbelief on Brooke's face. "All right. I'm tired of it, too."

"I vote we go to lunch and enjoy it." Claire glanced at her watch. "Twelve-fifteen. We've been at this steady since seven this morning. The chat is at six."

"You don't have to ask me twice." Brooke grabbed her purse.

"You won't need that. I'm buying," Claire said. "My last check from Middleton was in the mailbox when I got home last night."

Lorraine started to object and insist on paying until she saw the determined look on Claire's face. "Thank you," she said instead.

"Let me refresh my makeup and I'll be right with you. Might have a male waiter who can give us a hook-up." Brooke dashed into the small bathroom in the back.

"Brooke certainly has a way with men," Claire said as the two women strolled to the front of the store to wait. "I envy her sometimes. She always knows what to say, and how to charm them."

"If that's the case, why did Randolph dump me?"

Claire spun around. "Brooke, I'm sorry."

She waved the words aside. "I thought I had all the answers, too, but I'm not so sure anymore. Don't get me wrong, I enjoy the benefits this face and body give me, but I never thought much of how other people see me."

"Until John?" Claire guessed.

Brooke shrugged her shoulders in her black DKNY ribbed tank top. "I hate to admit it, but sometimes I catch myself thinking about him. Then I want to kick myself *and* him for making me doubt myself."

"Men are experts at that. I've been there." Lorraine wrinkled her mouth. "Who am I trying to fool? I'm still there. Thomas can be so encouraging and Hamilton such a goose."

They were silent as they left the store and started down the street. "Why aren't men straightforward and logical like science and computers?" Claire wanted to know.

Brooke hooked her arm with Claire's. "Because, although we get the rap, men aren't logical."

"You can say that again," Lorraine put in.

Going into the same restaurant where Claire and Gray had eaten, they sat in a booth. A waiter promptly appeared to take their orders. After the young man learned it was Brooke's first time there, he insisted on treating her to their famous buttermilk pie for dessert. He'd make sure it was big enough for her to share. Smiling he left to turn in their food orders. Almost immediately another young man served them their drinks.

Claire looked across the table at her friends' gloomy expressions. "We're getting free dessert, excellent service, yet we don't make a blissful-looking picture."

"Some men can sure mess up your day," Brooke said and lifted her glass of iced tea. "To more blissful days ahead."

Claire picked up her glass. "To making things happen instead of letting them happen to us."

"To staying the course no matter how long or how difficult." Lorraine touched her glass to theirs. "To success in and out of the bedroom."

Claire didn't hesitate repeating the toast. She had already begun working on the former, maybe it was time to get back to working on the latter.

M r. Livingston, Ms. Bennett is here to see you."

Gray's gaze zipped back to the speakerphone, forgetting the report on his desk.

"Sir?"

He heard the question in his secretary's voice. She expected him to have Claire sent in immediately. He'd told her that Claire was to have immediate access to him at any time. Being his secretary for the past five years she hadn't questioned his request nor had her face shown any indication that it was the first time he had given such a dictate. He'd always kept women at a polite distance. Even in intimacy, he always kept a part to himself.

"I can come back if he's busy," he heard Claire say.

Gray could almost visualize Claire chewing on her soft lower lip. That was the trouble, he could visualize too much about Claire and what he could do to her and with her. He'd finally figured out what Carl had seen the other day. He had been halfway through his plant inspection when he realized he was smiling at everything. He wasn't a dour person by any means, but he didn't normally go around smiling at nothing.

Being with Claire made him happy. He just didn't want it to make him a fool.

"Mrs. Hodge, please tell Ms. Bennett I'll call her later."

"I'm sorry, sir, but she's already gone."

"What!" He jerked upright in his chair.

"She mouthed 'bye' and left."

"Why didn't you say something?" He knew he was being irrational, but couldn't seem to help it.

"Shall I have security see if she's left the building?"

He didn't want to scare her. The trouble was he didn't know *what* he wanted with an inexperienced woman like Claire Bennett. "No. Did she say what she wanted?"

"With you, sir?"

He held on to his unraveling temper with sheer force of will. It wasn't his secretary's fault that for once in his life he wasn't sure which direction he wanted to take. "You did say she wanted to see me, didn't you?"

"Yes, sir, but Claire—Ms. Bennett, brought me a gift."

Gray was out of his chair and out the connecting door in three seconds. He spied the squat jar in peach netting tied with satin ribbon and a tiny peach-colored flower on his secretary's desk the moment he opened door. "I wasn't aware you knew Claire."

"I didn't," Mrs. Hodge explained, placing a possessive hand over the jar as if she expected Gray to take it from her. "She called the other day and you weren't in. I happened to have just lotioned my hands and commented how it didn't seem to help with my dry skin. She said she had something that might help."

"She told you about Bliss?"

His secretary's blank stare was his answer. "No, sir. I tried to pay her, but she said that was all right. She . . ." Her voice trailed off.

"Finish it."

Mrs. Hodge's hand flexed on the top of the jar. "She said she could never repay you for what you did for her so the least she could do was return the favor to your secretary." Her hand slid the cream to the far corner of her desk. "Do you want me to look up her address and return it?"

He rubbed the back of his neck. "You think I've gone off the deep end, Phyllis?"

"You haven't been your best since you came in Wednesday morning," she frankly admitted. Five years with an exemplary evaluation did give you some privileges.

"Go on. Open it up and tell me what you think of the product."

A big smile on her face, she oohed and aahed about the pretty wrapping, then dipped a finger into the creamy substance and rubbed it on her hands. The soft scent of peach wafted up. "Oh, it feels as good on my skin as it smells. Forgive me, sir, but I'm glad you didn't have me send it back. I wonder where she bought it."

"She made it."

Phyllis jerked her head up and around. Her sharp mind didn't take long to figure it out. "Bliss."

"Bliss."

His secretary's eyes looked more avaricious than his grandmother's when she went on and on about the products.

"Claire and a couple of friends have a store on East Bay Street. I'm sure she'd appreciate you spreading the word." He had almost seven hundred employees and the majority were women.

"Leave it to me, sir. By the way, after your next meeting, in about ten minutes, your schedule is clear until nine-fifteen in the morning and there's a flower shop down the street from here."

"Thanks for reminding me why I hired you."

Excuse me, ladies," Gray said, then expressed his thanks as the crowd of women parted in front of Bliss's glass door. He immediately saw why. Brooke was passing out samples in thumb-sized jars of what looked and smelled like the same product Claire had given to his secretary.

"That won't make up for what you did," Brooke said, eyeing with disdain the huge bouquet of fresh cut flowers in a crystal vase he held in his hands.

"I'll do whatever it takes," Gray said, aware that the chatter around him had stopped.

"This place is better than a soap opera," one of the women said. "First the Bliss Man and now this one."

"Wonder what he did?" asked another woman.

"Doesn't matter," voiced a third woman. "I'd take him back in a heartbeat."

Brooke's smile slipped for a split second on hearing all the comments, then blossomed again. "Thank you, ladies. Please don't forget about the chat tonight and the grand opening in two weeks." She stuck the silver tray beneath her arm. "All the information is on the sample of Peach Meringue moisturizing cream. Goodbye." She turned to reenter the store and Gray moved with her.

Brooke paused and glanced over her shoulder at him. Her look wasn't comforting. "The last man who crowded me found himself looking up at me from his back."

Since his mother and sister took self-defense classes and could hold their own, Gray decided not to test her. But neither was he leaving until he spoke with Claire. He took a half-step back. "I'm hoping you won't want to destroy Claire's flowers before she has a chance to see them."

Wordlessly Brooke moved aside. Gray quickly slipped past her. "Thank you."

"I didn't do it for you." She jerked her head toward the milling crowd.

"I just didn't want an audience when I tell you to leave and don't come back."

He wasn't leaving. "Don't you think Claire should be the one to make that decision?"

"She's more forgiving than I am." Brooke replaced the tray in the window and set the wine glasses on top. "Besides I feel responsible because I trusted you to know she hurts easier than the rest of us. She still expects the best of people."

Her jab hit the desired target. Gray's insides twisted. "I didn't mean to hurt her."

"And you think because you're rich and powerful that makes up for your behavior?"

The only person who got away with even a hint of reprimand was his grandmother. He considered seeing for himself if Claire was there. But his grandmother had taught him to always take responsibility for his actions and never make an enemy when you could make a friend. "My behavior was inexcusable. It won't happen again."

"You can say anything."

"My word is my bond. You trusted me once." At her unforgiving expression Gray tried again. "Haven't you ever regretted something you did or said and wished for a chance to take it back or change things?"

A myriad of emotions flashed across Brooke's face. "When I came to your office I became a part of this, so I feel responsible. I don't like thinking I had a hand in hurting Claire. Mess up again and you'll be sorry."

He didn't think she was making idle talk with the implied threat. There was more to Brooke than a beautiful face and sexy body. "Fair enough." Gray set the flowers on the counter nearest him and stuck out his hand.

Claire came out of the back to see if Brooke needed any help passing out the flyers and samples and saw Brooke and Gray holding hands. Her heart skipped a beat. Gray had come to see her, she thought. Then she saw the flowers on the counter. A pain sliced through her chest.

She had never been jealous of anyone but had no trouble recognizing the emotion. So that was why he hadn't wanted to see her. He was interested in another woman. She couldn't blame him for wanting someone who enjoyed the same lifestyle, who wouldn't have to search for a dress to wear or who wouldn't be embarrassed to talk about sexual desires.

He'd probably just left the florist shop down the street. Brooke must have seen him passing and invited him in. The urge was strong to leave before he saw her, but she'd hidden enough from life. "Hello, Gray."

His head snapped up, but Claire's gaze had already moved on to Brooke. Claire fought hard not to let the hurt show on a face that felt too stiff to smile. "I just came to see if you needed help."

Brooke frowned and went to her. "Claire, are you all right?"

She'd get through this. "I'm fine."

Brooke glanced back at Gray. Her frown deepened. "Remember what we talked about," she told him, then went into the back of the store leaving them alone.

"Hello, Claire."

She didn't want to be affected by the seductive pull of Gray's voice or look at him with flowers for another woman when no man had ever given her flowers, but she didn't have a choice. "The flowers are beautiful."

"They're for a very special woman," Gray said, picking up the bouquet.

Claire fought the stinging in her eyes and tried to swallow the growing lump in her throat. Gray deserved to be happy. "She's very lucky."

"I'm the lucky one," he said softly and handed the flowers to her.

Her eyes widened in disbelief. Wordlessly she stared at him.

"I nearly drove the florist crazy trying to assist him with the arrangement. I told him you liked yellow."

"F–for me." She looked from the most beautiful, the most perfect roses, chrysanthemums, and ruffled tulips she'd ever seen to Gray. Tears misted her eyes, but she blinked them away. This was too important. She felt as if she had swallowed the sun. Joy splintered through her.

"Aren't you going to take your flowers?" Gray asked.

Her hands trembled as she took the heavy crystal vase. Afraid she'd drop them, she quickly placed them back on the counter. The arrangement smelled wonderful. "I don't know what to say."

Neither did Gray at the moment. He thought he had it all figured out, but after what just happened he wasn't sure. The wounded look in her eyes had been painfully obvious when she'd thought the flowers were for another woman. He could easily hurt Claire if he wasn't careful. Because whatever happened between them wouldn't be long-term. "You don't have to say anything. Sorry I was busy when you dropped by. I was trying to work out a situation when you arrived."

"Did you get it worked out?"

He wasn't surprised that her first thought had been of him and his needs. "I'm still working on it."

She smiled up at him with complete confidence and openness. "You will. There's nothing you can't do."

He hadn't counted on what hearing her say that would do to him or how much hearing her words would make him want to pull her into his arms and hold her. He glanced around the brightly lit, attractive store, and although there had to be different scents in the air, he was positive he could distinguish Claire's, a clean aroma overlaid with a floral fragrance. "The place looks better each time I come in."

"Thank you. That means a lot coming from you."

He studied her for a moment, his gaze moving to her lips, glossed with a faint trace of mauve lipstick. He wanted to put his mouth there and countless other places on her body, but he hadn't forgotten about the audience. "What's all this talk about a chat?"

Excitement entered Claire's voice. "We're trying to keep interest and enthusiasm high by hosting a chat about the products. Brooke is going to give beauty points."

"Why aren't you doing it?"

She blinked, then nervously clasped her hands in front of her. "She's the obvious choice and she is the Bliss Woman."

Without thought, he tenderly grazed her cheek with the back of his hands. "Your skin is softer than anything I've ever touched. I think you should be on the chat as well. There's something to be said about a beauty that comes from within as well as without."

Claire swallowed. Trembling fingertips touched the spot where Gray's hand had been.

He shoved his hands in his pockets. Friendship was all he could offer until he figured out if he dared act on the invitation Claire unconsciously kept sending him. Yet, how could a man be expected to resist a woman who looked at him as if he was the embodiment of her every fantasy? Especially a man who had his own fantasies about her.

"Have you thought about doing mail orders?" he asked, trying to keep his mind on business.

Was that disappointment on her face or was it his imagination? She nodded almost absently, then moistened her lips. Gray barely kept from groaning. His hands fisted inside his pockets.

"It's already set up, but we're not taking orders until after the opening. We plan to fill orders after closing each night and one of us will drop them off at UPS the next day. Through Brooke's contacts from Middleton she was able to get us everything at a fraction of the cost, along with bags with the logo we're having trademarked."

Going behind the counter with the cash register, Claire held up a red, mid-sized shopping bag with a black-corded hanger. Bliss was in black cursive letters. The image of three women in red, arms linked, were near the last letter. "Lorraine came up with the logo to remind women they can do anything."

"All these are good strategies, but I don't recall seeing them in your original business plan." He crossed to her. "How is the cash reserve?"

"We'll make it," she said and returned the bag to a shelf.

He could almost hear her add *we have to.* "Why don't you have a pre-opening? It will bring in cash revenue and get women talking about Bliss. You can cut down on expenses by serving sparkling or flavored water instead of wine and say it's better for the skin. Between the three of you, I'm sure you can come up with finger food that won't put a dent in your budget."

Claire's eyes sparkled with interest. He could almost see the idea taking root. "Mama had a recipe for a mock shrimp salad that is delicious. That might work." She smiled up at him again. "I'm always thanking you."

Gray barely kept from touching her as he wanted to. "That's what a friend and mentor is for. What time are you leaving tonight?"

A frown crossed her face. "I'm not sure. The chat is at six and it's scheduled for a maximum of two hours. We're getting more and more hits on the Web site, so the chat should be a good one."

"I'll be back then to make sure you and the other women get to your cars all right," he said easily.

She turned stubborn on him. "That's not necessary. Since we get here so early we park next to each other and walk out together. And we call each other when we get home," she said, coming from around the counter.

"What about on the way home?" he wanted to know.

Her gaze dropped a fraction. "I don't have a cell phone, but I'm getting one tomorrow."

"Call me with the number when you get it."

Claire looked up at him through a sweep of lashes. "Is that your way of making sure I get the phone?"

Gray was pleased she felt comfortable enough to flirt with him. A ball of heat rolled though him. "Yes. Any objections?"

"Not a one. It's been a long time since someone worried about me."

The innocence and loneliness of her words went through him. He'd come from a big, extended family. No one had to tell him that her brother, Derek, was all about himself. "Just don't forget it."

"I won't."

C laire carried her flowers to the back and proudly placed them on the card table. She wanted to be able to enjoy them every chance she got. A big grin on her face, she touched a perfect rosebud.

"What beautiful flowers," Lorraine commented.

"Gray bought them for me," Claire said as she sat at the card table with Lorraine.

Brooke turned from the computer screen. "Told you he was interested."

"I'm still having troubled taking it all in," Claire said, touching the rosebud again.

"I'm pulling for you and Gray," Brooke told her.

"So am I," Lorraine said. "I'd say you two were off to a great start."

"I hope you're right," Claire confessed, then withdrew her hand. Time to get back to business. "He came up with another suggestion I want to discuss with you." Claire quickly outlined Gray's idea. Brooke and Lorraine thought it made sense, and the three decided to go for it. "How does A Night of Bliss sound for a theme?"

"Perfect," Brooke agreed.

In less than thirty minutes they had decided on the time, date and menu for the pre-opening. With so many colleges in the area they wouldn't have any difficulty finding a few students to serve the food. Lorraine was sure she knew enough people from her circle of friends and acquaintances to have a good turnout. She was just as sure she could count on Thomas.

Brooke came up with the idea of giving a five-percent discount for purchases over one hundred dollars. Claire, wanting to ensure that they kept track of their potential client base, thought of having an hourly drawing for free merchandise. There was one other thing.

"I think we should dress up," Claire said carefully. "In red and black, our signature colors."

"You're sure?" Brooke asked, obviously concerned about Claire's lack of funds.

"I should be able to get a dress for that night." Claire hoped she was right.

"Not necessary." Lorraine braced her arm on the table. "The Charleston Opera had a red and black fundraiser affair last year. Stacy's gown is still here and if you don't mind, Claire, you can have it. It is knee-length, strapless with a red rose at the cinched waist. Gray will be mesmerized."

"I'll take it," Claire said with a wide grin.

"This is going to be dynamite." Brooke tapped her pen on the pad she'd been taking notes on. "Next Thursday at six is perfect. The following Saturday will be the official grand opening."

"I have enough silver serving dishes and trays for the food," Lorraine mused. "I'll take care of the flowers. If there are no objections I'd like lilies, Margaret's favorites, and I'd like to always keep a fresh arrangement in the store."

"None," Claire and Brooke said at the same time.

Claire looked at her bouquet. "I still can't believe Gray brought me flowers."

"Believe it." Brooke said.

"He's so wonderful," Claire mused, then flushed in embarrassment at her outburst. "I mean . . ."

Lorraine patted her hand. "You won't get an argument from us."

"She's right," Brooke said. "He's definitely worth the effort. Some men take their time. Others just grab."

Claire had no difficulty figuring out that Brooke's thoughts were on John. "I'm not sure how you'll take this, but I wouldn't mind if Gray grabbed."

Lorraine leaned back in her chair. "What are you going to do if he does?"

"Grab him right back," Claire said with a wide grin.

CHAPTER SEVENTEEN

The chat was fun, risqué, and a success. Over a hundred potential customers signed on before it was over. All three women got a chance to answer questions when women wanted to know more about the owners and their backgrounds. The resounding message they sent was that Bliss's hypo-allergenic, animal-free, handmade products pampered women from head to toe in supreme luxury.

Taking a clue from Claire's idea, Brooke gave away a candle every thirty minutes to keep the women in the chat room and encourage them to sign Bliss's guest book and mailing list. Not wanting to leave anyone out and to thank everyone for making Bliss's first chat such a tremendous success they offered a ten percent discount on the first purchase within a month of the store opening.

When they walked out of Bliss it was almost eight-forty-five and the women were on a natural high. Brooke bumped hips with Claire, then Lorraine as they popped their fingers.

"Can I join in?"

They jumped and whirled. A smile on his handsome face, Gray stood a few feet away. "Sorry, I always seem to catch you ladies by surprise."

"Isn't that the truth?" Brooke finally said. "I'll pass, but I'll keep the offer in mind." She looped her arm with Lorraine's. "Night, Gray. Claire."

"Night, Gray. Claire," Lorraine said, getting the message.

"You want me to see you to your cars?" he asked as the women passed.

"We're fine," Brooke called over her shoulder, never pausing.

Gray returned his attention to Claire. "You did a good job on the chat."

Claire finally got her brain working. "You signed on?"

He held up the laptop and closed the distance between them. "I wouldn't be surprised if I wasn't the only man who was there. The opportunity was too good to learn what women think about men."

"What was your screen name?" she asked, trying to recall if her answers had been too revealing when she had talked about being single, and after being laid off, wanting more job security.

"I'll never tell." His hand lightly touched the curve of her waist and they started down the sidewalk.

Claire didn't start at his touch, but it was a near thing. She had to work to get the next words out in a normal voice. "You didn't have to check on me. I told you we had a plan."

"I don't like the idea of you not being able to contact anyone if you needed help for any reason," he told her as they started to cross the street to the parking lot.

"I'll be fine." Stopping by her car, she dug in her purse for her car keys.

"I'm going to make sure. Drive carefully. I'll be right behind you." He strode toward a black Porsche parked a short distance away.

By the time Claire arrived at home she was more in control of her emotions. If Brooke was right and Gray was trying to make up his mind about whether to grab or not, she'd just have to be patient. After all, she'd been waiting for most of her life. "Would you like to come in for coffee?"

"Thank you, but you need your rest." He slipped his hand into his pocket. "I'll expect to hear from you tomorrow with your cell number."

The phone rang before she could give him her answer. "Excuse me, it must be Claire or Lorraine calling to make sure I got home safely." Going to the family room she picked up the phone. "Hello?" she answered, noting that Gray had come inside and closed the door.

"Tell me Gray's there with you?"

"Yes, Brooke," Claire said watching Gray watching her.

Brooke screamed in delight. "I'll call Lorraine so you won't be disturbed again. We'll understand if you're late in the morning."

Claire flushed at Brooke's innuendo and shot a glance at Gray. Thankfully, Brooke hung up before she had to respond.

The corners of Gray's sensual mouth kicked up. Claire thought again of his statement that he had grown up with a lot of women and wondered if he had any idea about what Brooke had intimated. Her face felt hotter.

"Problems?"

"I, err, no," Claire said and wondered how a woman went about letting a man know she wanted to be kissed. Perhaps just do it?

The phone rang again.

"Lorraine checking in," Gray stated.

"Brooke said she would call her," Claire said before she thought of the implications of that statement. "Hello?"

"Hi, sis."

Her face lit up. She couldn't wait to tell him about the progress of Bliss. "Hi, Derek. You'll never guess what happened tonight."

"Baby sis, things aren't going well here for me." A deep sigh drifted out to her. "Bad luck keeps dogging me. I really hate to ask, but could you send me another hundred?"

The smile on Claire's face faded. Aware of Gray watching her, she walked deeper into the room. "What happened?"

"The guy I loaned money to help him and his family from getting evicted now can't pay me. I need the money to pay my cell phone bill. My clients need to be able to contact me."

Claire sank into the side chair. It would be comical if it wasn't so bad. The cell phone wasn't a frivolous item. He needed it for business, but so did she. "Derek, you know I lost my job. I need every extra penny to get Bliss up and going."

"At least you have another option. My job is my only source of income. You don't want me to lose mine, do you? I wouldn't ask you if I didn't need it."

In her mind Claire tried to shift money. Robbing Peter to pay Paul, her father had called it.

"Claire, we're family," Derek whined. "You aren't going to hold it against me because I couldn't repay your money, are you? I have no place else to turn."

The decision became easier. It was only the two of them left. It wouldn't hurt for her to go a few days longer without a cell phone. "I'll wire the money in the morning."

"Thanks, baby sis. I knew I could count on you."

Hanging up the phone, Claire turned and saw Gray a short distance away. His face was hard.

"How often does that happen?"

For a moment she didn't know what he was talking about, then it came to her. Derek would hit the roof if he learned Gray knew he was having financial trouble. The two had never liked one another. "Not often."

Gray didn't move. "Thinking of yourself first is not selfish."

Gray had never been slow and, unfortunately, Derek had always needed help in one way or another. "Thank you for seeing me home, but as you said, I'm rather tired."

"Is that your polite way of telling me to mind my own business?"

She didn't hesitate. "Please."

He went to the front door and opened it. "Lock up."

"Good night. Drive carefully." The door closed and Claire went straight to her desk. Derek was family. Somehow she'd make the money stretch, just as she always had.

She wasn't going to listen. Gray knew it even before the words had left his mouth. Claire would do anything for family, and as worthless and as opportunistic as Derek had proven himself to be, he was her brother. She'd lived in a one-bedroom apartment to buy her parents a home, done without and worked long hours to keep it.

She could have sold the house for a tidy profit and given herself some breathing room. The thought had probably never crossed her mind. Money didn't rule Claire. Family did. Her parents had been proud of the beachfront house, prouder of what it represented, a family member who had made it. Claire understood and accepted that responsibility better than anyone had ever known.

Taking one last look at the house, Gray got into his car and started back to Charleston. He couldn't get over the happy look on her face when her brother had called, then the despair later in the conversation. Familiar with Derek, Gray doubted if he'd even asked how Claire or Bliss was doing. First and foremost, Derek thought of Derek, and to hell with everyone else.

Just like his ex-wife.

Gray started over Ben Sawyer Bridge. Thoughts of Jana no longer filled him with rage. He was just thankful he'd found out early in his marriage instead of later. Anger had driven out most of the love he'd had for her, work had done the rest.

Or had it?

He made a quick turn. Ten minutes later he pulled up in front of a replica of an Italian Mediterranean villa and cut the motor. The opulent neighborhood was eerily quiet, as if nothing was allowed to intrude on the residents who lived there.

A light shone from the upstairs, balconied window of the house. He stared at the window and remembered how eager he'd been to get home to his wife, and how utterly devastated he'd been to see her in their bed with his business associate. Before, he would have shut the memory off, but tonight he let it play through his mind, let himself feel all the anger, the hurt, the loss and accept what nothing could change, then forget them and move on.

A flash of light from the street cut across Gray. His gaze lifted and he saw the police car. He rolled his window down as one policemen came toward him, while another stood by the car.

"Good evening, sir." The flashlight swept Gray's face, the interior of the car. "Do you have business at this residence?"

"You might say that since I own it."

The light came back to his face, then moved away as the policeman quickly straightened. "Mr. Livingston, I'm sorry, sir. I didn't recognize you."

Gray looked at the man, in his mid-forties, and mildly wondered if this had been his beat when gossip of him and Jana had stretched all the way to Virginia. The gullible, cuckolded husband.

He started the motor. "No problem. Good night."

The officer took the hint. "Yes, sir. Good night." Waving the other policeman back into the car, they pulled off.

Backing up, Gray went in the opposite direction. He'd probably given them and the men at the station a lot to talk about. For the first time since the incident, he couldn't have cared less. He had more important things on his mind, namely Claire Bennett, and doing his damnest to keep a smile on her face.

W e're having a pre-opening at Bliss next Thursday and I'd like you to be there," Lorraine told Hamilton casually the next morning over breakfast. The sky was as blue as the water in the swimming pool a few feet away.

Hamilton glanced up from the newspaper he was reading, folded it, then laid it aside. "You're talking to me again?"

"I can always stop." Lorraine sipped her coffee, watched a bee flit from one rose bloom to the other, and tried not to think this might be her fault for starting the silent treatment.

The scrape of the iron leg of the chair on the terrazzo floor sounded unnaturally loud. Her fingers clenched slightly on the handle of the porcelain cup. Hamilton had a golf game with one of their country club members in thirty minutes. He was always punctual.

"Why didn't you tell me this last night or this afternoon?" he asked.

Setting down the cup, she slowly turned to him. "I didn't want another argument."

"So you purposely told me when you know I had to leave," he accused, crossing to her. "You think more of Bliss than us?"

The hurt and uncertainty in his eyes kept her temper in check. "There's nothing more important in my life than you and the children, but I want to do this." Her voice strengthened. "I will do this."

Hamilton checked the step he was about to make to her. "Then, there's nothing else to say, is there?"

"I guess not." She picked up her cup to do something with her hands.

Where had the love, the trust, gone? They shared a deep bond she thought nothing could destroy.

"What time?"

The cup clattered as she put it down and ran to him, her arms going around his neck. "Thank you! Six o'clock. Oh, Hamilton, I would have hated you not being there."

"But you would have gone?" he asked quietly.

She closed her eyes briefly, then answered softly, "Yes."

He pulled her arms from around his neck. "I don't want to be late."

"Hamilton," she whispered, but too softly for him to hear. He kept walking.

Refusing to cry again, Lorraine sat down and picked up the cordless phone she had brought with her in case Claire or Brooke called and began to dial. More than ever she planned to succeed. The pre-opening had to be a resounding success. Thomas was the fourth friend she called. He answered almost immediately.

"Hello."

"Hello, Thomas. Bliss is having a pre-opening next Thursday night and I wanted to know if you'd like to come."

"Just try and keep me away," Thomas said, sounding excited.

If only Hamilton could be like Thomas, she thought, then pushed the idea aside. "Wonderful. I'd like to send Candace and Karen a gift basket since you can't use the products," she said with a smile.

"If they make a woman's skin feel as good as yours, they'll be ecstatic."

Lorraine hadn't expected the compliment and faltered for a brief moment. "That's the object of Bliss."

"I'd say you've achieved your goal," he said. "How about lunch if you can get off?"

She was surprised at how much she wanted to say yes. "We're stocking."

"Maybe some other time," he said, obviously disappointed.

"I'll hold you to that. Bye." Lorraine hung up the phone, then looked at the empty chair in front of her and sighed. If she thought it would help, she'd ask Thomas to talk with Hamilton. But it wouldn't. Hamilton kept his own counsel. Besides, she and Margaret might have been best friends, but their husbands weren't. She just had to keep hoping and praying that he'd come to understand and accept her choice. She wasn't sure what she'd do if he didn't.

Five minutes after arriving at Bliss that morning, Brooke knew Lorraine and Claire were not in good moods. She wasn't doing so well herself. Last night she had dreamed of John.

This time there was no camera, no crowd, just them beneath a moonlit sky on the beach as the rush of foaming Atlantic sea tumbled over their entwined bodies. This time he hadn't stopped with his wide hands on her thigh. He'd let them slide up her legs until they could go no further, then he had done things to her body that had caused her to moan and weep with pleasure.

"Let's listen to the radio while we work." For her efforts Brooke received a shrug from Lorraine and a nod from Claire. "You know, just yesterday we said we wouldn't do this."

That brought their heads up. Lorraine stopped doing inventory. "You're right."

"Sorry." Claire stopped making notes at the card table. "Thanks for the reminder."

"Anytime. Either one of you want to talk about it?"

"If I thought talking would help, I'd do it non-stop." Lorraine went back to the inventory. "It won't, but thanks for asking."

Claire's answer was almost the same. "I have to work this out by myself."

"All right." Brooke walked over to turn on the computer. "You have until noon to get it together."

As the day lengthened, Brooke was relieved to see the lines of strain on Lorraine's face and the worry on Claire's disappear. By the time they were ready to break for lunch, conversation was flowing normally again. Brooke decided to treat. On the way back a wrecker passed and Brooke strained her neck to see if it was John, then noticed the other women staring at her.

"So, he does something for me," she admitted with a wry twist of her mouth. "I don't have to like it."

"But you definitely like what he does to you," Lorraine said with such straightforward frankness that Brooke stopped and stared at her.

Claire giggled, then clamped her hand over her mouth.

"Well, since you asked." Brooke looped her arms through theirs and proceeded to tell them every naughty, delicious detail of her dream. When they arrived at Bliss, they had to turn up the air conditioner, and cool down with bottles of Brooke's Evian. Finished with that tale, she regaled them with her horror date stories. By the time Brooke wore down it was almost three, Claire had a stitch in her side from laughing so much, and Lorraine was holding her stomach with one hand, while she dabbed at her eyes with the other to keep from laughing.

"Please stop," Lorraine begged.

"He came out of the cabana wearing long black socks, sandals, and bunny rabbits on his swim shorts. I laughed so hard I couldn't get up from the side of the pool for five minutes," Brooke said. "That was my first and last blind date."

Claire finally straightened and wiped the tears from the corners of her eyes. "Tell me you're making that up."

Brooke held up her right hand. "On my honor as the Woman of Bliss."

"Hey, I've got an idea." Lorraine straightened. "Why not put a few of those incidents on the Web site? Not specific enough to embarrass anyone, but enough to show what you went through on your way to being the self-assured woman you are, the one who can take or leave the Man of Bliss."

Brooke who had been about to veto the idea sat up straighter. "John will burst an artery if he finds out."

"That means she'll start working on it immediately," Claire said.

"It's great when your friends know you so well," Brooke said, then thought that was exactly right. The day had certainly gotten brighter . . . for all of them.

'll be there in five. I want to take you someplace. Don't dress up."

Gray's cryptic message had Claire pacing the floor in her entryway later that night. He'd sounded all right, but she couldn't think of one single place he would want to take her. The phone had been ringing when she entered the house, almost as if he'd been calling every few minutes until he reached her, which was absurd. Why would it be that urgent for Gray to speak with her?

She didn't even think of not being ready. She'd raced into her bedroom and quickly changed her khaki pants and blouse for a sundress and flat sandals.

She heard the car and didn't wait for him to come inside. Her long legs carried her swiftly to him. "Are you all right?"

"I will be." His hand brushed her hair behind her ear. "Ready?"

"Yes." She clutched the handle of the worn brown handbag she'd had forever and allowed him to seat her in his car. "Where're we going?" she asked when he got inside.

"To bury the past." Giving her hand a squeeze, he put the Porsche in gear and pulled off.

Gray stayed quiet, Claire did the same. But when they turned into an exclusive residential area she'd been to once before in her life, tension rolled through her.

"You know where we're going?"

She wondered how he had sensed the change in her. "Yes."

"At one time it was as much a tourist attraction as Fort Moultrie," he related calmly as he pulled up in front of the house.

"That's not why I came," she said, willing her voice not to falter.

He angled his body toward her. "Then why?"

"To mourn for your loss," she said.

His eyes narrowed. "Thank you." Getting out, he circled the car and opened her door. Together they went up the curved walk. He stuck the key in the top, then the bottom lock. "I haven't been inside in two years."

"Why now?" she asked, ignoring the slight pressure of his hand at her back.

Once again, his hand touched her cheek. "It's time."

This time she didn't resist. She stepped over the threshold. The house was beautiful, but somehow cold. They went from room to room. At the top of the stairs he didn't pause.

"I don't want to go in there."

His hand slid to catch hers. "I wouldn't ask you if it wasn't important."

Claire recalled what he'd said about burying the past. She opened the door and walked in. The room was huge, with a recessed ceiling, artwork and heavy furniture. Directly in front of the door was the bed. Her heart constricted.

"That isn't the infamous bed. I tore it apart and pitched it piece by piece out the window along with most of the things in this room. Then I bought more furniture to replace it."

"But it didn't help you forget, did it?"

He looked at her. "No. It didn't help." He walked further into the room. "I thought I had everything. I was thirty-eight, vice-president of a multimillion dollar company, voted Man of the Year by top publications in the country, had a slew of honors both academic and civic, a beautiful wife that I loved, that I thought loved me. The world couldn't have been brighter."

Claire pushed aside the pain threatening to send her to her knees. This was for Gray, not her. "Then she betrayed you in the worst possible way."

"Did you know she initially said she was forced, but after the judge denied her alimony, and her suit, she told me how inadequate I was, then proceeded to give me dates and details of all the men she'd slept with while we were engaged. She even managed the pool boy while we were on our honeymoon in Bermuda."

"Gray, don't." Nausea rose in Claire's throat.

"Do you know how used and utterly stupid that makes me feel?"

Grabbing his arms, she turned him toward her. "She was the stupid one. She had you and your love and she threw it away."

His thumb grazed her cheek, lifted the tear he found there. "Don't cry."

"She hurt you." Claire cried, unable to stop the flow of tears. "Please, don't let her keep hurting you."

"She can't. Not anymore." Gray's head slowly descended until his lips gently touched hers. "Let's get out of here."

Claire was still trying to assimilate the brief kiss when they went back down the stairs and out the front door. She gasped as Gray picked her up around the waist and swung her around. She saw the open smile on his face and laughed. "The neighbors will think we're crazy," she said, then remembered.

Setting her on her feet, he took her face in his hands. "No, they'll think I'm finally coming to my senses. Come on, I'll take you home."

CHAPTER EIGHTEEN

Claire had a restless night. She dreamed of the tender kiss she and Gray had briefly shared. She dreamed of him walking away as she cried for him.

When she got up Sunday morning she was still unable to decide if he wanted friendship from her or something more personal. At times the intense way he'd look at her would cause her body to yearn even as her knees grew weak, her heart to pound. She didn't know if she was letting herself in for heartache or if she'd even stop the ever increasing awareness of him if she could.

Seeing Lorraine and Hamilton at church, the unmistakable sadness in both their faces showed her that love wasn't always enough to ensure a couple's happiness. So where did that leave her and Gray? She was pondering that question when she saw the black Porsche parked in front of her house.

Her foot automatically pressed on the accelerator. Gray sat on the middle step, his elbows propped on the wide porch as he leaned back. He waved and came to his feet as she passed. She almost ran off the road into one of the many palmetto trees dotting the island. She quickly corrected and pulled into her driveway and got out. No way was she taking time to put the car in the garage as she usually did.

"Hi."

"Hi." He was dressed casually again, in light brown walking shorts and a yellow Polo shirt. On his long, narrow feet were leather sandals. "I hope you don't mind my waiting for you."

"No. I'd love the company. You can join me for dinner," she said, trying to keep her words from rushing out, glad she was able to give him a reason for staying for a while.

"I'd like that."

"Come on in."

Inside she went directly to the kitchen. She'd never been more thankful that she'd grown up in the habit of fixing Sunday dinner before leaving for church. "I'll have it on the table in a minute."

"Can it wait?"

Claire glanced around from setting the baked chicken on the rack on the counter. He looked so serious. "Yes."

"It's about the other day when you came to my office." He went to her.

"You were busy," she recalled, trying to determine where the conversation was going.

His hands settled on her waist. "I was hiding from the first woman I can't get out of my mind."

If he hadn't been touching her so gently, his eyes staring into hers with such tenderness, she might have cried out in pain. "Do you want to get her out of your mind?"

"No. I may be slow, but I'm not that big of a fool," he said. "I'm not hiding any longer."

A sigh of relief rushed over Claire's lips as she allowed her body to sink more heavily against his. Her arms went around his neck. "I have one better. You're the first man in my life. Period."

Closing his eyes, Gray leaned his forehead against Claire's. "I figured that out. You have an honestness that sets you apart from other women. You look for the good in people. You have no built-in defenses."

"With you I won't need them," she happily told him.

His arms tightened around her. "Don't trust me too much, Claire."

She might be naïve, but she wasn't stupid. "I know you won't be here forever, but having you for a little while far outweighs never having you as a part of my life. I'll take it for as long as it lasts."

His face lost none of its harshness. "You shouldn't have to settle."

She brushed her lips across his chin, and was elated to feel his body shudder. "I don't plan to settle. Do you?"

His mouth took hers. Claire thought she would be prepared for their first real kiss. She'd dreamed, fantasized, but nothing compared to the rush of heat, of desire, that swamped her. His mouth claimed hers in the most primitive, erotic way. His tongue boldly mated with hers, causing her to shiver, to press closer, to want more, to demand more. His hand swept down her back then up again as if to reassure himself she was really in his arms.

He lifted his head a long time later. The sound of their ragged breathing filled the room. "I've never been one to settle."

Claire's eyelids fluttered upward. "That makes me very happy."

Gray chuckled and held her closer. "I'm going to enjoy getting to know you."

"Not as much as I am." She kissed him again.

C laire was definitely going to be a problem, but Gray looked forward to every moment. Whether testing his control with her soft kisses or looking at him through a sweep of her dark lashes, she made him want to keep her happy and safe, then take her to the nearest bed. He'd never had such a wide range of emotions for a woman before or dated one who was so determined to be independent. Claire might not mind asking for help, but then she wanted you to stand back. That wasn't always possible.

"I want you to take this until you have time to get one," he said Sunday night before he was about to leave. He'd let her walk him outside in order to give it to her. "I realize how busy you are. I kept you from getting one yesterday and with getting ready for the pre- and grand opening you might not have time to do it yourself."

She took one look at the cell phone box in his hand and her smile faded. "Gray, I thank you, but I'll get my own phone."

He'd eat dirt rather than embarrass her. "I know that. Livingston just upgraded and we're donating the old ones to shelters, so there's no reason for you not to have one," he said, which was the truth. He didn't think she'd accept one of the newer models.

"I'm not taking the phone." She folded her arms. "Please, let's drop the subject."

He would have argued if he thought she'd change her mind. "I'll worry about you."

"Don't." She stepped forward and curved her arms around his waist. "I'm careful, and John takes good care of my car."

He kissed her forehead. "I'll have to thank him when I see him again."

She nibbled on his lower lip. "I'm trying to get him to come to the pre-opening Thursday night."

Gray's breath hitched as the tip of her tongue slid into his mouth. "Keep doing that and we're going back inside."

"Promise." Her hot tongue slid inside his mouth. He grabbed her and held her close. Claire was a fast learner.

This is the beginning. A Night of Bliss," Lorraine said, as she stood in a circle clasping Brooke and Claire's hands Thursday night. All three wore the signature colors of Bliss: Lorraine in a black pure silk organza, embellished rajah tunic intricately embroidered with red threads, with a silk taffeta sleeveless shell and matching pants; Claire in the black, strapless gown with a blood red rose in full bloom at the waist; while Brooke opted for a red jersey gown with black chain straps and feather trim around the hem.

"I'm so nervous. I didn't sleep at all last night." Claire found it difficult to stand still. The only times in the last few days that she hadn't been worried were when Gray had been with her or kissing her. Thank goodness he visited almost every day after work.

"If only my family comes, they'll fill up the place," Brooke commented, but her laugh was a bit strained.

After a brief knock on the swinging doors, Gray stuck his head inside. "Ladies, your guests have started arriving."

Gray moved aside as the three women hurried past him. Perhaps now

Claire would stop worrying. He'd put in a few calls himself to ensure the success of the night. He was determined that Claire would have her chance.

"They'll be bankrupt within six weeks," Hamilton muttered, a few feet away from Gray.

Those were the first words the other man had said since he'd arrived thirty minutes ago. Gray didn't know why he was so set against his wife's business venture. Gray had heard of Hamilton and seen him at a couple of business functions, but had never met him. "If the number of women coming through that door is any indication, I'd have to disagree with you."

"It's just the novelty of the shop and the risqué promotion." Hamilton shoved his hands into the pockets of his tuxedo. "It will wear off and Lorraine will come to her senses and come home."

Now Gray understood Hamilton's problem. He'd made it a habit never to interfere in other people's business, especially married people, but he liked and admired Lorraine. "I wouldn't count on that. This is more than some little hobby to them. They've worked darn hard and from the jingle of the cash register, they're succeeding. They have a right to be proud and I'm proud of them."

"That's easy for you to say. Claire isn't your wife. You don't have to fix your own meals or come home to an empty house." Hamilton shook his head as a waiter offered canapés. "I want my life back to the way it used to be. I want my wife back."

Gray watched Lorraine, a glow on her face, assist a matronly woman in selecting bath products. His mouth twitched when he saw they were at the BTS display.

"I've never seen her like this."

Gray heard the fear, before he saw it in the other man's face. "The way I see it, you don't have much choice. Accept the new direction her life is taking her or try to stop her and risk losing her."

Hamilton gave one emphatic shake of his head. "I won't lose her and I won't accept this."

Gray had said all he planned to on the matter. "Excuse me. Some of my family just arrived." He moved through the growing crowd to his grandmother and her oldest daughter. He kissed his grandmother on the cheek. She looked lovely in an opalescent blue jacket framed with sequined flowers over a sleeveless shell and skirt. No one defied his grandmother. "Thanks for coming and bringing Marcia."

"It wasn't difficult," his grandmother replied with an indulgent smile. "All I had to do was let Marcia sample my lotion. For once, she was ready when the car arrived."

"I want some of everything," Marcia said, glancing around, looking attractive and much younger than her fifty-eight years in a gold Yves Saint Laurent gown that complimented her flawless golden brown skin and dark brown eyes.

Gray had expected as much. Marcia was a shopaholic. That's why he'd specifically asked his grandmother to bring her. Her husband, who owned three charter boats, adored her and could afford her passion for shopping. "Let me take you to meet Claire first."

He ignored the shared glances between mother and daughter, took their arms, and led them to Claire who was with two customers by the candles. "All of our candles are hand poured, made of soy wax so there are no animal products. The wick is cotton, not lead, and will burn for sixty hours. This scent is Winter Gardenia."

"I just can't decide," the woman said, picking up another candle scented with jasmine.

"Take your time." Claire saw Gray with his aunt and grandmother out of the corner of her eye. "If I can be of further assistance, you only have to ask."

"Good evening, Mrs. Livingston. Mrs. Wainwright." Claire extended her hand. "I'm so pleased you could come."

"Hello, Claire," Mrs. Livingston greeted her. Taking Claire's hand the older woman continued, "Bliss is lovely. Your parents would be very proud of you."

Pleasure went through Claire. "Thank you. Have you had a chance to look around?"

"Not yet," Gray's aunt said. "I'm not sure where to start."

"I can definitely attest that the candles are hand poured," Gray said, easily stepping beside Claire and curving his arm around her waist. "Claire almost splattered me while she was working."

Claire smiled at the memory. "If you'd allow me, I'll grab a basket and show you around."

"Gray can do that, can't you, dear?" his grandmother said with asperity.

Their gazes met, then he brushed a kiss to Claire's forehead. "Be back in a second."

Claire didn't know what to do. His grandmother knew she was his protégée, and the hug could be between friends. The kiss said something entirely different. She clasped her hands in front of her.

"Don't let Gray embarrass you, dear. The kiss was to tell me to go easy on you, and if I didn't we'd have a discussion later neither one of us would like very much," Mrs. Livingston said frankly.

Claire blinked.

"Entirely unnecessary. I've always admired you. Now," she opened her small beaded purse in the shape of a bee and pulled out a sheet of heavy vellum paper. "I'd like to get these items for myself, and Gray's mother wanted a few things. They're listed below mine."

"Don't forget about me," Marcia said. "Where is the Honeysuckle Soufflé moisturizing cream?"

Claire glanced at the list, then back at Gray's grandmother. There were at least twenty products on the list and some had quantities of two or three listed next to them. She didn't want to insinuate that Mrs. Livingston was trying to patronize her because of Gray, but she also wanted the business to succeed on its own merit. "The recommended shelf life is six months."

"I brought a couple." Gray rejoined the group with two of the handled sweetgrass baskets.

"I'll take mine," Marcia said, and promptly put two candles inside.

"Mrs. Livingston," Claire began cautiously. "There are a lot of products on this list. Some are duplicates."

"Will you have trouble filling it?" Mrs. Livingston asked, adding a candle to the basket Gray held.

"No," Claire said, then decided not to beat around the bush. "I don't want you to buy the products just to help Bliss, but because you want them."

Mrs. Livingston held out her hand. "Please, may I have the list back?"

"Yes, ma'am." There went a hefty sale.

Gray's grandmother studied it for a moment then went through the list, reciting aloud the names of the people she was buying the products for. Some of the names Claire recognized as the servants who worked at the Livingston mansion. "As I thought, it is correct. You may not remember, but I like to do little things for people while they can enjoy them."

"I don't, but I do remember my parents thought very highly of you, of the whole Livingston family."

"The feeling was mutual." She handed the list to Claire. "If you could give us a bit more of your time, I'd appreciate it."

"I'd be honored." Claire reached for the basket Gray held. "I'll fill the order from the back."

"Why don't I go with you?" Gray's eyes twinkled.

"You'll only distract me." Surprising herself and him, she kissed him on the cheek, removed the basket from his lax fingers, and walked away.

"Well," his grandmother said. "I do believe little Claire has grown up."

Brooke's close-knit family turned out as she'd known they would. They'd driven from Columbia and Myrtle Beach for her big night and bless their hearts, they'd brought their platinum cards. Besides her parents, her favorite uncles and the cousins from her mother's side showed up.

Of course she'd been apprehensive about them seeing the pictures, but after she explained the marketing plan, they'd seemed to take it in stride. Especially when she told them there would be no more photos and how they had created a buzz for the store. They had always been supportive of her.

"Brooke, this bill is wrong," her mother said, peering at the receipt her daughter had just given her. Delicate, like her daughter, she looked beautiful in a seafoam jacket trimmed with sequins on the double-ruffle collar and cuffs, with a long skirt repeating the double-ruffled hem. A registered nurse, she had a mind like a calculator. Brooke had gotten her mathematical skills from her mother. "Early Christmas gift. Mama, I love you, but there's a line of customers behind you."

"Well, you better run my credit card back through again or I'm not moving. You have a business and two other partners to consider." She held out her card. "When *The State* newspaper in Columbia does an article on the hometown girl doing well, I want to know I helped."

Her father, cuddly and handsome in his black suit, waited patiently beside his wife. He had refused to wear a tux and it had been more important to have him there than to argue. He'd promised he'd make the ultimate sacrifice for her wedding. "Run the card, Brooke."

She ran it because she knew they'd stand there until she did. As an only child she'd learned early when she could have her way and when she couldn't. She handed her mother the new receipt. "I love you."

"We love you, too." Her mother reached for the package, but her father was already picking it up by the black-corded handle. "I told you many times before, but I want to say again we're proud of you and we love you."

"Same here." She blew them a kiss. "Next."

Taking the woman's single bar of soap of honeysuckle-vanilla soap, Brooke rang up the sale with the same enthusiasm and friendliness as she had the other orders. She wrapped it in tissue paper, and reached for a Bliss shopping bag, then pulled a black ribbon through the top of the bag. The pre-opening had originally been by invitation only, but as word had leaked out about the event they had decided to let in anyone who wanted to come inside.

The next woman had a basket that overflowed. In her hand was a duplicate set of the candlesticks on the mantel. Lorraine's crystal and sterling were selling well. Brooke's mouth twitched as she placed a BTS product into the woman's bag.

The slim well-dressed woman who appeared to be in her late-sixties saw Brooke's expression. "If the claim is true, I'll be back to buy it in the fifty-gallon drum. George would rather watch TV than me."

"Maybe you haven't given George enough incentive," Brooke whispered as she leaned over to hand the woman the bag. "The moisturizing cream is for all over the body. I'm sure there are some places you can't reach. He might be interested in helping."

The woman chuckled. "It's worth a try."

The next woman moved up. "Start ringing that up. I think I want some of that cream."

"Certainly," Brooke said. "It's on the third counter with the rose and gardenia petals."

Business was good, and the women were certainly getting into testing the BTS products. It wasn't likely she'd have an occasion to test the products. This time it was much harder to keep the smile on her face when the woman came back.

Gray recognized Elaine Forest, a reporter from *The Post and Courier*, the South's oldest daily newspaper, as soon as she entered Bliss. He was pleased to see she had accepted his invitation and had a photographer with her. She was dressed casually in khakis and a white blouse. Spotting him, she waved and started in his direction.

"Hello, Elaine," he greeted, shaking the slender woman's hand. "Glad you could make it."

"Hi, Gray. So am I. You know Harold, my photographer," she said, glancing around at the busy shop. "If this crowd is any indication, Bliss is going to be as successful as you predicted."

"And you'll have reported it first," Gray put in smoothly. Elaine was fair, tenacious and her competitive spirit almost equaled his own. "Let me introduce you to the owners."

When Gray introduced Elaine to Claire her beautiful brown eyes widened in astonishment, but she quickly recovered. Smiling warmly, she introduced Brooke and Lorraine, all the while relating how Bliss had begun . . . out of despair and a dream to become a wonderful opportunity and the strong bond of friendship that had developed between them.

"What's your interest in Bliss, Gray?" Elaine asked, looking up from scribbling on her small memo pad.

He didn't shy away from the speculation in Elaine's face or her shrewd eyes. "Claire is an old friend of the family. She came to me for some business advice."

"We couldn't have done this without Gray," Claire admitted quietly.

Brooke and Lorraine quickly agreed.

"Let's get a picture and I'll get out of your way," Elaine said, and motioned the photographer forward.

Gray started to move aside. Elaine shook her head. "You'll give the picture and the piece more power."

It would also give rise to talk about his possible romantic interest with one of the two single owners. Gray accepted it and curved his arms around Claire's slim waist, the other went around Brooke's. "It seems I need another arm." Everyone around them laughed as Lorraine took her place beside Claire.

"Thank you for coming," Claire said when they'd finished. "Before you leave, please accept an assortment of Bliss products with our compliments."

Elaine grinned. "I thought you'd never ask."

This should be one of the proudest occasions of her life—the turnout was fantastic, the event would be in the newspaper, the cash register had been busy all night—but Lorraine couldn't enjoy it; Hamilton's attitude wouldn't let her.

He had greeted the mutual friends she'd invited, but it was obvious he wasn't happy. Several people had already asked why he didn't appear to be enjoying himself. She'd lied and said he was tired from all of his out-of-town business trips.

Thomas wasn't buying it. "I'm sorry, Lorraine. I thought he'd come around by now."

His comforting words made her feel worse. "So did I."

"He should be proud of you," Thomas told her tightly, then his voice softened. "I noticed Margaret's favorite flowers on the counter. With all you've been going through, you didn't forget her."

"No, and I never will," Lorraine said softly. "She helped me to believe my dream was possible." She smiled sadly. "You've done the same."

Thomas shook his dark head. "I did very little."

"That's not true. You've been there every step of the way." *Unlike Hamilton*, she silently added.

Thomas stared deep into her eyes. "Anytime you need me for Bliss or just want to talk, call."

"Thank you. It means a great deal to know you understand." Lorraine glanced at Hamilton, his mouth set in a disapproving frown. "I better go see if I can make Hamilton smile." Excusing herself, she went to her husband. "Things are going well."

"Looks that way. What were you and Thomas talking about?"

"We were both remembering Margaret, and he was complimenting me on the success of Bliss."

Hamilton's mouth grew sterner. Lorraine took a deep breath and tried again. "Did you see the basket of roses the children sent? Of course, Melissa and Stacy want me to send them a sample of everything."

"How much longer before we can go home?"

His curtness hurt as much as his refusal to share in her success. "It's my turn to take over the cash register," she told him, unwilling to bend any further. "You can go home if you'd like, and I'll get a ride."

"I'll wait."

"Suit yourself. Excuse me." *Hamilton, what is happening to us?*

John had told himself over and over that he wasn't going to attend tonight. Claire had called the other day and left the decision up to him. He'd fully planned to stay away. But somehow he'd asked his parents to come over and stay with the kids and here he was.

Now what?

He looked through the window at the milling, jovial crowd. The women seemed to have gone all out, but thank goodness a few of the men simply wore dark suits. He realized he was looking for more than what people were wearing when he saw Brooke laughing up into some guy's face. The dress she wore showed off every luscious curve of her body.

Of course, the guy she was with wore a tuxedo like he'd been born in one. Why that point irritated him, John couldn't tell. Opening the door, he started toward Brooke.

"The Man of Bliss!"

"It's him!"

A buzz ran through the shop and his steps slowed. He took a step back as several women surged toward him.

"Ladies," Brooke said, seeming to come out of nowhere to stand by him. "I present to you the Man of Bliss. I bet with enough encouragement we can get him to sign the bag your merchandise is in, to commemorate this occasion."

Gleeful shouts of approval filled the room. The murderous scowl John threw at Brooke didn't seem to faze her.

"Gray, will you get the ladies in some type of order?" she instructed. "Claire, please get a pen and we can set up here." She gestured toward the counter.

"Wouldn't you ladies like to have the Woman of Bliss's signature as well?" John asked. That would teach her.

"I know I would," replied the man she had been talking with earlier.

John's expression darkened. He'd like to toss the grinning hyena out on his ear.

Brooke winked at the suave-looking man, then went behind the counter and reached for the pen Claire held out to her. "John, we're waiting."

John went to stand beside Brooke. His arm brushed against her bare arm. She quickly moved away. Her response annoyed him. She hadn't been that adverse to that other guy touching her. "I don't have a pen."

"Use mine," Gray offered with a half smile. "I can probably sell it on eBay tomorrow for a small fortune."

John hesitated, then saw the teasing glint in Gray's eyes. "Thanks, man."

John held his pen ready, and when Brooke slid the red bag over to him and he had to sign his name next to Brooke's, it strangely reminded him of the afternoon he'd signed his marriage license. He'd been so nervous, so happy, his signature had been barely legible next to Linda's neat cursive.

Brooke was nothing like his first wife, but he wasn't looking for a wife. He was simply trying to figure out why this one woman had gotten under his skin. He quickly scrawled his name and reached for the next bag.

The impromptu autographing seemed endless. John felt foolish and a bit embarrassed by the hoopla, but he was enough of a friend and businessman to realized that he was helping Claire cement good relations with the customers. It was time life gave her more than a hard knock. Satisfied word of mouth was the best advertisement in his opinion.

"Let's give the Bliss Man and Woman a big hand for being so gracious," Claire said thirty minutes later. There was enthusiastic applause. "Thank you, John. Why don't you take your mother a few items? On the house, of course."

"She'd like that, but I'll buy them as soon as I figure out what she might like," he told her, placing his pen on the counter.

"I'll help you," Claire responded.

"Grandmother and my aunt are leaving and wanted to say goodbye," Gray said joining them. "Brooke, would you mind helping John?"

"Gray, we really will have to have a talk one day," Brooke told him through clenched teeth.

"I can't wait." Gray smiled and ushered an obviously concerned Claire away.

John stuffed his hands into his pockets. "You don't have to help me."

"How brilliant of you to come to that conclusion," Brooke said crisply. "What kind of bath and beauty products does your mother enjoy?"

He shrugged. "I don't know. The usual, I guess."

Brooke rolled her eyes and went to a grouping of honey bath products. "These are nice. It comes in a soap, bath gel, lotion and moisturizing body cream." Opening a jar, she held it out for him to sniff.

He started to shrug his shoulders again and noted the impatient look on Brooke's face. "I guess I'll take them."

Gathering the merchandise, Brooke placed them in a basket and handed it to John. "You mother will enjoy these."

She was certainly in a hurry to get rid of him. He shouldn't care. But he did. And there didn't appear to be anything he could do about it.

CHAPTER NINETEEN

W e did it," Claire said as the locked the front door after the last customer had left. Many of the shelves and display areas were bare. "We did it! And we're going to be in the newspaper thanks to Gray."

The women squealed and joined hands. "Looks like we'll be over tomorrow to make more products," Lorraine said, still smiling.

"Especially BTS. Although my uncles scoffed at the idea, two of them purchased a jar. I think there's going to be more test-marketing," Brooke concluded with a giggle.

"Just because tonight's sales were good doesn't mean they'll continue."

Hamilton's prediction put a pall on the celebration. They all turned to look at Hamilton, Brooke and Claire's expressions showing their baffled surprise.

"Hamilton, not tonight, please," Lorraine said, her voice a bit shaky.

"I just don't want you disappointed when the store fails," he said defensively.

"It's not the store I'm disappointed in." She turned away from him to Claire. "I'll be over around nine in the morning and we can start restocking the inventory."

Claire was well aware of Hamilton standing nearby, vibrating with anger. "If you can't make it, I'll understand."

"I'll be there. Good night." Without a word to her husband, she turned and left. Hamilton hurried after her.

"Claire, I'll follow you to the bank to make the deposit and then to your house," Gray said.

Claire smiled. She couldn't think of a more perfect way to end the night than in Gray's arms. "Thank you."

"I'll see that Brooke gets home all right," John offered.

"I can take care of myself better than you can," she said, giving him a hostile glare.

"Then if there is a problem, you can protect me."

Her lips twitched as she tried to keep from smiling. He could give as good as he got. "Don't count on it."

"I'd feel better if John followed you home," Claire said.

Brooke's first instinct was to disregard Claire's attempt to help her accept John's offer without appearing anxious for him to do so. She quickly changed her mind. She wasn't afraid of him or any other man. "I'll probably leave him in the dust."

"Won't be the first time," he said with a wry twist of his mouth.

Brooke was unsure if he meant that sexually or physically. "Just remember that and keep your distance." Spinning on her heel she went to get her purse.

"Give it a chance," Claire said to Brooke as she unlocked the file cabinet and removed the bank deposit and their evening bags. "He's a wonderful man."

"He makes me so angry." Brooke removed her key from a bag no bigger than her palm.

"Because he also makes you want to jump him."

Brooke's head snapped around. Laughter bubbled from her lips. "Girl, you are getting to be something else. Do you plan to do a little jumping of your own?"

"Of course." Laughing, the women returned to the front of the store.

Gray immediately went to Claire. John stayed where he was. He was keeping his distance . . . at least until they were alone.

orraine, please talk to me." Hamilton hated to plead, but he didn't
have much choice. Lorraine had refused to speak to him after they
left Bliss. She wouldn't even look at him. "We have to talk if we're going
to work this out."

Continuing to ignore him, she rubbed the fragrant peach moisturizer
on her arms and legs. It hadn't taken him long to figure out she was doing
it to torture him. They hadn't made love in weeks. He'd approached her
once and she'd claimed she was tired. It had been the first time she had
ever refused him. At first he'd been concerned, then once he'd realized
her little performance had been to punish him, he'd become angry. His
mother had used the same methods to bring his father to heel.

At least tonight she hadn't left the bathroom door partially open so
he'd see her as she bathed, dried herself and smoothed lotion all over her
body—in places he wanted to touch. However her closing the door made
him more concerned, just as the sight of her in a heavy silk nightgown
instead of one in a lighter fabric that clung to her nipples and slid sensu-
ously over her hips. "Lorraine, is that shop more important than our
marriage?"

Her hand paused. He swallowed. He hadn't meant to say that. He
didn't want to make her choose. He didn't know anymore what her
answer would be.

She turned in the chair that had replaced the vanity stool he'd seen tonight at Bliss and he tried to prepare himself for the worst. Seeing the sadness in her eyes almost made him tell her she could do what she wanted,
just don't leave him. He might have if he couldn't hear in his head, over
and over again, his father begging his mother and her laughter as she
walked out on them and into the night without looking back.

"How could you embarrass me in front of my friends?"

"I'm sorry about that." And he was. Putting his business in the street
had been his parents' way. Never his.

"I wish I could believe that." She came to her feet and looked straight
at him, seemingly to struggle with a decision. "I—"

"No, wait," he said, going to her, taking her hands in his, holding them
when she tried to pull away. "I've been thinking. Perhaps I was a little

abrupt in my judgment. You and the others obviously have a product women are willing to buy."

Seeing the hope in her eyes, Hamilton knew he was on the right track. He should have seen it before. All he had to do was bide his time. It would also be better if she didn't remember that he had predicted Bliss's failure when it went belly-up. "I won't say another word against it."

"You mean that, Hamilton? You aren't saying that just because you want to make love?" she asked with her usual directness.

Since his arousal was jabbing her, he could hardly deny the obvious. His hand lifted to her face, dear and beautiful. He'd lie if he had to, but this time there was no need. He spoke from his heart. "You're the love of my life."

He expected that to be enough, but when he tried to pull her into his arms she resisted. "I've always trusted you, Hamilton, believed in you. If you take that trust away I'm not sure where that will leave us."

He felt chilled. Unflinchingly, her dark eyes bore into him. She was warning him: Lie to her and it might be the end of their marriage.

"You can trust me," he told her, then kissed her on the edge of her mouth, letting his tongue stroke the corner the way she liked. He felt her shiver, felt his own arousal grow harder.

"Hamilton," she sighed.

"Yes." Tonight he wouldn't go to sleep hard and aching. He pulled the strap of her gown down to reveal her beautiful, firm breast. Her nipple was already hard.

"Hamilton."

Aware that once his lips closed over her pouting nipple conversation would be over for both of them, he lifted his head. "Yes?"

"Just remember what I said."

Stunned, he stared at her. She slipped the strap of the gown over her other shoulder and let the gown fall to the floor. She stood there before him in all her naked splendor. He licked his lips, then looked up into her sultry eyes.

"Remember. Because I won't forget."

"I'll remember," he said, reaching for her, forgetting the coolness of the porcelain tile. It had been too long, the constant fear of losing her too strong. He wanted her to remember this, their love, their passion, what they had always shared.

His hungry mouth moved from one breast to the other. His hand swept up the smoothness of her thigh. His probing fingers found her wet and hot. She cried out, arching against his hand.

Not yet. He moved down her body, his mouth kissing and taking tiny nips, lower and lower to the most intimate part of her. She cried out his name.

She'd remember and so would he.

Brooke had considered leaving John in the dust when she pulled out of the parking lot. She didn't because it would be too humiliating if he saw her getting pulled over by the cops. Besides, she was determined that he remain oblivious to the way he made her body hum. She glanced into the rearview mirror at the headlights of his truck. A truck.

Randolph owned two expensive sports cars and he'd never come close to making her feel anything close to what John did. She twisted uneasily in her seat. She would not let herself be interested in a man who couldn't give her the lifestyle she had come to expect.

Pulling off, she took the next corner sharper than intended. Her gaze automatically went to the mirror again. John appeared to be the same distance from her. Irritated, she started to press a little harder on the accelerator. Then she thought of what she was doing and tried to settle down.

She turned another corner and was never so glad to see her condo. Easing up to the black iron gate, she spoke into the security box. "Hi, it's Brooke and a guest."

"Hello, Ms. Dunlap. Welcome home. Have a good night." Laughter followed. The steel gate, twelve feet wide and eight feet high, started rolling from left to right.

She recognized the voice as Helen Williams, a divorced mother of two, who had a wicked sense of humor. "He's coming right back out."

"Can I have him, then?"

The flash of jealousy was totally unexpected. Helen always carried on foolishness with Brooke when she manned the booth by herself. "Be my guest."

"Since I like living I'll pass."

Even more annoyed with herself, Brooke drove through and parked in her designated spot. She waited as John parked in the visitor's area. She tapped the toe of her red and black Jimmy Choo impatiently. He was certainly taking his time. She was about to go on without him when he came around a parked car and started toward her.

Her heart thumped. Damn him. He had no right to look so good. Against her will she remembered them locked together in the back of the store. It had been a mistake then, and it was a mistake to let him near her now.

"Nice place."

"Thank you. You've done your duty. Good night."

"Claire said I was to see you home. That means your front door."

Her chin came up. "You're not getting inside."

"I don't remember asking."

His chin begged for her fist. Whirling, she pushed the elevator button behind her. For once, it opened quickly and she stepped on, then punched four. She took a deep breath, then another to calm herself, then abruptly stopped when she realized she was breathing in his scent. Heat rolled through her.

The gleaming iron doors opened. Brooke stepped out, her key in her hand. Her condo was at the end of the hall, allowing her a spectacular view of the Ashley River and harbor at night from her bedroom. Which the irritating man beside her would never see.

Opening the door, she turned. "I'm home. Goodnight."

"I probably shouldn't care, but why don't you like me?"

She didn't need to be asked twice. "Because you're rude and crude. Unlike those women tonight fawning over you, I have higher standards."

"Like the penguin in the suit."

It took Brooke a moment to figure out he meant Rafael, her uncle. "Yes. He knows how to make a woman happy."

She saw her mistake the second after the challenging words left her mouth. John swooped in like an avenging angel. If he had been rough, his mouth not so inventive, she might have stood a chance of resisting. With a little whimper, her arms went around his neck.

Dimly, she realized he had picked her up, holding her easily against his hard length. His strength sent another thrill of pleasure surging through her, but not as much as his saying her name between heated kisses that threatened to fry her brain.

"I did it again. I'm sorry." He lowered her until her feet touched the floor.

Brooke's mouth was searching for his, her hands tugging his shirt from the waist of his pants when his words finally penetrated her brain. She froze, then stepped back with as much dignity as possible. She tugged up and pulled down her dress. At least they were inside her apartment with the door closed.

"I just wanted to talk. No, that's not entirely true. I wanted to see if this would happen again," he said with as much bewilderment in his voice as she felt. "I don't even like you."

Since she felt the same way about him, she wasn't offended. "I don't like you either."

He nodded as if he expected as much. "How about grabbing a burger and a movie Saturday night?"

Randolph had flown her in a private jet to a movie premiere in Los Angeles. Afterwards they had been invited to the home of the producer. They'd been served a scrumptious buffet of smoked salmon, beluga caviar and champagne. "Pick me up at seven. I'll let security know."

"Goodnight, Brooke."

"Goodnight, John."

The door closed softly, and then it hit her. This was the first time they had called each other by their first names.

Damn!

Claire opened her front door and invited Gray inside. "Would you like coffee?"

"Just the usual." He pulled her into his arms and kissed her breathless.

"Thank you for coming tonight, inviting the reporter, your grandmother and aunt."

His arm around her waist, they went to the sofa and sat down. "They would never have forgiven me if I hadn't told them about the pre-opening."

"It was a great idea." She snuggled in his arms. "I can see why Livingston Catalogue is so successful. Your grandfather was right to pick you to run the company."

The corners of Gray's mouth lifted. "I think I won by default. My father loved teaching at Morehouse, and my aunt is more interested in shopping from a catalogue than trying to find merchandise to put in one."

"What about your sister and your aunt's three children?" she asked him.

"My younger sister found her career in publishing. My cousins found their niche in other avenues of business." Absently he played one of her curls. "From the moment I stepped into the warehouse I was fascinated. I never wanted to do anything else. I have a feeling you've discovered your calling."

She actually laughed. "I have to admit I enjoyed myself tonight . . . after the first scary moments, of course. More than I ever did while working at Middleton and Zexxis. It's a good feeling knowing women enjoy the products I make, knowing that I could accomplish so much."

"I knew you could do it. The bank deposit tonight proves it."

"We did, didn't we?"

"You did it." He leaned over to kiss her cheek, but the little gasp she gave caused his eyes to go to her mouth. His mouth closed on hers. Her mouth softened beneath his as it always did. As if she'd waited a lifetime for the kiss.

He wanted to savor the moment, to savor her. He'd come to expect the quick rush of need, the uninhibited response of her body that drove him close to the edge of control. Her skin tasted like sweet cream. He inhaled the unique scent that clung to her and lured him. "You feel and taste so incredible."

"It's . . . it's the beauty products."

Gray took her mouth again. Claire was with him all the way. He was breathing heavily when he lifted his head. He stared at her kiss-swollen lips, the glazed passion in her eyes, and wanted very badly to take her to bed. "I better go."

Claire didn't want him to. "Can't you stay a little longer?"

"Not without taking you to bed."

"Then stay," she said softly.

"Honey." He pulled her into his lap and hugged her. "We'd probably already be in bed by now if I didn't have to go out of town tomorrow for a few days."

"Oh." Her stomach rolled then settled.

His finger lifted her chin. "I want you, Claire, but I can't make any promises of forever. Can you handle that?"

She felt the proof of his desire beneath her hips. The dreamer in her wanted him to love her forever just as she knew she would always love him. Her practical side accepted that it might never be. She could have his body, but perhaps never his heart. The idea hurt more than she thought she could bear.

Was she that bold or that stupid to even consider being intimate with a man when she knew it could lead to nothing except misery. She had wanted a family. If she let Gray go, would she find another man to love? A man who made her heart soar and ache at the same time? She looked into his face and realized the decision had been made long ago.

"I'm not asking for forever."

Gray's eyes closed and he pulled her to him. "You should, but I'm bastard enough to take you any way I can get you." His mouth found hers in a boldly erotic kiss that spoke more loudly than words that she would be missed as well. "I'll call."

Her smile was tremulous. "Take care."

With one last touch of her cheek, he was gone. Claire pulled her legs beneath her and leaned her cheek against the back of the sofa, missing Gray already.

CHAPTER TWENTY

orraine and Brooke pulled up in front of Claire's house at the same time. Worried about both of them, Claire had been watching out the front window. She was on the wide porch when they emerged from their cars, a copy of the newspaper in her hands with the article of Bliss and their picture on the front page. Lorraine and Brooke emerged with their own newspapers. Lorraine had a pleased smile on her face; Brooke's was contemplative.

Claire didn't have to guess. "What happened with John?"

Brooke sighed. "I should be walking on air that we made the paper. My family probably bought every copy they could get their hands on. Bliss is bound to reap the benefit."

"But," Lorraine prompted.

"You'll never believe it. I can't believe it myself," Brooke told them.

"Let's go inside," Claire said, explaining to Lorraine about John taking Brooke home as they went inside. Folding tables lined with newspapers and topped with bottles and jars and molds were already set up in the family room. She handed each one a cup of coffee and picked up her own.

"I might as well spill it, so you can both tell me how stupid this is." Brooke set her coffee aside without tasting it. "We have a date tomorrow night for burgers and a movie."

"They must have been at each other again," Lorraine said with a straight face.

"That would be my take on it," Claire added.

Brooke bit her lip, appearing miserable. "He kisses me and I lose it."

"Speaking from personal experience, that's the way it's supposed to be," Claire said.

Brooke's and Lorraine's mouths gaped.

Claire couldn't keep the smug grin off her face. "I think you're right about BTS, but it's obvious only certain men have that ability. Isn't it fortunate that we've found three men that do."

"I'll drink to that." Lorraine lifted her cup.

Brooke snatched hers up. "Me, too."

"Me three." The cups clinked.

B rooke had been on more dates than she could remember, she thought as she went through her closet of designer clothes Friday afternoon. She'd made a habit of always choosing what she planned to wear the day before. There was nothing more irritating than wanting to wear a certain outfit and then finding out it was in the cleaners or needed to go there.

She'd been popular with boys since she was in kindergarten. Being the only child of the oldest son of five boys brought her into a home where there'd always been strong arms to soothe away the hurt, take her anyplace she wanted to go, and spoil her shamelessly. She'd grown up with the attitude that she could wrap men around her little finger. She tossed a blue floral skirt on her king-sized four-poster.

She'd been voted Homecoming Queen her freshman year in high school and had regained the honor her senior year. She had respectfully declined the nomination her sophomore and junior years because she had wanted something to look forward to. The statement hadn't endeared her to a lot of the girls at her high school, but Brooke hadn't minded. As she'd told Gray, she didn't have many female friends.

She couldn't help it if she was beautiful, had a certain way with men, and a brain. She'd learned early that charm and a hint of vulnerability went a long way in getting a woman what she wanted. Southern women had it like that . . . if they knew how to use it. And she did.

Randolph's defection was still a sore point and she definitely planned to make him regret his decision, but in the meantime it was rather gratifying to know she hadn't lost her touch. John couldn't keep his eyes or his hands off her.

She made a face. That she was the same way with him annoyed her to no end. Perhaps all the changes in her life had caused some kind of hormonal imbalance or shift in her brain wave patterns. Even as the thought came to her, she dismissed it as idiotic. Two chiffon blouses joined the skirt.

It was pure old-fashioned lust. She hadn't decided if she'd feed it or try to control it. She tossed a pair of linen slacks on the bed just as the phone rang. She wasn't sure what type of eatery John planned to take her to for hamburgers. She didn't want to be too dressy. Linen or cotton, skirt or pants, slides or heeled sandals?

Her mind on her wardrobe, she picked up the phone with one hand and fingered the sheer ruffled hem of an ankle-length black skirt with the other. "Hello."

"Hello, Brooke."

Her heart leaped at the sound of John's voice. *Steady girl.* "Hello, John." Why did just saying his name make her heart beat faster?

"I got your phone number from Claire."

He sounded tired or upset. She could think of only one reason. "Are Amy and Mark all right?"

"Yeah, thanks for asking. But there's a problem."

Apparently John was the type of man who had to work his way up to the point in a conversation. Brooke sat on the bed and tried to be patient. "Oh?"

A weary sigh came through the line. "We have this big calendar in the kitchen where I keep all the kids assignments and activities so I can keep track of them. I don't know how I missed it."

"What is it?"

"Mark's Cub Scout troop is going on a field trip tomorrow to the Children's Museum in Columbia, then to Saluda Shoals Park in the afternoon. I promised to chaperone. We won't get back until after ten that night. I have to cancel."

Brooke sprang to her feet. "You're standing me up?" No one had ever stood her up.

"I'm not standing you up, Brooke. They're going canoeing and fishing. I'd want to be there even if I hadn't promised Mark."

Brooke had spent a lot of fun-filled days at the 270-acre park. She'd even gone on dates to the amphitheater in high school. "Of course. You promised."

"I'm sorry. I'll call you tomorrow. Bye."

"Bye." Brooke replaced the receiver, then glanced at all the clothes she'd tossed on the bed. She felt foolish. She'd left the shop early, splurged on a manicure and pedicure, all for a man who . . . who loved his children.

Picking up the clothes, she returned them to her closet. It was for the best. They had nothing in common and she never dated men who couldn't give her not only the lifestyle she wanted, but also their undivided attention.

She closed the closet door with a snap. She was glad he canceled.

The phone rang again and she snapped her head around, making a mockery of her earlier thoughts. Recognizing the number on the caller ID, she smiled and picked up the receiver. "Hi, Rafael."

"Hi, Brooke. You doing all right?"

She plopped down on the bed. "I was until my date for tomorrow night canceled."

"His loved ones will mourn him."

She laughed, falling back on the bed and staring up at the chandelier in the recessed ceiling. Rafael was the youngest of her father's four brothers and, at thirty, closer to her in age and temperament. He could always make her laugh. They'd always been close friends. "Perhaps he should live. He has two adorable little children."

"Not your usual style," he commented.

"I forgot that until he called to cancel. I won't forget again," she said with determination, then changed the subject. "Thanks again for coming up for the pre-opening. We practically sold out of products, especially the BTS ones."

"That's the reason for my call. Simon and Marc called me this morning to say they were concerned about your advertising claim," he said. "They didn't want to be put in a position of arresting their niece for fraud."

She sat up. All the Dunlap men, including her father, were policemen. And women adored them. "They've test-marketed it already?"

"They had concerns, and that's all I'm saying."

And they all had a difficult time talking to her about sex. "We've already figured out that it doesn't apply to all men."

"What do you mean, 'We.'" The snap of disapproval in his voice had her scrambling to explain.

"Lorraine, the married partner," she emphasized. "She already told us that."

"Ah." He sounded relieved and so was Brooke. "Then why keep promoting the product that way?"

"Because all women aren't fortunate enough to have found a man who can rival the product. Some women don't want to find one. Then there are the ones who've enjoyed the side benefits of their man proving the product wrong," she explained.

He chuckled. "Simon and Marc certainly did. I mean—"

"I know exactly what you meant," she said, trying to hold back laughter. "You want me to send more?"

He snorted. "You always did have a smart mouth, and I was about to drive up and take you out to dinner."

Myrtle Beach was an hour and a half away. "I'm fine. Besides I don't want to be the cause of another woman being stood up." Rafael always had some woman waiting in the wings.

"What are you going to do?" he asked.

Brooke only had to think about her answer for a moment. "Forget him and go on."

D addy."
John jumped upright, turning around at his desk to see Mark in

his Spider-Man pajamas. Concerned, John knelt in front of his son and put his hand on his forehead. Amy might roam at night, but not Mark. "You feel all right, son?"

"I'm a big boy, now. You don't have to go with me tomorrow."

So he'd overheard the conversation with his grandmother when John had asked her to keep Amy. John had been afraid of that. He just hoped Mark hadn't overheard his earlier conversation with Brooke as well. The lady wasn't too happy with him. "I want to go."

Mark looked at him, then away. "I didn't mean to, but I heard you talking to Grandma today when you asked her to keep us tomorrow night because you had a date."

"Then you heard me tell Grandmother when she reminded me about the field trip that I was going with you instead."

"Because you promised."

John's hand lifted his son's chin. He was so darn sensitive and loving, just like his mother, and always on his best behavior. "That and because I love you, and I'd feel better if I was there when you go canoeing and do all the other fun things we're going to do tomorrow."

Mark's head came up a fraction. "You can go on the date if you want to. I'll wear my life jacket. Mr. Johnson never has to reprimand me like the other boys."

No, and that worried John. Mark was too self-contained. John tipped Mark's chin up the rest of the way. "You're a better young man than I was at your age. Did I ever tell you the time I almost got kicked out of the Cub Scouts?"

"You did?" His eyes widened.

"I threw rocks into the Grand Canyon before the scoutmaster could get it out of his mouth not to. Then that night when no one was looking I put firecrackers into the campfire before it was lit. Grandma and Grandpa both spanked me good when I got home."

"Amy gets spankings all the time, but I never get spanked," Mark said as if he regretted it.

John playfully swatted Mark's backside and watched his son's eyes grow huge in surprise. "Consider this your first for getting out of bed. I ought to give you another whack for even thinking I didn't want to go with you tomorrow. You and Amy are the most important people in the world to me. Never forget that."

"My social studies teacher says women are important, too, and Miss Dunlap is a woman."

That she was. John pushed to his feet and took his son's hand. "Come on, let's get you back into bed. We have a big day ahead of us tomorrow."

"I'm glad you're going, Daddy."

"Me, too, son. Me, too."

B rooke woke up Saturday morning determined to have a wonderful day. She breezed into Claire's home in one of her favorite outfits, a gauzy coral-colored blouse and white, hip-hugging jeans, as if she didn't have a care in the world. She chatted with Claire and Lorraine, glued the cotton wicks exactly in the center of the glass jars, labeled merchandise, checked e-mail, then went back to check the wicks to make sure they remained in the center as the wax hardened.

"You want to talk about it?" Lorraine asked.

"What do you mean?" Brooke asked, moving to the next candle. Jasmine Whipped Meringue.

"Something is bothering you," Lorraine persisted.

"I'm fine." Twenty or so candles left.

"We're not prying. We care about you." Claire placed her loosely folded hands on the table where she and Lorraine had been bagging moisturizing lotion into netted bags. "Remember our pledge to each other? You haven't said two words in the last two hours." She looked at Lorraine. "If it's money and the check yesterday won't cover your expenses, we—"

"John canceled on me," Brooke interrupted. "He went on a camping trip with Mark today."

Lorraine picked up a length of yellow satin ribbon. "Hamilton was always too busy to take Justin anywhere."

"Derek was never the outdoors type." Claire began carefully putting the bath gel she'd finished labeling in the packing box. "I made turkey salad for lunch."

"That's all?" Brooke asked. "You aren't going to shred him to pieces or at the least tell me how immature it is of me not to understand?"

"Anything we would say would be redundant." Lorraine stretched, then stood. "Claire, you make the best turkey salad."

"It's the scallions and my special dressing." Claire went to the kitchen and took out the salad while Lorraine set the table.

Brooke had no choice but to follow. "You aren't going to let me sulk?"

"You've done enough of that. We all have," Lorraine said. Removing the plastic lid, she set the bowl on the L-shaped island.

"But I have to admit, if I'd known all the self doubts and hours I'd spend wondering about Gray's feelings for me, I might have run the other way when he kissed me."

Brooke took a box of crackers from the cupboard and set them beside the salad, then she slid onto one of the white slat-back stools around the island. "You can say that again."

Placing flatware beside the plates, Lorraine took her own seat. "All we can do is play this out and play to win."

Brooke was already shaking her head. "Maybe for you two, but I've decided to end it now. There's nothing for me with John except hot sex."

"I'm beginning to wonder if that's all Hamilton and I have left," Lorraine said quietly. "Although he hasn't said anything since Thursday night at the pre-opening, I catch him watching me and I just know he still resents Bliss. But I'm afraid to confront him."

Claire placed a small plate of fruit and cheese by the salad and took her own seat at the end of the counter. "When Gray returns, I'll be able to tell you my take on it."

"About time," Brooke said, biting into a strawberry. "As for me, I'm bailing. I'm putting on my sexiest dress and going out tonight. It's time I got back into the game."

CHAPTER TWENTY-ONE

B rooke left her apartment that night in a cloud of Rouge by Hermes. The Prada red slip dress clung to her figure like a possessive lover. There was a trendy new club she'd heard about that she wanted to check out. Now that Bliss was off to a good start she could relax a bit, even pay more than the minimum on a couple of the credit card bills. She had a right to kick up her red four-inch Manolo Blahniks a little bit.

Inside the Blue Note she found the music loud, the smoke stifling, and the men boring. She decided to leave before she finished her Evian. Fifteen bucks wasted. Going to the bathroom to repair her lipstick, she listened to the chatter about men, how to get them, how to dump them, how to drive them crazy with sex. The usual.

"Let's check out The Loft. It's more upscale. There are no cute guys here."

Brooke agreed with the redhead in a dress that showed everything she was born with. Brooke felt almost overdressed. Washing her hands, she opted to pass on putting lotion on them. There was a big sticky yellow glob beneath the pump dispenser.

Outside Brooke asked the doorman for the address of The Loft, laughed off his request to go with her, and got into her car. Seven minutes later she saw why there weren't a lot of people in the last place. They were all trying to get in The Loft.

She cruised in front of the club intending to check out the men and see if there was one that might possibly interest her, but she found herself studying the women instead. Most of the women in the line that wrapped around the building were there hoping, like the women at the Blue Note, to meet a non-violent, gainfully-employed heterosexual man. They were looking their best to attract and entice. Bliss could help them do that.

The idea popped out of nowhere and with it a whole new marketing plan emerged. Making a U-turn Brooke called Claire on her cell phone. "Fill up several pump bottles with Pear Vanilla moisturizing cream, make sure they have Bliss's address and web site on them. I'll be there in twenty minutes to pick you up. We're about to widen our client base."

Brooke, are you sure you can get in?" Claire glanced at the long, jovial line of men and women in evening wear waiting to get inside The Loft.

"No." She adjusted the V of her dress so more of her cleavage showed. The red slip dress stopped mid-thigh. "But I'm going to give it my best shot. Worse comes to worse, I'll let the women in line sample the product. The scent is soft enough that it won't interfere with whatever fragrance they're wearing."

Claire wasn't convinced. She'd counted at least four policemen patrolling the area on foot. "You could get arrested."

"That's the least of my worries. My family is full of uniforms." She picked up the two slender plastic bottles. "Here goes."

Trying not to chew on her lip, Claire sat in the driver's seat of the Jag. She saw Brooke stop and briefly speak with a couple of the policemen, before moving on to the front door. When Claire thought her nerves were stretched to the breaking point, Brooke disappeared through the black front door.

Claire didn't draw an easy breath until Brooke came back out empty-handed. Waving, she ran lightly back to the car. The gaze of the policemen followed. "Let's get out of here," Claire said.

"Not yet." Reaching into the back seat, Brooke picked up the box with the remaining bottles. "Gotta repay the men in blue."

"You bribed policemen? You can't do that!" Claire could hear the clinking of the jail cell door.

The look on Brooke's face was one of pure devilment. "Of course you can't. I'm simply donating these to those nice policemen for protecting the city. If anyone needs to blow off a little stress between the sheets, it's those who protect and serve. Be right back."

True to her word, Brooke came back directly. Claire went around to the passenger side and got in. "You enjoyed almost giving me a heart attack, didn't you?"

Brooke let the top down on the Jag, then pulled off. "You know you had fun."

Claire laughed, leaning her head back against the headrest and letting the cool evening breeze blow through her hair. "Certainly beats how I planned to spend the evening." She threw a worried glance at Brooke. "Sorry."

"I'm not going to crumble. Tonight could be the beginning of a source of new revenue. Some clubs won't care about lotion for their customers, but the upscale trendy ones will. Those are the ones we want to go after." Brooke headed for Highway 17. "I think we should contact several of them and suggest placing complimentary lotion in the ladies room. All with Bliss's information of course. Some of the attendants might not be as accommodating for a twenty as the one tonight, or think nothing of taking it home."

Claire nodded. "I'll start working on the list tomorrow. I think we should also include the four- and five-star hotel ladies rooms. Some of Lorraine's women's organizations may have had events at a few of them and she might have some contacts."

"I agree. I'll take the clubs. You can keep working on fine-tuning the site and producing the products. We're going to need them."

H i, sis."
Sitting in her home office Sunday afternoon working on the list of clubs and hotels, Claire tensed on hearing her brother's voice. She

couldn't afford to give him any more money. She felt ashamed at the thought and even more that she wished it was Gray calling. "Hello, Derek."

"You just get back from church?"

"About an hour ago. Did you go this morning?" she asked although she was sure she already knew the answer.

"I overslept. Maybe next Sunday," he explained. "Boss down at the job is on my case all the time. If that isn't enough, my girlfriend is always after me about one thing or another."

Standing, Claire walked to the French doors and looked out at the calm blue waters of the Atlantic. She could see two people fishing from the shore. "I'm sorry to hear that."

"I can't sell cars if nobody is buying. The economy is tight. Sheila is always pissed because I don't have the big bucks to take her to some fancy restaurant. She probably wouldn't even know which fork to use," he said snidely.

From the way it sounded, Claire didn't think there was very much affection between the two. "I thought your girlfriend was named Tonya."

He tsked. "Had to cut that crazy woman loose."

A couple strolled by, hand in hand. Perhaps one day that would be her and Gray. "How long have you dated Sheila?"

"Heck if I know. Met her at a club downtown. She was hot. All nice and smiling. Now every time she opens her mouth, she's nagging."

Claire massaged her temple, trying to keep her mind on Derek and not on how much she missed Gray. "I don't know what to tell you, Derek."

He tsked again. "I wasn't asking for advice, Claire. You don't know the first thing about relationships."

His words stung. She almost blurted out that he didn't either from the sound of it. "I'm dating someone."

"Who?" There was derision mixed with disbelief in his voice.

"Just someone I met." She didn't want to hear Derek get on Gray's case again. The couple she was watching embraced and Claire went back to the computer.

"Be careful, Claire," he warned. "Don't let some fast-talking dude dupe you into giving him money or moving in with you."

The only men Derek thought she'd attract were users. "Yes, you've told me that before."

"For your own good, baby sis," he lightly replied." Either he didn't catch the annoyance in her voice or he didn't care. "Well, gotta go, but how is the business going? Making any big money?"

She tensed again. "With three partners, it will be a long time before that happens."

"You never can tell. Bye."

"Goodbye." Claire hung up the phone, dismissing Derek's warning as she did so. He didn't know Gray the way she did. Life had certainly been simpler before they started seeing each other, but she had to admit as she sat back down to the computer, not nearly as exciting.

Lorraine had to get out of the house. Changing into slacks and a white sleeveless blouse, she told Hamilton she was going for a walk and left. Since he was the cause of her leaving, she wasn't about to ask him if he wanted to go with her.

She set off at a leisurely pace, waving to her neighbors, smiling despite the ache in her heart. She'd always loved living here and in the past had enjoyed looking at the beautiful, landscaped homes. Until today. She wasn't surprised when she ended up in front of Thomas's house. She and Margaret had talked about everything. But Margaret was gone.

She bowed her head, then lifted it, and started up the steps of the gray limestone Spanish Revival house. She didn't want to go home and she couldn't wander the neighborhood. The door opened seconds after she rang the doorbell. Thomas greeted her with a pleased smile.

"Lorraine, what a wonderful surprise." He stepped back. "Please come in. I was going to call later. Nice article in the newspaper."

"Hello Thomas. Thank you. We were pleased. It will help business." *And add to the troubles of my marriage.* Dragging her hands out of her pockets, Lorraine stepped inside the wide foyer. Overhead was an immense wrought-iron chandelier. To her right and circling in front of her was a gracefully carved iron-banistered staircase. Ahead of her was the family room, where she'd spent many wonderful hours. "I hope I'm not bothering you."

"Never. I just came to get a glass of wine, then I was going back to the pool. Care to join me?"

"I'd love to," she said.

"Good."

Lightly taking her arm, Thomas steered her into the family room, and then went to the built-in bar. Directly behind him was a built-in eight-foot-tall saltwater aquarium. Handing her a glass, he indicated she should precede him.

Although she had been inside the pool room hundreds of times it always took her breath away a little bit. Stretching one hundred feet, with a vaulted ceiling three stories high and formal colonnades, the wing held the indoor pool, a fully equipped gym and spa, and a wide deck for pool parties. Amid oversized light honey rattan furniture with plush cushions were three live palm trees.

Thomas indicated a lounger big enough for three people. Lorraine sat and propped her feet up. Her back sank against the cushion. She sighed.

"Bad day?"

She sipped her wine. "Try several bad days."

"I wish I could help."

She smiled over at him. "You have, just by being there."

He nodded, then sat back and sipped his wine as if deep in his own thoughts. That was all right with Lorraine, she had a lot on her mind as well.

"I was going to run out for a bit to eat later. How about going?"

She hesitated, then smiled. "You got yourself a dinner partner."

Lorraine hadn't meant to stay out past six, but the time had gotten away from her. After dinner, they'd gone to Charleston Harbor and watched the cruise ships dock.

"Sorry, I kept you out so late," Thomas said, pulling to a stop in front of her house. "You want me to go in with you?"

"No, thank you." She had called Hamilton when she'd noticed the time. Unbuckling her seat belt, she got out of the Navigator and hurried up the walkway. Hamilton jerked open the door just as she reached for the knob. His angry gaze went from her to the black SUV still parked at the curb, then his gaze flicked back to her. Without a word, he turned and walked away. Disheartened, Lorraine turned and waved to Thomas, then watched him drive away, almost wishing she could go with him.

He'd rehearsed what he planned to say, but somehow when John heard Brooke's voice over the phone Sunday night he went blank for a few seconds.

"Hello?"

"Ah, hi, Brooke. It's John."

"I'm rather busy at the moment," she said a bit impatiently.

She had a man there with her, he knew it. Cutting a glance at the kitchen door, John walked out into the backyard. Mark and Amy were watching *The Lion King* for the thousandth time and should be all right. "I'm sorry about last night. Would you like to go to dinner tomorrow night?"

"No, thanks. I really have to go. Bye."

"Brooke—" He was left talking to the dial tone. She wasn't going to give him another chance. Maybe that was for the best. He just wished he could believe that.

After dinner Claire decided to take a walk on the beach. Maybe it would help her sort things out. Sticking her feet into the rubber thongs she kept on the wooden back porch, she set off along the beach. The night was beautiful, the sky filled with a thousand stars. Seeing the couples on the beach had her thinking of Gray and missing him. She listened to the sounds of the gentle waves lapping the wide sandy beach, watched the seagulls search for food then, as the sun dipped behind the ocean, she started back.

She'd almost reached the steps leading up to her house when she noticed a figure sitting on them. It wasn't unusual for someone to stop to rest or simply enjoy the view. As she neared, the figure moved and she saw the broad shoulders of a man. Her heart thumped in her chest. Her hands came out of her pockets and she began to run.

She didn't think, she just leaped. Gray's rich laughter surrounded her.

"I guess you missed me," he said.

"Terribly."

Their mouths met, each greedy for the other.

She was trembling when he pulled back. He'd kissed her as if he was starved for her.

"I'm here now."

"Have you eaten?" she asked.

His hand brushed the hair from her face. "On the plane. How have things been going?"

"Wonderful." As they started back into the house she told him about Brooke's new ideas. "I have a list of clubs and hotels. We're going to select two each and see how it goes."

He watched her brush the clinging sand off her long legs and imagined them wrapped around him. She looked up and her entire body went still. He turned away and went into the family room. He hadn't planned to pounce on her as soon as he returned. Folding tables were set up, as they had been the first time he visited. He picked up a candle. "Once Bliss opens, you're going to be too busy making products and helping run the shop to do this by yourselves."

She nodded. "I figure we can get part-time help at the shop if we need it. I'd rather just Brooke and Lorraine know the formulas for the products. I'm teaching them."

He pulled her to him. "So if Bliss is doing well, why did you look so sad walking on the beach? I watched you for a long time."

She tried to distract him by kissing his cheek. "I was missing you."

"I'm here, and you're still sad. Bliss is doing well. The article in the newspaper was glowing. So, that leaves Derek." Gray's eyes narrowed when she tucked her head. "He isn't asking for more money, is he? He's worse than a parasite."

Incensed Claire pushed out of his arms. "He's not! How can you say something so cruel?"

"Claire—"

She shoved his reaching hands away. "He loves me!"

"Derek loves himself. The only time he showed up after he took off to Los Angeles was to borrow money from your parents or you after you got out of school. He probably hasn't changed much since he's in Orlando."

"He's hit some rough times," she said defending him.

"He's always hitting rough times, and now that your parents are gone you're the one who always bails him out," Gray flared. "It's past time for him to shoulder his responsibilities like a man instead of living off you. You giving him money every time he asks is not helping him. The only way to do that is to cut off the funds and the shoulder on which to dump."

It was too close to her own thoughts. "That's easy for you to say. You've never had to worry about money or a job or to scuffle the way Derek has. You've always had plenty. Your name guarantees that."

Gray's head snapped back at the accusation. "I worked hard and earned the right to be where I am. Every summer from my tenth birthday on, while other kids were enjoying their break from school, I was inside being taught the business by Granddad. My position wasn't given to me; I earned it."

Irritated with herself, she ran a distracted hand through her hair. He was right. She'd seen him skip enjoying the pool or sailing with his cousins countless times to sit with his grandfather in the study. "I'm sorry. I guess I'm not in a very sociable mood. Perhaps you should go."

"If that is what you want."

It wasn't. "Yes."

He nodded curtly. "Goodnight."

Claire shut her eyes as the door closed. Gray was home and she was as miserable as ever.

Her arms wrapped around her, she sat on the couch, remembering them being there together. She rose quickly and headed for the door leading to the beach. She had to get out of there. By the time she was on the sand tears were sliding down her cheeks.

"Gray, I'm sorry," she whispered to herself.

"So am I."

She spun and he was there, holding her so tightly in his arms she could barely breathe. She didn't care.

"I couldn't leave. I came around the back because I was afraid you wouldn't let me in," he said against her hair. "I had no right to say what I said. Forgive me."

She shook her head. "Let's not talk about it."

"Claire—"

She put her fingers against his lips. "Please. I missed you too much to have a fight your first night home."

He kissed her fingertips. "Then we'll do something I've thought of every hour I've been gone." His mouth claimed hers.

CHAPTER TWENTY-TWO

ohn wasn't the type of man to beg or grovel, so why was he here? Shoving his hands into the pockets of his jeans, he stared at the revolving stream of women going in and out of the glass door of Bliss Saturday night. The grand opening appeared to be even more successful than the pre-opening.

He checked his watch. It was almost eight. The sign on the door said the store closed at seven, but he guessed sales were so good they'd opted to stay open. Just his luck.

He thought he'd catch Brooke on her way out and try to talk to her. He wasn't doing it for himself. Mark had been asking about Brooke since they returned from their camping trip. His son had wanted to know when his father and Brooke were going out again. Never, would be John's guess. But he'd give it another try. He didn't want Mark thinking it was his fault. Not a night passed that Mark didn't ask him about the date so he could put it on the calendar. He'd even stapled the newspaper picture of her to it. John didn't need the reminder. However, he didn't have the heart to ask Mark to take it down.

In the distance, thunder rolled. John glanced up and watched dark clouds chase each other across the sky. The weatherman had predicted rain. With his luck, he'd get drenched for his trouble.

"Hello, John."

John didn't jump, but it was a close thing. He pulled his hands out of his pockets and whipped around to see Gray, immaculately groomed as usual. He scowled. The type of guy Brooke probably went for.

Gray held up his hands palm out. "Perhaps you should tell me what I did before you try to rearrange my face."

John shook his head as if to clear it. "Sorry."

Gray lowered his hands. "You going in?"

"Haven't decided yet." Getting the heck out of there seemed more appealing with each passing second.

"I was just about to. You could go with me and we could give each other moral support in a shop full of women," Gray said with wry amusement. "They should be closing soon. You could follow Brooke home."

John tugged his cap down on his head. "She's ticked at me because I had to cancel out last week."

"Ah," Gray said as if that clarified everything. "Try flowers and groveling. And if that doesn't help, kiss her until she forgets about being angry."

John wrinkled his mouth. "She knows karate."

Laughter rumbled from Gray's chest. He slapped John on the back. "Then you had better make that kiss count."

John laughed. "Maybe I will. I think I'll join you after all."

Brooke knew the instant John entered the shop. It had nothing do with him being recognized and the excited buzz of conversation, which still irritated her, it was the sudden leap of her heart, as if her body recognized his in some primitive way.

"Hi, Brooke."

She tried for disinterest, but it was difficult with him looking hot in jeans that cupped his long muscled legs and tight butt, and a white shirt that emphasized his wide chest. "Can I help you with something?"

"My mother likes the things you picked out."

"I'm glad. Now if you'll excuse me." She started past him and he grasped her arm. Spears of sensation shot through her. She snatched away, but the warmth of his hand lingered. "Do that again and you'll find yourself on your back again."

"We need to talk about Saturday night."

Her nose went up. "Saturday night is forgotten, just like you."

"This is about Mark."

His comment stopped her in her tracks. "What about Mark?"

"He wants us to go out," John said, just as his cell phone rang.

"What!" Brooke's outburst had several heads turning.

John recognized the number as his mother's. "That's probably him now." He activated the phone. "Hello. Hi, Mama, I thought—" Then his world went crazy. "What! Oh, no! No!"

"What's the matter?" Brooke asked, forgetting that she had promised herself that she would remain indifferent to him, that he hadn't made her heart lurch when he'd walked through the door, that she didn't care about him. "John, what is it?"

"I've got to get out of here," he said, turning around as if he had forgotten which way the door was. "I've got to get to Amy."

Taking John by the arm, Brooke pulled him with her toward the back of the store to get her purse. "You're in no shape to drive."

He pushed ineffectively at her hand. "She's hurt. I need to get to the hospital."

Brooke's hand clenched and her knees shook, but she pushed the fear from her mind. John needed to get to his daughter. "That's where we're going."

A sea of concerned faces met them as they reentered the store. Claire and Lorraine were in front. "Amy's hurt, and I'm taking John to the hospital. Stay here and I'll call as soon as I know something."

Brooke's father pushed his way through the crowd, took one look at his daughter and John, and took her purse from her shaking fingers. "I'll drive. Rafael, follow in Brooke's car."

"Let's go then." She didn't have time to argue.

John didn't say anything when they urged him into the backseat of her father's big Lincoln. He had a death grip on Brooke's hand. She didn't even try to break it. Her parents in the front seat were silent as well.

Luckily the hospital was only a short drive away. As soon as her father pulled into a parking space John was out of the car pulling Brooke right along with him. She didn't know if he had forgotten he still held her hand.

They hit the door running. Down the busy corridor a tall, slim elderly man in a khaki shirt and pants rushed toward them.

"She's all right, John. It's just a sprain. Just a sprain."

John seemed to sway as he took in the news. "Daddy, are the doctors sure?"

"They're sure." John's father placed a comforting hand on John's trembling arm. "She had a pretty big bump on her head from falling out of the bed. They want to keep her a couple of hours to make sure she doesn't have a concussion, but the doctors feel confident she can go home tonight."

"Thank God." He closed his eyes for a brief moment. "Where is she? Where's Mark?"

"Taking care of his sister, holding Amy's hand until you got here, where else? I'll show you."

John lifted his hand to rub over his face and seemed surprised to find it curled tightly around Brooke's. He shifted his questioning gaze to hers as if just realizing she was with him.

"We, uh, my father, actually brought you. My uncle followed in my car," she said by way of explanation. "I'm glad Amy's all right."

John glanced around at the two men and woman who stood just behind them. He recognized one of the men as the man Brooke had been talking to when he arrived at the pre-opening. "Thank you," he told them.

"I'm glad we could help." Her hand flexed in his, but she didn't try to free herself.

No one had to tell him that he couldn't have driven himself. He wasn't worth warm spit when one of his children was hurt. After all he has said to Brooke, done to her, she hadn't hesitated to help him when he needed it the most. There was only one way he could think of to make it up to her and show his thanks. "Why don't we both go see her?"

Brooke's smile came slow and beautiful. Somehow it helped to steady John just a little bit more.

"I'd like that." With one hand, she took her purse and gave her mother a brief hug. "Please let everyone know that Amy is all right."

"I certainly will," her mother said, then she left with her husband and brother-in-law.

Brooke stepped closer to John. "Let's go see Amy."

The news that Amy's injury was not serious put the opening back into full swing. The crowd didn't begin to thin until almost nine. The grand opening was an unqualified success.

Brooke's handsome uncles certainly did their part. When one of the women customers expressed concern that she had to park so far away, Simon Dunlap had politely offered to escort her. Claire was sure that it had helped that the woman was beautiful, leggy, and wearing black spandex. The next thing she knew, almost every woman was afraid she'd be attacked. When Rafael came back with Brooke's parents, his aid was enlisted as well.

"Looks like we have four more candidates for the Man of Bliss and quadruple that number of women wanting to be the woman," Claire commented to Brooke's mother.

"Happens all the time." She smiled indulgently. "They love women and women seem to love them. They're wonderful men. Every one of them helped spoil Brooke."

"She's wonderful, and a marketing genius," Lorraine put in, finally able to take a break from the cash register. "We couldn't have done this without her."

"I was worried about her after she lost her job and Randolph," Mrs. Dunlap said. "Although I wasn't that sad to learn they'd broken up. I'm glad she had friends like you two when she needed them."

"We complement each other," Claire said. "We're just as glad to have her as our friend."

"I can tell. We're spending the night at Brooke's and then driving back to Columbia in the morning." She glanced around, caught her husband's eye, and he started over.

"Ready to go, honey?" Mr. Dunlap said as he stopped by his wife.

"Yes. Claire, Lorraine, I think you and our baby have a hit on your hands. Good night," Mrs. Dunlap told them and left with her husband.

Claire smiled after them. "I like Brooke's parents."

"They seem very happy," Lorraine said, thinking wistfully of Hamilton.

"Hamilton loves you, Lorraine," Claire told her. "Some people just aren't comfortable with change."

Lorraine patted the hand that rested gently on her arm. "What hurts so much is that he won't even try. Even before our marriage I supported him. The children are happy for me; why can't he be?"

"Perhaps because they have lives of their own and Hamilton's is tied so closely to yours. Maybe your independence scares him after all those years of marriage when you had to depend on him," Claire said.

"You could be right. But I've given up enough. I refuse to give any more."

Hamilton was waiting in bed when Lorraine returned home. He'd driven by Bliss earlier that evening and seen how busy the shop was. Gray was right. There was a strong possibility that it would succeed. "How was the official opening?"

"Fine."

The weariness in her voice had him laying aside the reports he had been going over. "I saw Roger Myers today. He's disappointed that you had to cut back on your volunteer time at the museum. They need you. I got the impression you're missed since you've cut back on so many of your obligations."

She pulled off the pearl necklace and earrings he'd given her at the birth of their youngest daughter. "If I'm not happy I'm no good to anyone."

Hamilton didn't know what to say as she went into the bathroom and closed the door softly behind her. She wasn't happy. He'd failed her, just as her parents had predicted he would. He was no longer enough. Then there was Thomas Holmes. Hamilton didn't like that the man seemed to be spending so much time with Lorraine, but he had a feeling if he mentioned it, it would only cause more problems. He just had to remember that Thomas's wife and Lorraine had been best friends.

Most importantly, he had to remember that Lorraine wasn't like his immoral mother. He'd grown up hearing the nasty whispers about her sleeping around. When he went to junior high, boys began openly teasing him. The parents of the nice, respectable girls didn't want their daughters anywhere near him. He'd grown up alone and lonely. He sometimes thought he might be that way forever until he'd walked into the student union at Baylor and seen Lorraine. He'd known instantly she was the one woman for him and that he'd never have to be lonely again.

But that may have changed.

Lorraine came out of the bathroom in a heavy silk nightgown, got in bed, then turned her back to him. "Goodnight."

Hamilton cut off the light. "Good night."

Lorraine lay awake thinking that she'd be the happiest woman in the world if Hamilton could be pleased at her success. Tonight should have been one of celebration. Thomas had stopped by and purchased several products for his daughters, who had loved the things Lorraine had sent them. He was becoming such a wonderful friend. Her husband was becoming a stranger. And her heart was breaking in two.

CHAPTER TWENTY-THREE

The black limousine was waiting at Claire's house as instructed. Gray pulled up behind her car and got out. He got a kick out of the wide-eyed look on her face when she came out of the garage. "Who is he waiting on?" she said.

"Us."

Her head whipped back around. "Us?"

He kissed her on the lips. He couldn't help it. "We're going someplace special, but casual, to celebrate."

Her eyes lit up. "Where?"

"It's a surprise." He turned her toward the house. "You might want to change into tennis shoes. I'll give you ten minutes since I grew up in a house full of women. Bring a scarf and a light jacket."

She grinned at him over her shoulder as she opened the front door. "We're going to have a picnic on the beach, right?"

"You'll find out."

"I don't suppose you're worried about the forecast for rain. But what about the way you're dressed?"

The silk tie and tailored coat came off. He unbuttoned the first four buttons on his blue cotton shirt. Armani was supposed to take you anywhere. "Any other questions?"

Laughing, Claire went inside to her bedroom, unbuttoning her blouse as she went. She didn't know what Gray had planned but if this was to be their first night together she wasn't wearing cotton. Opening a drawer, she pulled out the black demi-bra and panties she'd bought a week ago.

Going into the bathroom, she took a quick bath, then applied the perfumed moisturizing cream, a mixture of the sensual fragrance of jasmine and orange blossoms that her mother had named "C" for her. Finished, she slipped on the lingerie she hoped Gray would have a chance to take off her. Laughing at her thoughts, she pulled on a ribbed black knit top and clam diggers. At the mirror, she quickly reapplied her makeup the way Brooke had taught her, put a scarf in a canvas tote bag she'd already dumped the contents of her purse into, grabbed her windbreaker, and was back out the door.

"How did I do for time?" she asked.

"You could give the women in my family lessons." Gray kissed her, then opened the door of the limo.

She gasped when she saw the huge bouquet of long-stemmed yellow roses on the seat. "Thank you!"

"My pleasure. Now let's get this celebration on the road." He climbed in beside her. As they pulled off he opened a bottle of champagne, filled two glasses, then handed one to her. "To the continued success of Bliss."

The bubbles tickled her nose. "This tastes wonderful." She took another sip.

"Don't drink too much," he warned, easing an arm around her shoulder. "From the looks of the crowd at the shop when I arrived, you probably didn't have a chance to eat lunch."

She relaxed against him. Over the speaker she heard the wail of a sax. "We only got to eat a couple of bites of the finger sandwiches Lorraine prepared."

"Good thing I thought that might happen."

She leaned up. "Picnic under the stars, right?"

"In a manner of speaking."

Claire knew her mouth was hanging open. She snapped it shut. "Under the stars, just as you said."

Claire's eyes filled. In front of her was a table for two on the deck of Gray's yacht, *Destiny*. The twin flames from the candles flickered in the evening breeze. In the center was a lotus bowl filled with yellow roses. Two white-coated waiters stood nearby. "Gray, it's beautiful, and much more than I could have imagined!"

"Good. We'll have our picnic next time." He guided her to a seat and sat across from her. Immediately their wine glasses were filled.

"I'd like to make a toast." Claire picked up her glass.

Gray followed suit, his mouth already curving into an indulgent smile.

"To a night to remember."

Something flickered across his face as he repeated the toast, then drank. "I'll do my best."

He signaled the waiters and they began serving. Claire caught the strains of a violin, then saw a lone violinist above them on the bow of the yacht. Her hands went to her face again. Tears sparkled in her eyes. She'd never imagined that she'd feel so special, or that Gray would be the one to make her feel that way.

"The chef is going to be very disappointed if you don't eat," he teased.

She picked up her fork. "It's hard to tell you how much this means to me."

"There's more to come."

As the scrumptious five-course meal was served, Claire realized just how much he had spoken the truth. The food, from escargot to black sea bass, was delicious. Every now and then thunder would rumble.

"It can't rain," she said, staring overhead as lightning forked in the distance.

Getting up, Gray pulled her to her feet. The violin was replaced by the music of a full orchestra. "Let's make the most of the evening in case it does."

She looked around him as he pulled her into his arms. She saw no one. Even the violinist was gone. Even now the waiters were quickly rolling the table and serving cart away. They were alone.

"What are you looking for?"

"To see where the music is coming from." He tucked her into his arms and her eyes drifted shut. "On second thought, it doesn't matter."

"You're good for my ego," he murmured against her hair.

She smiled, then lifted her head. "You're good for mine. With you I feel as if I can do anything."

He stared down into her upturned face and they both came to a stop. His mouth slowly descended to hers and the heavens opened up.

Both yelped as the deluge of rain peppered them. "Come on."

Catching Claire's hand Gray ran down the side of the yacht, then downstairs. Claire was laughing all the way. She got a fleeting glimpse of opulence and luxury. Gray opened a door and they were inside a cabin.

Claire pushed her dripping hair out of her face. The cabin was beautiful, with honeyed wood paneling, brass fittings and a large bed. "It's fantastic. Is this the guest bedroom?"

"It's mine."

Claire went very still, but her eyes were drawn back to the large bed with the midnight black covers turned down and a yellow rose on the pillow. She gulped.

"The guest bedroom is two doors down. I'll take you." Gray reached for the door.

"What if I'm where I want to be?"

He tenderly palmed her face and looked deeply into her eyes. "Then this will be one night I won't take a cold shower."

Claire swallowed. In his eyes she saw the passion that excited her and made her relax. This was Gray. He would take care of her. Her arms lifted to slide around his neck. "The rain was cold."

He pulled her to him, letting her feel the unmistakable proof of his desire. "Not cold enough."

She shivered.

"You should get out of those wet clothes."

She laughed at that. He joined in. Then as they stared at each other the laughter stopped. His large hand swept the hair from her face. "I want you."

"Then take me."

He caught her against his hard body. His mouth took its time to relearn the essence and pleasure of hers. Her top came off and he gasped softly.

"You're beautiful."

She thanked her foresight in wearing the lingerie, then her thoughts scattered as his thumb and fingers closed over first one nipple then the other. Both hardened even more.

"Your body is so responsive."

"Only with you."

An unfathomable emotion flashed in Gray's eyes, then he picked her up and carried her to the side of the bed. He stooped to pull down her soggy pants, and kissed the inside of her thigh. Claire's legs quivered and she sank down on the bed.

"Perfect." He removed her shoes, then came to his feet and shoved off his pants.

She swallowed. Gray wearing nothing but a pair of snug black briefs was an awesome sight. "We'll get the bed wet."

"It'll dry." He stripped off the briefs and lay down on the bed, drawing her to him. He took his time playing, nibbling, until she was trying to pull him closer to deepen the kiss.

"We have all night."

"But I want to kiss you now." She grabbed him around the neck and took the kiss she wanted.

His mouth moved to her breast and suckled gently through the thin material. She moaned, her legs moving restlessly. Gray's hand swept down her body and cupped her. She was damp and hot. One finger slipped inside.

Claire whimpered and lifted her hips off the bed. Pleasure swirled through her. She wanted Gray to feel the same way. Her hand sought him. He was hot and hard, the length of him awesome. She snatched her hand back.

Gray lifted his head and stared into her wide eyes. "Do you trust me?"

"Yes." *With my heart, with my life*, she added silently.

"Change your mind?"

"No."

"You may have saved my life," he said. "Close your eyes and just feel."

Her eyelids fluttered closed. There was the barest touch on her cheek. The sensations continued growing in pressure and strength over her body until she was completely relaxed.

"Open your eyes."

Her lashes fluttered upward as he slowly filled her, stretched her. Claimed her. Her hands clasped him around the neck. With each measured stroke the pain lessened and the pleasure built.

Her hips lifted to meet his before she was aware of it. Sensations spiraled through her, building like a storm cloud. Like the clouds, she was powerless to resist, although she tried.

"Trust me, Claire. Come with me."

Resistance fled. Her legs tightened around his waist and she let her body go free, reaching for the sun, knowing Gray would be with her.

Completion came, and it was like soaring over the edge of a mountain.

Gray had just enough presence of mind to roll and tuck her against him. "You all right?"

When she didn't say anything after a moment, he lifted her chin and his heart stopped. Tears were in her eyes.

"Oh, baby, I'm so sorry." He pulled her to him, his mind trying to think of way to ease the pain he'd caused her.

"I'd fantasized, but I never dreamed it could be so absolutely beautiful and wonderful," Claire murmured.

"What?" Gray tilted her face to his. "I didn't hurt you?"

She shook her head. "How could you think that?"

"Because, despite my reassurance to you earlier, I was scared spitless that I'd mess this up for you." His voice softened. "I couldn't have stood that."

"You can put your mind at ease on that count. But I seem to remember we toasted to a night to remember." She looked out the porthole at the darkened sky, then back at him. "Morning is a long way off."

Thousands of miles away in a chateau in the south of France, Jana Louise Carpenter Livingston Murphy Franklin stared at a picture of Gray in a newspaper. He was embracing two women while a third stood close by. Her latest lover, a wealthy financier, was asleep and sated in a bed big enough for seven people. Until an hour ago there had been five people in it.

Jana's lips curled at the man's loud snores. In the morning he was taking his private jet back to London. She hadn't decided if she would join him. He was becoming clingy and boring. Perhaps it was time to move on to her next conquest. There was always another gullible fool out there. But first there was a more pressing matter that demanded her attention.

Jana's attention switched back to the newspaper she'd received earlier that day by special courier. She dismissed the women in the photo after only a momentary glance. They were no match for her in beauty or sensuality. It was Gray, his handsome face, the easy smile she never wanted to see again, that held her entire attention.

He was happy.

Rage surged through her. With jerky, agitated motions, she shredded the newspaper. After what he'd done to her she'd sworn he'd never be happy again. No man would ever get the best of her or forget her.

Perhaps he needed another reminder.

CHAPTER TWENTY-FOUR

ohn walked out of the emergency room with Amy asleep in his arms at 2:14 Sunday morning. The mind-numbing terror that had gripped him when his mother first called was gone. He'd seen the X-rays, talked to the doctors. They assured him that there had been no mistake. This time. He hugged his daughter's precious body just a little bit closer. They hadn't been able to tell him that with Linda.

"Here's my car. Good night, everyone," Brooke said

John turned around slowly so he wouldn't awaken Amy or jostle her arm in its sling. Brooke waved to his mother, who had been walking beside her, and his father, who carried a sleeping Mark. John was just beginning to realize how she had helped him through tonight. It seemed every time he was ready to lose it when Amy was in pain and he couldn't help her, Brooke was there to place a reassuring hand on his back or his arm. She'd gotten them coffee, enlisted Mark's help, praising and reassuring him, as well, that his sister was going to be all right.

"It's too late for you to drive home alone," John said. She was out this late helping him help his children. For that he'd always be in her debt.

"I thought we'd already had this discussion. I can take care of myself." Brooke pulled her keys from her little bag. "I'm glad Amy is all right."

John took a couple of steps toward her. "You're not driving home by yourself."

Her eyebrow lifted. She opened her mouth, but the clearing of his father's throat caused her to snap it shut.

"John, if Brooke doesn't mind, she can drive me to where you left your truck. I'll see that she gets home safely and come back to your place afterwards," John's father suggested. "You get in the back seat of our car with Amy and Mark. If she wakes up, she's gonna want you." He faced Brooke. "Do you mind dropping me off at John's truck?"

"No, sir, not at all, but it's unnecessary to follow me home."

"Brooke, I'm too old, too tired, and too grateful for you helping John to argue. I'll put Mark down and be right back." He walked away.

John followed.

Brooke groaned.

"They mean well, Brooke." Mrs. Randle came up beside her. "We're just so thankful that Amy's all right and to you for helping John through this. Scraped knees do him in."

"He lost it," Brooke admitted, recalling how she had very nearly lost it as well. She would have if John hadn't needed her.

"It was mentioning that Amy was in the hospital that did it," she said. "I knew what my phone call would do to him and I just prayed for the good Lord to help him." She gently touched Brooke's shoulder. "And like always, He did."

Brooke was about to ask John's mother why he had an aversion to hospitals when an older-model sedan stopped a few feet away and John's father got out of the driver's side. "Ready."

"Good night, Brooke, and thanks again." Mrs. Randle got inside the car, made a U-turn, then pulled off.

"Let's get to it," Mr. Randle said, going to the passenger's side of the Jag.

Brooke reluctantly gave in and opened her car door. Polite, Southern-reared children didn't talk back to their elders. "Did anyone ever tell you how much alike you and John are?"

His grin was slow. "The handsome part or the stubborn part?"

Being polite didn't get you far in this world. "Guess?"

"You'll do." Chuckling, he got inside the car.

Frowning, Brooke did the same. John's parents certainly left her with some unanswered questions.

Claire woke slowly. A languid smile forming on her face, she stretched her arms over her head. Muscles protested. With her arms in mid-air, she froze. The torrid night with Gray came rushing back. They'd made love in this bed. Several times, if she remembered correctly. And in the shower.

She took a cautious glance over her shoulder and saw the rumpled, empty bed. Loneliness hit her. He had left her. Clutching the sheet over naked breasts, she pulled herself up in bed. Why hadn't he awakened her? Was he tired of her already?

The cabin door opened and she shrank back in bed. The clatter of dishes preceded Gray as he pushed the cart that had been used to serve their food last night into the room. Seeing her, he smiled.

"Good morning. I was hoping I'd be back before you woke up."

He looked refreshed in gray slacks and crisp shirt. He looked, as always, immaculate and beautiful. She wanted to slink away. Sunlight poured though the porthole. She didn't need a mirror to know her hair was a tangled mess after getting wet. Her makeup was gone. She tucked her head and tried to scoot out of the bed. Maybe she could make it to the bathroom and do something with herself. She had no idea where her clothes were.

"No, you don't." He playfully grabbed her foot beneath the covers. "You're getting breakfast in bed."

"Please, Gray." She refused to look at him.

Releasing her foot, he came around the side of the bed where she was. "You're trembling. What is it?"

She shook her head. *You're beautiful and I look like a castaway.*

"Is it something I did?"

Her head came up. She saw the gorgeous face that any woman in her right mind would fall in love with, and down went her head again.

"Please, Claire, what is it? Is it last night? You regret making love with me?"

She looked up at him. "No! How can you think that?"

"Then what is it?" He reached out and tenderly brushed her hair from her face. "You'll have to help me on this because you're the first woman I've been the first man with, the first woman that's spent the night in my bed on *Destiny*, the first woman I'd walk through hell not to hurt."

By the time he'd finished she was clinging to his neck. "I don't have a comb for my hair, no fresh clothes, and my eyes . . . I probably look like a raccoon."

"Claire, you proved last night that you trust me. Right?" he asked softly.

"Yes," she managed.

"Then believe me when I say you could never be anything but beautiful in my eyes. It's not just on the outside, it's on the inside, which is just as appealing to me." He leaned her away from him. "I'll get you a robe so you can go into the bathroom. I hung up your underthings last night so they should be dry. Everything you need should be in there. No clothes, but you can wear one of my shirts until I have Jay launder your clothes."

The idea of wearing Gray's shirt appealed to her. "I'd rather do them myself."

"I'll show you where the laundry room is after we eat."

Her eyebrows lifted. "You know where the laundry room is?"

"Yes, I want to know everything about the things I care about." He touched her cheek gently, then stood to scoop up a black silk robe from the foot of the bed and held it out to her.

She hadn't noticed the robe because it had blended in with the bedding. But if she stood to put it on he'd see her in the revealing light of day.

"Do you want me to leave the robe?"

"No."

"Good, because I like looking at you." He smiled and her heart turned over. She loved him so much.

"I like looking at you, too." Her hand loosened on the sheet and she stood quickly and shoved her arms into the robe. Gray belted it.

"Don't start breakfast without me."

He brushed his mouth across hers. "I wouldn't dream of it."

She went to the bathroom with a smile on her lips.

B rooke couldn't make up her mind.

She looked around the aisle of the toy store and felt overwhelmed. If she were in the couture section of one of her favorite haunts she'd have no problem. She knew exactly what looked good on her, how to coordinate and accentuate. Finding the right accessory or clothes often took time, but she recognized what worked the instant she saw it. Toys were out of her league.

She picked up a doll that needed its diaper changed, a doll that cried real tears, and a doll that crawled. And put them all back on the shelf.

She was hopelessly out of her element. Perhaps if she'd had girlfriends she'd have a smidgen of an idea. But she'd always been closer to men. Of course, she'd had associates who were mothers. If she'd been invited to a baby shower or a child's birthday party, she'd probably sent a gift certificate and gone on with her life. The thought made her sad.

"Can I help you, miss?" A young sales clerk grinned at her.

Brooke put his age at seventeen, vibrating with hormones he probably had no idea what to do with. "I'm looking for a toy for a four-year-old girl."

His gleeful expression fell. "I don't know about girls." His expression brightened. "At least, not at that age."

She went with her gut. "What's the gift older girls like best?"

He glanced around as if he were imparting the secret to cure the ills of mankind. "Teddy bears."

Amy had impressed Brooke as a four-year-old going on fifteen. "Lead the way. And while we're at it, how about something for a studious eight-year-old in accelerated classes."

B rooke found John listed in the phone book. Thirty minutes later she pulled up behind a late-model Ford in front of John's house in a quiet neighborhood. The streets meandered around grand oaks, water marshes and nature preserves. The big front yard was expected. The rows of azaleas bordering the front and a couple of the trees in the yard were not. The roof and exterior of the house were blue, a legendary color in the low country. The three gabled dormers, wide porch, railings and posts were white.

Brooke realized she was studying the house and putting off going inside and reached for the twelve-inch brown teddy bear. She'd ignored Cy the store clerk's advice to buy a bigger one. She wanted Amy to be able to carry it with her without dragging it or tiring. Mark's gift, however, was a different matter entirely.

Getting out, she went up the steps. It was a nice home, but it could be fabulous with a few simple additions. The cool area of the porch cried out for wicker furniture for relaxing after a hard day at work. Perhaps interspersed Boston ferns with baskets of geraniums. She'd take up the straight walk; make it more interesting with a curve and . . .

A car passed and she blinked. What was she doing? John did not need nor had he asked her for any home improvement tips. The only reason she could think of was that next to clothes, she and her mother both loved to redecorate. Maybe her mind had wandered in that direction because she'd been with her mother that morning.

Refusing to think anything else, Brooke rang the doorbell. A young woman in a dark brown suit, her hair pulled back from her slim face, answered the door. She frowned, "Yes?"

"Good evening, my name is Brooke Dunlap, I came to see Amy."

The woman's unfriendly gaze flickered to the toys in Brooke's hands. "She's in the den with her father." She opened the door wider and stepped back.

"Thank you."

Brooke wanted to tell the unsmiling young woman that she was no threat to her. She didn't want John. Wouldn't take him on a silver platter overflowing with platinum cards. Then she saw John on the floor with Amy and her heart rapped out a beat that seemed to say liar, liar.

"Brooke." He came to his feet with Amy in his arms. In a white tee shirt and snug jeans, he looked more tempting than any man had a right to.

"Hi, Brooke," Amy and Mark greeted with wide smiles. After last night their father had finally let them call her by her first name.

"Hi, guys. I brought you a present."

"Let me down, Daddy." Amy wiggled out of her father's arms.

Mark watched her with solemn eyes. "For me, too? But I didn't hurt myself."

Brooke had never been happier about an impulsive buy. She hunkered down to eye level with him. "You held your sister's hand and took care of her. For that, you deserve a present, too."

"Thank you." Mark took the present and sat down to slowly tear off the paper. Aware of Amy's impatience, Brooke opened the large shopping bag and allowed Amy to peek in. "Like it?"

The little girl squealed and made a motion with her bandaged hand to pick up the bear.

Brooke was already reaching for the toy when John squatted down to help. Their hands brushed. They both jumped. Brooke's eyes went to John's.

"Daddy, I want my teddy."

"Sure, honey." Pulling the animal out, he handed it to Amy, who promptly hugged it to her with her good arm. "Thank you, Brooke."

"You're welcome." Brooke looked anywhere but at John.

"The children were about to eat," said the woman who had answered the door, watching from the entryway with obvious disapproval. "I'm sure you'll understand."

Brooke pictured the sour-faced woman flat on her back. Two seconds max. John pushed upright. "Brooke just arrived, Mary. A few more minutes won't hurt. I thank you for dropping by, but I can manage the dinner Mama brought over this morning."

Although she knew it was wrong, Brooke looked up and grinned. "Goodbye."

"Don't think I don't know who you are!" Mary said with heat. "You're that woman in those disgraceful pictures."

Brooke's assessing gaze swept up the woman's thin frame, her tight mouth. "I get the feeling you wished it were you instead."

Mary gasped. An intake of breath she held so long her body trembled.

Brooke remembered too late there were two children listening. She came upright. "Gotta run. Bye, kids. Enjoy."

"Brooke—"

She waved John's words aside, heading for the door as fast as her feet would take her. Opening the door, she made her escape.

CHAPTER TWENTY-FIVE

What John knew about women he could put on the head of a pin. He refused to let that be the case with his two children.

John cut a quick glance in the rearview mirror of his truck into the back seat of the cab where Mark and Amy were seated. Neither had said anything since they left their grandparents' house ten minutes ago. He pulled to a stoplight, and glanced in the mirror again. Their somber expressions remained the same. Mark might sit still, but never Amy. Her grandmother lovingly called her a wiggle worm. John had to agree. Amy's motto was, why walk when running was so much more fun.

"You kids, all right?"

"Yes, Daddy."

"Yes, Daddy."

The car behind him honked and John pulled off. He wanted polite children like everyone else, but something was wrong here and had been since Brooke's visit. He'd broken a cardinal rule for a school night, and kept them out past their bedtime of eight in a futile attempt to cheer them up with a visit to their favorite fast-food restaurant and then to their grandparents. It hadn't helped.

Amy had an armlock around the teddy bear Brooke had given her. At Mark's feet was the motorized car he'd taken with him everywhere.

Brooke had made as big an impression on his children as she had on him. He glanced into the mirror again, then took the next right to Highway 17. He was doing this for his kids.

Less than ten minutes later he pulled the truck into the driveway of the luxury condominium and stopped at the security gate. "John, Mark, and Amy Randle to see Brooke Dunlap."

"One moment, sir."

"We're going to see Brooke?"

"Brooke lives here?"

"Yes." *And if she refused to see us I really will wring her beautiful neck.*

"Have a good night, sir." The black steel gate started to retract.

John drove through. They were in, but what would he say once he saw her?

B rooke was waiting at the elevator for them. She couldn't imagine a protective father like John being out with his children on a Sunday night just driving around. Maybe Amy was sick again? Or Mark?

The elevator slid open and the two she had been worried about shot out. "Brooke! Brooke!"

She automatically squatted to hug them both, careful of Amy's arm. "Are you all right?"

"They are now."

Brooke's gaze shot up to John, all mouth-watering, six-foot-plus of him. "What happened?"

"We wanted you to stay for dinner instead of Mary. She always—"

"Amy," John said quietly.

"She's not any fun," Amy finished.

Same thing Brooke had thought. She stood with her hand on Amy's head and Mark's shoulder. "Have you had a chance to test the car, Mark?"

"Not yet." He drew the Corvette closer to his chest. "I was afraid it would run into something."

She threw John a chilling glance, then smiled down at Mark and lifted the car from his arms and put it on the carpeted hallway. "My condo is straight ahead. Go for it."

His fingers moved over the control. He looked up at his father. "Can I?"

"Let it rip."

"Wait!" Amy laid her teddy beat across the seat. "Mr. Bear wants to ride."

"If he falls off, you won't cry, will you?"

"He won't fall off. Mr. Bear is smart."

Brooke hid a smile behind her hand. John pretended to be rubbing his nose, as he tried to hide his smile.

The 'Vette took off with a whirr of its motor. Brooke flinched as the car came perilously close to hitting the wall.

"Hold on, Mr. Bear!" Amy cried and started after the car and her stuffed animal at a dead run.

John scooped her up and kept going, careful to stay to one side so Mark could see. "Slow it down, son."

With his tongue in the side of his cheek, Mark brought the car to a halt inches from her door. "I did it!"

There was awe and wonder in his face and voice. Brooke hugged him before she thought better. "Never had a doubt. Come on. Let's go inside and see what else that baby can do."

A lot, they soon learned. Amy had long since decided she didn't want Mr. Bear to have a boo-boo like she did, so he stayed safely in her arms.

John watched his son forget his shyness as he and Brooke put the car through its paces. He wasn't surprised to hear her say she'd had one as a child. She'd wanted to do what the boys did. This, of course, got Amy's attention. As soon as her arm was better, she said, she was driving it. Mark said nothing. John knew a fight was in the making.

"Time to go, kids." The expected protests were ignored. "Thank Brooke and let's go. Neither one of you is going to want to get up in the morning."

She hugged and kissed both children. John had never been envious of his children, but he wouldn't have minded a hug at the moment. Hell, he wanted the kiss, too.

He hefted up Amy. "Thank you," he told Brooke.

"I enjoyed having them." She stroked Amy's cheek and placed her hand on Mark's shoulder.

"Can you come to supper tomorrow night?" Mark asked. "She can, can't she, Dad?"

"I'm sure your father has other plans."

He could read her like a book. She had gone all stiff on him. "I didn't invite Mary for dinner and if you hadn't left in such a hurry you would have heard me tell her how rude she was."

"We all wanted you to stay," Mark said, catching her free hand with his.

"What do you want, John?"

A thousand erotic things. None of which could be said in front of his children. "I try to get home for dinner around six. It's lasagna."

"Thank you. I'll be there."

The children cheered. Mark reminded Brooke of the address before John could open his mouth.

She smiled down at him. "You're such a smart and courteous young man. Good night, John. Be careful of your arm at school tomorrow, Amy. Mark, I expect to hear about the camping trip tomorrow night. You went to my hometown."

John appreciated that she had included both his children, made them feel that she cared. Nodding, he headed for the elevator. The caring side of Brooke might be even more dangerous than the seductive one.

L̲orraine was determined that Hamilton not spoil the success of Bliss. She'd left home early on purpose. She didn't think she could stand the tension again that morning. Hamilton's anger was such a startling contrast to the support and encouragement Thomas gave. She paused in front of the display window of Bliss. She was not giving up her dream.

"Morning, Lorraine."

"Morning."

Lorraine looked over her shoulder to see Brooke and Claire coming toward her. There was no mistaking the happiness shining in their faces. "Well, you two are walking advertisements for the store."

Claire's smile widened. "I wish every woman could feel at least one time in her life the way I do this morning."

Brooke grinned. "I want to hear every detail about the weekend."

Claire blushed, but she didn't tuck her head. "I wouldn't want to make you jealous."

Brooke hooted and bumped her shoulder against Claire's. "That's my girl."

Lorraine opened the door, happy for them. She just wished her life wasn't in such turmoil. "Let's get inside and make some coffee."

Arm and arm, Brooke and Claire entered the shop in front of Lorraine. "Good thing we all decided to come in early," Lorraine said. "It will take us at least that long to straighten up the place and restock."

In the back office Brooke filled the carafe with tap water, instead of the spring water she'd always used before she lost her job. "I have to confess I came early in hopes that I can leave a bit early."

"Hot date?" Claire asked, putting all their purses away.

Brooke shrugged her shoulder. "Not exactly. I'm having dinner with John and the children. It's no big deal."

Lorraine and Claire traded looks.

"Is that why you're wearing that sexy blouse with a double ruffle that's guaranteed to draw a man's attention?" Lorraine asked.

Brooke cut off the water. "Do you think it's too much? I decided on the pants instead of the short skirt. The jacket is in the car."

The other two women laughed. Brooke had never been in doubt of what to wear. "You look beautiful, sophisticated, seductive," Lorraine said.

"That's what I was aiming for." Brooke hit the coffeemaker's switch. "I decided to give John another chance. He might irritate the hell out of me, but he's a wonderful father."

"That he is," Claire said, picking up a box of Honeysuckle Soufflé square pillar candles. "I've said it before, but thanks for going with him, and letting us know Amy was all right."

"She's a character," Brooke admitted with a chuckle. "But Mark is the one that steals your heart. He's so serious all time that you want to help him cut loose."

"You can certainly teach him that," Lorraine said, a bottle of glass spray and paper towels in her hand.

"That's what I figured." Brooke took the box from Claire. "So give with your disgustingly happy self."

A dreamy smile came on her face as Claire walked into the store. "Gray is the most wonderful, considerate man in the world. We had a celebration dinner on his yacht. It rained. We got wet."

"And?" Brooke prompted.

Claire began stacking candles on the glass shelf. "You sure you want to hear?"

"As long as I'm not getting any, I might as well hear about it." Brooke began helping.

Claire squatted to fill the lower shelf. She glanced up at Brooke. "Being with Gray was the most frightening, exhilarating experience of my life. It was like catching the perfect sunset again and again, sheer joy, sheer pleasure, where all your senses are alive, reliving that perfect moment again and again."

There was a long silence. "You love him?"

"Yes." Claire didn't even try to deny Brooke's statement.

Brooke came down beside her. "Be careful."

"Too late. I won't give up what we have worrying about tomorrow. I'd rather spend the time loving Gray," Claire declared.

"I wish I had your courage," Lorraine said softly. "I don't know what to do anymore."

Claire went to Lorraine on the other side of the counter. "You have more courage than either of us. Despite everything, you keep going. You won't give up."

"She's right. Anyone who can look adversity in the eyes has my vote." Brooke came up beside her. "Besides, I've seen Hamilton watching you. He loves you no matter what comes out of his mouth."

"Some men can be so trying at times," Lorraine said with feeling.

"You won't get an argument from me," Claire said.

"We just have to be smart enough to teach them better," Brooke said with an emphatic shake of her head. "My money is on us."

Hamilton couldn't find the black pinstriped suit he wanted to wear, the white cotton shirt with the monogrammed French cuffs to go with it, nor his black silk underwear. He shoved a dresser drawer closed then opened another. He liked silk underwear, but had never been comfortable with the housekeeper laundering them. Lorraine always made sure he had plenty. Until now.

He opened and slammed another drawer. Red, blue—polka dots his children had given him as a gag—but not black. It might be crazy to some, but once he could afford to do so, he always matched from the skin out. He'd grown up wearing patchwork clothes. He promised himself he'd never do so again.

If Lorraine hadn't been so busy with Bliss this wouldn't have happened. He didn't consider the consequences, he just went to the phone on the bedside table and dialed.

"Bliss. May I help you?"

Hearing Lorraine's cheery voice wanting to help some stranger when she hadn't helped her husband, the man who loved her, hit Hamilton the wrong way. "You forgot to wash my black briefs."

There was a distinct pause. "You have others."

"I want to wear those with my black Hugo Boss pinstripe that you were supposed to get out of the cleaners last week."

"I see."

"You see," Hamilton said, pacing the floor, his anger growing by the second. "What does that mean?"

"Simply that you will have to rely on yourself to pick up your laundry and dry cleaning, wash your briefs and all the other things I've done for you over the years. It's my time, Hamilton, and I'm going to get my business going," she said. "You never had to worry about the children nor the house when you opened Corporate Revitalization LLC, did you?"

He didn't want to answer, but didn't see how he could get out of it. They both knew the answer. "No."

"Then be as resilient as I was and take care of yourself. Goodbye, I have a company to run."

Hamilton hung up the phone and sat on the bed. He didn't want to take care of himself. He wanted Loraine to do it, but it no longer looked as if he had a choice.

Lorraine slammed the phone down. "Hamilton, I take it," Brooke said, entering the back room.

Lorraine closed her eyes and counted to ten, then ten again before she opened her eyes and said, "Yes. Can you believe he actually tried to scold me for not picking up his dry cleaning and washing his briefs?"

Brooke picked up a case of BTS products. "As a matter of fact, I can. Mom and Dad both worked, but Daddy would come home from work and sit on the couch and wait for Mama to cook, then bring him a plate. I asked her why she did all the housework and she said it was too late to train him, and if she acted differently he might think she didn't love him." Brooke shrugged her shoulders. "I asked Daddy why he didn't do more for himself and he always said Mama enjoyed taking care of him. My uncles are the same way."

Lorraine stared at the ceiling. "I did the same with Hamilton. I haven't worked since the oldest started kindergarten. That's a lot of years to overcome."

"You ask me, they just enjoy being waited on hand and foot." Brooke harrumphed. "When I get married, we're hiring a housekeeper and cook from day one."

"We couldn't afford it when were first married and I have to admit I enjoyed taking care of Hamilton and the children," Lorraine told her, then quickly added, "But now I want my freedom to do what I want. Thomas sees it. Why can't Hamilton?"

"I don't know, but you might have waited too late," Brooke told her. "Sounds as if Hamilton is thoroughly spoiled. If my mother told Daddy to start taking care of himself, he'd be lost. Just as Hamilton appears to be."

Lorraine considered what Brooke had told her. "You think the change was too abrupt?"

"If he's getting on your case about his briefs not being clean, it is. He probably has a drawer full."

"Make that two."

"Exactly," Brooke said. "It's not the briefs he's upset about, it's that it's one more thing he sees that's changing that he can't control. Men hate change, and being out of control of their lives, worse than any woman who ever lived."

"What do you suggest?" Lorraine asked. Brooke certainly seemed to know more about men than she did.

"Pick out a couple of things you know Hamilton goes bonkers over, do those and give the rest to him. If he still balks, tell him what you can do and let him choose two, that way you make him think he's still in charge," she finished.

Lorraine gave her a hug, then laughed. "You're brilliant."

"No, I just grew up surrounded by men." Brooke smiled, then sobered. "That's why I can't understand why I can't figure John out or why he makes me want to tear off his clothes every time I see him."

"Maybe you'll find out this afternoon at dinner," Lorraine said, wondering if Brooke realized she hadn't mentioned Randolph's name in weeks.

A wary sigh drifted from Brooke's lips. "I hope so. It's humiliating knowing he knows I'm a heartbeat away from dragging him to the floor."

"If the photo shoot is any indication, you may be closer than that."

Monday morning Gray stepped off the elevator whistling and started down the wide hallway to his corner office. He felt loose, energized. He'd gotten a chance to call Claire before she left for work. Her sleepy voice had him wishing he were there with her. The end of the day couldn't come soon enough so he could see her again.

It was all he could do this morning to leave her sleeping while he slipped out of her bed. If he hadn't, he would have made love to her again and he wanted her to have some rest before she went to work that morning. He couldn't get enough. No woman had ever affected him so strongly. Loving Claire was a sweet addiction that he had no intention of seeking a cure for.

Opening the outer door to his secretary's office, he strolled inside. "Good morning, Phyllis."

Gray's secretary glanced up from the folder in her hand. "Good morning. I can see that you had a good weekend."

Since he was grinning, there was no sense denying the obvious. "Yes, and yours?"

"All right. My husband's parents came up for the weekend and I didn't get a chance to attend the grand opening of Bliss." She swiveled toward him in her chair. "How was it?"

"The shelves were practically bare by the time they closed." There was pride in his voice.

Phyllis looked pained. "I hope they have more of the hand cream Ms. Bennett gave me. My mother-in-law loved the way it smelled and made her skin feel soft."

Claire's skin was as smooth as velvet. He'd loved and tasted practically every delectable inch of it. His body hardened and he was glad he had his attaché case in his hand. He reached for his door. "I'm sure they have more."

Phyllis turned back to the file. "I better finish up this report you wanted this morning, then I can run over there on my lunch break. Maybe I'll get a couple of friends to go with me."

"You do that." Gray pushed open his door.

"FedEx delivered an overnight package this morning. I put it on your desk." Slipping a disk into the computer tower, she reached for the mouse. "I'll have this financial report into you in fifteen minutes."

"Thank you."

Entering his office, Gray placed his attaché case on his desk and picked up the package. He wasn't familiar with Trinity Merchandising in London. He reached for the tab and pulled. Out tumbled a tiny bit of black lace and with it, Jana's cloying scent. His entire body went still as he stared at the underwear on his desk. Fury swept through him. The last package she'd sent from New Orleans had contained a black lace thong as well. Phyllis had been the unlucky one that time.

Picking up the notepad on which it had fallen, Gray tossed everything, including the envelope, into his trash can and went into the outer office. "Have Housekeeping come up immediately and dispose of this. Don't accept any more packages from that address and check all of the overseas mail."

Frowning, Phyllis glanced from the trash can to her boss. "Yes, sir."

"It's from Jana." His voice was clipped.

Anger flickered in her gaze. She picked up the trash can and wrinkled her nose. "I'll take care of it. Maybe I'll pick up a candle or two from Bliss and burn them in here."

Tight-lipped, Gray nodded as she went out the door. Claire had certainly helped erase the bitter memory of Jana's betrayal. But just as Jana destroyed their marriage, the package, as she'd wanted, had reminded him that nothing lasts forever. One day, he'd have to leave Claire and move on.

He never wanted to be that vulnerable again.

CHAPTER TWENTY-SIX

H e wasn't going to make it.

John resisted the urge to check his watch again. It couldn't have been more than five minutes from the last time he'd checked at six-ten. This wasn't the first time he'd been late for dinner with his children, though he did his best to keep those occurences to a minimum, but this was the first occasion Mark had invited a woman.

John came to a stop behind a small compact car and impatiently flexed his hands on the steering wheel. He'd planned to arrive home in time for a quick shower and change, but that was out now. His last client *would* need to have a tire change with bolts that had rusted on. By the time he'd finished, dirt and grime was all over his shirt and arms. No one had to tell him Brooke dated men who wore expensive suits and had manicures. All he'd had time for was a degreaser to get the dirt off his hands.

The Beetle inched forward and John pulled off behind it. Brooke would probably turn up her pretty little nose at him. He shouldn't care that she saw no further than what was on the outside, but he did and there was no sense fooling himself any longer.

John turned off into his housing development as restless and anxious as any sixteen-year-old picking up his first date. Seeing Brooke's Jag in front of his house increased his anxiety. Pulling up behind it, he jumped out of the wrecker. Long, ground-eating strides carried him up the walkway. He heard the laughter before he put his key in the door and shoved it open. They were all around a card table set up in the middle of the family room. Brooke was directly in front of him. His parents were on either side.

All eyes converged on him, but somehow his gaze never made it past Brooke. Amy was in her lap. Mark leaned against Brooke's chair. His pulse accelerated. Even wearing a suit that would probably equal his house payment, she looked perfectly natural sitting with his children.

"Daddy!" Mark and Amy exclaimed and both ran to him. Bending down he hugged them.

"We waited dinner for you," Amy said. "Even Mr. Bear."

"About time you dragged home after inviting a guest for dinner," his mother admonished. "You know how I don't like reheating food."

"He could have waited until I was winning," his father grumbled.

Brooke lifted a skeptical brow. "Got any other jokes, Mr. Randle?"

"I want a rematch," his father said and began putting the dominoes back into the worn box.

"We helped Brooke beat Grandpa at dominos five games to one," Mark volunteered. "I kept score."

"And helped me figure out which piece to play," Brooke said. "Amy was our good luck charm. I couldn't have done it without my team."

Once again she had included his children. John's father had trounced him on many occasions. He didn't pull back for anyone, young or old. Brooke had to be a shrewd player.

Amy and Mark went back to Brooke. She picked up Amy as carefully as she had put her down moments ago. Mark leaned against her chair, his arm touching hers.

Brooke had won his family over as effortlessly as she won over every male that breathed. And she was ignoring him again.

"Hello, everyone. Sorry I'm late. I'll go take a shower and be right out."

"Then we'll be leaving." Mrs. Randle came to her feet and folded the chair she had been sitting in. "Mission meeting tonight. You can drop them off if you have to go back out later."

"Greg is picking up the wrecker and bringing my truck later. I'm in for the night." John crossed the room and took the chair from her. "Thanks for staying and for dinner."

His mother affectionately patted his cheek. "I'd disown you if you tried to keep me from doing it." She turned to her husband. "Come on, Hiram. You can try and beat Brooke next time."

"I won't try," Hiram said, coming to his feet and folding his chair. "It's going to be total annihilation."

Smiling sweetly, Brooke set Amy on the floor and folded her chair. "Name the date and place, and me and my team will be there."

"Sunday at one-thirty," was his quick comeback. "Evelyn and I'll feed you first before I take you down a peg."

The smile slid from Brooke's face, as she realized that she'd committed herself to Sunday dinner.

"Afraid?" John's father taunted when seconds passed and she didn't respond.

Brooke moistened her lips. "I . . . er . . ." She threw a quick glance at John. No help there. His face was expressionless and she could have kicked him for it. "Maybe John has other plans for his family?"

"Then it's settled, because they eat dinner with us every Sunday the Lord sends," Evelyn said. "Come give Grandma some sugar, and I'll see you two tomorrow after school."

Brooke blinked as if she hadn't known what hit her. Unfortunately John did. His parents had decided he needed to move on and the woman they'd selected he needed to move on with was Brooke.

Brooke did not have supersonic hearing, but she swore she could hear the water from John's shower running in rivulets down his muscular body, over his wide shoulders, down his chest, sliding over his flat stomach to his—

"Brooke, are you all right?"

She jumped guilty and stared at Mark, who had stopped filling the water glasses. "Of, course, sweetie."

"You face is all funny," he said.

"Like you've been out in the sun," Amy added, sitting at the kitchen table with Mr. Bear.

Erotic thoughts in front of a man's children were definitely a no-no. She considered making an excuse and leaving for all of two seconds. There was no reason to hurt the children because she couldn't get her mind off their father's body, his hands, his mouth, his—

"Ready to eat?"

Brooke whirled around with the salad bowl in her hand. John stood in the doorway in a snug pair of blue jeans, a white tee shirt. He hadn't taken time to dry thoroughly. Water glistened in his hair and dampened a couple of spots on his impressive chest. The alluring combination of his clean male scent and soap reached out to her. She was ready all right and it wasn't for food.

His face went from carefree to lusty.

"Daddy, you face looks like Brooke's," Amy said. "You hot, too?"

John's stricken gaze flew to his daughter.

"She means from the sun," Brooke interjected and put the tossed salad on the table.

"Yeah. Right."

Brooke didn't think she'd ever seen a grown man blush. They were certainly a pair.

"Let's sit down and eat," John said and started to sit. He hung suspended in mid-air when Mark went around and held Brooke's chair.

"Thank you, Mark. You are such a gentleman."

The little boy flushed. "Daddy would have done it, but he's tired and he's got a lot on his mind."

Brooke lightly touched the little boy's shoulder to reassure him that she hadn't taken offense. "Then he's lucky to have you, just as I was."

Beaming from ear to ear, Mark took his seat.

John's bottom finally settled in the cushioned chair. "Thanks, son. It's nice knowing you always have my back." Folding his hands, he bowed his head and said grace.

Brooke said her blessings, then silently asked for strength to resist temptation. Opening her eyes, she looked across the small table separating her from John. He was looking right back at her. Desire slammed into her full force. She glared at him as best she could, considering the fact that if the children weren't there she'd probably drag him to the floor.

This was all his fault.

L orraine, please go on home," Claire ordered, adding up the day's receipts.

"I'm staying and following you to the bank and tomorrow you're getting a cell phone," Lorraine said, refusing to budge from beside Claire at the cash register.

Claire lifted her head long enough to throw Lorraine a quick look of exasperation before continuing with the receipts. "Lorraine, I'll be fine. You want to go home to show Hamilton you'll still be there for him. You can't do that here with me."

Lorraine shook her head. "I won't shirk one responsibility for another."

Shoving the receipts and deposit slip into a money bag, Claire gave Lorraine her full attention. "You're not needed here; you are at home. Go home."

A knock sounded on the door and both women jumped and glanced around sharply. Seeing Gray with another man, Claire's face creased into a wide smile and she rounded the counter to open the door. Memories of their lovemaking flushed her skin and made her wish they were in bed together. She should have known she'd be insatiable with Gray after waiting so many years.

Unlocking and opening the door, she had just enough presence of mind not to fling herself into his arms since she didn't know who the other broad-shouldered man, dressed in a short-sleeve shirt and slacks, was. Gray had on a charcoal and red pinstriped suit that she'd have liked to take off. "Hello, Gray."

"Hello, Claire," he greeted, a smile curving his mouth as if he knew exactly what she was thinking and couldn't agree more. "I've brought someone I wanted you and the ladies to meet."

"Brooke is not here, but Lorraine is."

Coming inside, Gray closed the door and introduced everyone. "Lee

Roy is a security guard with Livingston during the morning shift. He's available at a rate I think you'll find agreeable to escort whomever to the bank. He can start tomorrow night."

"You're hired," Lorraine quickly said. "But can you start tonight? I have to go home."

"Yes—"

"That won't be necessary," Gray cut in smoothly. "I'll see to it tonight. Lee Roy, please escort Lorraine to her car, and thanks for taking the job."

"I'll get my purse." Lorraine took off for the back.

Gray held out his hand to the big man. "Thanks. I appreciate you."

"Thanks for the confidence," Lee Roy said, his large, calloused hand a startling contrast to Gray's slender, manicured ones. "I won't let you down."

"Ready." Lorraine hugged Claire and then she and the security guard were out the door.

Gray hadn't taken his eyes off Claire since Lorraine had reappeared. "Hello, beautiful."

She replied without thinking, "Hi, handsome."

He pulled her into his arms and kissed her until they were both gasping for breath. "I wasn't sure I'd be able to last much longer."

She nuzzled his neck. "Me either. My first thought was to jump you."

"Keep that thought." He gave her a quick kiss on the lips. "Grab the deposit and let's get out of here."

After the first awkward moments at dinner, John's libido cooperated enough for him to carry on a normal conversation and look at Brooke without wanting to give her everything her hot gaze was asking for. The children's happy conversation about their day at school helped most of the time, but then Brooke would say something and his gaze would travel back to her, and no matter how hard he resisted temptation the V of ruffles framing her breasts always drew his attention. His imagination would kick in and he'd visualize burying his head there, and another part of his body that was hard and aching for release someplace else.

"More water, John?" she asked sweetly, but her eyes shot daggers at him.

At least she couldn't kick him anymore. After the second kick, he'd finally wised up and moved his long legs out of harm's way. He'd be black-and-blue for a week.

He glanced at the glass she kept full. He'd be sloshing if he drank any more. "No thanks. Mark, any problems with homework?"

His son grinned at Brooke. "Brooke checked it and said it was all right. She's smart."

"I bet if I had homework, she would have said the same thing," Amy put in and yawned.

"Time to get ready for bed," John announced. Protests and groans sounded from both children. "We were out late last night to see Brooke. I'd like to think if the occasion came up again you wouldn't mind going to bed a little early the next night."

Both children got up from the table without further protest. "Say goodnight to Brooke, and I'll be in to help you with your bath, Amy."

"Can Brooke help?" she asked, leaning against her father and staring up at him.

A smile tugging the corner of his mouth, he kissed her on the forehead. "No, but nice try. She'd get her pretty suit wet."

Mark and Amy both hugged Brooke, told her goodnight and left the kitchen. John watched them go and then turned around. A hunk of garlic bread hit him in the face and plopped into his plate. He was so surprised he simply stared at Brooke. She was seething.

"How dare you let Amy think that a suit is more important to me than she is." Brooke shot up from the table. "Thank goodness they have your parents to help you raise them or they'd be as insensitive as their father."

She was halfway out of the room before John reacted. Recalling vividly that she could put him on his back, he grabbed her around the waist with both hands, quickly saying "The kids" in hopes that she wouldn't want to put up a fight and frighten them. She didn't say anything, but she kicked him.

"If I fall, guess who is going to be on the bottom," he whispered into her ear. Immediately she stilled.

In five steps they were out the back door and in the oversized yard that had been a must when he was looking for a house three years ago. A swing set, a sandbox, and a little club house were in the far corner of the yard. The security lights winked on. He continued until he was out of the direct line of the light. "I'm going to put you down and I want you to listen to what I have to say for Mark and Amy, if not for me."

Brooke grunted. Since she didn't punctuate the sound with a kick, he loosened his hold by increments, then quickly stepped back realizing even before she whirled on him with her small fists clenched that he had to talk fast. "Amy is like a water buffalo when she takes a bath. You would have been soaked in minutes."

"It will dry clean and, if it wouldn't DKNY and Saks would have heard from me."

He shoved his hand over his head. "That's not the only problem, as I see it."

She braced her hands on her hips. "What is?"

"If you had gotten wet I would have had to let you use my bathroom to dry off, since the children share a bath, then loan you something of mine since it would be the only thing close to fitting you." He blew out a long breath. "I'm already having enough problems sleeping at night from thinking about you without visualizing you undressing in my bedroom."

Her hands dropped to her side. She looked stricken. "T–This shouldn't be happening."

"That doesn't seem to stop it." John stepped closer. He couldn't help himself. "I don't think we'd be fighting this so hard if we hadn't gotten off on the wrong foot."

Brooke's eyes went lethal again. "You blame me for that?"

He didn't have to think. "You got mad because you tried to con me and it didn't work."

She opened her mouth, closed it, and looked away. "I wasn't having a good day. You ignoring me made it worse."

"Believe me it wasn't easy," he admitted.

Her head whipped back around to him.

If she hadn't looked stunned instead of triumphant he might not have been able to tell her the rest. "Every time you're within a foot of me, I want you. I have from the first moment I saw you, and it gets worse every time I see you."

"From the first?" she asked in amazement.

He nodded, then reached out and took her hand, felt the leap of her pulse which caused his to settle a bit more. "Don't you know when a guy is playing hard to get?"

She glanced at their two hands together, then back at him "My judgment hasn't been what it once was."

He didn't want to hear about another guy. "Do you want me to go beat him up or, better yet, take you to beat him up?"

A smile broke over her face. "That might be difficult to do since he's in London."

"Do you wish he was here?" John forced himself to ask.

"No. He wasn't who I thought he was or what I wanted." Brooke stared up into John's face. "He didn't care that I lost my job or how frightened I was. You did and we'd just met. I've moved on."

"Good." Breathing easier, John pulled her closer, fitting her body effortlessly to him. "We can concentrate on each other."

Standing easily in his arms, Brooke rested her hands on his chest. "This is the longest we've ever been together without fighting."

"I know," he replied, brushing a kiss across her forehead. "Tell me about Brooke Dunlap, who can put a man down in seconds or bring him to his knees, then help that same man keep it together for his kids with equal ease."

Her hands trembled. "I was scared."

"I'll always be thankful you were there with me," he said. "Have you always been bossy?"

"Decisive," she said, and told him about her family with uncles who were always there for her.

"So men have been catering to you since you took your first breath," he said matter-of-factly.

She shrugged her shoulder. "I guess."

He laughed and hugged her to him. "Don't go modest on me."

She wrinkled her nose at him. "You could certainly use some modesty."

"I've got a feeling you're going to teach me some." His fingers traced the delicate curve of her jaw. He felt her shiver. "I want to see you again. Just the two of us and I don't think I can wait until Sunday."

"Me either," she breathed. "Breakfast at my place Wednesday at nine."

"I could be there at eight-fifteen."

"Even better."

Lorraine opened the back door leading from the garage and saw Hamilton sitting at the kitchen table, seemingly staring into space. "Hamilton?"

He jerked toward her and came to his feet. He took a couple of steps and stopped. "Hello, Lorraine."

Her throat stung. So much formality when there had once been so much love. She closed the door. "I see Betsy made dinner for you."

His glanced back at the half-eaten almond trout, grilled vegetables and roasted rosemary potatoes. "She's not as good a cook as you."

Censure and complaint. Lorraine took a seat on the other side of the table. "That's why I came home early."

His eyes lit up. "You decided to quit?"

A pain sliced through her that he could be so happy to hear she'd given up on her dream. "No."

"Oh." He leaned back in his chair.

Lorraine swallowed the growing lump in her throat. "I came home to do the laundry. If possible, I'll try to be here when you get home in the evenings. I'm not sure about cooking. I realized today that this is difficult for you."

He stared across the table at her. "Knowing that, you won't give up the shop?"

"Knowing how much it means to me how can you ask me to give it up?" she countered. She started to add that Thomas hadn't asked Margaret to give up her dream, but didn't think it wise.

Hamilton flinched as if she had struck him, then he came around the table and drew her into his arms. "We'll get through this."

"Yes, we will." Lorraine held him as tight as he held her. Brooke's plan hadn't been a total failure. But her marriage was still in trouble.

As soon as they entered Claire's house, Gray pulled her into his arms and kissed her until both were starved for breath and even more starved for each other. It took Claire considerable willpower to pull back and ask, "How much is Lee Roy's salary and are you matching it in some way?"

Gray stopped dropping little kisses on her face and lifted his head. "I thought about it. Then I recalled how stubborn and how independent you are and decided not to. He earns $16.50 an hour. I think he should get there at least fifteen minutes before closing, walk whoever is not making the deposit to their cars, then escort the person making the deposit to the bank for night deposit, then follow for at least ten minutes to ensure she's not being followed, then head home. You're looking at an hour-and-a-half."

Claire strained away from Gray when he tried to kiss her again. "So he's willing to do so much for less than $25 a night, most of which Uncle Sam will get?"

"Which, monthly, will help him pay for the fishing boat he wants. Plus the side benefits." Gray kissed her forehead since that was the only part he could reach. "He's hoping you'll consider him for the next Man of Bliss. He likes the ladies."

Claire frowned and let him pull her closer. "We don't need one now."

"He's there if you do." Her blouse came out of her skirt. "How hungry are you?"

She chuckled then moaned as his teeth nipped her earlobe. "I suppose I could wait an hour."

"That should give us just enough time."

CHAPTER TWENTY-SEVEN

This was it.

Standing in front of Brooke's door Wednesday morning, John glanced at the small bouquet of fresh-cut flowers in one hand, the fresh-baked croissants in the other and swallowed. This wasn't what Brooke was used to. Everything from the expensive clothes to the Jag to the upscale address testified that she was used to the best. She had style, grace, elegance. So why was he standing in front of her door with flowers and croissants from a grocery store?

Because he didn't seem to be able to stay away.

The answer wasn't settling. He'd always been able to control his emotions. Until now. Until Brooke. Worse, he wasn't able to keep from revealing those feelings to her. Being vulnerable was new to John.

And he didn't like it one bit.

He stared down at the bouquet. He recognized a daisy but that was about it. Maybe there was something in there that she was allergic to. Perhaps he should stash them. Too hokey. He was trying too hard to please. He couldn't compete with her other dates and he wasn't about to try. Brooke either accepted him for himself or not at all. He was leaning over to hide the flowers by the door when it opened.

Caught, he glanced up and his breath snagged. Brooke might be petite, but she was filled out in the most wonderful, arousing places. She packed a wallop in the short white sheath she wore. Great legs went along with the mouth-watering rest of her. She looked beautiful and more tempting than any woman had a right to . . . at that time of morning . . . unless she was in a man's bed. And that's exactly where John wanted her to be.

Slowly he straightened and caught a whiff of the elusive fragrance she wore. The ache that had awakened him that morning worsened.

"Good morning, John," Brooke greeted, hoping she didn't sound as breathless as she felt. "Come on in."

"Good morning," John said, entering.

"Are those for me?" she asked.

Wordlessly he thrust the flowers he was clutching toward her.

"They're beautiful." Taking the bouquet, Brooke brought them to her face and inhaled. She looked at him over the top. "No one has ever brought me flowers for a breakfast date. Thank you."

An odd mixture of relief that she liked the flowers and irritation that she had known other men went through him. He wasn't the jealous type. Another trait he'd acquired since meeting Brooke. "I was about to hide them when you answered the door."

John's honesty and obvious nervousness went a long way in settling her jumpy nerves. She had tossed and turned most of the night wondering about this. "I asked security to let me know when you arrived so I'd have everything ready." She turned away. "Come into the kitchen and I'll put these in some water and we can have breakfast."

"Smells good," he said following her into the stainless steel kitchen. He took a seat at the glass-topped table set with crystal, and china trimmed in pewter—or was it platinum?—and linen napkins.

"Canadian bacon, cheese grits, scrambled eggs and French toast." She placed the cut-crystal vase full of flowers on the edge of the table so it wouldn't impede their view of each other and put the croissants on a tray. Finished, she reached for a high-backed chair covered in soft gray-and-black stripe.

John jumped up from his seat to pull out her chair.

She glanced up to thank him and the nerves that had just begun to settle went on full alert. He looked so mouth-wateringly tempting. Clean-shaven, crisp white shirt and dress slacks. She wet her lips. His gaze followed. Heat shot through her. It was either have John for breakfast or talk fast. "Thank you. If you'll take a seat I'll say grace."

He blinked, then tore his hungry gaze from her lips to her eyes. "W–what . . . sure. Sorry."

Brooke bowed her head to say grace and for deliverance from the lure of John's body. She heard a strangled sound from across the table and glanced up; realizing as she did that she had spoken out loud.

"If you don't mind, that's one prayer I hope He doesn't answer," John said. Staring at her intently.

"I think you can put your mind at ease."

John made a motion to stand. Her hand shot out toward him.

"Don't you dare. I was up at six-thirty cooking this breakfast and we're going to eat it."

John eased back into his cushioned seat. And picked up his small black checked napkin. "Bossy, just like I said."

"Decisive." She served him, then herself. "How are Amy and Mark this morning?"

"Better than usual." He reached for a croissant. "I only had to tell them once on the way to school to stop arguing."

Smiling, she picked up her orange juice. "They're great kids."

"In spite of their father," he said, a teasing glint in his eyes.

She made a face. "Sorry about that remark."

"Don't be. I probably wasn't at my best. Being in a state of perpetual arousal tends to make a man testy."

She sighed. "It's not very good on a woman either."

He choked on his bacon. Jumping up from the table, Brooke pounded him on his back. He stopped coughing and stared up at her. "You're trying to kill me?"

"Not until I'm finished with you."

He pulled her into his lap, his mouth fastening on hers. The hands holding her were as desperate as hers holding him. The kiss rocked both of them. His tongue swept inside her mouth, mating with hers.

Gathering the off-the-shoulder collar of her dress in his fists he pulled the soft, stretchy material down. He almost groaned on seeing the tiny bit of white lace barely covering her lush breasts. He did moan when his lips brushed across her silken flesh.

She moaned right along with him, then her hands were on him, small and demanding. She pushed his shirt up and ran a delicate tongue across his nipple. He shuddered.

Bowing her backwards, his teeth closed delicately around the hard nipple pushing against the lacy fabric of her bra. Sensations rocketed through him. He wanted; he needed.

A buzzer sounded. He thought it was in his head until the sound continued. Finally he recognized it as the oven timer. Lifting his head, John breathed in gulps of air and tried to control the desire racing through him. Brooke's breathing was just as erratic.

"I–I need to cut it off, but I'm not sure I can stand."

"Don't look at me."

She laughed and he joined in. She palmed his face. "You have a strange effect on me. You can make me madder than any man I've ever met. You can also make me laugh more."

"I want to make you hot and wet."

"That, too." Her voice quivered.

His gaze narrowed. Getting up, he sat her in her chair, then went to turn off the timer. "What time do you have to be at the shop?"

Biting her lip, she glanced at her watch. "Thirty minutes."

John's head fell forward.

"I can get off early," she quickly told him.

His head lifted, but there was disappointment in his face. "I always try to have supper with the kids and tuck them in."

"I'll guess we'll see each other Sunday," she said softly

"I'll never make it."

Brooke sighed. "I don't think we have a choice."

know you'll enjoy these," Claire said, as she handed the slim young woman a Bliss shopping bag filled with Honeysuckle Meringue bath gel, soap, candle, and moisturizing cream.

"I'm sure I will," the customer said, then headed out of the store.

Claire glanced around and felt a burst of pride. They were going to make it. Their dream had become a reality. If only Hamilton was able to get past Lorraine being an active partner in the store, Claire wouldn't have a complaint in the world. Seeing Lorraine helping a customer with a pair of silver candlesticks, she headed for the two women browsing by the candle display and yawned for the third time in as many minutes.

"You didn't get very much sleep last night, I take it," Brooke said with a twinkle in her dark eyes.

Claire smiled. "I'm not complaining."

Brooke laughed. "You go, girl."

Taking another look at the two women, Claire decided to leave them alone for a few minutes since they seemed to be systematically going through the various scents. Nothing she disliked worse than pressure when shopping . . . the few times she had gone shopping. "How are you and John doing?"

Brooke bit her lower lip. "I'm not sure. He came by for breakfast, but I had to leave for work and at night he likes to have dinner at home and put Mark and Amy to bed." Brooke sighed. "We're seeing each other Sunday for dinner at his parent's house, but I'll be ready to tear off his clothes by then or be a nervous wreck."

Claire might have blushed, or not understood the concept of sexual frustration, before she and Gray became lovers. "As a partner, you can set your own hours. Why didn't you call me or Lorraine?"

"I thought you might have been involved," Brooke said.

"Point taken." Claire glanced at her watch. "One-fifteen. The lunch crowd will be dwindling soon. As I see it, there's only one way to handle this."

"What?"

"Have John make a service call."

The battery you replaced is defective and I think you should come over and check it out."

Brooke had been pacing the floor since she'd called John fifteen minutes before. She'd taken Claire's advice and hurried home. Thank goodness he was in and had taken her call. He'd said he'd be right over. What if he thought she was too forward? She'd never made sexual overtures like that before.

The doorbell rang and she swung around. Rubbing her hand on her dress, she went to answer the door.

He came inside and closed the door behind him. "You have a complaint about a defective battery. I pride myself on customer satisfaction." He swung her up in his arms and continued to the hallway on the immediate right. "I'll do whatever it takes for as long as it takes to put a satisfied smile on the customer's face."

The tension eased out of her. "I'm going to hold you to that."

"I wouldn't have it any other way." He entered the bedroom and set her on her feet beside the turned-down bed. "How long do we have to work on the problem?"

Her arms circled his neck. "For as long as it takes."

"I certainly plan to take full advantage of it." His mouth closed her over. Once again white hot heat rippled through them. His mouth feasted on hers.

His hands fisted on the off-the-shoulders dress and dragged it down, stopping on the slope of her breasts and capturing her arms. "I was hoping you were wearing this so I could take it off you. An inch at a time." His head bent and he kissed the slope of her neck, the swell of her breast.

John made good his promise and paid homage to her body as he stripped her of her clothes and left her panting and hungry. When he finally moved over her and his eyes locked with hers, she was quivering with need. She watched him as he slowly entered her, filled her.

When completion came, they reached it together. Brooke had never felt so wonderful, so bonelessly delicious.

"I hope you haven't gone to sleep." He kissed her shoulder.

"Mmm."

I'll just have to wake you up." His mouth moved down her stomach to the most intimate part of her. She bucked and came off the bed, felt herself come undone, then the hard length of him was pressing into her. All she could do was lock her legs around him and enjoy.

t's five-fifteen," Brooke said, her hand stroking John's head as he lay on her breast. He needed to be home by six.

"I know." His arm tightened around her for a fraction.

She didn't want to let him go either. She was surprised how relaxed and at peace she felt after all the arguments they'd been through.

"I don't suppose you want to come home with me?" he asked casually.

Her hand paused for a fraction of a second. "I don't think that would be a good idea."

His head lifted and he stared at her. "No, but I don't want to leave you. Nothing else has ever come close to keeping me from my kids."

Her heart turned over. She palmed his face. "That's the most beautiful thing anyone has ever said to me."

Catching her hand, he kissed her palm. "How about breakfast in the morning? I'll take care of it. Then Friday night it's the kid's night to eat out and give Mama a break. I know they'd want you to come. Saturday afternoon you can come watch me play baseball and cheer me on."

She lifted a delicate brow. "You certainly aren't shy."

"Not when I see something I want." He nibbled on her neck.

She didn't know whether to purr or sigh. "I'm the same way. Is there something you'd like besides what you're bringing for breakfast?"

"You in this bed," he said, rolling on top of her.

"I think that can be arranged."

Surprise and delight widened Lorraine's eyes on seeing Thomas enter Bliss Thursday evening. Excusing herself from a customer, she quickly walked over to him. They hugged each other without thought or hesitation. She smiled up at him. "Thomas, what are you doing here? I know your daughters don't need any more bath and body products."

He smiled down at her, his hands on her arms. "I happened to be passing and stopped to see if you wanted to grab a bite to eat."

She'd only picked at her lunch. "Well, I—"

"Please, don't say no." His face clouded. "I just don't feel like going home to that empty house again."

In a way, she knew how he felt. She didn't want to go home either and she could use some good company. "Brooke is doing the deposit tonight so I'll be free to grab a cup of coffee at least, after we close. If you won't be bored, you can wait."

"How can I be bored waiting on a beautiful woman?"

Lorraine blushed and silently chastised herself for doing so. "Hamilton hates waiting."

"I'm not Hamilton," Thomas told her, staring down at her.

This time Lorraine didn't blush; she felt an odd sensation in her chest. To give herself a moment to collect herself she glanced at her watch, then back up at Thomas. "I'll be ready to go in about twenty minutes."

"Take your time. I'll just look around. Christmas is coming."

Lorraine watched him move away. She wondered what had happened to her moments ago, then she dismissed it. She turned and almost bumped into Brooke, who was staring at Thomas with narrowed eyes.

"What's he doing here?"

Lorraine frowned at the abruptness of Brooke's question. "Waiting for me. He's feeling sad and doesn't want to go home to an empty house."

"You're sure that's the real reason?" Brooke questioned, watching her friend closely.

Lorraine looked away. "What other reason could there be?"

Brooke brought her attention back to Lorraine then shrugged. "Don't mind me. I'm not looking forward to going home to an empty apartment either. Tomorrow night will certainly be different. We're all going out for burgers."

Lorraine smiled, relieved that Brooke wasn't pushing the issue. "Try to be good in front of the children."

"I will." Laughing, Brooke walked away.

Lorraine went back to the customer, completely dismissing from her mind Brooke's comment.

Thomas and Lorraine found an all night coffee shop and took a seat in a booth next to each other. They were silent until the waitress had brought them their coffee. "I must be getting old if I have to order decaf," Thomas said, his large hand almost hiding the plain white mug.

"Speak for yourself," Lorraine admonished, taking a sip of hers.

He chuckled, then leaned back in his seat. "How is business?"

"Wonderful." She sat her cup on the Formica table. "The web site continues to grow and, with the holidays approaching, we're should continue to do well."

"Then why do I see sadness in your eyes sometimes," he asked softly. He leaned forward, his arm brushing against hers as she tucked her head. "Hamilton?"

She nodded. "I keep hoping and praying he'll change."

"I remember hoping and praying when Margaret was sick. It didn't do a bit of good," he said tightly.

Twisting toward him, she put her hand on his tense shoulder. "Things happen that we don't understand, but there's always hope. Never forget or give up."

Thomas's eyes darkened as he held Lorraine's gaze, his hand covering hers. "What if it's something you're not sure about?"

She withdrew her hand. "Then pray about it and wait for an answer." She reached for her purse. "I should be getting home."

He slid out of the booth and reached to help her stand. "Sorry. I didn't mean to keep you so long. I'll follow you home." Thomas paid the bill and escorted her to her Mercedes.

As she got inside and pulled off, Lorraine tried to figure out if perhaps Brooke had been onto something. Could there be a woman Thomas was interested in? Was the beginning of a new relationship what he wasn't sure about? Lorraine glanced in her rearview mirror at Thomas following her in his Navigator. He couldn't be expected to mourn forever, and he was certainly an attractive, supportive man that most women would jump at the chance to have.

And she had to tell herself that of course she wasn't jealous.

Friday was a busy day at the shop. Claire was glad for more than one reason. She and Brooke didn't want to discuss the men in their lives since Lorraine was having problems with Hamilton. She had made Bliss possible. It seemed a cruel twist of fate that the woman who changed their lives for the better was going through such a rough time.

Claire had noticed that Lorraine hadn't eaten the day before. She planned to see that she did today. She was about to order from the deli around the corner when Thomas entered the shop with a large carry-out bag containing succulent roast beef subs, potato salad, cole slaw, and iced tea. They had just enough time to thank him before he was gone again. Lorraine couldn't stop talking about how considerate he was. Claire had to agree. They took turns eating.

Finally it was almost seven. Claire kept looking for Gray to enter the shop as he usually did, but as the clock ticked past seven she had to accept that he wasn't coming. Disappointed, she said goodbye to Lorraine, who was making the night deposit, and left.

She understood he had a company to run, but she had quickly grown accustomed to him being there at closing, taking her home and spending most of the night with her. If she was having difficulty with one night, how was she going to handle it when he was gone for good?

Not wanting to think about that time, she hurried to the parking lot. She'd entered into the relationship with her eyes wide open.

Arriving home thirty minutes later, she came in the back door and headed for her bedroom. She suddenly stopped, then raced to open the sliding glass door. She was in Gray's arms in two steps. "I missed you."

Kissing her, he lifted his head. "We never had our picnic."

Her eyes misted. How was she going to go on without him?

He frowned. "What's the matter?"

Shaking her head, she smiled up at him. "Nothing. You're just so sweet."

His eyebrows knitted. "Men are not sweet."

"I didn't say men, plural. I said you singular."

He turned her toward the door. "Go change."

She smiled over her shoulder at him. They still had time. "I'll go, but you're still sweet."

Gray watched her go, then turned to gaze out at the blue waters of the ocean. She wouldn't think he was so sweet when he walked away. He went to the edge of the wooden deck and clamped his hands around the balustrade. That time was coming. He'd sworn he'd never let any woman be so important to him that he couldn't walk away. He couldn't allow that to happen.

"Ready."

He turned as Claire came toward him. He just hoped it wasn't too late already.

Where was she?

Hamilton glanced at his watch every few minutes as he paced the floor in the living room. It was past nine and Lorraine wasn't home.

She'd never been this late since the shop opened. He'd tried to call her on her cell phone, but it was off. He'd picked up the phone to call Bliss, then slammed it down. The store's phone hadn't been answered the last two times he called; why did he think it would be now.

They could have been out doing God only knows what. Claire and Brooke were both single. As a married woman Lorraine shouldn't be socializing with them.

Hamilton's hand ran over his head. That was the crux of the matter. He was afraid Lorraine might become interested in another man. She was an attractive woman. He'd never even entertained such a thought until she'd changed so completely from the woman he'd married. Just like his mother had changed.

Going to the window, he stared out into the darkened night. His mother had told his father that she had found a part-time job in the evening to help with expenses. That should have alerted his father, since neither one of them liked to work. It hadn't, since it meant he could sleep late and the refrigerator always held beer even when there was no food. His father couldn't control her.

Then one night there was a fire at the local no-tell motel and his mother and the deputy mayor of the city had been overcome with smoke and had to be rescued. By morning the whole town knew. His father had crawled even deeper into the bottle.

Hamilton thanked God he'd been a month away from graduating from high school and had an academic college scholarship. He'd left for Baylor University in the fall and could count on one hand the number of times he'd gone back home.

He heard the back door open. Wheeling sharply, he hurried in that direction. "I was worried about you."

Lorraine continued past him. "I had to make the bank deposit."

He stared after her. "Is that all you have to say? I was worried sick."

In the middle of the spiral staircase, Lorraine turned to face him. "Apparently you got over it quick enough. Goodnight, Hamilton." She resumed going up the stairs.

He wouldn't be the fool his father was. "It shouldn't have taken this long. What else were you doing?"

She turned again, her expression incredulous. "I don't like what you're inferring."

"Then tell me why it took you two hours past the shop's closure to make a deposit," he demanded. He wasn't backing down.

"You really want to know?" she asked.

Hamilton couldn't decide if she was challenging him or questioning him. "Yes."

Opening her purse she took out a box wrapped in gold foil with an emblem from an upscale jewelry store, then came down the stairs separating them and thrust it at him. "The gold cuff links you wanted. Happy birthday, Hamilton."

He didn't know what to say. The pain and hurt in her eyes made it worse. He'd completely forgotten he'd be sixty in a couple of weeks. Or perhaps he had just pushed it out of his mind. He couldn't think of anything that would make up for his accusation.

Picking up his hand she slammed the box into his open palm. When she started to turn away, he pulled her into his arms despite her struggles. "I'm sorry. I'm sorry. I was worried then . . . then I became angry because I couldn't reach you on the phone."

"Please, let me go."

His arms tightened. There wasn't a shred of warmth in her voice. "I don't want to lose you, Lorraine."

"Then why are you pushing me away?" she asked, her voice surprisingly steady. "Why do you make me not want to come home?"

Fear swept through him. "That's not what I want."

She pushed against his chest until he loosened his hold and she stared down at him from her higher perch on the stairs. "It's no longer about what you want, Hamilton." Turning she continued up the stairs.

CHAPTER TWENTY-EIGHT

Hamilton didn't know what to do.

He was just as lost as ever in trying to reach Lorraine. He was thoroughly baffled. It was affecting his work. He glanced down at Reynard's financial report. He was no closer to finishing up his recommendations than he was three days ago.

Reaching into his drawer, he flipped through one of the three books on menopause he'd purchased from the bookstore. Lorraine was certainly cranky and unpredictable, but she wasn't having the night sweats. He was.

He slammed the book back. He wanted to make love to her, but was afraid she'd turn away from him and he was too big of a coward to push it. It would just be another wedge between them.

He'd just slumped back in his chair when his phone rang. He picked up the phone. "Hello?

"Hello, Dad."

For the first time in days Hamilton experienced real joy. "Hi, son. Nice to know you haven't forgotten us."

Rich laughter flowed though the line. "Mother already beat you to making me feel bad for not calling regularly."

Hamilton drummed his fingers on the report. "When did you speak to your mother?"

"Just before I called you." Justin laughed again. "She was busy at the store, so we didn't talk long."

Hamilton jumped on the opening. "That's what I've been trying to tell her. She's busy all the time. I've asked her to give it up, but she won't."

"Whoa, Dad, calm down. I mean no disrespect, but Mother put her life on hold for all of us. If she wants to have a career now, I say let her go for it."

"Go for it?" Hamilton repeated incredulously. "She doesn't need the money and it takes time away from home and me."

"Dad," Justin said, then after a long paused continued, "it's not the money. It's the satisfaction of accomplishing something on your own, knowing you did it."

Restless, Hamilton stood and paced in front of his desk. "Taking care of me and the house should be enough."

"Some women, your daughters and the women I'm presently dating included, want a career *and* a marriage. Mother just wants her time in the sun," Justin said. "We're all pulling for her. Melissa and Stacy are both talking up the products to their friends."

Hamilton didn't have one ally. "You know as well as I do that the economy is worse than it's been in years."

"Yes, but certain businesses, like personal care, are booming and that's exactly what I told Mother when she called about Bliss."

"She called you?" Shock radiated from Hamilton.

"Yes, didn't you know?" Justin asked, sounding worried.

Hamilton didn't know if he felt more hurt or angry that she had listened to their son and not him. "No, but it doesn't matter. Your mother loved the flowers you kids sent." He would not let this ruin his relationship with his children.

"She told me." Relief sounded in his son's voice. "I have to run. Take care of yourself and let Mother try her wings a bit. She always supported us."

"And you think it's time we supported her?" Hamilton stopped and stared out the window at the bright blue sky.

"Yes. She deserves it."

"If I could give Lorraine the world, I would," he said, meaning every word.

"I know. Take her out to dinner tonight and tell her in case she's forgotten," Justin advised. "If it's one thing I learned out here it's that women don't like to be taken for granted. Bye, Dad."

Hamilton disconnected the call, then began pacing again. He was actually considering taking his son's advice. That just showed how desperate he was. Although Justin certainly had an inordinate amount of practice dating, he had no concept of what it took for a relationship to work long-term. Hamilton would stay the course. Lorraine would come to her senses.

She had to.

don't suppose we should expect you for dinner tonight," Gray's grandmother said, looking at him over the rim of her delicate porcelain cup.

Gray glanced up from eating his breakfast and merely lifted an eyebrow. Most people would back off. His grandmother wasn't most people.

She sat her cup on a saucer rimmed with 24K gold. "Frankly, I was surprised you were still here when I came down to breakfast. You come home late and leave early."

"I've always put in long hours," Gray said, folding his napkin and placing it beside his plate.

"Do continue eating or I'll be forced to get the answers out of you at the office instead of here," she said, a sweet smile on her face that fooled no one. Behind it was a will of steel.

"What answers?" he asked although he had a pretty good idea what.

She eyed his plate of ham and grits, then lifted her gaze to his. Gray eyed her right back.

A sigh drifted from her lips. "You're too much like me."

He laughed.

"You haven't eaten dinner at home all week and you haven't gotten home before two in the morning."

The laughter abruptly ended. He lived in a separate wing of the house, but he'd forgotten his grandmother had a keen sense of hearing and never rested until everyone was safely home.

"I'm not checking up on you, criticizing, or being nosey. I like Claire and I'm glad you're finally settling down with one woman."

Gray paused in reaching for his coffee cup. A mild panic swept through him. "I don't think a few dates signifies settling down."

His grandmother's gaze didn't waver. "Claire impressed me as the type of woman who'd want a committed relationship."

No longer wanting the coffee, Gray gave her his full attention. "Grandmother, this is between me and Claire."

"All women aren't the same."

His mouth flattened into a grim line. He didn't want to talk or think about Jana. He didn't want to remember what a fool he had been to believe she loved him or what that belief said about him. "Grandmother—"

"Don't let what she did keep you from finding happiness with another woman," she talked over him. "Nothing would give her greater pleasure. Although she knows you won't take her back, she purposely keeps sending you those packages to disrupt your life so you can't move on."

And it upset his grandmother when it happened. Mess with a Livingston and you had her to deal with. She didn't know about Jana's latest maneuver and he planned on keeping it that way.

"Claire is a wonderful young woman."

Gray fiddled with the spoon by his coffee cup. He liked Claire, but he had no intention of their relationship lasting. He'd played the fool once where a woman was concerned and didn't plan to do so again. He'd trust Claire with anything . . . except his heart. "We're just dating."

His grandmother sat back in her chair. "Every night since the pre-opening."

He tried to bluff. "Who says?"

"You do," she said, then went on at his surprised expression. "You're bubbling over with happiness. You whistle. You bound up the stairs at night."

"So I'm happy," he said, wondering if he'd just been going through the motions of living before Claire.

"She has a good heart, and although you're my grandson and I love you, I don't want you to break that heart."

Astonishment mixed with anger flared in Gray's eyes. "I'd never hurt Claire."

"What do you think will happen when you decide it's time to leave?"

His mind went blank. He couldn't imagine not seeing Claire, not being with her, not seeing her smile.

His grandmother stood. "I admire Claire; I always have. If you don't plan to stick around, then break it off now."

"I won't do that."

Her face saddened. "Then both of you will be hurt."

He frowned. "Both?"

Rounding the table, she palmed his cheek. "Whether you want to admit it or not, you care about Claire, and the crush she had on you as a young girl has matured into a woman's feelings. I could tell from the way she looked at you the night of the pre-opening. You'll both lose unless you're willing to accept the second chance God has given you."

Gray's eyes darkened. "I'll never fall in love again."

Her hand fell to her side. "You're wrong about that, Gray, but you'll have to learn that for yourself."

Gray watched his grandmother walk away. What was she talking about? He knew his own mind. Love, a wife and family, wasn't for him. It hurt too much when it fell apart.

Gray had thought long and hard since his talk with his grandmother that morning. Perhaps she was right. Perhaps it was time to pull away. He didn't want to hurt Claire. Picking up the phone in his study around one that afternoon he called to tell her he might not be able to make dinner that night. Something had come up.

She'd been disappointed, but she'd accepted the lie without question and had ended the conversation by telling him, "If you can come by later, just come. Don't worry about the time. Just know I'll be waiting."

He had tried to work after the phone call, but he hadn't been able to concentrate. He'd finally gone by the warehouse in Charleston, then the one in Columbia. It was almost six when he returned. He hadn't been able to resist going to the third floor piazza and looking out at the lighthouse on Sullivan Island in the distance. His hands had gripped the iron balcony across the front. He longed for what he couldn't have. Slow steps had taken him back downstairs. His grandmother was sitting down to dinner in the small dining room. Her lifted brow showed her surprise.

They talked about the upcoming Christmas catalogue and hiring part-time help for the holidays. Claire was not mentioned. The seared tuna had been tasteless, as was his favorite wine. Tired of pretending to eat, he'd excused himself and gone into the study to try to do the work he hadn't done that morning. Their busiest season of the year was fast approaching and he had his mind on a woman instead of work. An uncomfortable first.

Determined to work, Gray opened the prospective items for the Christmas catalogue file, but after flipping through a couple of pages he caught himself staring at the Seth Thomas clock on his desk instead of the merchandise for the catalogue. He turned the clock around, only to turn it toward him again. He turned another page and saw an afghan that made him think of Claire curled up on her sofa or in bed reading. A candle set and he recalled them making love with only the light from the candles on her dresser. The yellow roses on the writing pad reminded him of the rose on his bed the first time they made love.

He slammed the book shut, then looked at the clock. 9:57. He didn't want to be here; he wanted to be with Claire. So what was stopping him? Fear of hurting her, of getting in too deep? But was the edgy rest-lessness he felt any better? He surged from his desk and out the study's door. He took the stairs two at a time. He didn't stop until he stood in front of his grandmother's door on the east wing of the second floor to knock.

"Come in, Gray."

His mouth twisted wryly. He might have known. Opening the door he saw her sitting up, reading, in the hand-carved bed that his grandfather had made especially for them. "I'm going out and I may not be back until morning."

Placing the book on her lap, she didn't bat a lash. "Drive carefully, dear, and give Claire my best."

Crossing the room, lavishly decorated in eighteen-century antiques, he kissed her on her unlined cheek. "Goodnight, Grandmother."

"Goodnight, Gray."

CHAPTER TWENTY-NINE

n a matter of minutes he was in his car and on the road. He didn't call until he had crossed Ben Sawyer Bridge. The phone was picked up before the second ring.

"Hello."

Just hearing her voice made the restlessness cease and his heart to race. "I'll be there in five minutes."

"It's after ten. Are you hungry?"

"Just for you."

"Then hurry."

Gray disconnected the phone with one hand. Minutes later he pulled up in front of Claire's house. Before the engine died, she was out the door and running toward him. He had barely closed the door before she was in his arms, her mouth on his. The kiss was hot, erotic. He wanted to kiss her all over and start again.

"I'd hoped you'd come," she said, staring up at him in the moonlight.

He couldn't stay away. Even as the thought formed in his brain he was kissing her again. She was worth the risk and, for the time being, he was taking it.

Inside the bedroom, need driving him, he quickly undressed them both. He'd take his time the next time he loved her. Now he needed her satin heat, needed her arms and legs locked around him, driving him, beckoning him, answering him.

Their completion came together. He lay there as the haze of passion drifted away, leaving an odd feeling. He shifted to lie on his side and draw her into his arms and kissed her on the head when he heard the even sound of her breathing. She was asleep. He smiled. He'd have to wait for seconds, he thought, then realized what the feeling was. *Peace.* He didn't try to fight it or rationalize it or deny it. He simply pulled the covers up over them and drifted off to sleep.

D omino!" Brooke exclaimed, slapping her last domino on the card table set up in the small den of John's parents' house Sunday afternoon. "And give me fifteen."

"We win again, Grandpa," Mark exclaimed as he grinned up at Brooke, then wrote down the score. "That's four to nothing."

Mr. Randle grunted, then narrowed his gaze at Brooke, who sat across the table grinning at him. "It's impolite to gloat."

She laughed. "I know, but I can't help it. We're awesome."

"Awesome," Amy repeated, sitting in Brooke's lap, and clapping her hands since she'd gotten rid of the sling a few days before.

"If you want, Grandpa, I'll be on your side," Mark said slowly, obviously torn between wanting to be with Brooke and feeling sorry for his grandfather.

"Hiram." It was one word, but his gaze went to his wife sitting on the sofa next to John watching the baseball game

Mark's grandfather held out his left arm and Mark went to him. He hugged him tightly to his chest. "If I took you I'd have unfair advantage. I'm feeling a little sluggish from eating all your grandmother's good chicken and dressing. Maybe I'll take a rest and let your daddy have a go at it."

John had been enjoying the interaction between Brooke and his family. She enjoyed them as much as they enjoyed her. She wasn't the first woman his parents had invited to dinner in hopes of jump-starting a romance, but John couldn't remember a single one of them that his children or his parents had taken to so quickly or been so happy to be around.

"How about it, John? Can you take her?"

Brooke blushed and John's own body heated. Before he allowed his mind to remember all the times they'd made love, he rose to his feet. They'd met for breakfast every morning. Once they actually ate. He hadn't seen her Saturday because he'd been busy working. He fully planned to make up for it when he followed her home tonight. "I'd consider it my pleasure."

A warm flush spread up from the scooped neck of Brooke's floral sundress. "You're welcome to try."

"We're awesome, Daddy," Amy said. Then she leaned toward him as he took his seat. "It's OK to lose; Mrs. Johnson says so."

John took his father's seat and began shuffling the dominoes. "Your pre-kindergarten teacher is absolutely right. So when you, Mark and Brooke lose, I don't want you to cry."

"Ha!" Brooke cried. "Shuffle."

John lost three straight in record time. Amy gave him a kiss to make him feel better. "I love you, Daddy."

"I love you, too," He told her, then set her down when she pushed against his chest. She promptly got back up in Brooke's lap. They looked perfectly at ease with each other, their heads close together, giggling at something Brooke whispered in his daughter's ear. Mark eased up beside her chair and she hugged him to her side and had him laughing, too. They'd sat in a booth Friday night at a local burger joint and had had a wonderful time. It was as if they'd always known each other.

It was strange watching his children playing and happy with the same woman. Amy could make friends with a rock, but with Mark, it took longer. Not with Brooke. She had won him over from the beginning. John had always wondered what it would have been like if Linda had lived. She'd loved him and their children so much. She shouldn't have died. She was too young and too good.

Brooke glanced over at John. The teasing smile on her face froze. She was taken aback by his hard, angry stare that drilled into her. Stunned, hurt, she came unsteadily to her feet. "It's almost six. I should be going."

John's parents and the children protested. "Dinner was wonderful. Thank you for the invitation." She set Amy on her feet, gave her a hug, then hugged Mark. "Be good, you two."

"We enjoyed having you, Brooke," Mrs. Randle said. " 'Bout time Hiram learned a little humility."

"I'll get her next Sunday," he said.

Brooke's gaze flickered toward a silent, grim-faced John, who had stood when she had. "Thank you, but I may go home to Columbia. Goodbye."

"I'll walk you to your car." John pushed the chair under the table.

"Not necessary." She picked up her small Fendi clutch from the end table and headed for the front door. She'd hoped to escape, but she could feel John's presence right behind her. She kept her head high and her steps unhurried, but there was nothing she could do about the tightness in her chest.

Deactivating the lock on the Jag, she reached for the door handle. John's hand closed over hers, trapping her between him and the car. His body bowed over hers. Air hissed from her lungs. She trembled. Despite everything that had just happened, she couldn't prevent her body from still wanting him.

"I'll follow you home."

"I'm perfectly capable of taking care of myself." She didn't want to look at him and see the anger in his eyes again.

"Why are you running away from me?" he asked.

She would get through this. "What do you expect after the way you looked at me? If you don't want me around your children—"

"No. Never that." His body gently touched her, then he straightened, his hand closing around hers on the door handle. "Come with me to the backyard. Please."

Refusing to look at him, Brooke allowed him to lead her into the backyard to a picnic bench. She didn't want to create a scene in front of his parents' house. Otherwise he'd be on his back again. The security light snapped on the moment John opened the Cyclone gate.

They sat on a redwood picnic bench with their backs to the house. In the daytime it would be shaded by the nearby oak and magnolia trees. She was just glad the thick, leafy branches cast shadows on her and hid the emotions on her face. Randolph had made her angry and hurt her pride when he'd shown her that she didn't matter to him. She was afraid John would hurt her heart.

"Well?"

"I'm not sure how to say this."

"Just say it." Her hand flexed in his. Perhaps if he had ended it with some tact, she'd leave him standing instead of spitting out Bermuda grass.

Sighing, he leaned back against the table. "Seeing you with Amy and Mark made me think of Linda, and what it might have been like if she had lived."

Pain twisted in Brooke's chest. He resented her. This was worse than she had imagined.

"I've tried so many times to envision her laughing and playing with them, us being a family. Sometimes I'm more successful than others, but I can always see her face." His hand tightened on Brooke's. "Tonight I couldn't see her. Her picture kept slipping away."

Brooke heard the pain in his voice and ached for him. "Tell me about her."

John reared up and stared at her in disbelief.

"I saw her picture on your desk and in your house," Brooke said softly. "She was a beautiful woman with Mark's serious eyes and Amy's smile. You loved her."

"More than my life." He swallowed hard. "She was the best part of me. It was her idea to open the garage instead of my working for someone else. She ran the front office, took care of Mark, and still kept the house. She always had faith in me. Six weeks after Amy was born Linda began having these bad headaches." His free hand rubbed across his face.

"The doctor thought they were migraines until she passed out driving, a month later. They did a series of tests and found a brain tumor. By that time it was inoperable. Everyone was sorry. Near the end she was in and out of consciousness and in a lot of pain. Over and over she kept telling me to take care of myself and the kids, that she loved me. I took off work and stayed with her the last month."

"John." Tears slid down Brooke's cheeks.

"I don't want to forget her." The words sounded torn from him.

Brooke understood what he was saying. No woman would ever come first in his life again. Hurt she didn't expect went through her. There had been no promises. Yet she knew what she felt for John went beyond simple caring. "Do you want us to stop seeing each other?"

"No." The answer was sharp and decisive. He took her face in his. "I wake up longing for the taste of you and go to bed wishing you were next to me." His forehead leaned against hers. "Even when you're trouncing me at dominoes I enjoy being with you. But the next time I'm coming out on top."

For now that had to be enough. "Weren't you in that position Friday morning?"

John's head came up, his gaze hot. "I can be that way again in thirty minutes."

"If we hurry we make it in twenty."

Man, we needed you at the bat Saturday," Sam Carlson told John as he sat in a folding chair in front of John's desk Monday afternoon. "The Sharks creamed us five to one."

"Sorry, but I told you when I joined the team that work came first." John kept working on a customer's bill, and it would be a hefty one with a complete overhaul on his vintage 'Vette.

"Yeah, it's just that you're our best player and we need you if we're going to finish in the division." Sam, lean and balding at forty, leaned forward. "You're coming to the next game on Saturday, aren't you?"

"I'll be there if I can." John reached for another customer's invoice. He was leaving on time tonight. After he got the kids in bed his parents had agreed to come by and he was going to see Brooke.

"You're sure it's work that's keeping you away?"

John lifted his head. His eyes were flat. "Meaning?"

Sam shifted. He and John had gone to elementary school together. John didn't like his integrity questioned. "The guys in the shop mentioned you and some woman who's been in a couple of times. Talk is, she's off the hook, and I thought she might be the reason you didn't make it."

John was on his feet before he realized it. "I don't lie. Anytime you want my uniform you can have it."

"Now, John—"

"If you question me again you won't have to ask for it."

"I didn't mean anything." Sam came to his feet. "We'll see you at the game . . . if you can make it." He reached for the door. "Sure hope you can. Invite your friend. I'd like to at least see the woman who had me seeing my life flash before my eyes."

John took his seat. "If you try to hit on her, you'll pay full price for your parts from now on."

Sam winced. He had a '72 Caddy he loved almost as much as he loved women. "Enough said. Later."

"Later." John leaned back in his chair, then picked up his phone and dialed.

Brooke's breathless voice answered on the second ring. "Bliss, your first stop for a more blissful you."

"How'd you like to go to a baseball game Saturday night around five?" he said. Then he explained about the team's loss.

"I'm not sure I can get off that early, but I'll try."

"Good. Now, about the days in-between," he said casually, but he had a death grip on the ballpoint pen in his hand. "Mother called this morning and said they'd stay with Mark and Amy once they were down for the night so you and I could go out. Where would you like to go?"

"I think you know the answer to that."

"I was hoping. I'll be at your place at eight-thirty."

"I'll be waiting."

Hi, Claire."

"Derek!" Claire gasped and ran across the shop to hug her brother. Taller by five inches, he had her dark brown eyes and nut-brown complexion. Always on the thin side, his suit coat hung loosely on his frame. She wished he had worn the suit she sent him the three hundred dollars to buy six months ago while he was job hunting. "When did you get in? Why didn't you tell me you were coming?"

He smiled at her enthusiasm. "Thought I'd surprise you. A partner of mine was heading this way and he wanted some company for the drive. This is some set-up."

"Thank you," she said. "The other partner, Brooke, is gone, but I'd like you to meet the woman who talked me into this." Looping her arm through his, she took him to Lorraine, who was working on restocking bath gels and soaps.

"Lorraine Averhart, my older brother, Derek," Claire said proudly.

Smiling warmly, Lorraine extended her hand. "I've heard so much about you from Claire. It's nice meeting you."

He tossed Claire an affectionate smile. "She always looked up to her big brother."

"That's as it should be," Lorraine said. "A customer just came in. Excuse me."

"Sure." He glanced around again, noting the glass, the display, the chandelier. "This is some set-up," he said again. "You must be making money hand-over-fist."

Claire tensed in spite of herself. "The first year is always rough. We've only been open a little over a month. You pile all the profits back into the business. The rent takes a big chunk."

"Hmmm." Derek picked up a jar of moisturizing cream and flipped it over for the price tag. "Thirty bucks. How many of these have you sold today?"

Claire's smile wavered. "I don't know. Perhaps five or six."

Once again he glanced around the shop. "And that's just one product." His attention switched to Lorraine ringing up a sale. "I think you're going to be rich."

"Hardly." Claire laughed it off.

"I know about these things." He picked up a bottle of lotion. "My old lady would sure welcome me back if I brought her some of these products." He picked up a couple of candles. "You don't mind, do you?"

Claire remembered Brooke's family insisting on paying full price for merchandise; and the number of customers her family continued to refer to Bliss. They wanted to help, not take. Lorraine paid for her daughter's products as well.

"I mean, technically, it's half mine anyway since you got the formula from Mama," he said.

Claire's mouth gaped. He'd never wanted to help, never poured one mold, never brought one thing their mother needed.

Derek laughed. "Just kidding. You should see the look on your face. You know how I like to joke. You go on and help your friend. I'll just look around."

Still reeling from the shock of her brother's words, she walked away. Yes, she remembered how he liked to joke, but she also remembered how much he liked money . . . sometimes to the exclusion of everything else.

Claire tried without success not to be annoyed with her brother for the amount of products he'd picked up. The sweetgrass basket overflowed. She threw a glance in Lorraine's direction and was happy to see she was helping another customer and not paying attention to them. "Derek, you have over two hundred dollars worth of merchandise."

"So what?" He shrugged his shoulders under a thin black suit that had seen too many dry cleanings. "You're a partner and I'm just like one."

There it was again, the inference that he deserved a portion of the profits. "Derek, we share equally. It isn't fair to them."

Immediately he was offended. His eyes narrowed angrily. "If you don't want me to have it, just say so," he said, his voice rising. Customers turned in their direction.

Claire flushed with embarrassment. "I didn't say that."

"Then put them in a bag and take them home with you. I'll get them tomorrow before I leave." He straightened the lapels of his suit. "Right now I have to meet Ronnie. We're going to check out the action around here."

She stopped ringing up the merchandise. "I thought you had a lady friend."

"What she doesn't know won't hurt her." He winked. "Don't wait up for me."

"You're staying with me?" she questioned, her eyes widening.

He frowned. "I always do, don't I?"

"I have a date," she blurted.

He looked incredulous. "You'll be home long before I will, so it won't be a problem. In any case, I have my key. Bye, Claire."

Claire watched him saunter from the shop and felt like shaking some sense into her brother's insensitive head. She felt like crying because she would have to cancel her date with Gray. Telling Lorraine she had to make a phone call, she went into the back and dialed.

"Gray, I'm sorry, but Derek is in town. I have to cancel."

"What's he done?' Gray asked sharply.

"Nothing," Claire said, then saw no way to put it delicately. "You two don't like each other and he's staying with me."

"Knowing Derek, he won't be there for long."

She took a seat. "Gray, please."

"Do you want to see me?"

"Of course I do."

"Then I'll see you at eight as planned."

She dropped her forehead into her hand. "He won't like it."

"All I care about is what you like. Goodbye."

Hanging up the phone, Claire returned to the shop. She wasn't looking forward to her brother and Gray meeting.

W hat is he doing here?" Derek asked the instant he walked into the house that evening and saw Gray sitting on the sofa.

Claire took a deep breath and closed the front door. "Gray and I have a date."

"Date? The daughter of the hired help going out with old man's Livingston's grandson?" Derek sneered. "The only place he'd want to take you is to bed."

Gray came off the couch in one controlled motion. Rage filled his eyes.

Embarrassed for herself and angry at her brother, Claire stepped in front of Gray and braced her hand against his chest. "Please."

A muscle leaped in Gray's jaw as he stared at Derek, then he brought his attention back to her. "Let's get out of here."

"She ain't going nowhere with you," Derek said. "I noticed the way you used to look at her, but you never asked her out until she stood to make money for your company. You're not using my sister."

"You're the one doing that," Gray said tightly.

Derek bristled. "How many society things has he taken you to, Claire? You certainly don't look like you're ready to go to any ball." Her gaze flickered down to her khakis and cotton blouse, then away.

"Thought so. Leave, Livingston, and don't bother my sister again."

Gray kept his attention on Claire. "Claire, you don't believe him, do you?"

"She's got your number now." Derek went to the door and opened it. "Take your lying self someplace else."

"Do you believe him?" Gray asked, unmoved.

Claire finally lifted her head. "No."

The back of his knuckles brushed across her cheeks. "That's my girl."

"The door is waiting for you, Livingston," Derek told him.

"I'll be back," Gray told her.

Derek slammed the door after Gray, then stalked over to his sister. "What's the matter with you? I know you always watched him with those big eyes, but didn't I tell you that all he wanted was some action between the sheets."

Claire winced at his crudity. "I don't want to discuss it, Derek."

He threw up his hands in the air. "All right. Just don't come crying to me when it's all over. At least you're too old to get pregnant."

She whirled on him and he stepped back.

"Your friend is waiting on you," she told him.

He licked his lips. "Yeah, yeah. You'll thank me one day." He hurried out the door.

Wrapping her arms around herself Claire sank onto the sofa in the family room. Derek's last taunt had gone straight to her heart. She'd always wanted a husband, children. She just realized how much she wanted Gray to be that man and the father of her child.

Derek was right about one thing. Gray would never stay and when he left she'd lose twice: him and any hope of her dream for a family coming true.

The doorbell rang and she pushed herself up. Derek must have forgotten something. She'd let him in then go to her room. She didn't want to see or talk to him now.

"Gray," she said in surprise.

"I didn't think he'd stay long." He closed the door and put his hands on her shoulders. "I have a confession to make."

"All right," her voice trembled. She'd never seen him look so serious.

"I didn't ask you to go to places at first because I selfishly enjoyed being alone with you. But if you want to go out, I'll have my secretary fax you the list of invitations I've received for the next month and you can pick out which ones you want to go to. Or we can go wherever you want."

The vise around her heart eased. "Bliss is running smoothly. Perhaps a couple of dinner dates out might be fun."

"Is tomorrow night too soon to have dinner at the Peninsula Grill or would you rather wait until later in the week?"

The five-star restaurant was ultra chic, expensive, and served exquisitely prepared low country dishes. She'd need a dress, shoes, a trip to the salon for her hair and nails to be done. "Perhaps later in the week. Maybe Saturday."

"It's a date. Come on, let's go for a walk on the beach, then we can come back here and eat popcorn and find a sad movie on TV so you can cry on my shoulder and I can comfort you."

Her arms circled his neck. "You're an amazing man."

"You make it ridiculously easy." His lips sought hers.

CHAPTER THIRTY

e was gone.

When Claire came home from church early Sunday afternoon the house was empty. Derek had left his bed unmade, his breakfast dishes were on the table. A note was propped on the yellow salt shaker.

"See you. Don't forget what I told you. Derek."

Claire's fingers clenched, then loosened. She gave the note as much consideration as she thought it due. She tossed it in the trash, then cleaned up the kitchen. Derek hadn't changed. He was still jealous of Gray, of anyone who had the financial success he craved but hadn't achieved. He couldn't see that Gray worked hard for his success, while Derek worked hard at playing.

Loading the dishwasher, she finally admitted to herself that Gray might be right in his opinion of her brother. Perhaps she had helped him to remain weak instead of becoming strong. But it was difficult to turn her back on him. She'd like to think he'd get it, that one day he'd be the self-sufficient man she could be proud of, instead of tensing every time when the phone rang thinking it might be Derek wanting money.

Finishing up in the kitchen, she went to the bedroom to change, her thoughts shifting to Gray. He was taking her out on his yacht. A smile touched her lips as she remembered them snuggled up on the sofa last night. He'd been so tender and gentle with her. She wasn't going to let Derek's warning or anything else keep them apart. This time she was grabbing what she wanted with both hands and holding it for as long as heavenly possible.

She quickly changed out of her suit into a pair of white clam diggers and a blue and white striped tee. Gray cared about her. He wasn't using her. The real threat to them came from his past. Jana.

Sitting on the bed, Claire pulled on her blue canvas sneakers and tied them. Jana had done a number on Gray and, whether he admitted it or not, her betrayal made him distrust women. He was making progress, but he had a long way to go before he allowed himself to be vulnerable again and love a woman.

She had to believe that one day he would, that he'd want her and a family. In the meantime, she'd cherish each moment with him. Saturday night she planned to look her best and continue to show him that she'd be there a lifetime if he let her. For Gray she even planned to wear heels.

The doorbell rang and she hurried out of her room. As soon as she opened the front door, Gray pulled her into his arms and his mouth came down on hers. She let herself tumble mindlessly into the passionate kiss. Whatever happened she'd always know what it felt like to be cherished and desired by the man she loved.

Brooke was in her element. Shopping. With controlled precision she went through the racks in the stores Monday night after Bliss closed. She hit pay dirt in the fourth shop. "This is it. Simple, yet elegant and sensual. Plus it's on sale."

Claire's eyes rounded as Brooke turned the dress around. The short black, three-quarter sleeve wrap dress had the back cut out in an alluring V. "You don't think it's a bit much?"

"No." Brooke held the dress up to Claire. "You've got great legs and it's time you showed them and some skin. Think of it as advertising for Bliss."

"I don't know," Claire mused, trying to visualize how far down the cut of the dress would hit in the back.

"Trust me. If Lorraine hadn't had to make the deposit, she'd be here and she'd tell you the same thing." Brooke took matters into her own hands and steered Claire into the oversized dressing room. "Just try the dress on."

Claire unbuttoned her blouse. "You're going to look for something?"

"No." At the surprise on Claire's face, Brooke smiled. "I don't need couture for family restaurants and the movies."

Pulling off her black knit top, Claire paused, then removed her black cotton bra. The way the dress was cut there was no way around it. "You miss it?"

"I thought I would, that there was nothing like shopping, but now I'd much rather spend the time with John and the children." Taking the dress off the hanger, she handed it to Claire. Once it was on, she pulled up the tab of the five inch zipper in the back. "Wow! When Gray sees you in that dress he may decide to stay in and dine on you."

"I think I'd rather stay in and let him," Claire said. She turned and gasped when she saw herself in the mirror. She had shapely legs, rounded curves and full breasts. Hands outstretched, she twisted first one way then the other. She looked totally different. "I can't believe that's me."

Brooke laughed. "Believe it. Gray's going to love you in it."

Claire's smile only slipped for a second. "If only he would."

Brooke touched her arm lightly. Their eyes met in the mirror. "Gray is a smart man. He won't let you get away. And in that dress you'll certainly give him a lot to think about."

"But will it be enough?" Claire whispered. This time there was no answer from Brooke.

You need your eyes examined!" Brooke yelled at the umpire Saturday evening as he called strike one on John. "The ball was wide!"

"The ball was wide!" Mark yelled.

"The ball was wide!" Amy repeated.

John's father, and family members and fans of The Hawks, John's softball team, grumbled their displeasure as well. They were down by one run at the bottom of the ninth with two out and two men on base. John was their last chance.

Brooke cupped her hands. "Knock it out of the park, John!"

Her "team" chorused her sentiment and so did those sitting around them. She'd arrived at the game in the bottom of the fifth inning. Amy and Mark had immediately beckoned her to sit between them in the space they'd saved. Of course Mr. Randle hadn't been able to keep quiet about her being late.

"About time you showed up. My boy is gonna have a stiff neck with as many times as he'd looked up here."

Despite the warmth his words caused, she winked. "It's good for him to wonder."

John swung and missed. "Strike two!" yelled the umpire.

The other team cheered. John's team groaned. His head down, he walked out of the box.

Brooke remained on her feet and yelled, "You can do it, John." He looked up at her. "Hit the ball and win this game!" she ordered, her hands on her hips.

The bill of his cap shadowed his face so she couldn't tell if he smiled or grimaced just before he walked back into the box.

"John's their best hitter. The last game they played he was working and they lost," Mr. Randle said quietly. "This game means a lot to him."

"I know," Brooke said. She'd come as fast as she could. She reached for Mark and Amy's hands. The pitcher eyed John, rubbed the ball in his glove, then brought his left arm up and sent the ball over a hundred miles per hour straight over the plate. John swung. The crack of the bat on the wood sent the stadium to its feet.

John watched the ball arc high and keep going over the twelve-foot back wall. He glanced back at Brooke, casually tossed his bat to the ground and started a slow run around the bases.

"Arrogant," she said between screams, grinning for all she was worth.

The celebration moved from the softball field to a family pizza parlor with John as the man-of-the-hour. His back was sore from all the slaps he'd received from people, and his neck was getting sore from trying to keep up with his children and Brooke. He'd admitted ruefully as she and her "team" played in the arcade that his children weren't the problem. Brooke was. Two or three men in the place had tried to pick her up. All of them had left with a wistful smile on their face.

"Just like I heard, she's off the scale," Sam said with a deep sigh. "And she doesn't know any man in this room exists besides you. Man, what wouldn't I give to trade places with you for just one hour?"

"Not if you want to see tomorrow."

Sam's head whipped around. He stared at John. "Man, I've never known you to be so touchy about a woman."

"I've never known a woman like Brooke."

Casually John eased through the small crowd—mostly men—standing around watching Brooke play pinball on the old-fashioned arcade game. He couldn't blame them. She played with her entire body, her hips moving this way, then that. He was glad he'd taken his shirt out of his tight pants so he wouldn't embarrass himself or her. He wanted her, and thanks to his parents agreeing to let Mark and Amy spend the night, he didn't have to rush home. They'd have all night to make love. But first they were going out on the town.

He'd never been possessive or jealous, but he couldn't resist slipping his arm around her waist. "Ready to leave?"

"No, Dad. Brooke's almost got the record beat," Mark protested from beside her.

"She gets points and prizes and she said we could pick out anything we wanted," Amy, his little mercenary, chimed in from the other side.

John looked at Brooke, read her dilemma in the quick look she threw over her shoulder at him before she resumed playing. She was torn between him and his children. He stepped back to give her room. "Then win the game."

Brooke won the game.

The middle-aged manager with a receding hair line and a big stomach from eating too many of his own products took one look at Brooke and insisted they take a picture together to commemorate the occasion. She insisted just as strongly that Amy and Mark be in the photo as well.

"What about the prizes?" Amy wanted to know as soon as the flash-bulb went off. The people around them laughed.

John shook his head and picked her up. "We're going to have to have a talk about your avariciousness."

Amy frowned. "Since it's a big word, does it mean I'm not going to get prizes?"

"It means you're greedy and you should wait until Brooke offers," Mark told her.

Her big eyes widened. "But she already did. Didn't you, Brooke?"

Brooke's mouth twitched. "Yes, I did. You have half the ten thousand points and your father can help you pick out what you want. I'll go with Mark."

John was already shaking his head. "She gets one prize and that's all. We'll meet back here in five minutes."

Reading the heated look in John's face, Brooke flushed. She was almost at her limits as well. She'd never wanted a man as much before. Just a look and she was hot.

"You going to try out for the Y's year-round softball team next week?" she heard a boy ask Mark.

"No. Daddy wouldn't have time to take me."

Brooke came out of her lustful musings to see Mark talking to another young boy about his age, and frowned. Mark had to know his father would move heaven and earth for his children.

"Maybe your grandparents could bring you?" the boy continued.

Mark shook his head. "They always go to church on Wednesday night. Besides, practice starts at six and Daddy makes a special effort to be home to eat dinner with us and put us to bed. It's important to him. Softball practice would throw off the schedule. The calendar is already full with things for him to do for us. I'm in Cub Scouts. He works hard and I don't want him to have to do more."

"Bummer. Wish you could play," the little boy said. "See you at school Monday. Your dad sure can hit the ball."

"Thanks. He's the best."

Brooke's heart went out to Mark, trying to make life easier for his father even if it meant not having things he wanted. "Mark."

He looked up from staring at the floor. The smile came, but it was slow. He walked over to her. "You ready to go pick out your prizes?" he asked.

Even now, he didn't put himself first. She wanted to hug him, but was afraid it might embarrass him. "No, I'm ready to go with you to pick out your prizes. Consider it a math lesson."

The smile grew. "Really?"

"Really, and I'll take care of your father so he'll let you keep them. We're friends and teammates, aren't we?" She held out her hand.

"Thanks, Brooke." He took her hand, took a couple of steps, then stopped and beckoned her to lean down. When she did he whispered. "I'm glad you're my friend."

She blinked away the tears. "Me, too."

Mark wants to play year-round softball, but he thinks you work too hard to have anything added to your schedule."

"What are you talking about?" John asked. Moments after he'd come back from putting the children down for the night, she'd dragged him into the backyard. "Mark would have told me if that was true."

"I overheard him talking to his friend tonight," she said, then went on to tell him about the conversation. "He loves you so much, John. He's trying to be the perfect son, to not bother you or make life more difficult."

John stared at her for a long moment, then blew out a breath. "Thank you." Brushing by her, he went into his old bedroom where Mark and Amy always slept. Amy slept soundly with her arm wrapped around Mr. Bear. Mark was playing with the Spider-Man stuffed toy he'd chosen as one of his prizes. The instant he saw his father, he was up and putting the toy away.

"Sorry, Dad. I'll get right back in bed." He climbed into the twin bed and got under the covers.

John swallowed. He'd known that Mark was too serious, but he hadn't tried to talk to him about it. Filled with remorse, he sat on the side of the bed.

"You know I love you, don't you, Mark?"

"Yes, Daddy," he said, staring up at his father. "Thanks for letting me keep the toys Brooke helped me pick out. I'll share with Amy."

Always so polite. "You never ask for much. Why is that, Mark?"

Mark's gaze flickered away. "I don't know."

John was afraid he did, and the knowledge went straight to his heart. "Look at me, son."

Mark's head turned. "Yes, sir."

"All I am, all I ever hope to be means nothing if you aren't happy. I don't mind the hard work, the long hours. What I would mind was if there was something you wanted and you couldn't talk to me about it. Is there something you want that you haven't told me about?"

Mark's squirmed in bed. "Maybe."

John waited patiently, but Mark didn't say anything else. "Maybe to play softball?"

His son's eyes lit up, then dimmed. "There's no time in the schedule."

"We'll make time," John promised. "What position do you want to play?"

"I really can?" Mark sat up in bed.

"I'll never break a promise."

"I want to pitch," he said, coming out from under the covers to kneel in front of his father. "I'd send the ball so fast they couldn't see it."

John chuckled. "Tomorrow after church you can practice on me. When are try outs?"

Mark's smile faded. "Wednesday at five-thirty at the Y."

"I'll take you. Your grandfather will probably want to go, too."

"But that's prayer night, and we eat at six." Mark said.

John stared at his son in surprise. Had he become so rigid? "This is important. Dinner can be late. We can grab a bite afterwards, and your grandfather wouldn't mind being late, too, if it means seeing his only grandson try out for the softball team."

"Wow? Can I go ask him? Maybe Brooke can come, too?"

"Sure." He might have known Brooke's name would pop up.

Mark scrambled out of bed and ran into the den where his grandparents and Brooke were watching a sitcom. "Daddy said I could try out for year-round softball. Granddad, he said you might want to come, but it's Wednesday night at five-thirty at the Y."

"I'll be there," his grandfather told him from his easy chair.

Mark's attention switched to Brooke. "Maybe you can come, too."

She didn't hesitate. "I wouldn't miss it."

"I think I'll be there, too," his grandmother said from beside Brooke on the sofa.

Still smiling, Mark looked back over his shoulder at his father who had come up and placed his hand on his shoulder. "Daddy is going to let me practice my pitching tomorrow after church."

"Why wait? If your grandfather has a softball, John can get his bat and glove from his truck." Brooke stood. "The back is well lit and I can be the catcher."

His eyes as round as saucers, Mark's gaze flicked from Brooke to his father. "Can we?"

"Not in your pajamas."

He raced out of the room to change.

John stared across the room at Brooke and saw their plans for a cozy dinner and dancing fade away. He didn't regret it, but he wasn't sure how she felt. This was the first time they would have gone to a really nice restaurant. Afterwards they were going dancing. He had planned it all week. Mark had happily put it on the calendar. "They're not going to hold our table."

Brooke gave him a look. "If you think I'd miss Mark striking you out, you're crazy."

Carrying his tennis shoes, Mark raced back into the room, his shirt unbuttoned and went straight to Brooke. "You really are going to catch?"

She began buttoning his shirt. "We're friends and teammates. Your father won't have a chance against us."

Grinning, Mark sat down on the sofa to put on his tennis shoes.

"Don't just stand there. Go get the things out of the truck," Brooke ordered.

Shaking his head, John went to his truck. Brooke didn't seem to mind that she wasn't going to the fancy restaurants and parties she once had.

But for how long? That bothered him almost as much as the guys coming on to her all the time. He'd never had to constantly be on guard for a woman's attention. He didn't like it, but he'd like it less if Brooke wasn't in his life. Opening the truck's cab, he took out his bat and glove and headed back into the house.

CHAPTER THIRTY-ONE

Gray simply stared. "You're beautiful."

Gray had called her beautiful before, but he'd never sounded as if the words were a reverent vow. She closed the front door with an unsteady hand. "Thank you. I'll get my purse."

He gasped when he saw the back of the dress. She turned back to him, biting her lower lip.

"You look exquisite. And I wish I could take that dress off you and take you to bed."

A smile broke over Claire's face as she came to him. "We can stay home if you want."

"We're going out. I want to show people what a desirable woman I'm fortunate enough to be dating." He kissed her on the forehead. "Go get your bag."

Smiling, she started toward the family room, her steps slow and deliberate. His gaze traveled to her feet in the sexy high heels. He looked up and their eyes met.

She flushed. "I've practiced every day."

He went to her and placed his hands on her waist. "And I don't suppose the dress would look right with anything but four-inch heels."

"I'm afraid not. As long as I go slowly, I'm all right."

"Then slow it is and I'll be right beside you all the way, just where I planned to be."

"You don't think I'm vain or silly?"

"No," he answered softly. "I think you're the most loving and giving person I know. I think the world is better because you're in it. I think I'm a lucky man."

Tears crested in her eyes. "No one has ever said anything so beautiful to me. You touch me in ways I didn't know possible. I've never been happier."

Gathering her hands in his, he kissed them. "I'm glad. Now, let's go show you off."

The Peninsula Grill was elegant, posh and romantic. They'd entered through a gas-lit, tree-enshrouded courtyard. The maitre'd greeted Gray by name, then immediately showed them to their intimate table by a window. Antique landscapes hung from velvet-upholstered walls, and chandeliers cast a rosy glow. Claire didn't breathe easier until Gray had personally seated her. She smiled her thanks across the white-linen-draped table. He hadn't let her go until the last possible second. Handing them their menu, the maitre'd withdrew.

Claire's eyes widened at the prices. "There's definitely a difference between living and living well."

Gray chuckled. "Tonight let's go for living well. What tickles your fancy?"

She chose Chilean Sea Bass. She glanced around as Gray gave the waiter their order, then selected their wine from the steward. She couldn't help but notice two women who were following the maitre'd abruptly stop when they saw them, and begin whispering.

"What's the matter?"

Her gaze went back to Gray. He always read her so well. "Two women were staring at us, but they're gone now."

"Probably trying to figure out if they'd look as great as you do in that dress. The answer would be no," he said. The wine steward appeared and showed Gray the label. At Gray's nod, he poured. Gray picked up his glass. "To a wonderful evening."

Claire picked up her glass and thrust the women out of her mind. "A wonderful evening."

And it was. Gray was a charming and attentive, the food wonderful, and the service impeccable. Claire thoroughly enjoyed herself.

"You want dessert?" Gray asked, setting his coffee cup down. "Their coconut cake is six layers perched atop a swirl of crème anglaise."

Claire smiled. "Not if I don't want to pop out of this dress. This was wonderful, Gray."

A shadow crossed his face. "I'm sorry we haven't gone—"

"Please, don't say anymore." She reached across the table and this time his hand captured hers. "We needed the time with just the two of us. Now, on order from Brooke, I need to go scope out the ladies room to see if they have hand cream."

"And if they don't?"

She grinned across at him. "Send management a few jars of our products and see if we can't get him or her to stock them."

"Spoken like a true entrepreneur." Getting up, Gray went to her chair.

Rising, she touched him lightly on the shoulder when his arm curved around her waist. "I can handle it, but if you hear a crash come running."

He kissed her lips. "Always.".

Warmth coursing through Claire, she started toward the bathroom. Either she was finally getting used to the high heels or the wine was mellowing her, but she didn't feel shaky anymore.

Pushing open the door she stepped into luxury: Chinese paintings in heavy gold frames, lush padded benches, gold faucets and silk-covered walls in the palest shade of blue. In between each of the five round sinks was an arrangement of birds-of-paradise in cylindrical crystal vases. Cloth towels rested neatly in square sweetgrass baskets with a larger basket underneath for the used towels.

But there was no lotion. Deciding to test the soap, Claire pumped a couple of squirts into her hand, then rubbed it with her fingertips. The white liquid didn't feel as luxurious as hers. Sticking her hand beneath the automatic faucet, she washed and dried her hands. Whatever they were using was good, but theirs was better. Brooke and Lorraine would be delighted. She turned to leave just as the door opened and the two women she had seen earlier came in.

Both wore expensive dresses and jewelry that glittered and sparkled at their throats, wrists and their ears. From the way their gaze went directly to her, Claire suspected they had followed her. Deciding to test her theory, she turned back to the mirror and checked her lipstick. In the mirror Claire saw them move further into the restroom, whispering, their eyes on her.

Claire faced them. "Is there something I can help you with?"

The two appeared startled that she had spoken to them. "You were whispering and staring earlier and now you followed me in here. Why?"

"You won't be able to keep him," one of the women blurted. Lines radiated from her narrowed eyes.

Despite the chill that went through Claire, she casually folded her arms. "Could you be more specific?"

The woman who had spoken jutted her pointed chin. "Gray. Jana wants him back, and she always gets what she wants."

Claire didn't even blink. "Not a chance in hell."

The women's eyes widened at the venom in Claire's voice. Jana wouldn't get a chance to hurt Gray again.

"And if Jana's your friend you must be hard up for a friend, and between men."

They flushed and Claire knew she had guessed correctly. "Now, if you'll excuse me, Gray doesn't like me to be away from him too long and neither do I."

The two moved aside. Head high, breasts thrust forward, Claire left the bathroom and went to the table.

Gray rose when he saw her. The smile on his face disappeared when his gaze went beyond her. He quickly went to her. He glanced at the two women as they hurried past them.

"Are you all right?"

Claire smoothed the frown from his face. "I'm always better in your arms."

His arm curved around her waist, they stopped to get her purse then went outside. He handed the valet his ticket and pulled her aside.

"What happened? Kathy and Shiloh are friends of Jana's. They haven't caught on yet that she keeps them around because they're less attractive and insecure. They stay because men gravitate to her and neither has been able to keep a man."

Claire's arms twined around his neck. "I'm not going to let them ruin our evening."

"What happened?" he asked, his voice curt.

She saw no way around making him even angrier. "One of them said Jana wanted you back and she always gets what she wants."

Gray swore softly.

"I told her there wasn't a chance in hell."

Gray's hands tenderly palmed her face. "You're incredible."

"You are pretty incredible yourself." Her hands covered his. "Now, please take me home. These shoes are killing me."

"Shall I carry you?"

"Why don't we wait until we get to my place?"

He quickly led her to his waiting Porsche. As they drove off, several people watched them. One of the women from the restroom pulled her cell phone out of her Prada bag. "Jana, I think you better plan on coming down to Charleston sooner than you planned."

John had heard The Loft was the hottest club in the city. It certainly had to be the most crowded. Seeing the line wrapped around the building, he thought his plans to go dancing wouldn't pan out either. They'd had hot dogs for dinner in honor of Mark trying out for the soft-ball team.

"Maybe it will move fast," he said, although he didn't hold out much hope. It had been close to nine-thirty when they'd left his parents' house. Mark was excited because he had struck his father out. John had to admit it wasn't too difficult to fake it. By the time he'd gone home to shower and change, then drop by Brooke's place to pick her up, it was a little after ten-thirty.

"Yancy is on the door; he'll let us in."

John's head whipped around, but the valet was already opening Brooke's door. As usual, when Brooke was within five feet of a male, they fell all over themselves to please her. She greeted the teenager by name.

"How do you know everyone?" John asked more abruptly than he meant.

Her eyebrow arched. "I'm the commercial rep for Bliss and this is one of our first clients. In fact, I got the idea from The Loft." Her head twisted to one side. "You still want to go in? I know several people inside, too."

"Men, you mean."

Brooke's eyes glittered. "Yes. Is that a problem?"

It was, but John didn't think it wise to point it out. "Let's go inside."

As she'd promised, she had no trouble getting them in. Loud music and cigarette haze greeted them. It was Brooke who snagged them a table when another couple got up to leave. Against overwhelming odds, she got the attention of a passing waitress who took their drink orders.

John simply stared at her. She seemed to go through life effortlessly. She made things happen and attracted men like a homing device.

"You want to dance?" asked a young man with a diamond earring and twenty pounds of gold chains hanging around his neck.

"Perhaps later," Brooke said. The man left and she glanced around the crowded club, trying to recall what had attracted her to such places in the past.

"Why didn't you just tell him no?"

She looked at John, his shoulders stiff beneath his sports coat, his jaw tight. "It never hurts to be nice. What is the matter with you? It was your idea to come here."

He shoved his hands impatiently over his hair. "I thought you'd enjoy going out."

"You want to dance?" another man asked Brooke.

"No, she doesn't," John snapped.

The man abruptly straightened and walked away.

Brooke stared across the table at John. Her natural instinct was to snap, but something about the droop of his shoulders, his troubled expression, wouldn't let her. "Do you want to talk about what's upsetting you?"

John's mouth pursed.

"When the waitress gets back, we can leave." She glanced around the crowded, smoke-filled room again. "Frankly, I recall enjoying this better."

"Would you be having a better time if you weren't with me?"

Brooke's head snapped back around. She was stunned for all of two seconds. "What a stupid thing to say. If I wanted to be with someone else, I wouldn't be sitting here with you."

"You can't go two feet without some guy coming on to you," John grumbled.

"Have you looked around to see how many women are sizing you up?"

Surprise flickered across his face. "They're not."

Her mouth tightened. "There are two at the far corner of the bar and the Hoochie Mama in the red dress a couple of tables back for a start."

John didn't look at them; he looked at Brooke. She was steamed. The night took a sudden turn for the better. "You're jealous."

She stuck up her nose. "You wish."

He scooted his chair next to hers, then curved his arm around her stiff shoulders. "I'll admit I am if you'll admit you are."

She snuggled closer. "Maybe just a little."

"Try a lot." His hand threaded through her hair. "I think I'd throw a bag on your head if I could."

She might have laughed at the idea if she hadn't sensed he was half serious. Sitting up, she gazed at him. "This won't work if you can't trust me. I can't change the way I look or avoid men. I wouldn't if I could. Some of my best friends are men."

"Here are your drinks." The waitress sat the drinks on the table.

John leaned over to pull his wallet from the hip pocket of his slacks when the first man who has asked Brooke to dance returned. "How about that dance now?"

"Sure," she said and placed her hand in the man's. Grinning, the man popped his fingers and sashayed all the way to the crowded dance floor. Brooke winked at John over her shoulder.

"Would you like to dance?"

John looked around to see a slim young woman half-wearing a red dress. So much skin was showing he almost felt the urge to offer his coat. "Someone might get the table if I leave, too."

"Sure." Shrugging, she melted into the crowd.

Picking up his draft beer, John leaned back into the chair. So Brooke had been right. He hadn't paid any attention to other women because he only saw Brooke. Sam's words came back to him and he realized that it was the same way for her. He sipped his drink and leaned back in the chair. He didn't have to worry about some guy beating his time. If she didn't want to be with him, she wouldn't be.

The bottle was near his mouth again when he saw Brooke push her way through the crowd. Her eyes were narrowed and she was no longer smiling. John had seen that look before. "Should I expect the police?" he asked when she reached their table.

"No, but I bet it will be a long time before he tries to grope another woman."

The bottle of beer hit the table with a thud. John came to his feet. Brooke caught the tail of his jacket and tugged until he sat back down next to her, then whispered in his ear. "Would you rather spend the night in jail or putting a smile on my face?"

He was torn. "That's not fair."

She blew into his ear and smiled when he shuddered. "You ever see hand-painted lingerie, John?"

He was out of his chair in an instant. His eyes blazed. "Let's go.

Laughing, she allowed him to pull her from the club.

CHAPTER THIRTY-TWO

Half-asleep, Claire's head pillowed on his chest, her leg thrown over his, Gray groped for the ringing phone. "Hello," he said, his eyes remaining closed as he absently stroked her back. Her skin was so soft, he'd never tire of touching her.

"You bastard! What the hell are you doing there?" Derek asked.

Gray tensed and came fully awake. Claire's head came up and she stared at him.

"I guess I know the answer at eight in the morning," Derek snapped. "Let me speak to my sister. Now!"

Claire stiffened against Gray. Sitting up, she clutched the sheet to her naked breasts. Gray would have given anything to take away the stricken look on her face. "I'm sorry. I answered it on instinct."

Nodding, she swept her hair back from her face and took the phone he extended. "Yes, Derek?"

"You didn't listen, did you? I might not have known if Red hadn't called me this morning to tell me you were with Livingston last night."

Her gaze flickered to Gray who watched her closely. "Red?"

"Your waiter!" Derek snapped. "You probably didn't notice him since you were with Livingston. How could you be so gullible?"

From the sudden narrowing of Gray's eyes, he'd heard her brother. "My life is my own. I've never interfered in what you do."

"That's because no woman is going to use me like Gray is using you."

She flinched. Her grip on the phone tightened. "I'm going to hang up the phone if you persist in attacking me and Gray."

"You'd pick him over me? Over your brother?"

"I'm not making that decision; you are." Her hand raked through her hair again causing the sheet to slip. She quickly grabbed it.

"I can't believe you'd turn your back on me. That hurts, Claire. Hurts bad."

"Der—"

The line went dead.

Closing her eyes, she clutched the phone.

Gently Gray removed the phone from her hand and pulled her into his arms. "If he wasn't your brother . . ."

His voice trailed off, but from the tone Claire didn't need him to finish. "He means well."

"If we don't want to argue I won't comment on that. Instead, why don't I cook us breakfast?" He wanted to take the shattered look from her face.

Her eyes rounded with pleasure. "You can cook?"

"Yes, and I'll show you . . . in about thirty minutes or so."

He drew her down into the bed, kissed her gently, then began to build the passion, the need that, no matter how many times sated, would come again. Claire was with him and nothing or no one was going to change that or hurt her.

Claire and Gray returned from a walk on the beach to a ringing phone. Her hand flexed in his.

"Let it ring," he said. His mouth, which had been smiling moments ago, settled into a tight, disapproving line.

"It's all right," Claire said. She went to the phone on the end table by the sofa. "Derek has to learn that my life is my own." She picked up the phone dreading the confrontation. "Hello."

"Claire, I'm sorry if this is a bad time to call," Gray's grandmother said.

Claire's head whipped around to Gray. "No, Mrs. Livingston. It's fine. I just wasn't expecting it to be you."

The frown on Gray's face changed to one of puzzlement. He crossed the room to stand beside Claire.

"It's a shame the way solicitors bother people even on Sunday," she commented.

"Yes, ma'am?" Claire said and moistened her lips. She almost felt embarrassed by the call. There wasn't a doubt in her mind that his grandmother knew they were sleeping together.

"But I didn't call to talk about those worrisome solicitors; I called to invite you to the Business Professionals of Charleston's monthly luncheon a week from Wednesday. I hope you don't have other plans. A lot of important people will be there and it pays to have contacts," she said. "You need a sponsor to attend and join, and I'd be so very pleased if you'd let me have that honor."

Claire couldn't believe it. "Mrs. Livingston, I don't know what to say. I'm the one that's honored. I've admired you for so very long."

"What is it?" Gray asked.

Claire put her hand over the receiver. "She's invited me to the Business Professionals of Charleston's luncheon next Wednesday. She wants to sponsor me."

Instead of the pleased smile she expected, he frowned. "I can sponsor you. You're my protégée."

Claire was loathe to point out that he was also her lover.

"Claire, is there a problem?" Mrs. Livingston asked.

She removed her hand from the mouthpiece. "Gray wants to sponsor me."

"I'm sure he does, but please remind Gray that he hasn't attended one of the meetings in months, plus you'll need the support of the women and men in the organization. Since some of those women might have a history with Gray or simply wanted one, they might not warm up to his protégée whereas they have no reason to be less than friendly if I sponsor you. And if they are, I shall take care of them as well they know," Mrs. Livingston said, her soft voice overlaid with steel.

"I trust your instincts and gratefully accept your sponsorship."

"I like a woman who can make up her own mind," Mrs. Livingston said, warmth in her voice.

"Thank you," Claire said, ignoring the frown Gray was giving her. She listened as Mrs. Livingston gave her the time and place. "I'll be there and thank you again."

"Why can't I sponsor you?" Gray wanted to know the instant she hung up the phone.

Claire's arms circled his neck. "In a nutshell, because we're lovers and some women are bad losers." She almost laughed at the shocked expression on his face. "But in this case I can't blame them. I'd be upset if you got away." She'd meant it as a joke, but the sudden tensing of Gray's body against hers said it was anything but. Her mind scrambled for something else to say, but nothing came to mind.

"Claire, I—"

She pressed her fingers against his lips. "No promises. No regrets."

He caught her hand and clutched her to him. "I keep telling myself that I won't let anything hurt you, yet I stay knowing one day I will hurt you most of all. You should hate me."

How can I when I love you? she thought, knowing she could never say those words aloud. Nor could she tell him she had begun falling in love with him when she was eleven and he was a shy, sensitive boy. "I can't ask you for more than you can give."

Gray's head lifted. Anger shone in his eyes. "You should. If any other man treated you this way I'd take him apart."

"You mean you wouldn't want a man to help me to be the best that I can be? A man to respect me? A man to make me laugh? A man to cherish my body and nurture my spirit?"

He stilled as her words sank deeply into him.

"You give so much to me. Yes, letting go and saying goodbye will be difficult, but never having been loved by you would be the real tragedy."

"I wish . . ." His voice trailed off. Shutting his eyes, he drew her tightly to him.

Claire didn't ask him what he wished for. The desperation of his arms was enough. One day he'd be gone and there was nothing she could do to keep him.

Monday morning Claire arrived at Bliss a little after nine with a smile on her face and Gray on her mind. He had spent the night again. After eating a leisurely breakfast on the deck, he had helped her clean up the kitchen, then followed her into the city before he passed her on East Bay to continue on home to change. He'd casually mentioned he'd call her after work to see if she was too tired for him to come by. That, she told him, would never happen. He had appeared relieved.

She could have wept for both of them.

Entering the shop, she relocked the door and went into the back to put the coffee on. No matter what he said, Jana's betrayal continued to dictate how he felt about lasting relationships. Claire would just have to show him how good it could be with them and let his heart do the rest.

He cared about her. She felt it in the way he touched her, the way he looked at her. She just prayed he'd soon realize it, too.

Taking the carafe, Claire began filling it. Brooke had long since stopped insisting it be bottled water, or that they do espresso. Claire set the carafe on the stand and wondered if Brooke realized how much she had changed. Shopping and looking for a rich husband no longer were the focus of her life. As far as Claire knew Brooke hadn't gone shopping in weeks. She didn't have time. If she wasn't at the shop, she was with John or his children. And apparently enjoying herself tremendously. Now, if only Lorraine could be happy.

Putting away her purse, Claire got the sweeper for the hardwood floors out of the closet. She never would have thought Hamilton would act the way he did. If ever there was a man who loved a woman, it was Hamilton. Going into the shop, Claire began running the sweeper over the floor. Unfortunately caring for another person didn't guarantee a happily ever after.

It was a life lesson she could have lived without experiencing.

They didn't get many men in the shop, but when they did, they usually stopped a few feet inside, looked around and if they saw too many women, headed back out the door. Since the shop was fairly crowded with lunch shoppers, all women, Claire expected the man in a tailored suit, with a well-worn attaché case in his hand, that had just entered to do the same.

Claire started around the counter to try and reassure him. Brooke who'd just finished with a customer reached him first. "Welcome to Bliss. I'd be delighted to help you or answer any questions you might have."

He gave her a friendly smile. "Thank you, but I'd just like to look around if that's all right?"

"Of course," Brooke said. "There are shopping baskets available if you'd like."

"I'll keep that in mind." He went to the display of BTS products, picked up the sample jar of moisturizing cream and sniffed. Moments later, he moved to another display, this one of the orange-pear products.

Brooke went to stand beside Claire at the counter. She waited until she had rung up the sale. "He looks like he knows what he's doing."

"Same thing I thought. Whoever he's shopping for is very lucky," Claire said.

The shop's door opened and a couple came in. The man had the same long-suffering look she'd seen countless times before in the six weeks the shop had been opened. "I'll take this one," Claire remarked.

"All right," Brooke said. "It will be kind of interesting to see what he buys."

He purchased nothing. The man had wandered leisurely around the shop for forty minutes, often talking with customers or asking them a question about a particular product. They couldn't decide if they should be concerned or not. Men, as a rule, hated shopping and usually were much more decisive and faster.

"You think we should call someone?" Lorraine asked as she helped Claire restock the shelves.

"I don't think so." Claire placed the last candle on the glass shelf, then stood.

Lorraine came to her feet as well. "Brooke says she can take him, but . . . he's coming this way. Empty-handed."

"And only a few customers are left," Claire said, her hand unconsciously closing on the candle she'd just shelved.

"Ladies," he said in greeting. "You have quite a business here."

"Thank you," Brooke said, moving to his left. "Is there something we can help you with?"

"As a matter of fact, I think we can be of mutual benefit." He reached into the inside pocket of his suit. Claire and Lorraine tensed. Brooke shifted her weight to one foot, and lifted her hands to her waist. He pulled out a business card and handed it to Claire. "My name is Reginald Turner, Director of Acquisition for Livingston Catalogue."

Lorraine gasped. Brooke stepped around in front of him. Claire felt her heart plummet.

"I'd like to talk to you about our catalogue carrying a few of your products. When would be a good time?" he asked.

"After closing," Brooke and Lorraine said almost in unison.

"Is that convenient with you, Ms. Bennett?" he asked.

"How did you know my name?" Claire asked. Had Gray sent him because they were sleeping together?

Before he could answer, Brooke said, "I have to check out a customer. I'll be back."

"Mr. Turner?" Claire said.

"Research," he told her. "I should have announced who I was at first, but I wanted to see if all I had heard about Bliss was true."

"Who'd did you hear it from?" Claire's voice was sharper than intended.

"Claire?" Lorraine said, in surprise at her defensive tone, touching her arm to calm her.

"Perhaps it would help to say that I have complete autonomy in choosing products. Management can certainly offer suggestions, but the final decision is mine," the man said, his gaze steady. "However, your shop came up because my secretary received a jar of moisturizing cream from Mrs. Livingston and couldn't stop raving about it."

Claire and Lorraine's eyes rounded. "Mrs. Livingston?"

"Gray might be in charge, but she still makes her presence known. But I have to tell you that I have an appointment with Gray in an hour to go over several new products we plan for the Christmas issue. He often has suggestions." He glanced at his watch. "Can I call you later or can you tell me now if you're interested?"

"Of course, we're interested," Brooke said, rejoining the group.

"It has to be Claire's decision," Lorraine said.

Brooke opened her mouth, then closed it and nodded. "It's Claire's decision."

Now it was Claire's turn to stare. A listing in Livingston Catalogue was what they had hoped for from the first. The potential profits were staggering.

"Ms. Bennett?" the man was the one now prompting her.

Apparently more people were aware of her and Gray's relationship than she had suspected. It wouldn't matter if his grandmother did sponsor her; everyone would know. She'd always been a private person. With Gray in her life, that was no longer possible.

"One of us will call you, Mr. Turner," Lorraine said.

Obviously disappointed, he nodded. "Please do. I had hoped I could report that we had an appointment at the meeting. Goodbye."

"Wait!" Claire called as he turned to go. Gray and his grandmother believed in her, believed in Bliss for good reason. She and her partners had made their bath and body products concept work It was time to take it up a notch. "Would seven-thirty this evening be convenient or would nine in the morning be better?"

Brooke and Lorraine squealed, drawing the attention of the shoppers. Excusing themselves, they went to relieve the customer's concerns.

Relief swept across the man's face. "I'll see you at seven-thirty."

CHAPTER THIRTY-THREE

orraine had never felt lonelier than she did when she drove home that night. Bliss would have two lines of bath and body products in the Livingston Christmas catalogue. They'd have to hire help to get the thousand sets Livingston had ordered ready, find storage, and fifteen other things, but none of them doubted they'd succeed.

Gray, who had stayed at his office and out of the negotiations, wanted to take Livingston's newest business associates out to celebrate. Brooke had called John to join them. He'd been able to get his parents to stay with his children so he could meet them at the Peninsula Grill. Lorraine had called Hamilton, but he said he was too tired. He'd congratulated her, but hadn't sounded as if he meant it.

She swallowed and eased on her brakes at a stop sign. Not wanting to put a damper on the celebration, she'd left after a couple of sips of champagne. There should be a person she could share her triumphs with. She didn't have to think long before Thomas came into her mind. The light changed and she pulled off. Picking up the cell phone, she punched in his number.

"Hello?"

Just hearing his voice made her feel better. Margaret had been lucky to have such a supportive husband. "Two of Bliss's product lines will be in the Livingston's Christmas catalogue."

"Wonderful!" he exclaimed. His warm laughter boomed through loud and clear. "You ladies are certainly making your mark."

"We're trying. Thank you. I wanted to ask you if you had a property we might lease to make and store the products."

"I think I have just the place. But first, we should celebrate. How about lunch tomorrow?"

As always, he was there. "I'd love to. Is eleven-thirty all right?"

"It will be. I'll see you then."

Lorraine hung up the phone, no longer feeling lonely.

Three bouquets of flowers were delivered to Bliss by eleven Tuesday morning. The largest and much more elaborate was from Livingston, welcoming Bliss. The second, a mixture of peach and white roses, was from Thomas. The third, a spring bouquet, came from John. All the notes congratulated the "Ladies of Bliss," but each woman knew they were for her.

Lorraine was even more appreciative of Thomas's friendship. She'd never been one to compare herself or be jealous, but she realized that if only Claire and Brooke had received flowers, she would have felt left out, especially after Hamilton's refusal to attend their impromptu celebration. He'd left that morning on another business trip. They'd barely said good-bye. He certainly hadn't sent flowers. Thomas was more considerate. He'd chosen a wonderful restaurant and the salmon was fabulous.

"Thomas, this is marvelous. The roses were perfect and beautiful."

He sipped his wine and smiled across the table at her. "I'm glad. I seemed to remember you liked roses."

Her brow lifted in surprise. "How could you remember something like that?"

He paused. "Most men notice what beautiful women enjoy."

Lorraine was even more startled by his announcement. She wasn't sure what to say.

"If my compliment surprised you, I'll have to have a talk with Hamilton," he told her easily.

Sighing, Lorraine leaned back in her chair. Brooke and Claire were aware of her increasing problems with Hamilton, but Lorraine hadn't wanted Thomas to know the extent of her marital problems. She was tempted to change that.

"Lorraine, you looked so sad for a moment," he said, reaching across the table to place his hand on hers. "Is everything all right?"

Lorraine glanced at the large hand covering hers, the offer of comfort it represented. How long had it been since Hamilton has been there for her? Aching a little inside, she pulled her hand from beneath his. "Just thinking of all the work ahead in getting the products ready."

"I can take you to see the property I think will be ideal anytime you want," Thomas told her.

"Perhaps Thursday. They're doing the photo shoot Wednesday."

"I can pick you up around ten Thursday morning. The photo shoot sounds interesting." He picked up his fork. "Mind if I drop by and watch?"

"Of course not," she said. "We'd love to have you."

Something flickered in Thomas's eyes, then it was gone. But her breathing went off kilter and she began to wonder just what in the world she was doing.

It took the photographer from Livingston Catalogue longer to decide the angle and positions of the shot than to shoot the actual picture. She wanted seduction and sensuality, and decided on a tight shot with ribbon, potpourri trailing from its bottle, and a couple of the flowers from the bouquets amid the orange-pear products. BTS products were grouped on the vanity seat.

The photographer had barely finished when Mr. Turner phoned. A reporter from *The Post and Courier* was doing a piece on the catalogue and, when she'd heard about the photo shoot, she wanted to interview the Bliss owners. This article was scheduled to go in the business section next Wednesday. Would it be all right? If Knight Ridder picked up the piece it would go nationwide.

The answer had been a resounding yes. Less than an hour later, the reporter and photographer were there. As with the freelance photographer for Livingston, the reporter and her photographer left with products in Bliss's signature bag.

"Looks like you have more to celebrate," Thomas said to Lorraine. "I'd like to take you and Hamilton to dinner."

The happy smile faded. "He's out of town."

"Well, there's no reason for you not to celebrate. I could pick you up at your place at eight and we could have dinner."

She debated only for a moment. "All right."

"Good. See you at eight." Lorraine stared after him as he left the shop.

"He's a handsome man," Brooke said from beside her.

"Yes, he is, and considerate," Lorraine said, a soft smile playing around her mouth.

Brooke's brow lifted. "I think we need to talk." Without giving Lorraine a chance to balk, Brooke took Lorraine by the arm and pulled her to the back of the shop.

Lorraine frowned all the way into the storage area. "What is it? We shouldn't leave Claire by herself."

"I'm more concerned with you handling yourself." Brooke finally dropped the other woman's arm. "I may be out of line, but I've seen it happen too many times." As the puzzled look on Lorraine's face grew, Brooke continued, "Inattentive husbands and neglected wives."

Lorraine gasped. "How dare—"

"I dare because I like you and respect you," Brooke interrupted. "You're vulnerable now and some guys can see that."

"Thomas is just a friend."

"A friend who lost his wife six months ago. He can't be more than fifty-five and from a couple of the looks he threw at you, sex is still on his mind."

Lorraine's mouth gaped.

"Cancel the date, Lorraine," Brooke said gently.

"I—I'd never betray Hamilton."

"Intentionally no, but sometimes the unexpected can happen." Brooke took her purse from the file cabinet. "Soft music, slow dancing, then—wham—you're in a situation you hadn't counted on. I had a couple of close calls when Randolph was out of town, but I have to say, if one of them had been John, I wouldn't have been able to hold back."

"But . . . but you care about John," Lorraine said.

"My body wanted him before my mind caught up." She touched Lorraine's shoulder. "Call off the date. After Mark's try outs we'll probably grab a pizza. I'll be home if you want to talk."

Lorraine closed her eyes. Brooke had already said enough.

B rooke arrived home that night at eight-seventeen. Mark had made the team as the alternate pitcher. He'd been more worried that his father would be disappointed than anything. After John had reassured him, he was all right. She and John had managed to steal a goodnight kiss, then he had taken the kids home. She had gotten in her car and tried to call Lorraine at home. There had been no answer.

Pacing in her apartment, she hit redial, then dialed Lorraine's cell. "Lorraine, pick up." She was seriously considering calling Claire to see if she knew where they were having dinner when the phone was picked up.

"You had no right to say those things to me." Lorraine's voice wavered.

Brooke sat on the arm of the sofa. "Before Claire, I never had any close female friends. You're the second."

"Claire might need your advice, but I don't."

To debate that would cause even greater friction. "Of all of us, I think Claire is the only one who has a clear picture of what she wants and accepts that she may not get it. I'm not sure I'm that strong."

"You're right. She's proven to be the strongest of the three of us."

Brooke slipped off her shoes. "Loving Gray was a big part of it, but we helped. We helped each other."

"I was so angry with you this afternoon. I still am."

"And I was so worried about you, I only took time for a pitiful goodnight kiss. I wouldn't do that for just anyone."

"Brooke?"

"Yes."

"I think you're wrong, but I canceled the dinner engagement."

Brooke relaxed against the back of the sofa, a slow smile growing on her face. "Lunch is on me tomorrow. What shall it be?"

"Slightly North of Broad."

Brooke smiled. S.N.O.B., as most of the locals called it. They served wonderful low-country cuisine. Expensive, but that was all right. "You're in luck. I just paid off my MasterCard."

Hanging up the phone, she headed for bed, hoping Lorraine stopped seeing Thomas completely until she was less vulnerable. If she didn't, she could still find herself in trouble.

Lorraine was almost afraid to see Thomas again. She didn't want to think she could be so needy that she was attracted to another man, especially the husband of a woman who had been her oldest and dearest friend. She'd always detested women who ran after men before their wives were even cold in the grave.

Bliss's door opened and Thomas walked in right on time for their appointment to see the property. Her heart didn't thump, she didn't feel breathless, but it was a near thing. He stared at her for a few moments. She really looked at him this time and saw the interested way he looked at her. Brooke has been right.

He crossed to her immediately. "Morning, Lorraine. I hope you're feeling better."

Because this morning she really did have a headache, she rubbed her temple. "A bit."

Reaching out, he placed a gentle hand on her shoulder. "I hate to see you in pain."

The warmth of his hand seeped through her blouse. His hand was larger than Hamilton's, softer. Aware of what she was doing, she stepped away. "Thank you." She glanced around the shop and saw Brooke watching her. She flushed.

"Would you rather we put off looking for a place?" he asked.

"No. I'll get my purse and we can leave." She passed Brooke on the way to the back, and wasn't surprised to find that she had followed her.

"You sure this is wise?"

No. "We need to find a place so we can order the supplies and begin production. You know that as well as I do."

Brooke came further into the room. "I can go, or Claire, or we can find another realtor."

Lorraine's chin lifted. "Thomas is a friend. I won't hurt him that way."

Brooke sighed. "Is the risk worth it just to keep his feelings from getting hurt? Besides, I think he knows you're conflicted. A real friend would make himself scarce."

Not wanting to think she might be right, Lorraine brushed by her and went to Thomas. "I'm ready."

"Let's go," he said. With a friendly wave to Claire at the cash register and Brooke, who had followed Lorraine out of the back, they left.

"What's the matter?" Claire asked Brooke. "Why the frown?"

Folding her arms, Brooke whispered her suspicions to Claire. "She won't listen and she's headed for trouble."

Deeply troubled Claire asked, "What can we do to help her?"

"Absolutely nothing." Brooke's hands came to her side. "Lorraine is on her own on this one, and I think she's out of her league."

Despite being in Thomas's roomy Lincoln Navigator, Lorraine felt almost claustrophobic. She kept fidgeting with the neck of her blouse, the hem of her short skirt. She felt odd in her own skin.

"I think this property will suit you best and it's not because I own the building," Thomas said as he pulled into the parking lot of the five-story white brick building. "It has twenty-four-hour security so you ladies can come and go at will and feel perfectly safe." Pulling into a parking space, he got out and came around to open her door and help her down.

Lorraine hesitated a fraction too long before placing her hand in his.

"Lorraine, what's the matter?"

She didn't want to meet his gaze. What kind of friend and wife was she? Was she attracted to Thomas, or what he represented: a man to comfort her?

"Lorraine?"

"I–I think my headache is coming back," she said evasively.

He stepped closer to her. Too close. "It wouldn't be any trouble to put this off for another day."

Try forever. "No, I'd like this settled."

He reached out his hand again and this time she didn't hesitate. As soon as her foot touched the concrete she withdrew her hand. He lightly took her elbow and they entered the building. Lorraine's nerves didn't settle until they were inside the office suite on the first floor.

"I think you'll be comfortable here. It already has a few office pieces like the sofa, desk and file cabinet. I think you should take this one." Releasing her arm, Thomas went to open the door in front of them. "This room has plenty of storage and electrical outlets for your equipment."

Lorraine made her feet move toward him. Thomas moved back, but not far enough and her breast brushed against his arm. She jumped. She stared up at him with horror-filled eyes. "You did that on purpose."

He looked away. "Yes."

"Why, Thomas? Margaret and I were friends."

His head whipped back around. This time she could see the passion and desire there. "She's been gone almost six months. I loved her, but I can't deny I have feelings for you. Helping you these last weeks have shown me that I'm not dead."

"I'm married," she cried, half-wondering if she'd said it for her or him.

"To a man who doesn't appreciate what he has."

The truth of his words hurt. "I'd like to leave."

He clenched his hands. "Please, don't be angry."

"I'm not, I'm just . . ." Lorraine swallowed, then pushed the hard words out, "I'm not entirely immune to you."

His eyes lit and he started for her. She quickly backed up.

"No. Please, let me finish. It's because you were there when Hamilton wasn't. You've been my anchor, my solace when he hasn't. But I love my husband. I substituted you for him, and for that I'm sorry."

"We could build on that," he told her.

"Nothing can be built on lies and deceit." Her chin lifted. "And I won't shame Margaret's memory. She loved you and your children so much."

His head fell forward. "I miss her so much. Sometimes I catch myself listening for the sound of her voice or looking for her in the gardens she loved."

"Perhaps you're attracted to me because I was so close to Margaret," Lorraine offered.

His head came up. "That would make it nice and neat, but that isn't the case. Come on, I'll take you back."

Lorraine didn't protest when he led her back to his SUV. Thankfully, the ride back to Bliss didn't take long. As soon as he parked, she was out the door.

He also got out and came around to the passenger side. With a weary sigh he pulled a key out of his pocket and held it out. "Take Claire and Brooke back to see what they think. This place suits your needs and I'd feel better knowing you're safe."

She moistened her lips. "Thomas, perhaps I should get another realtor."

He was already shaking his head. "Please don't make me feel worse than I do already."

She'd been just as wrong as he had. She accepted the key.

"Thank you. I think I may go visit the children for a couple of weeks. Call the office and ask for Helen Steins if you decide to take the place."

He was giving her space and notice that he wouldn't be there for her to lean on. She was extremely grateful. She could have wrecked so many lives by turning to another man instead of her husband. "I'm sorry if I led you to believe we could be more than friends."

"I won't lie. I am, too. Goodbye, Lorraine." Getting in his vehicle, Thomas drove off.

Lorraine crossed the busy street against the light and entered Bliss. The second she opened the door, Brooke and Claire's heads came up and they rushed to her. She looked at Brooke. "I was a fool."

Brooke put her arms around her shoulder. "Most women have been at one time or another. Now, go put up that purse and get busy."

Lorraine's smile trembled. "No feeling sorry for myself, huh?"

"Nope. Rule of Bliss," Brooke said, then her eyes widened in excitement. "I just had a great idea for our Web site. Rules of Bliss, and the first one is giving yourself permission to make a mistake."

Lorraine shook her head. "At least something good has come out of the mess I almost made."

"That's the beauty of a mistake," Claire said. "We learn and move on and we're lucky to have each other. Now, lets all get back to work."

CHAPTER THIRTY-FOUR

The bath gel slipped from Brooke's hand and landed with a thud on the floor. Claire saw the stark expression on her face, glanced in the direction she had been staring and rushed to across the room to the handsome, well-dressed man who had entered the shop. "Can I help you?"

He flicked a dismissive glance at her. "No. I came to see Brooke," he said and walked up to the counter. "Hello, Brooke. You look more beautiful than I remember."

Randolph Peterson III was exactly as Brooke remembered: handsome, charming, and impeccably dressed in a tailor-made Italian suit. He favored Gucci. The mauve silk pocket square perfectly matched the faint mauve stripe in his shirt and the tiny dot on a gold background in his tie.

Pleased that shock, not affection had caused the reaction, she picked up the bath gel and placed it on the shelf. "You were always smooth, Randolph. Can I show you around?"

He reached for her arm and she deftly evaded his touch. His eyebrow lifted. "Is there someplace we can go and talk?"

There were a few shoppers, but Claire and Lorraine could handle them. "In the back."

"I've missed you," he said, reaching for her as soon as the louvered doors swung closed behind him.

Holding up her hands, Brooke stepped back. "What do you think you're doing?"

"Trying to kiss the woman I love."

Brooke simply stared. Randolph had said he cared, but he'd never admitted to loving her.

He took advantage of her stillness and circled his hands around her arms. "You're the most resilient woman I know. You thrive on challenge. If I had babied you, you would have folded instead of fighting back and becoming a part of this."

"You want to take credit for Bliss?" she asked incredulously.

He laughed. "No, darling. The credit belongs to you and the other two ladies, but if I had made the calls as you wanted you'd be stuck in corporate instead of riding high on the success of your own ingenuity. My mother has even ordered online. She sent me the article in the newspaper. It was picked up by several papers. The family is thrilled for your success. Mother was pleased to learn I'm bringing you home with me this weekend."

"What?" she gasped. Randolph had never mentioned her meeting his parents in the past. She'd met them by accident when they came to Charleston for a Jack and Jill charity function. They had barely spoken before his parents moved on.

Reaching into the inside pocket of his coat Randolph pulled out an oblong blue jewelry box. "I had this made especially for you."

Brooke gaze flickered from Randolph to the box. Her stomach felt jittery. "I don't understand."

"You mean a lot to me and I don't want to lose you." Opening the box he lifted a diamond bracelet and put it on her arm.

Brooke gasped at the stones, A-1 flawless and glittering, circling her wrist in a fiery display of beauty and perfection.

"I hope this proves my sincerity and my love." Reaching into his pocket again, he pulled out an airline package. "First class tickets to Atlanta. A limo and driver will be waiting at baggage claim to bring you to the house to meet my parents. And I'll have another surprise that will put that one to shame."

Her eyes widened. "A ring?"

"You'll have to come and see." He pulled her into his arms. "I've missed you, Brooke." His mouth lowered.

At the last second, she turned her head. "Wait! This is too fast."

His lips brushed her cheek. "This is what we've both wanted. Come to Atlanta."

Everything she ever wanted was within her grasp. Randolph was practically begging her to be his wife. So why wasn't she shouting with joy? *John.* "I need time."

"I have to leave this afternoon. I'm taking over new accounts at Daddy's bank. Today is Tuesday, I expect to see you no later than Saturday. You can catch an early flight and be there by noon." He smiled indulgently. "I probably shouldn't tell you, but Mother is planning a little dinner party with some of our closest friends to introduce you to, but I know how women like to dress up for such things so I wanted you prepared."

Or did you want to make sure I wouldn't embarrass you by not dressing appropriately? "I didn't think your mother cared for me."

A brief frown marred the perfection of his handsome face. "You're mistaken." He glanced at his eighteen-karat gold watch. "I have to go. I'll see you Saturday morning."

Brooke watched him leave, then looked at the bracelet, weighing heavily on her arm. She wanted to cry.

B rooke's phone call, that it was urgent she see him, had John on edge. There was something in her voice that had him pacing the floor since she'd called thirty minutes ago. At the knock on his office door he swung around. He'd already told everyone he didn't want to see anyone, no matter what. "Come in."

The door opened and Brooke came inside and closed the door behind her. Her face was haunted. Instead of running to him as she always had, she remained by the door. His gut twisted. "What is it?"

"I—" Her hand shoved over her head and the light flashed off the diamond bracelet on her wrist.

He knew. "He's back, isn't he?"

She swallowed convulsively before speaking. "Yes."

The pain almost sent John to his knees. "Thanks for telling me in person." Ordering his feet to move, his knees not to buckle, he went around to his desk and sat down. "Goodbye, Brooke."

"That's all you have to say?"

He kept his head down, staring at papers he couldn't see. "Good luck."

Crossing the room, she swung his chair around. "Look at me!"

Slowly he lifted his head. He'd carry her face with him always. And the regret. It had taken losing her to realize how much he loved her. Leaning back in his chair he folded his arms across his chest to keep from grabbing Brooke and begging her to stay.

"If . . . if I thought this was going someplace—"

"It's not." He cut her off. He couldn't compete financially with the other man and he was unwilling to risk Brooke leaving later because she was tired of the simple things. He wouldn't do that to his children or himself.

She swallowed. "I thought you cared." Her voice trembled.

"Not enough." *Please leave*, he thought, *while I can still let you go.* He wheeled in his chair and picked up his pen. The door closed and his head fell forward.

She was gone and he felt as if his heart had been ripped from his chest.

Wednesday at eleven in her new Albert Nipon fashionable black suit, Claire walked into the meeting for the Business Professionals of Charleston. Although Gray said he'd be there, her pulse hammered erratically when she saw him. Seeing her, he excused himself from a group of people that included his grandmother and went to her.

"Hello, beautiful."

"Hi, handsome."

His gaze swept down to her feet in their stylish three-inch heels. "Looks like you're getting the hang of it."

She smiled into his teasing face. "Practice."

"Come on, I want you to meet some people." He took her by the elbow. "Many have already read the two newspaper articles. You won't have any problem gaining membership."

Gray's words proved correct. She was warmly accepted. However, Claire was smart enough to know that it was Gray and his grandmother who the people didn't want to offend, not her.

Taking a seat at the round table for eight between Gray and his grandmother, Claire ate the surprisingly delicious chicken and mixed vegetables, and tried to keep straight the names of the many people who stopped by. After the speech by the president it was time to introduce potential new members by going from table to table. Finally they reached them. Under the table Gray squeezed her hand in reassurance.

Mrs. Livingston started to stand. Gray got up to assist with her chair.

There was a collective gasp, then whispers grew. Claire turned as everyone in the room did and felt the floor shift beneath her feet. Beautiful and seductive as ever, Jana stood in the doorway, her eyes trained on Gray.

The swift hatred and rage on Gray's face was frightening. Claire instinctively reached for his hand. He seemed oblivious to everything except Jana. Claire looked back at the woman and saw her smiling. She wore couture and she wore it well. She was stunning in an Armani lavender and charcoal suit with a draped collar that seductively curved over her full breasts. There wasn't a woman in the room who could match her for beauty or sensuality. Brooke's appeal was subtle; Jana's demanded attention.

"Gray, please sit down," his grandmother told him.

His body rigid, his jaw tight, he didn't move.

"Gray, please," Claire said. Her voice trembled, her heart cried out for the pain he was enduring. Jana had planned her reappearance well. But Claire wasn't going to let her hurt him anymore. She came to her feet, then stepped in front of him. "Don't let her do this to you. Please." She placed her hand on his chest, felt the thud of his heart. "Don't let her win."

Slowly Gray brought his gaze to Claire. The rage was still there, and the lingering pain. His hand lifted to squeeze hers, then he held her chair for her and took a seat beside her. He didn't release her hand. If those in the room suspected Gray and Claire were more than business associates, they had just proven them right. Claire couldn't have cared less. Gray was all that mattered, and helping him get through this.

"Thank you, Amanda," Mrs. Livingston began as if the interruption had never occurred. Ignoring Jana was the best way to deal with her. "In my lifetime, I've had the privilege to meet some dynamic people, who by their very presence make the world a better place and those around them happy. The person I'm about to introduce is one of those individuals. Her honesty and integrity are unquestionable. She is destined to make her mark in the business world. Indeed, has already begun to do so." She smiled warmly at Claire.

"I've known her for many years and am honored that she first approached us about her business venture." Her gaze ran over the crowd. "She is a friend of mine and the Livingston family. We support her fully and humbly ask that you do the same."

Mrs. Livingston paused and Claire could almost hear the unspoken threat, *If you don't, you'll have us to deal with.*

The older woman's attention came back to Claire. "I'm honored to present Claire Bennett."

Claire stood as the applause began, aware she still held Gray's hand, but she had no intention of releasing it and it appeared he didn't plan to release hers either. As if drawn, her gaze went to Jana in the back. She wasn't smiling any longer. If looks could kill, Claire would be in need of a hearse. Claire smiled.

Gray didn't say a word as he, Claire and his grandmother left the luncheon. By tacit agreement, they walked to the Livingston Building a couple of blocks over. The silence continued as they rode the elevator, then went down the hall and into his office.

"Hold all my calls. Let security know that my ex is back and may try to see me."

His secretary's eyes widened. She reached for the phone. "Right away, Mr. Livingston."

In his office he was ready to explode, then he looked at Claire, saw the worry on her face and pulled her into his arms. "I'm sorry she ruined it for you."

"Me?" Leaning back, Claire palmed his face. "It's you she wants back. I could hurt her for the pain she's put you through."

"Pain?" he said, frowning. "What pain?" Claire remained silent. "You think I still care about her?"

"N–Not exactly."

"Then what?" he demanded.

"She's very beautiful."

"So is a coral snake, but I wouldn't want to snuggle up with one." He scowled. "I was concerned about you, not me. Moments before, you were so happy. She did it on purpose. She's as vindictive as ever."

"You were worried about me?"

"Of course." Couldn't she see he'd do anything for her?

"Gray!" she cried and kissed him.

"I can see my presence is not necessary," Mrs. Livingston said to the abashed Claire and smiling Gray. "I'll see you when I see you."

Leaving Claire, he gave his grandmother a hug. "Thank you. As always you came through."

"One does what one must." She looked at Claire. "Come to dinner Sunday and we can talk."

"Yes, ma'am. I'd like that."

The door closed and Gray pulled Claire back in his arms. "Now, where were we?"

Jana Louise Carpenter Livingston Murphy Franklin was back in Charleston. Fifteen minutes after the business meeting was over the news had run through Charleston's elite society. Every detail, from the time she walked into the meeting until Gray, his grandmother, and Claire Bennett, his protégée/lover left, was repeated. They'd walked right by Jana as if she were a bump on a log. The two little friends with her seemed nervous. They had a right to be.

It was obvious to everyone in attendance that they had invited Jana. Mrs. Livingston didn't make idle threats. The women's clothing boutique certainly wouldn't see any of Mrs. Livingston's cronies shopping there. They'd be lucky if they didn't close before Christmas.

Jana, her black eyes cold, stood outside Bliss later that afternoon. She wanted Gray back and she planned to have him. She didn't love him. She loved no man. Love made you vulnerable. Just look at the men she had tossed aside who begged her to come back to them. All but Gray.

He was a challenge. No matter how many men came and went in her bed, he was the one she couldn't forget. A man could be wild in bed, driving her to the height of ecstasy, but sooner or later she'd feel the need to move on and dominate another man. They might think they were using her and having sex, but to her it proved that she was stronger, more powerful. Perhaps that was why she could never forget Gray. She had never been able to dominate him. Not once.

There was restlessness in her that she knew was caused by that omission. She had to bring Gray to his knees. Once she did, she'd move on to another fool who thought he could make her love him exclusively. Men were such fools. Her mother was right about that. Some called them amoral, but they were realistic. She might have been conceived in sin, but sin was her redemption. Giving control to a man made you weak and vulnerable. Even now her mother was discreetly carrying on an affair behind the back of husband number four.

Jana knew she could only depend on herself to ensure her well-being. Her father might have cut her off, but there was always another man waiting and she knew just how to win him. Her skill as a lover had served her well. Amazing how a mouth and tongue in the right place drove a man crazy and made him generous. She might have taunted Gray about a pool boy, but she'd never stooped to the working class. She only went after men with money and influence.

The banker in London had been a side diversion while her real target was in Brussels on business. She neither knew nor cared if the banker came looking for her when she left the next morning while he snored. She'd heard him talking to his girlfriend, Brooke. He was cheating, also. He just didn't know how to play the game as well. She did, and she was about to show the drab woman clinging to Gray that she didn't have a chance now that Jana was back. As long as she drew breath she'd never allow him to be happy with another woman. A smile on her face, Jana crossed the street and entered Bliss.

———

laire glanced up as the door opened and froze. There was only one reason why Jana would come to Bliss—to make trouble. Excusing herself from a customer, Claire met the other woman a few steps inside the shop.

"Please leave."

Jana's perfectly brow arched. "I go and do as I please."

"Then do it someplace else."

"Are you that insecure of Gray or of yourself that, after seeing me, you know you'll never be able to keep him?"

Claire laughed at the absurdity of Jana's statement. "And what do I see? A woman without morals, without worth. If Gray wanted a beautiful shell he would have overlooked your immorality and kept you. He didn't want you then or now."

Rage flushed her cheeks. "You bitch!"

Claire's smile died. "Leave, Jana. You won't like it if I have to help you."

"You—"

"Leave," Brooke said, coming up beside her friend.

"Please let me handle this, Brooke," Claire said.

Jana's attention snapped to Brooke, she laughed. "Brooke? This is rich. I've had both of your men and could have them again if I wanted." She smirked at the astonishment on Brooke's face. "Randolph Peterson, the third. London, in his flat. You were moaning about losing your job. I had him moaning about something else entirely."

Brooke returned Jana's nasty smile with interest. "No wonder he came running back to me with an eighteen-karat diamond bracelet. He's promised a wedding ring. What did you get besides a toss in the sheets?"

Fury glittered in Jana's eyes. "I can have him back if I want."

"You have my blessings and Randolph my sympathy, but Gray's too smart. Otherwise you wouldn't be here," Brooke said.

Lorraine joined then, and went to open the door. "Don't come back."

"I'll ruin you," Jana hissed, drawing the attention of the few customers in the store, who had long since stopped shopping to watch the fireworks.

"You can try, but whatever happens, you'll never have Gray, and you'll always regret you lost him," Claire said with complete confidence and assurance.

"You won't keep him!" Jana predicted with a snide smile. "The only reason he's with you is that he doesn't have to worry that another man would want an ugly woman like you."

"Shut up or I won't be responsible!" a male voice snarled.

Jana whirled as Gray entered the shop. Rage emanated from him. "Claire is more woman that you could ever be. You're right. I don't have to worry about Claire. She's too honest to ever be the liar and cheat you were. She has something you never will, a heart." His eyes narrowed dangerously. "Go after me all you want, but don't get in Claire's face again. Don't mistake my silence for weakness."

"Gray, I . . ."

Jana reached for him and he stepped back as if from something vile. "It's over. It has been for a long time."

"You loved me once!" she cried. "You can't choose her over me."

"I already have." He stepped to Claire's side and circled her waist. "What makes it so wonderful is that she chose me as well."

Brooke and Lorraine cheered. The other women joined in. Jana stared from Gray to Claire, then ran from the shop. Lorraine shoved the door shut behind her.

Gray stared down at Claire. "I'm sorry."

Her arms circled his neck. "I'm not. She's finally out of your life. You're free."

But the memory of her betrayal lingered, Gray thought. The avid attention he was receiving from the other customers brought it all back. He wondered if he'd ever be completely free.

Claire opened the door to the ringing phone. Thinking it was Gray, she rushed to answer it. He hadn't been his usual self since the confrontation with Jana at Bliss yesterday.

"Hello."

"Hi, sis. You hit the big times," Derek greeted, his voice booming.

Claire tried not to be disappointed that it wasn't Gray, but failed. "Hello, Derek."

"You could have knocked me over with a feather when one of the guys at work showed me the newspaper with you in it." He chuckled. "Seems I didn't have to worry about Gray taking you after all. You played him like a fiddle."

Frowning, she continued into her room with the cordless. In the background she heard a baby crying. "What are you talking about?"

"You're going to be in Livingston Catalogue. That will bring big bucks."

Her mouth tightened at the implication. "My dating Gray has nothing to do with the catalogue."

"If you say so."

From his snide tone he obviously didn't believe her and it grated on her nerves. The baby's screams had accelerated to a high, disturbing pitch. "What's wrong with that baby? She sounds as if she's in pain."

"She sick. Running a temperature and can't keep any food down," he said.

Concern drew Claire's brows together. "What did the doctor say?"

There was a discernable pause before he said, "We haven't taken her. No insurance. Brandi belongs to my girlfriend. The baby's father won't help and I don't have the money. Sheila hasn't got paid because she's been home with Brandi. She's only nine months old and as cute as a button. I hate to see her sick, but I lost wages when I came to see you."

Since Claire didn't think it would do any good to point out he hadn't come to see her, she asked, "How much is the doctor's visit?"

"I guess a couple hundred should be enough to see the doctor and get her prescriptions filled," he told her. "Well, I better go help."

"I'll wire you the money," Claire said. She couldn't stand the thought of a sick child, and she had done nothing to help.

"Claire, I don't know what to say," Derek said.

"I'll go do it now. Just take Brandi to the doctor as soon as you get the money." She grabbed her purse.

"I will. Thanks, Claire. You sure are a good sister."

Hanging up the phone, she was out the door. Claire hurried to wire the money. She didn't begrudge sending it for a child in need. Perhaps Derek was learning to stand on his feet. He hadn't even asked for the money. Hurrying back home, she saw Gray's car parked in front of her house. Not taking time to put the car up, she went around the back of the house. He was there as she'd expected, his hands deep in his pockets as he looked out at the moon-draped ocean.

"Gray."

He pivoted at the sound of her voice, but he didn't move toward her or take his hands from his pockets. His unsmiling face, his pose said it all. Tonight was their last night. She wanted to scream out her protest, beg him to stay.

"You know, don't you?"

Too numb to speak, she nodded.

He looked up the empty beach, then back at her. "I'll be working from Columbia for an indefinite period of time."

"You're leaving Charleston?"

"I'm driving up tonight. Christmas season will be here before you know it and I want to make sure the warehouse is able to meet the demand for the increase in incoming and outgoing merchandise," he told her.

Claire had told herself she'd accept his decision calmly, but now she found she couldn't. "If Jana hadn't come, would you be leaving me tonight?"

His head drew back. "She had nothing to do with my decision."

Claire's laugh was ragged. "She had everything to do with it. You won't trust me because you can't forget she betrayed your trust."

"I trust you."

She took a step closer to him. "Then stay and prove it."

"I can't," he whispered. "I can't."

Can't or wouldn't, it made no difference. He was going to leave her. If she thought telling him she loved him would make him stay instead of adding to his burden she would have shouted it.

"We'll miss you at dinner Sunday." She thought he flinched.

"You better go inside."

"I'd like to stay out here for a while. Goodbye, Gray."

"Goodbye." His hands still in his pockets, he disappeared around the side of the house.

Claire dropped to her knees as pain swamped her. Jana had won after all. Gray still wasn't free of her.

Gray got inside his car and leaned his head back. He had expected the pain, but he hadn't known it would be this intense. Nothing had prepared him for leaving Claire with moonlight and tears on her cheeks. He hadn't planned it this way. He'd foolishly thought they'd both walk away unscathed. He'd quickly found out different, but by then he hadn't wanted to think of a day without her in his life.

He did trust Claire, but there was some tiny part of him that resisted being that vulnerable again. He had to make the break now. Claire slipped into his mind too easily.

Standing at his office that afternoon he'd come to a hard decision. He and Claire had to break up. He'd cut back on his out-of-town business because he didn't want to be away from her, because he wanted to spend the nights with her. He couldn't let himself fall in love that deeply again. It hurt too badly when it was over.

He lifted his head as she came around the side of the house. She stopped when she saw his car, then continued to hers. He sat there until the garage door came down, until all the lights in the house winked out. He imagined Claire in her bed and clamped his eyes shut.

He knew she was crying. He felt it, hated it, and tried to accept it. Starting the motor of his car, he made a U-turn. She'd get over him.

He wished he could be certain he'd get over her.

Claire woke up the next morning with red eyes and puffy, sore lids. Crying most of the night would do that to you. Because she didn't want to wallow in self-pity, she dragged herself out of bed to the shower. To prove to herself that she wasn't dead, she ate a piece of toast for breakfast. Since every time she thought of Gray, tears would start falling, she tried to think of the shop, the new products they planned, the building they were going to rent.

She pulled her keys from her purse and the receipt from wiring the money fell out. Concerned for Brandi, she picked up the phone and called

Derek's apartment. There was no answer. Deciding to call later, she left the house.

A rriving at Bliss later, she saw that Brooke's eyes matched hers. Since both were sniffing, their excuses of allergies worked well. Thankfully, they were busy. Around noon, Claire finally got a chance to call Derek at his place again, and when there was no answer, she called him at work.

"Derek Bennett please."

"He no longer works here. Is there anyone else who can help you?" asked a crisp, efficient voice.

Stunned, it took Claire a second to respond. "He doesn't work there?"

"No, ma'am. Is there someone else who can help?"

"Robert Johnson," Claire said, then paced until Derek's friend came on the line.

"Robert Johnson. How can I help you?"

"Robert, this is Claire, Derek's sister. The receptionist just told me he doesn't work there. We spoke last night and he said he was still working there."

A long sigh drifted through the phone. "I don't like to get in another man's business."

Anger had long since overtaken pride. "I wired him two hundred dollars to take Brandi to the hospital. I want to speak to him and find out how she's doing."

"Brandi?"

"His girlfriend's little daughter."

"Claire, the woman Derek dates doesn't have any children, but I think her sister does. Derek was fired a couple of weeks back for poor performance and coming to work late and leaving early."

Claire plopped down in a chair. Same story, different employer. "He's not at home."

"When I saw him the other day he said he and his lady were going to Myrtle Beach for a few days before he started looking for another job."

Claire felt utterly stupid. "Did he mention which hotel?"

"The Sheraton."

"Thank you." Claire hung up the phone and dialed information. In minutes she was connected to his room.

"Where are those extra towels I asked for? I didn't shell out good money for lousy service."

"You didn't shell out any money," Claire told him.

"Claire," he said shocked, fumbling for words. "I—I can explain."

"Don't bother, Derek. Just know that Claire's Bank and Trust is permanently closed."

"Now, wait a minute. I just needed a little down time before looking for another job. You know how it is when you're let go and it's no fault of your own."

"I do, but you don't have a clue. Stop the lies, Derek," Claire said, her voice quivering. "All this time you've been trying to denigrate Gray's character when it's you who have taken from me, lied to me. It stops now. From now on, you're on your own."

"Claire. No."

She talked over him. "If you ever get your act together give me a call, but in the meantime, I wish you well. You've conned your last penny from me." She slammed the phone down.

It rang almost immediately. She picked it up, heard Derek's frightened voice and down it went again. He had used her for the last time.

CHAPTER THIRTY-FIVE

Bliss is a success, but our lives could certainly use some," Claire commented as the three women sat around the table after closing Friday night. They'd told Lee Roy they needed to discuss business and to return in thirty minutes. Derek had called back several times. From Gray there had been nothing.

Brooke brushed a tear away from her eye. "I miss John and the children so much."

"Hamilton grows more distant each day," Lorraine said. "I'm not sure how to reach him, but at least I'm not leaning on Thomas any longer."

"At least Hamilton is back in town for you to keep trying. Gray is in Columbia."

"I think he's hiding," Brooke commented. "He's afraid if he sees you he'll weaken."

Claire brightened. "You really think so?"

"Immediately after he calls it off, he gets out of town. I'd say it was to keep temptation out of the way." Brooke lobbed another tissue in the wastebasket.

Lorraine nodded. "It makes sense."

"Then you think he cares?" Claire asked, wanting to believe they still had a chance.

"The question is, are you willing to go find out?" Brooke asked, then swallowed. "But be prepared if you don't get the answer you want."

Claire placed her hand on Brooke's. "John is a good man."

"If he weren't I wouldn't waste all these tears over him." Brooke reached for another tissue. "After I go to Atlanta tomorrow to return the airline ticket and bracelets, I may give him another chance. Whatever happens, I'm not shutting Mark and Amy out of my life."

"Once he hears you've given Randolph back the jewelry and paid for your own way to do so, he should come around," Lorraine suggested hopefully.

"I don't plan to tell him. He has to have faith in me or this will never work. If I didn't know how cruel it is to break up with someone on the phone, I wouldn't go."

Lorraine sniffed and grabbed a tissue. "I'm going home and take an aspirin and go to bed. Hamilton isn't coming home until late tonight from a business meeting. I'll open in the morning." Lorraine came to her feet.

Brooke stood with her. "I'll be back in time to close."

"Neither of you will do any such thing," Claire said, picking up the day's receipts. "Lorraine, stay and have a leisurely breakfast with Hamilton. When you get back, Brooke, you find John and make him listen."

"What are you going to do?" Brooke asked.

"Work on a strategy to make Gray realize I'm the best thing that could have happened to him," she said. "He won't know what hit him."

Despite the somber mood of moments ago, they all laughed.

amilton opened the front door and closed it behind him. It was a little past nine. The house was eerily quiet. Perhaps Lorraine hadn't gotten in from work. He'd ended the business meeting early because she'd sounded so tired this afternoon on the phone. After hanging up he hadn't been able to get out of his mind that perhaps it was him she was tired of.

If he lost her, he wouldn't know what to do. Gripping the briefcase tighter, he started up the stairs. They couldn't go on like this. Both of them were miserable.

He pushed open the bedroom door and stopped. Lorraine was in bed. The covers tossed back as if she'd kicked them off . . . or someone else had. Fury swamped Hamilton. He recalled his mother's affairs, his father turning a blind eye so long as he had enough beer and whisky to drink. Dropping the briefcase, he started across the room.

Lorraine jumped and sprang up in bed, her eyes filled with fear until she saw who it was. "You startled me."

His knees were already on the bed when he saw her red puffy eyes. A different kind of fear took hold of him. "Lorraine, we have to talk."

She threaded her fingers through her already tousled curls. "What good will it do? We've talked and we're both miserable. I guess there is only one thing left to do."

"No!" He grabbed both her arms in desperation. "You can't leave me. I won't let you."

"Ham—"

"No, listen to me. I know you care more about the shop than our marriage, but . . . but if that's the way it has to be, I'll accept that."

Her eyes widened. "Care about the shop more than you? Why would you think such a thing?"

"Because with it, you don't need me." He swallowed, then continued. "You don't need me anymore. I've always worked hard so you wouldn't think I was a failure, so you wouldn't miss having the things you were used to, the things I desperately wanted to give you."

"You dolt."

His head fell forward, and she lifted it up none to gently. "Listen to me, Hamilton Averhart, I'm proud of you. I always have been. I admit that since I opened Bliss there have been times I wanted to brain you, but that's beside the point. You don't have to give me things. All I've ever wanted is your love."

"You have that."

"Do I?" she questioned. "Then why can't you see that Bliss makes me happy? The same way your business made you happy. I didn't make you choose a nine-to-five or denigrate you when I had to raise the children mostly by myself. Why are you making me choose?"

He drew back. It was time to tell her everything. "My parents didn't die in an automobile accident the summer I graduated from high school. My mother had a succession of lovers for as long as I could remember. When I was a sophomore in college she dumped my father in a nursing home after his heavy drinking led to cirrhosis and left town. I haven't heard from her since. I didn't even know how to contact her when he died six months later."

Stunned, she stared at him. "Why did you lie?"

His face filled with pain. "Didn't you just hear me? Why would you want me after you learned what type of people I came from? My father never worked a day. He might have once cared about her, but not enough to try and stop her as long as she kept a bottle of booze in his hand. The whole town knew exactly what kind of 'work' she did. I grew up ashamed and studied hard so I could leave all that behind me."

"Look at me, Hamilton." Slowly his head came up. "I'll say this once and then we forget it. First, you were wrong to lie to me—"

"Lorr—"

"I haven't finished." She waited until he slowly nodded. "You should have known me better, trusted me not to judge you because of what your parents did. But you committed a worse sin in my sight by thinking I could be like your mother. And if I didn't love you so much, I might hold it against you."

His eyes widened, and she went into his arms.

"I'm sorry, Lorraine. So sorry."

Her hand rubbed up and down his back. "It's over. We move on."

He set her away from him. "Can you forgive me?"

"I already have."

He shook his head. "I mean about Bliss? I hope you can. From now on, you have my full support."

• "Hamilton—"

"Wait." He came off the bed, opened his attaché case, then came back with a magazine in his hand. "Best magazine is one of my clients. What if

I put a full-page color ad in here for Bliss? The circulation is over nine million."

Her eyes rounded. "Hamilton!"

"I have Marion's private number in San Francisco. I'll call in the morning."

She launched herself into his arms. "I love you so much."

"I love you, too." His hold tightened. He knew he'd have a lifetime to prove it to her. His mouth took hers as they tumbled onto the bed. He felt as if his life was starting all over again . . . just like the first time he'd held her.

W hen do you plan to tell Mark?" John's father asked as they stood behind the catcher's box at the softball field waiting for Mark's team to take the field to warm up Saturday afternoon. "The coach is putting him in since Kerry didn't do so hot the last game. This is Mark's first time pitching. She wasn't at his practice Wednesday. He wants her here and keeps looking for her."

John's fingers clamped and unclamped on the wire fence. "I don't know how. He was so excited about starting today. I wish I'd never met her."

"Son, that's a lie and you know it."

"We'll forget her," he said.

"Another lie."

His father never pulled punches. John straightened. "She wasn't cut out for hamburgers and dresses from Sears. We couldn't have made it work."

His father put his hand on his son's tense shoulder. "You just described a vain woman and that's not the Brooke who played mud pies with Amy, took off work to be with you or your children, was happy to sit at an old card table with me or whose eyes lit up when she saw you."

"Leave it alone, Dad." He didn't want to think or talk about her. He hadn't had a good night sleep since she left. There wasn't an hour in the day that he didn't think about her.

"Wish I could, but there's Mark and Amy to consider. He's taking the field now."

John turned around to see Mark walk to the pitcher's mound. With almost every step he looked back, first at them and then into the stands where his grandmother and Amy sat. The hopefulness in his face and eyes was replaced by disappointment by the time he reached the mound. "I should have never let her into our lives. This is what I get for forgetting Linda."

"That's nonsense, and you know it," his father told him with some heat. "Don't you go blaming the mess you made of this on Linda. She loved you and the kids more than anything. She'd want you happy and, if that meant another woman in your lives, so be it."

John felt ashamed. He had put the blame on Linda because, as much as he'd loved her, he loved Brooke more. And that shamed him, scared him that he couldn't keep Brooke happy for a lifetime. He should have fought to keep her. Now it was too late. Misery weighed heavily upon him, because his children would have to pay the price as well. And for that, he didn't know if he could ever forgive himself.

He watched Mark throw the pitch half-heartedly. "Put some fire into it, Mark!" he yelled.

Mark nodded, but the next warm-up pitch didn't have the zip it had the day before as they'd practiced at home.

"You gonna call her?" his father persisted.

"She's with him," John said tightly, then gripped the wire fence. "Come on, Mark. Straight down the middle."

"Mark, you heard your father. Send one over the plate."

John's head whipped around. Brooke was standing directly behind the catcher. She wore a red jacket trimmed in black and red braid, black pants and a white shell. Chunky gold and black jewelry glinted around her throat and on her ears. A slim gold chain belt hung loosely from her tiny waist. He knew squat about clothes, but he knew the outfit was high dollar.

Mark's head came up. He grinned from ear to ear.

"Show me what you got!" Brooke encouraged. The next one zoomed over the plate. "Whoo!" Brooke yelled, her hands in the air. "That's what I'm talking about."

"Seems she got back. Dressed fancy for a game. I guess she'd rather be here than wherever it was she was at and didn't take time to change,"

John's father said mildly. "It takes a good woman and a loving one to come here today knowing you don't want to see her, but she's doing it for Mark. You think she hadn't figured out he can't buy her anything? The only thing he can give her is his love and trust."

"You've made your point, Dad."

"Hope so, but can you make yours?" Whistling, he strolled over to Brooke.

The sultry heat had long since demanded Brooke remove her jacket. She'd purposely worn St. John's couture to see Randolph. She'd wanted him to see she didn't need or want him. His mouth had gaped like a fish on the bank when she'd given him his bracelets and the plane ticket back two seconds after she'd walked through the door of his parents' Georgian mansion.

"What about the guests waiting?"

"Tell them it didn't work. Tell them anything." She glanced at her watch. "I have a plane to catch."

He caught her arm as she started out the door of the home in the exclusive Buck Hill division in Atlanta. True panic was in his face and in his voice. "You can't do this to me. I can have any woman I want."

Her smile was cold and baiting. "I wasn't going to go there but since you insist, I know all about your affair in London. Jana was all too anxious to tell me."

His mouth gaped again. His hands came to his sides. "She didn't mean anything to me."

"Your problem and hers. I'm leaving."

"Brooke, it doesn't have to end this way. We're both sensible," he cajoled. "With the right kind of financial backing my father's bank can provide, Bliss can go nationwide. I can help you do that."

She stared at him in his ten-thousand-dollar suit, his heart and soul bankrupt. She stared at what she had almost ended up marrying. She might have if she hadn't lost her job. They'd both seen dollar signs instead of each other. "You won't use Bliss to make a name for yourself."

"Think of all we can have together."

She opened the door. "Goodbye, Randolph."

"You're making a mistake by walking out that door."

"I'd make a worse one if I stayed." The door closed behind her.

Coming out of her musing, Brooke cut a quick look at John. He was talking to the father of one of the other boys. She caught him watching her, but he'd made no move to come over as his father had. Even his mother and Amy had come down. Stubborn mule.

The roar of the crowd brought her attention back to the game. Mark's teammate had struck out and they were taking the field for the bottom of the ninth and last inning. The score was one even. It was up to Mark.

"You can do it, Mark!" she yelled.

Mark nodded, then glanced at his father, then back at her.

Brooke didn't know if he was seeking reassurance or wondering why they weren't together. She did know he didn't need any distraction. Taking her jacket from the wooden bench, she started for John. As if sensing her, he lifted his head.

"Hello," she greeted. "This is for Mark."

John's gaze flickered to the mound. Mark was watching them. John reached out and pulled Brooke against him. "Might as well make it look good."

She'd kick him if her knees weren't so weak. How could she love such a sneaky, overbearing rat? Her legs might be weak, but she glared up at him. How could he have done that to her? Making her fall in love with him and then not love her back? He would though, or suffer the consequences.

John had felt Brooke tense and it had gone straight through him. She didn't even want him to touch her now. Tough. She was in his life, the life of his children, and she wasn't getting away.

The first batter came out of the dugout. Brooke stopped glaring at John and grabbed the fence. Behind her, John did the same, bracketing her body. "Just like we practiced!" John yelled.

"You can do it!" Brooke joined in.

Mark nodded, studied the batter, then let the ball fly straight across the plate. The batter swung so hard he turned in a half circle. He struck out in three swings as did the next batter. The third batter came to the plate, stared at Mark and when the pitch came he stepped into the ball and sent a line drive straight at Mark.

Brooke gasped.

John tensed, pressing closer to Brooke.

Mark's hand came up. The ball smacked into the center of the glove. He seemed amazed to look down and see the ball in the glove.

The crowd went crazy. Mark's teammates swamped the field and him.

It took John a few moments to notice Brooke was silent. "Brooke?" When she didn't respond he turned her to him. She was trembling. "Brooke, what's the matter?"

"The . . . the ball was going so fast . . . I was afraid." She swallowed. "If he hadn't caught it . . ."

His hand tenderly cupped her cheek. "You love him, don't you?"

Her eyes snapped. "You can be such a doofus."

He looked over her head at Mark's teammates, who still surrounded him, then found his parents with Amy coming out of the stands. "We have a few minutes. Come on." Without waiting he pulled her to a clump of trees a short distance away. As soon as they were out of sight he took her into his arms. "Stop squirming or you're going to get a response that will embarrass both of us."

She stilled.

"I'll make this quick since we don't have much time." He picked up first one wrist then the other. "He's out of your life?"

"Yes."

He stared into her eyes. "Was there another reason you came here today besides for my children?"

"Maybe," she said, her heart thudding.

He pulled her closer to him. "I hope so, because I don't think I can go on if you aren't in my life. I'm not letting you move until you agree to marry me."

"W–what?" Her legs almost went out from under her.

"I loved Linda and she'll always have a part of my heart, but you are my heart. I love you, Brooke. I can't give you the things you want—"

"Shut up," she ordered, then threw herself into his arms. "I love you. I'm holding all I want. Mark and Amy are special gifts and I love them, too. Just try and stop me from marrying you."

John threw his head back and laughed. "I might have known you wouldn't accept the proposal in a traditional way."

"Disappointed?" she asked, grinning up at him.

"Never. I've got a feeling there are going to be a lot of firsts in our lives just like the first time we met and I can't wait to experience them," he said, then lowered his head to kiss her waiting lips.

A short distance away, Mark and Amy and their grandparents turned away from watching the kiss and started for the parking lot. All of them were smiling.

M rs. Livingston, I love Gray and I need your help to make him realize he loves me, too," Claire said Sunday afternoon as she sat across from Gray's grandmother in her opulent living room. They'd finished dinner and were having tea.

Corrine Livingston had always liked people who came to the point. She also liked that she had been right about Claire. She had spunk and the good sense not to let Gray get away. She picked up her cup and sipped. "What did you have in mind?"

Since Mrs. Livingston hadn't so much as batted an eyelash when Claire told her she loved Gray, she saw no need to tread lightly. "Seduction."

Brown eyes twinkled. She set down the cup and patted the seat beside her on the Chippendale sofa. "Come and tell me how I can help."

Claire explained her plan and was thankful that Gray's grandmother listened attentively and agreed to help. Thirty minutes later Claire was in her car and on the way to Columbia.

G ray didn't want to go to his apartment, but he had no other place to go that wouldn't remind him of Claire. Every day there was something that reminded him of her. A breeze. A flower. The moonlight. He thought he'd be free in Columbia since they'd never been there together, but he carried her in his heart and that was much more difficult to rid himself of.

Opening the door, he continued to the bedroom. He'd change and go for a run. Perhaps the jarring pace on concrete would get clear his mind.

Eighteen holes of golf certainly hadn't helped. He'd shot a 67. He'd never played that badly. The guys at the club kept asking if he was all right.

How could he be when part of him was missing? Opening his bedroom door he froze, blinked, then blinked again. The image remained.

"Hello, Gray."

Not only was she still there, with a black sheet draped seductively between her thighs and just skimming her beautiful breasts, she was talking to him. His unruly body hardened in an instant.

"I've come to make you a business proposition and we're not leaving this room until you say yes."

Since Gray had been able to do little else but think about her, he gripped the handle of the golf bag to keep from going to her. He had to put her needs first. "You shouldn't be here."

"Where else should I be than with the man I love?"

The clubs plopped to the floor. Gray grabbed the straight-back chair near the door and dropped heavily into the padded seat.

Claire breathed a little easier. "Here's the proposition. We can either live together or get married, but I'm not letting you go. In the past I've allowed too many things to come before what I really wanted."

"What you really wanted," Gray repeated.

"You. I've wanted you since I was eleven. I don't intend to give you up now." Claire held out her hand.

Gray didn't move. He simply stared at her. Her hand trembled, then firmed. She refused to break eye contact.

He realized she was risking everything for him. She had more courage than he did. She really loved him. For the first time a woman loved him for himself. And what a woman. Claire was like no other woman and to think otherwise was sheer stupidity. He might be a bit slow to realize how fortunate he was, but he'd like to think he wasn't stupid.

Standing, he pulled his Polo shirt over his head and reached for his belt buckle. By the time he got to her, he was as naked as she was beneath the sheet. "Lady, you got yourself a lifetime deal."

His arms greedily pulled her to him and they tumbled to the bed. Just like the first time.

EPILOGUE

Bliss, a year later their lives were still filled with it.

Bliss's appearance in the Christmas issue of Livingston Catalogue might have given Claire, Brooke, and Lorraine a wider audience, but it was the fabulous products and savvy marketing of the three owners that kept their profits rising. But who could argue with the walking advertisement of the three happily married owners. That two of them had found their husbands as a direct result of Bliss had other women anxious to find their own man and do their own test marketing.

The three pictures on Bliss's Web site certainly attested that the owners' husbands enjoyed being guinea pigs. Gray and Claire, who was six months pregnant and ecstatically happy and healthy, were captured strolling on the beach in back of their home on Sullivan Island. John, Brooke, and their two children, Amy and Mark, posed for their shot after Mark's team won the Y's district softball championship. Hamilton and Lorraine's picture was taken in their garden with her holding a rose he had just given her.

Just like the first time, like every time love found a way.

Reading Group Guide

1. Initially, Claire thought her parents had been wrong in teaching her that a college education would ensure success, but she eventually saw that her education helped her unexpected business venture. What other things did they teach her that helped her just as much or more? Do you think some lessons your parents taught you are outdated?

2. Have you ever been faced with a life-changing "leap of faith" the way Claire, Brooke, and Lorraine were? If so, did you go for it? Which of the three women had the most to lose? To gain?

3. Claire was the "good daughter," but Derek was definitely a selfish user. When you love someone, it is very difficult to determine when you cross the line from loving and supporting to enabling. What signs should Claire have seen and heeded? Would you have acted any differently in her circumstances?

4. Brooke's philosophy early in the book was that you could just as easily fall in love with a rich man as a poor man. Did thinking that make her a bad person? Do you agree with her?

5. Lorraine was the perfect executive wife and mother who finally decided she wanted to have a life for herself. Was there anything she could have done to help Hamilton accept her decision? When is it all right to give in to your husband on some issues and when is it not? Give examples.

6. Three women had a profound effect on the men in the story that in turn influenced their relationships with Claire, Brooke, and Lorraine. Gray by Jana's betrayal, John by his wife's death, and Hamilton by his amoral mother. Emotional baggage has sabotaged many relationships. Why do you think Gray and Claire, John and Brooke, and Hamilton and Lorraine survived?

7. Brooke and John thought they were in lust, not love. How can you tell the difference?

8. Should women use withholding sex as a way of teaching their husbands a lesson as Lorraine did? If problems can't be resolved before going to bed should the discord stop at the bedroom door?

CPSIA information can be obtained at www.ICGtesting.com
Printed in the USA
LVOW08s1930280116

472728LV00001B/35/P